Outcast

BY **KIRKMAN** & **AZACETA**

VOLUME **6**: INVASION

OUTCAST BY KIRKMAN & AZACETA
VOL. 6: INVASION
August 2018
First printing

ISBN: 978-1-5343-0751-3

Published by Image Comics, Inc.

Office of publication: 2701 NW Vaughn St., Ste. 780,
Portland, OR 97210.

IMAGE COMICS, INC.
Robert Kirkman—Chief Operating Officer
Erik Larsen—Chief Financial Officer
Todd McFarlane—President
Marc Silvestri—Chief Executive Officer
Jim Valentino—Vice President

Eric Stephenson—Publisher / Chief Creative Officer
Corey Hart—Director of Sales
Jeff Boison—Director of Publishing Planning
& Book Trade Sales
Chris Ross—Director of Digital Sales
Jeff Stang—Director of Specialty Sales
Kat Salazar—Director of PR & Marketing
Drew Gill—Art Director
Heather Doornink—Production Director
Nicole Lapalme—Controller
IMAGECOMICS.COM

For SKYBOUND ENTERTAINMENT
Robert Kirkman - Chairman
David Alpert - CEO
Sean Mackiewicz - SVP, Editor-in-Chief
Shawn Kirkham - SVP, Business Development
Brian Huntington - VP, Online Content
June Alian - Publicity Director
Andres Juarez - Art Director
Jon Moisan - Editor
Arielle Basich - Associate Editor
Carina Taylor - Production Artist
Paul Shin - Business Development Coordinator
Johnny O'Dell - Social Media Manager
Sally Jacka - Skybound Retailer Relations
Dan Petersen - Director of Operations & Events

International inquiries: ag@sequentialrights.com
Licensing inquiries: contact@skybound.com

WWW.SKYBOUND.COM

Robert Kirkman
Creator, Writer

Paul Azaceta
Artist

Elizabeth Breitweiser
Colorist

Rus Wooton
Letterer

Paul Azaceta
Elizabeth Breitweiser
Cover

Arielle Basich
Associate Editor

Jon Moisan
Editor

Rian Hughes
Logo Design

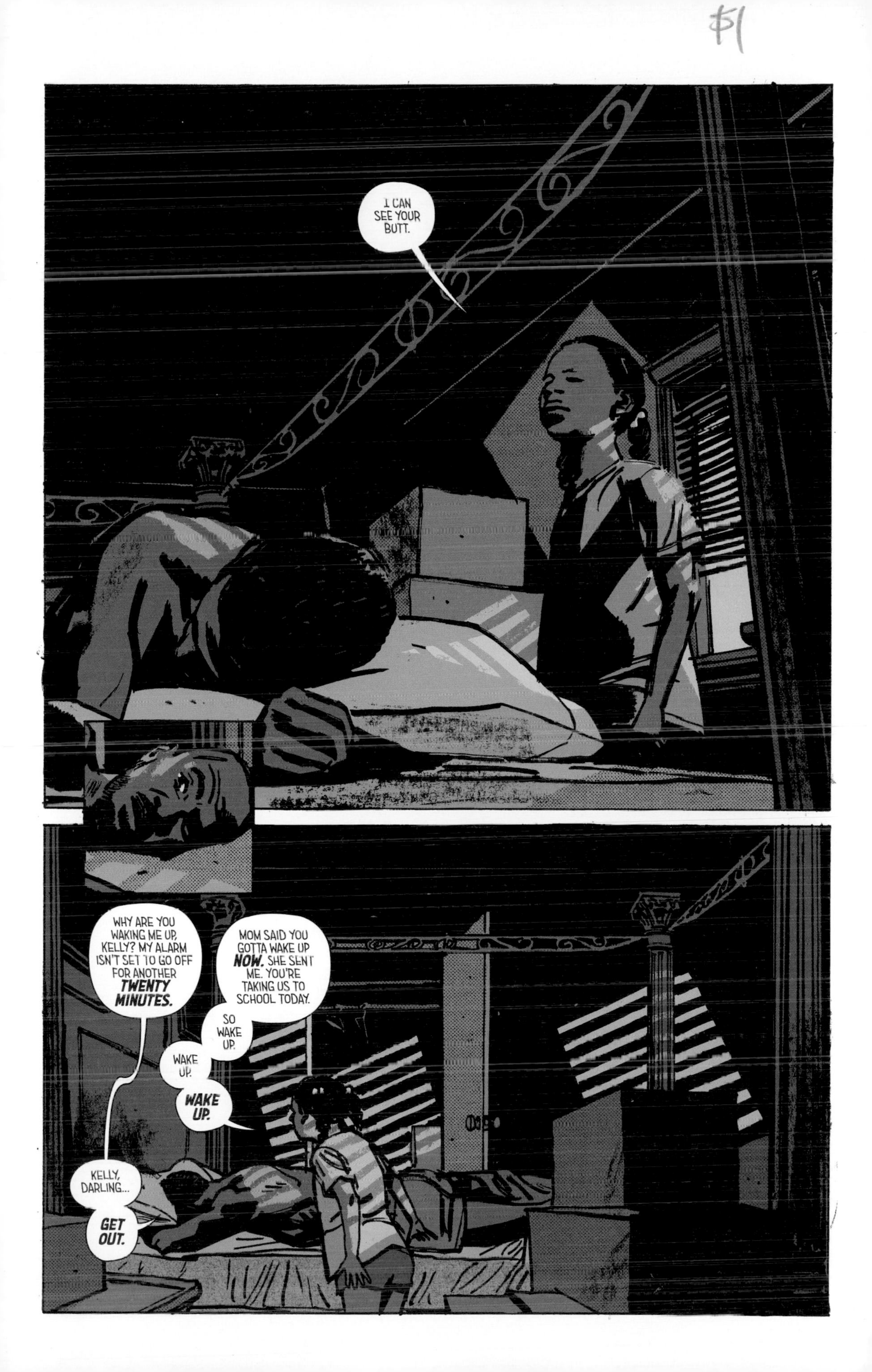

5 1
I CAN SEE YOUR BUTT.
WHY ARE YOU WAKING ME UP, KELLY? MY ALARM ISN'T SET TO GO OFF FOR ANOTHER **TWENTY MINUTES.**
MOM SAID YOU GOTTA WAKE UP **NOW.** SHE SENT ME. YOU'RE TAKING US TO SCHOOL TODAY.
SO WAKE UP.
WAKE UP.
WAKE UP.
KELLY, DARLING...
GET OUT.

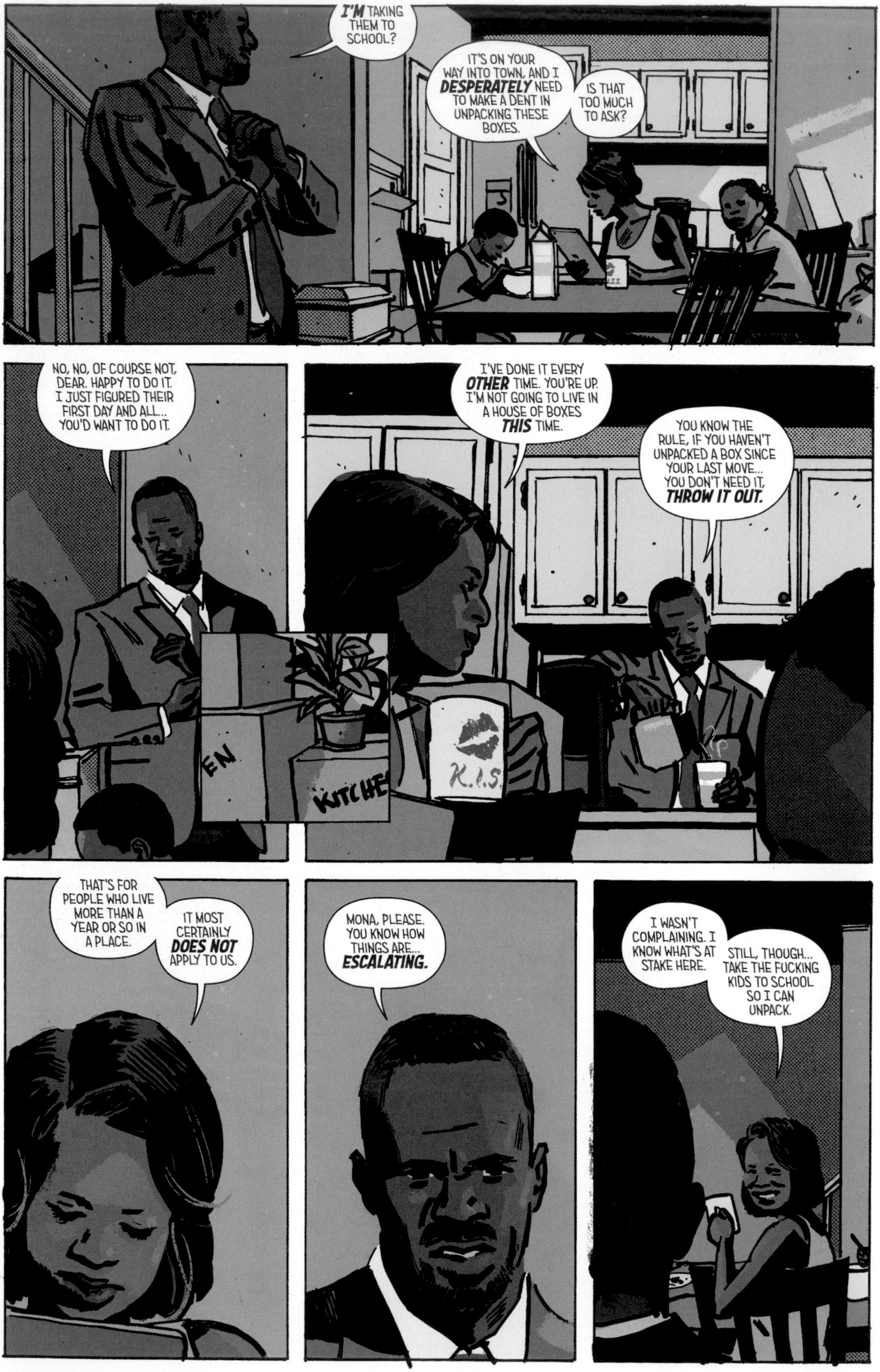
I'M TAKING THEM TO SCHOOL?
IT'S ON YOUR WAY INTO TOWN, AND I DESPERATELY NEED TO MAKE A DENT IN UNPACKING THESE BOXES.
IS THAT TOO MUCH TO ASK?
NO, NO, OF COURSE NOT, DEAR. HAPPY TO DO IT. I JUST FIGURED THEIR FIRST DAY AND ALL... YOU'D WANT TO DO IT.
EN
KITCHE
I'VE DONE IT EVERY OTHER TIME. YOU'RE UP. I'M NOT GOING TO LIVE IN A HOUSE OF BOXES THIS TIME.
YOU KNOW THE RULE, IF YOU HAVEN'T UNPACKED A BOX SINCE YOUR LAST MOVE... YOU DON'T NEED IT, THROW IT OUT.
K.I.S.
THAT'S FOR PEOPLE WHO LIVE MORE THAN A YEAR OR SO IN A PLACE.
IT MOST CERTAINLY DOES NOT APPLY TO US.
MONA, PLEASE. YOU KNOW HOW THINGS ARE... ESCALATING.
I WASN'T COMPLAINING. I KNOW WHAT'S AT STAKE HERE.
STILL, THOUGH... TAKE THE FUCKING KIDS TO SCHOOL SO I CAN UNPACK.

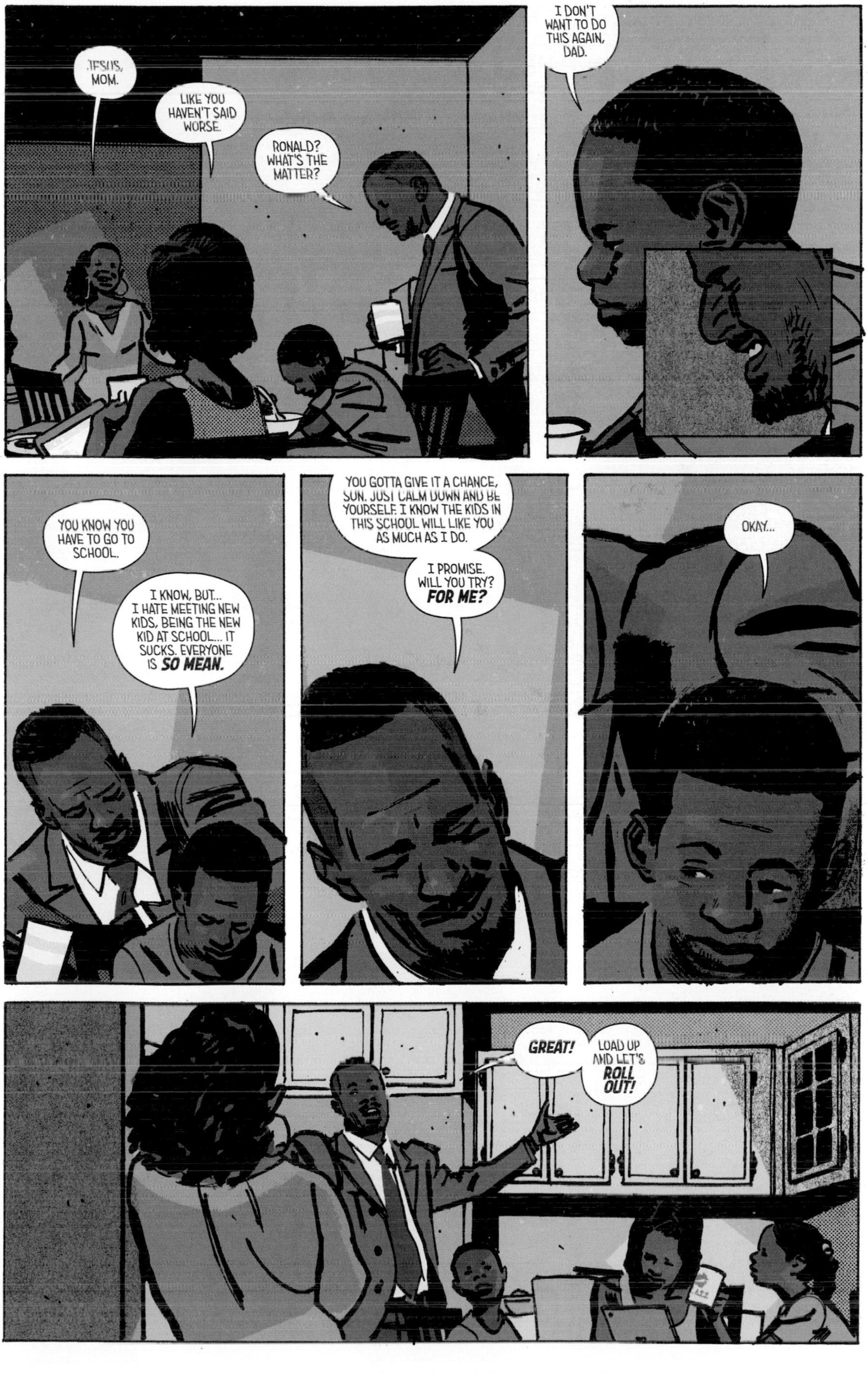
JESUS, MOM.
LIKE YOU HAVEN'T SAID WORSE.
RONALD? WHAT'S THE MATTER?
I DON'T WANT TO DO THIS AGAIN, DAD.
YOU KNOW YOU HAVE TO GO TO SCHOOL.
I KNOW, BUT... I HATE MEETING NEW KIDS, BEING THE NEW KID AT SCHOOL... IT SUCKS. EVERYONE IS SO MEAN.
YOU GOTTA GIVE IT A CHANCE, SON. JUST CALM DOWN AND BE YOURSELF. I KNOW THE KIDS IN THIS SCHOOL WILL LIKE YOU AS MUCH AS I DO.
I PROMISE. WILL YOU TRY? FOR ME?
OKAY...
GREAT!
LOAD UP AND LET'S ROLL OUT!

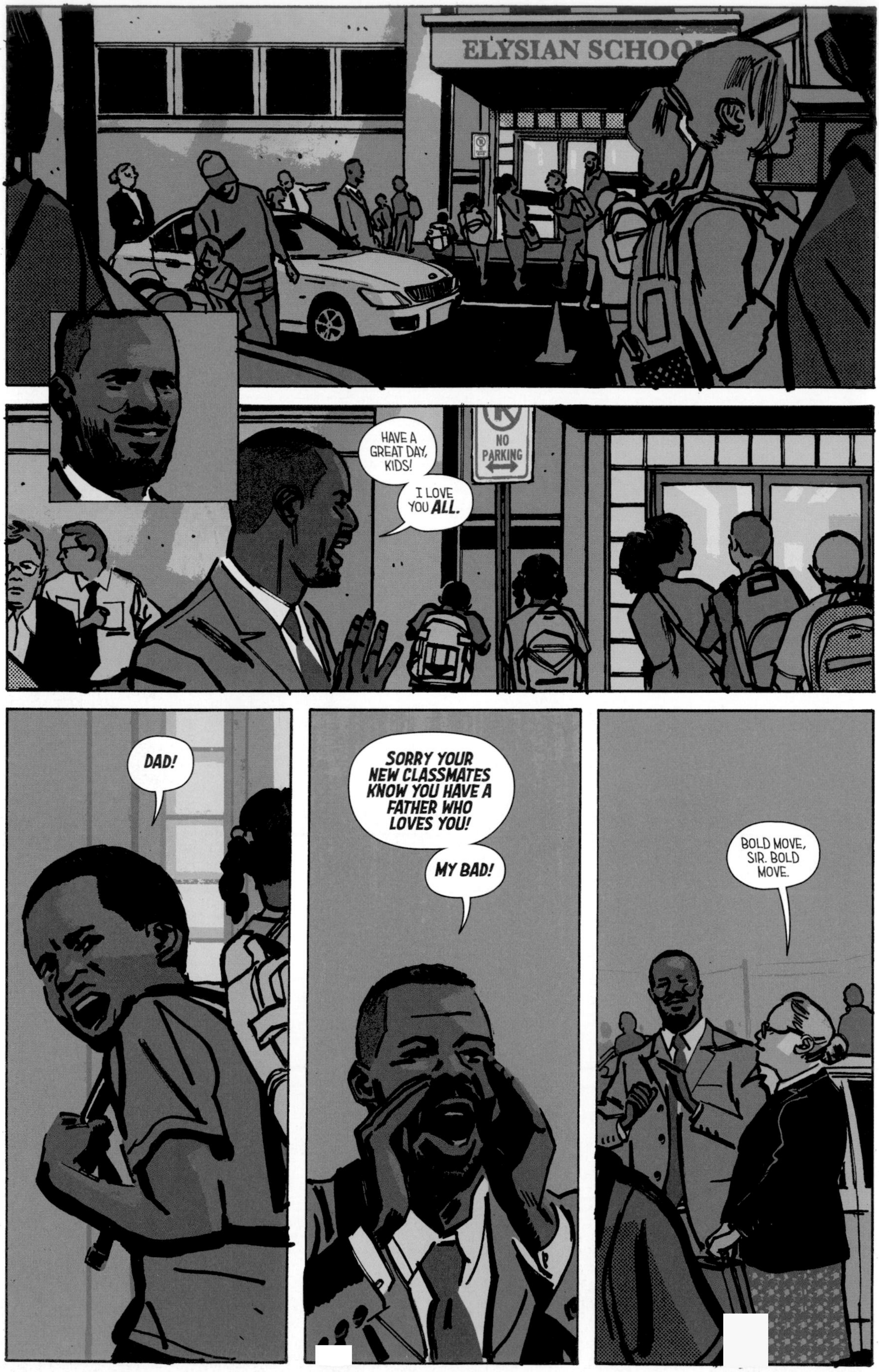
ELYSIAN SCHOO
NO PARKING
HAVE A GREAT DAY, KIDS!
I LOVE YOU ALL.
DAD!
SORRY YOUR NEW CLASSMATES KNOW YOU HAVE A FATHER WHO LOVES YOU!
MY BAD!
BOLD MOVE, SIR. BOLD MOVE.

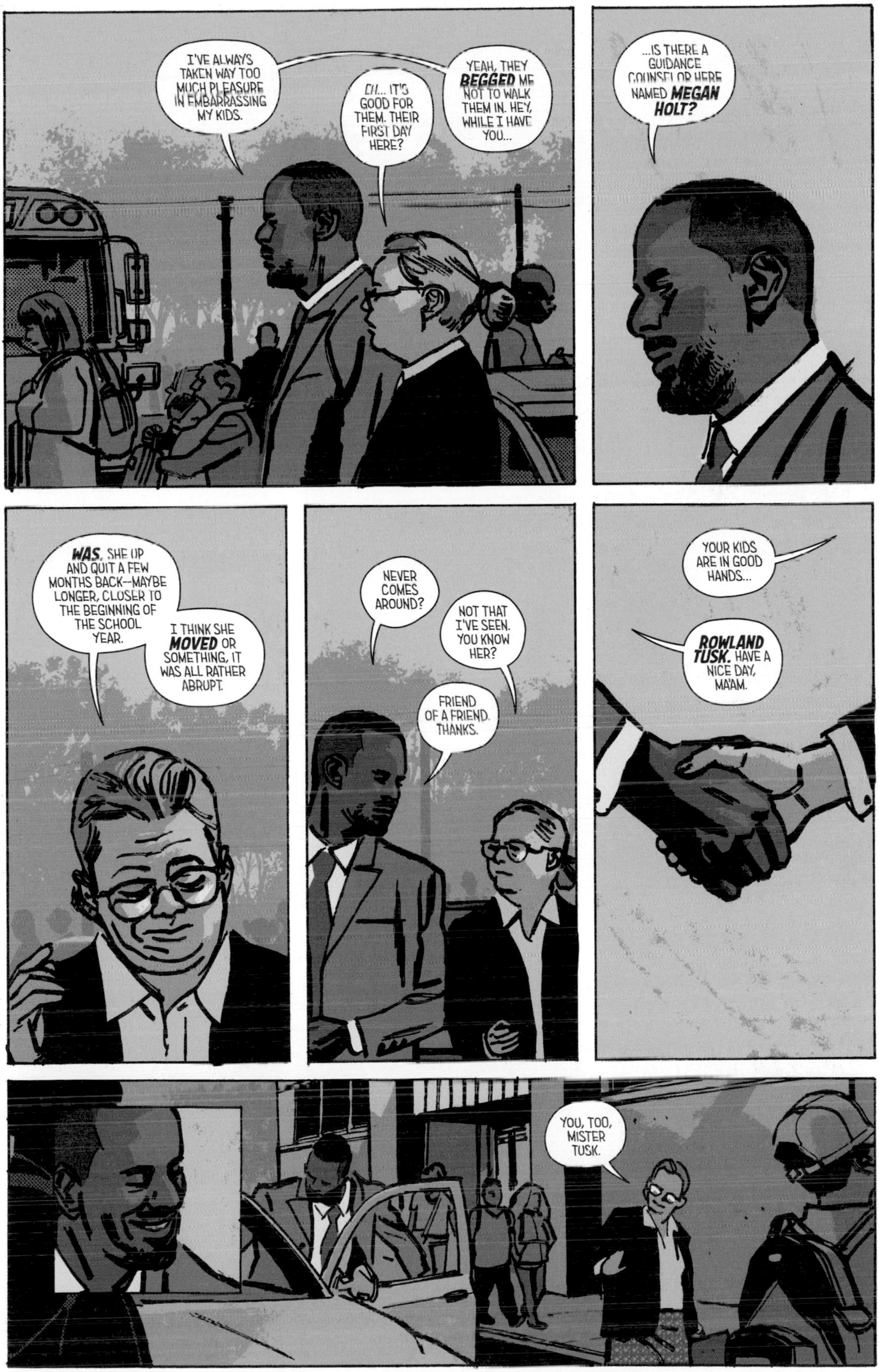
I'VE ALWAYS TAKEN WAY TOO MUCH PLEASURE IN EMBARRASSING MY KIDS.
EH... IT'S GOOD FOR THEM. THEIR FIRST DAY HERE?
YEAH, THEY BEGGED ME NOT TO WALK THEM IN. HEY, WHILE I HAVE YOU...
...IS THERE A GUIDANCE COUNSELOR HERE NAMED MEGAN HOLT?
WAS, SHE UP AND QUIT A FEW MONTHS BACK--MAYBE LONGER, CLOSER TO THE BEGINNING OF THE SCHOOL YEAR.
I THINK SHE MOVED OR SOMETHING, IT WAS ALL RATHER ABRUPT.
NEVER COMES AROUND?
NOT THAT I'VE SEEN. YOU KNOW HER?
FRIEND OF A FRIEND. THANKS.
YOUR KIDS ARE IN GOOD HANDS...
ROWLAND TUSK. HAVE A NICE DAY, MA'AM.
YOU, TOO, MISTER TUSK.

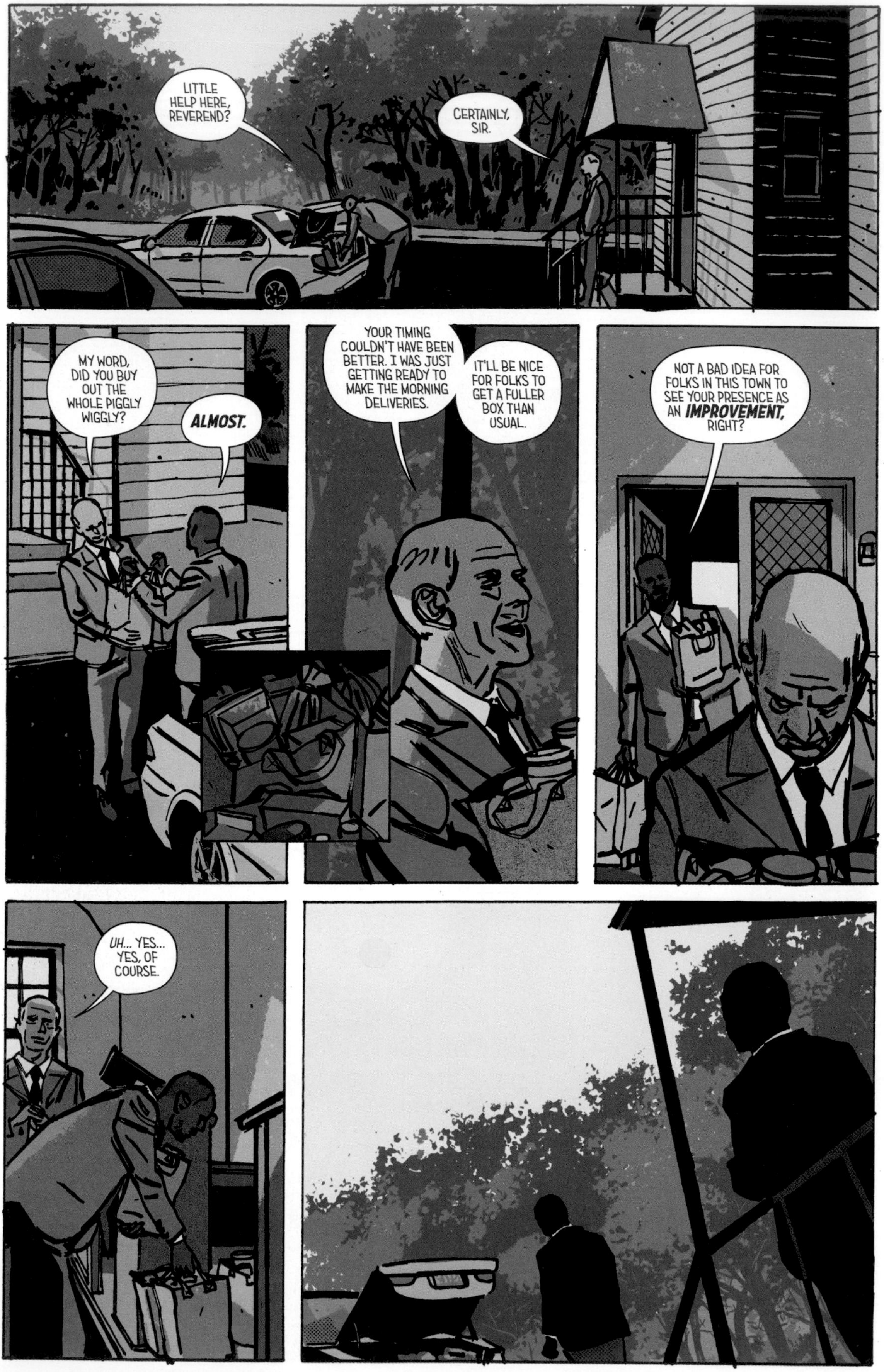
LITTLE HELP HERE, REVEREND?
CERTAINLY, SIR.
MY WORD, DID YOU BUY OUT THE WHOLE PIGGLY WIGGLY?
ALMOST.
YOUR TIMING COULDN'T HAVE BEEN BETTER. I WAS JUST GETTING READY TO MAKE THE MORNING DELIVERIES.
IT'LL BE NICE FOR FOLKS TO GET A FULLER BOX THAN USUAL.
NOT A BAD IDEA FOR FOLKS IN THIS TOWN TO SEE YOUR PRESENCE AS AN IMPROVEMENT, RIGHT?
UH... YES... YES, OF COURSE.

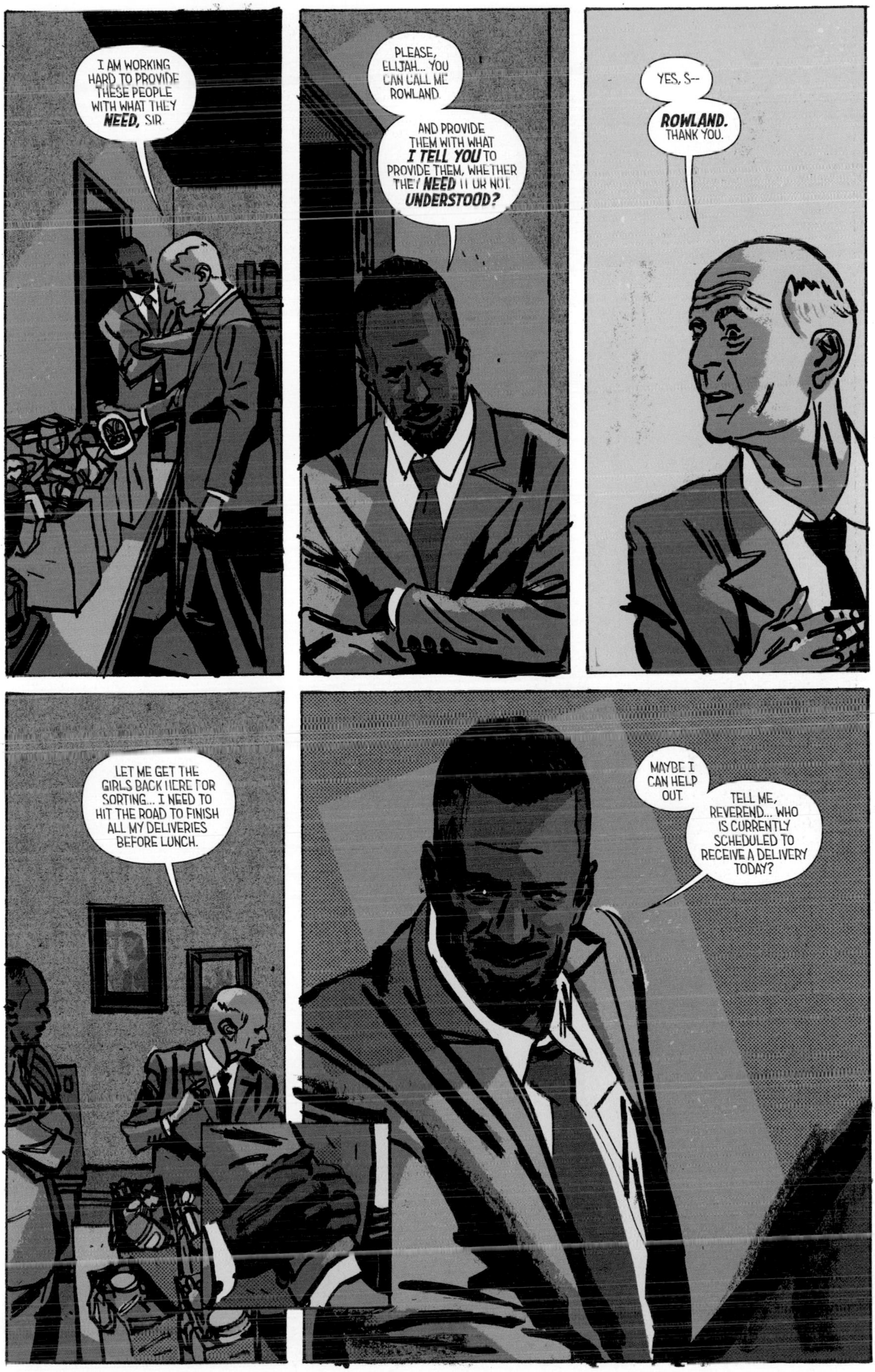
I AM WORKING HARD TO PROVIDE THESE PEOPLE WITH WHAT THEY NEED, SIR.
PLEASE, ELIJAH... YOU CAN CALL ME ROWLAND.
AND PROVIDE THEM WITH WHAT I TELL YOU TO PROVIDE THEM, WHETHER THEY NEED IT OR NOT. UNDERSTOOD?
YES, S--
ROWLAND. THANK YOU.
LET ME GET THE GIRLS BACK HERE FOR SORTING... I NEED TO HIT THE ROAD TO FINISH ALL MY DELIVERIES BEFORE LUNCH.
MAYBE I CAN HELP OUT.
TELL ME, REVEREND... WHO IS CURRENTLY SCHEDULED TO RECEIVE A DELIVERY TODAY?

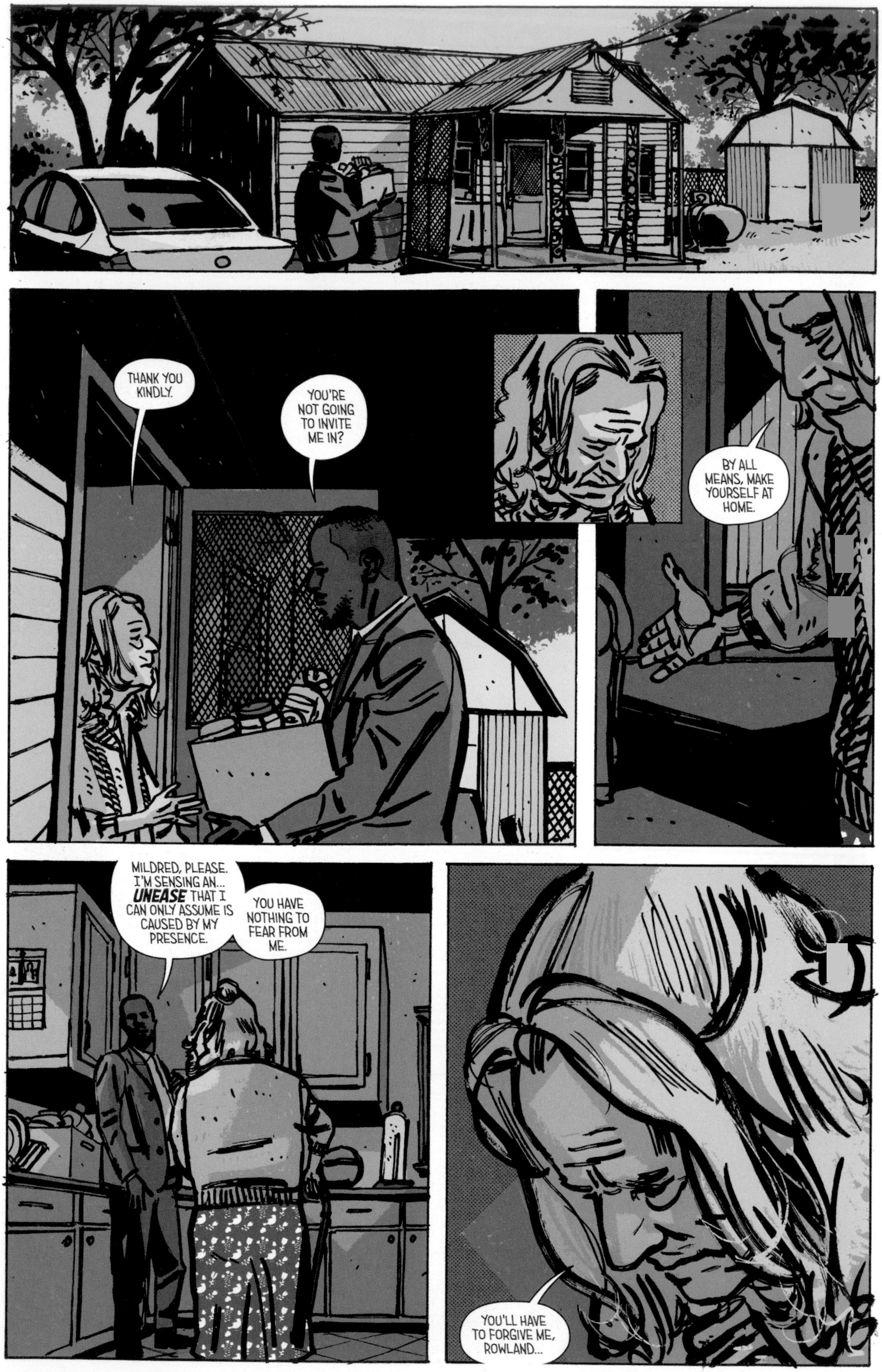
THANK YOU KINDLY.
YOU'RE NOT GOING TO INVITE ME IN?
BY ALL MEANS, MAKE YOURSELF AT HOME.
MILDRED, PLEASE. I'M SENSING AN... UNEASE THAT I CAN ONLY ASSUME IS CAUSED BY MY PRESENCE.
YOU HAVE NOTHING TO FEAR FROM ME.
YOU'LL HAVE TO FORGIVE ME, ROWLAND...

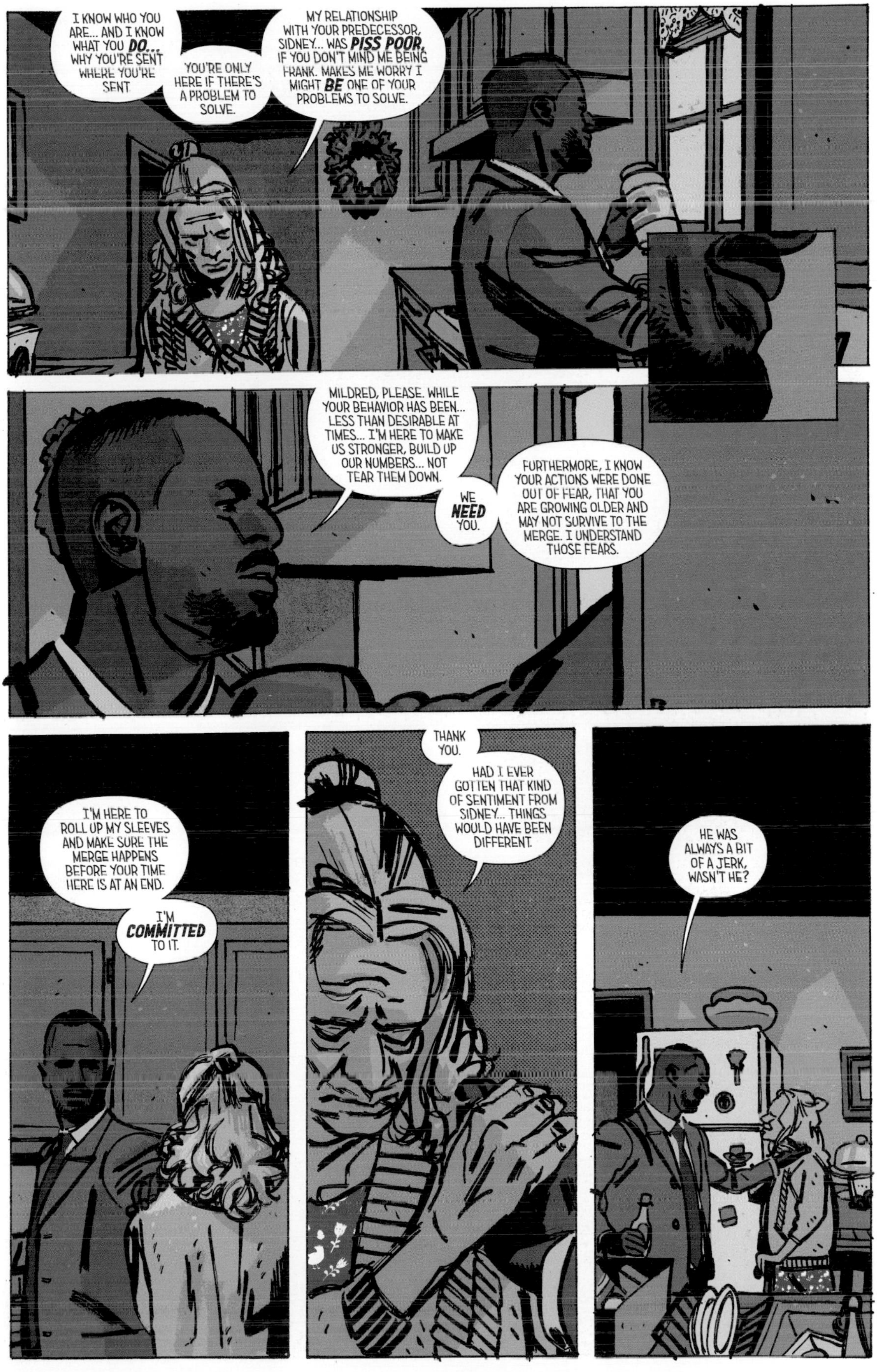
I KNOW WHO YOU ARE... AND I KNOW WHAT YOU DO... WHY YOU'RE SENT WHERE YOU'RE SENT.
YOU'RE ONLY HERE IF THERE'S A PROBLEM TO SOLVE.
MY RELATIONSHIP WITH YOUR PREDECESSOR, SIDNEY... WAS PISS POOR, IF YOU DON'T MIND ME BEING FRANK. MAKES ME WORRY I MIGHT BE ONE OF YOUR PROBLEMS TO SOLVE.
MILDRED, PLEASE. WHILE YOUR BEHAVIOR HAS BEEN... LESS THAN DESIRABLE AT TIMES... I'M HERE TO MAKE US STRONGER, BUILD UP OUR NUMBERS... NOT TEAR THEM DOWN.
WE NEED YOU.
FURTHERMORE, I KNOW YOUR ACTIONS WERE DONE OUT OF FEAR, THAT YOU ARE GROWING OLDER AND MAY NOT SURVIVE TO THE MERGE. I UNDERSTAND THOSE FEARS.
I'M HERE TO ROLL UP MY SLEEVES AND MAKE SURE THE MERGE HAPPENS BEFORE YOUR TIME HERE IS AT AN END.
I'M COMMITTED TO IT.
THANK YOU.
HAD I EVER GOTTEN THAT KIND OF SENTIMENT FROM SIDNEY... THINGS WOULD HAVE BEEN DIFFERENT.
HE WAS ALWAYS A BIT OF A JERK, WASN'T HE?

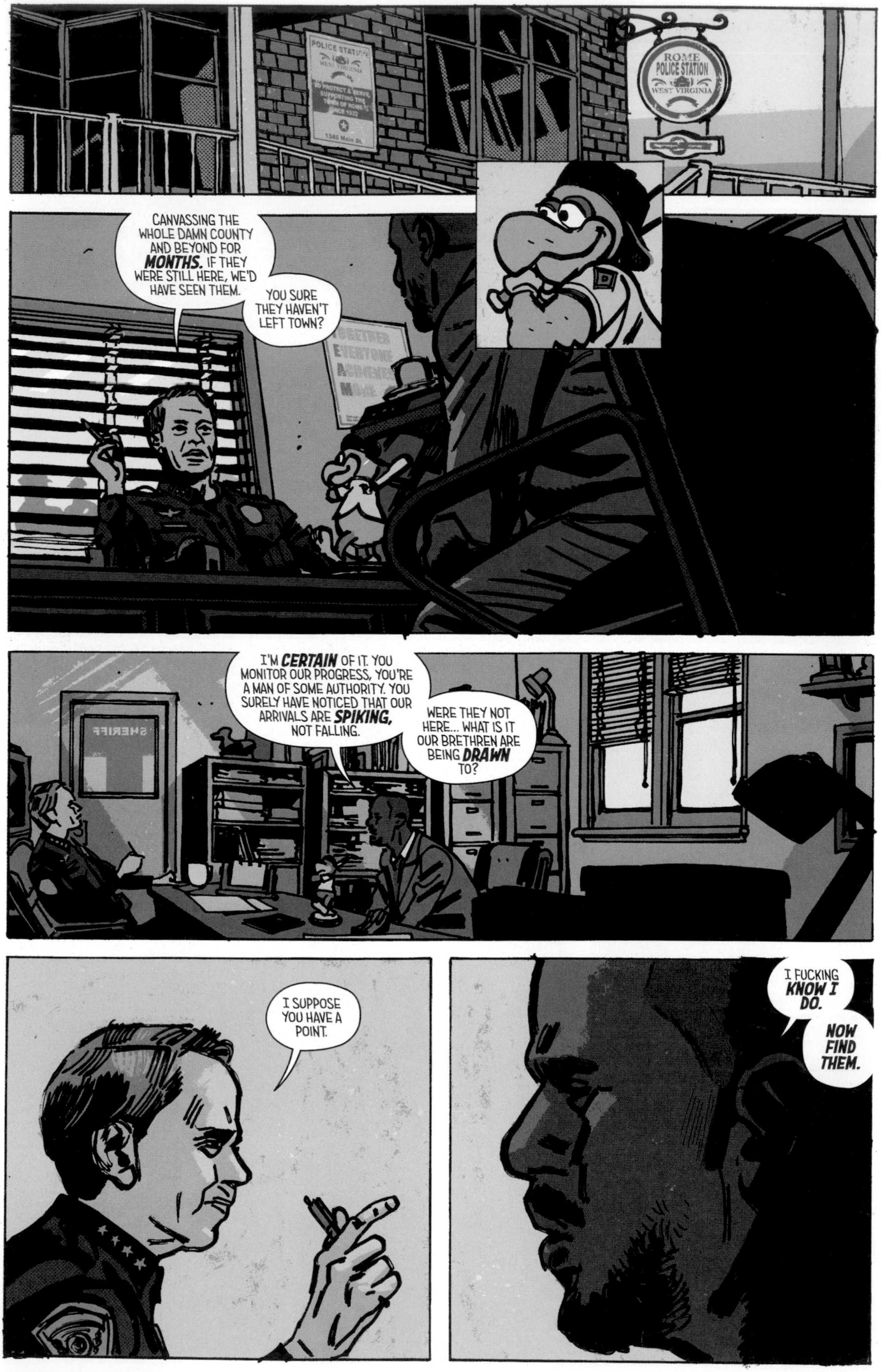
POLICE STATION
WEST VIRGINIA
TO PROTECT & SERVE, SUPPORTING THE TOWN OF ROME SINCE 1922
1345 Main St.
ROME POLICE STATION WEST VIRGINIA
CANVASSING THE WHOLE DAMN COUNTY AND BEYOND FOR MONTHS. IF THEY WERE STILL HERE, WE'D HAVE SEEN THEM.
YOU SURE THEY HAVEN'T LEFT TOWN?
TOGETHER EVERYONE ACHIEVES MORE
SHERIFF
I'M CERTAIN OF IT. YOU MONITOR OUR PROGRESS, YOU'RE A MAN OF SOME AUTHORITY. YOU SURELY HAVE NOTICED THAT OUR ARRIVALS ARE SPIKING, NOT FALLING.
WERE THEY NOT HERE... WHAT IS IT OUR BRETHREN ARE BEING DRAWN TO?
I SUPPOSE YOU HAVE A POINT.
I FUCKING KNOW I DO.
NOW FIND THEM.

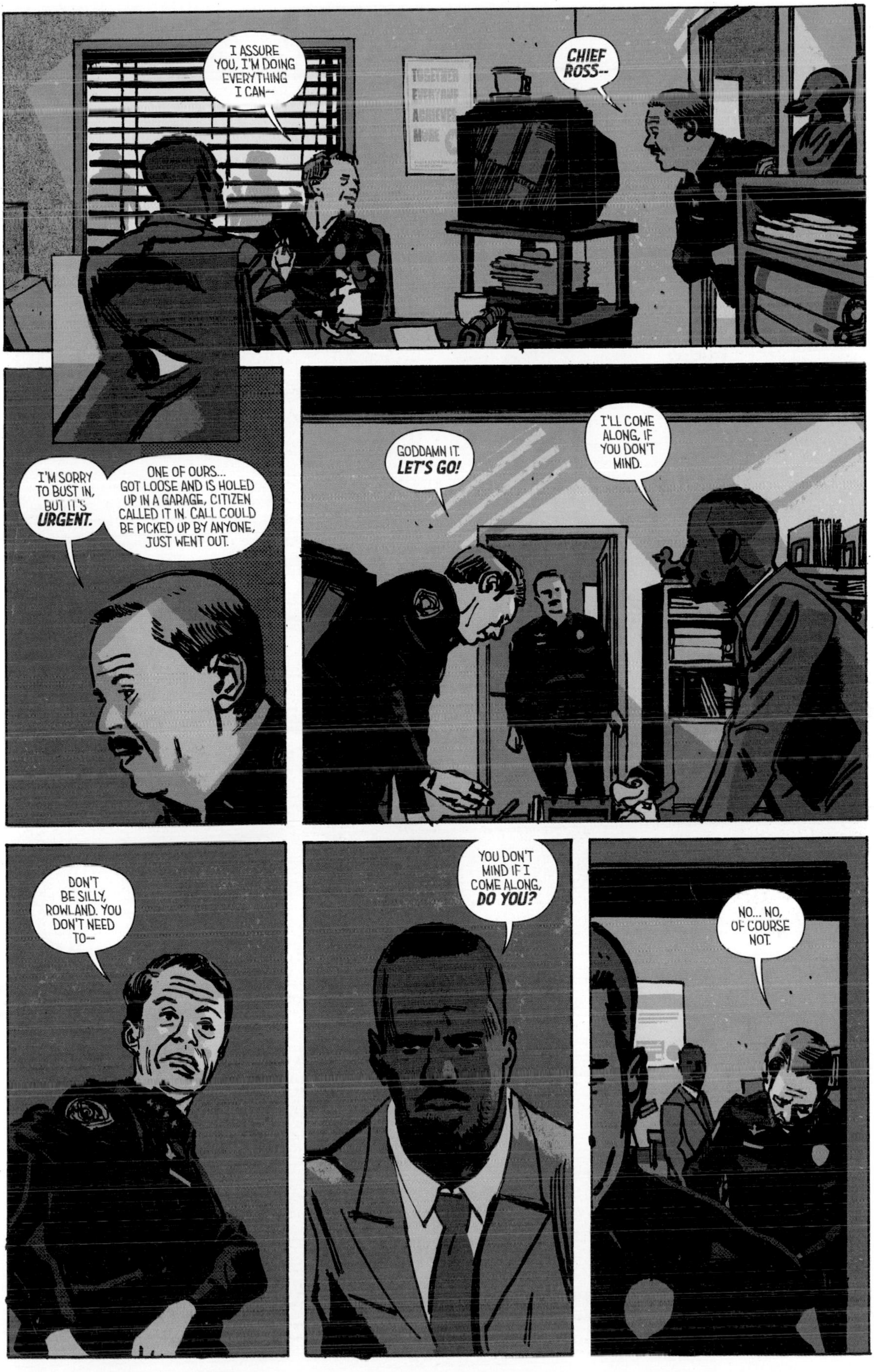
I ASSURE YOU, I'M DOING EVERYTHING I CAN--
CHIEF ROSS--
I'M SORRY TO BUST IN, BUT IT'S URGENT.
ONE OF OURS... GOT LOOSE AND IS HOLED UP IN A GARAGE, CITIZEN CALLED IT IN. CALL COULD BE PICKED UP BY ANYONE, JUST WENT OUT.
GODDAMN IT. LET'S GO!
I'LL COME ALONG, IF YOU DON'T MIND.
DON'T BE SILLY, ROWLAND. YOU DON'T NEED TO--
YOU DON'T MIND IF I COME ALONG, DO YOU?
NO... NO, OF COURSE NOT.
TOGETHER EVERYONE ACHIEVES MORE

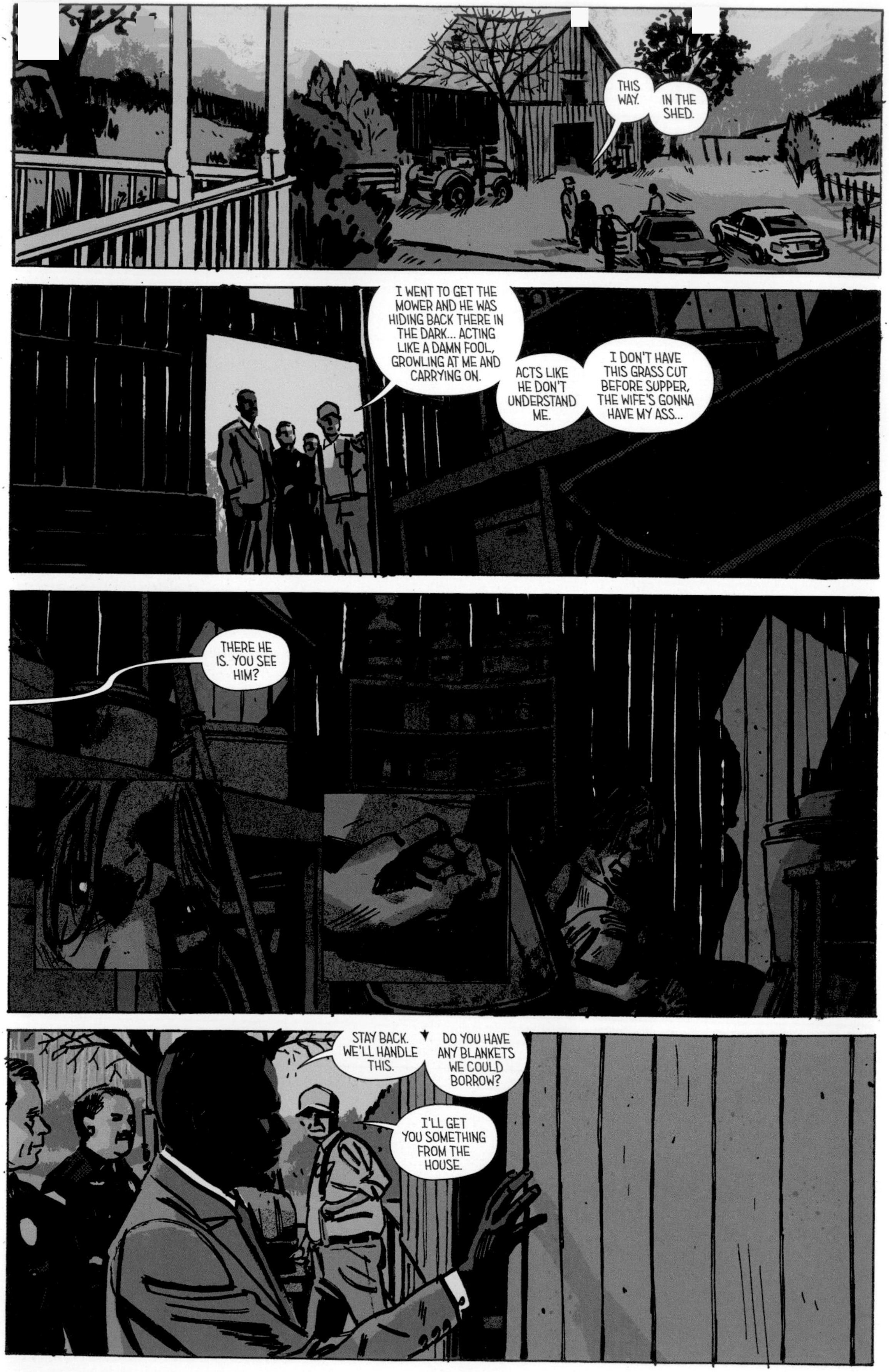
THIS WAY.
IN THE SHED.
I WENT TO GET THE MOWER AND HE WAS HIDING BACK THERE IN THE DARK... ACTING LIKE A DAMN FOOL, GROWLING AT ME AND CARRYING ON.
ACTS LIKE HE DON'T UNDERSTAND ME.
I DON'T HAVE THIS GRASS CUT BEFORE SUPPER, THE WIFE'S GONNA HAVE MY ASS...
THERE HE IS. YOU SEE HIM?
STAY BACK. WE'LL HANDLE THIS.
DO YOU HAVE ANY BLANKETS WE COULD BORROW?
I'LL GET YOU SOMETHING FROM THE HOUSE.

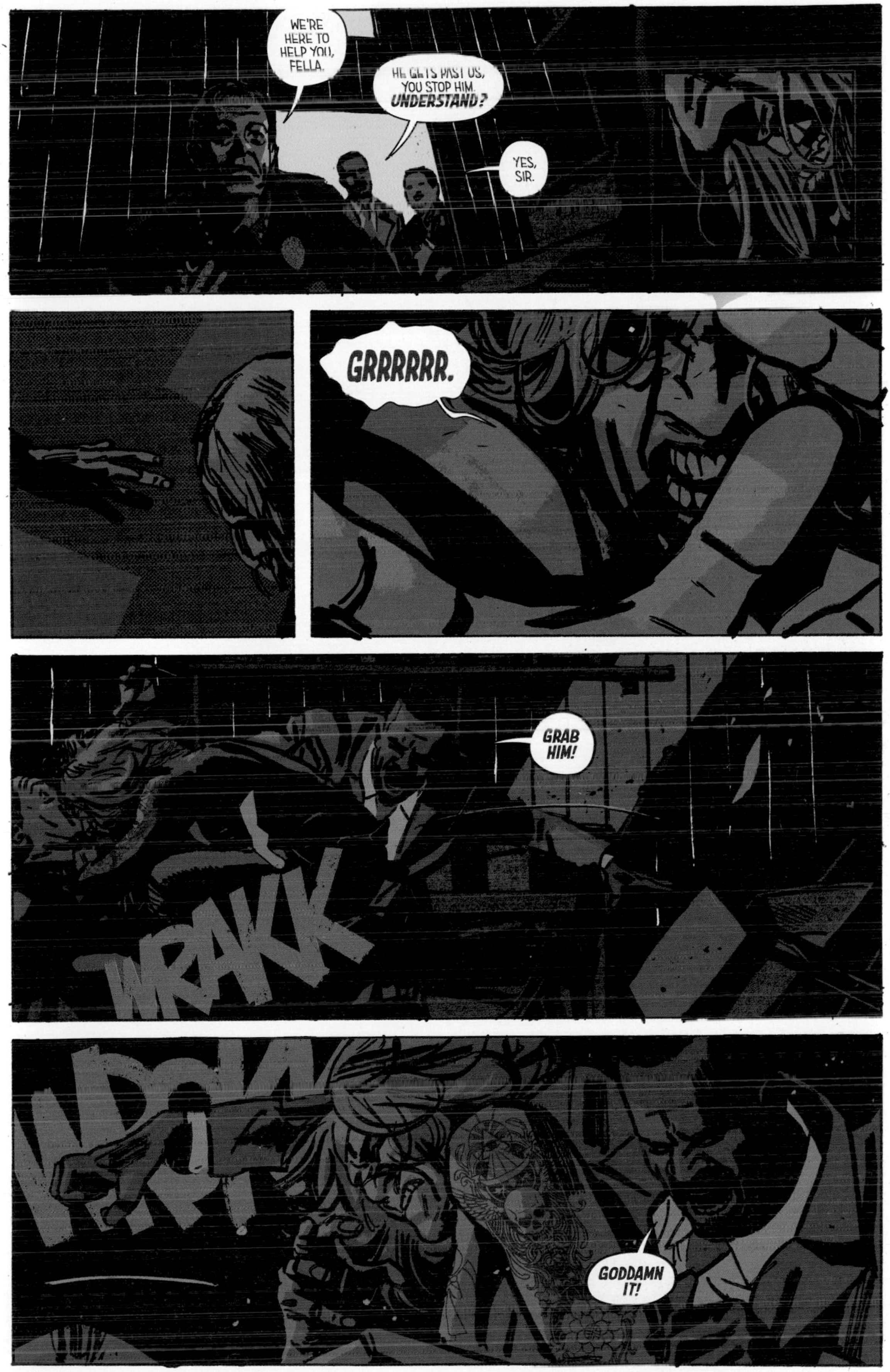
WE'RE HERE TO HELP YOU, FELLA.
HE GETS PAST US, YOU STOP HIM. UNDERSTAND?
YES, SIR.
GRRRRRR.
GRAB HIM!
WRAKK
GODDAMN IT!

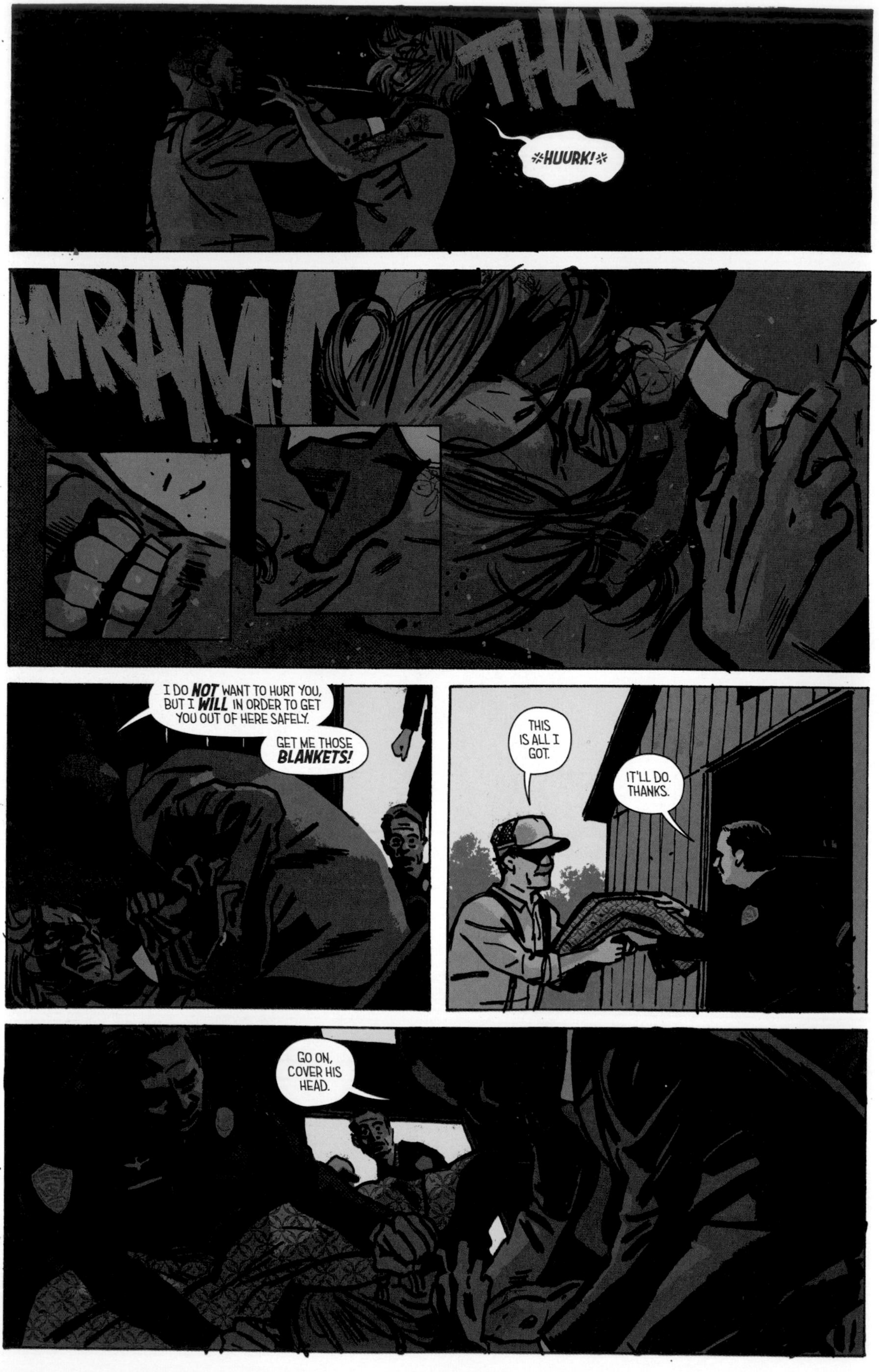
THAP
HUURK!
WRAMM
I DO NOT WANT TO HURT YOU, BUT I WILL IN ORDER TO GET YOU OUT OF HERE SAFELY.
GET ME THOSE BLANKETS!
THIS IS ALL I GOT.
IT'LL DO. THANKS.
GO ON, COVER HIS HEAD.

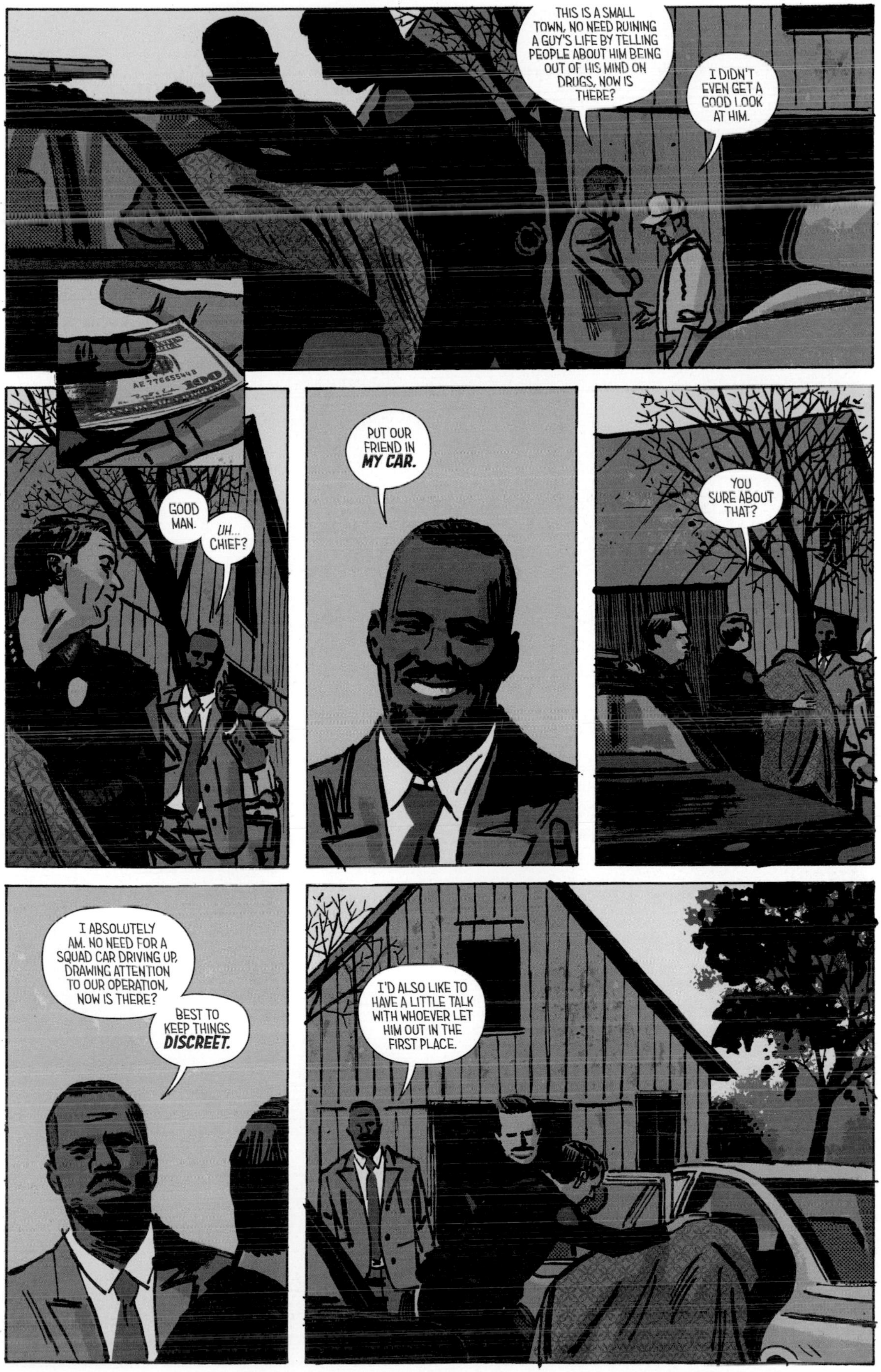
THIS IS A SMALL TOWN, NO NEED RUINING A GUY'S LIFE BY TELLING PEOPLE ABOUT HIM BEING OUT OF HIS MIND ON DRUGS, NOW IS THERE?
I DIDN'T EVEN GET A GOOD LOOK AT HIM.
AE 77665544 B
100
GOOD MAN.
UH... CHIEF?
PUT OUR FRIEND IN MY CAR.
YOU SURE ABOUT THAT?
I ABSOLUTELY AM. NO NEED FOR A SQUAD CAR DRIVING UP, DRAWING ATTENTION TO OUR OPERATION, NOW IS THERE?
BEST TO KEEP THINGS DISCREET.
I'D ALSO LIKE TO HAVE A LITTLE TALK WITH WHOEVER LET HIM OUT IN THE FIRST PLACE.

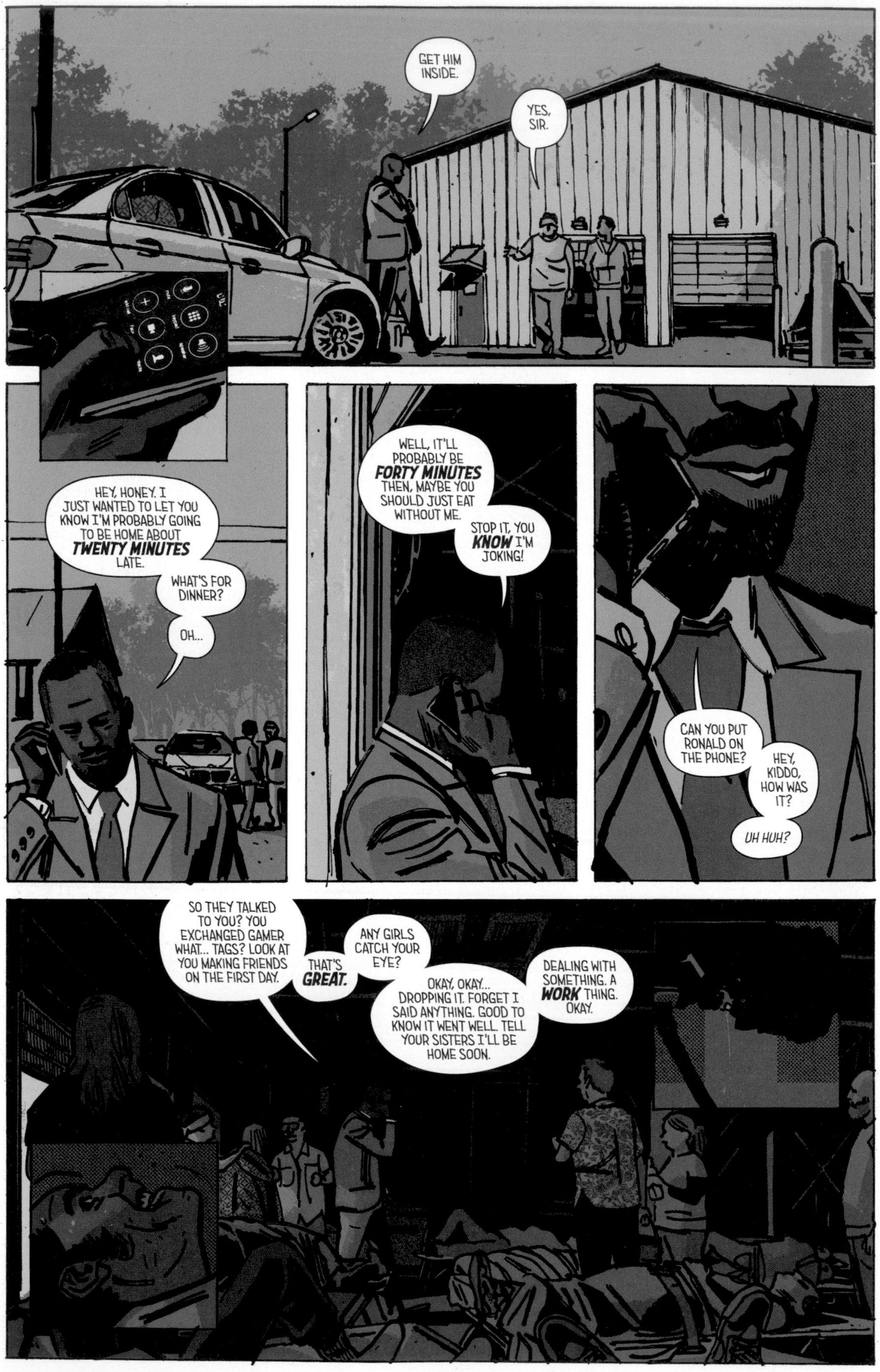
GET HIM INSIDE.
YES, SIR.
HEY, HONEY. I JUST WANTED TO LET YOU KNOW I'M PROBABLY GOING TO BE HOME ABOUT **TWENTY MINUTES** LATE.
WHAT'S FOR DINNER?
OH...
WELL, IT'LL PROBABLY BE **FORTY MINUTES** THEN, MAYBE YOU SHOULD JUST EAT WITHOUT ME.
STOP IT, YOU **KNOW** I'M JOKING!
CAN YOU PUT RONALD ON THE PHONE?
HEY, KIDDO, HOW WAS IT?
UH HUH?
SO THEY TALKED TO YOU? YOU EXCHANGED GAMER WHAT... TAGS? LOOK AT YOU MAKING FRIENDS ON THE FIRST DAY.
THAT'S **GREAT.**
ANY GIRLS CATCH YOUR EYE?
OKAY, OKAY... DROPPING IT. FORGET I SAID ANYTHING. GOOD TO KNOW IT WENT WELL. TELL YOUR SISTERS I'LL BE HOME SOON.
DEALING WITH SOMETHING. A **WORK** THING. OKAY.

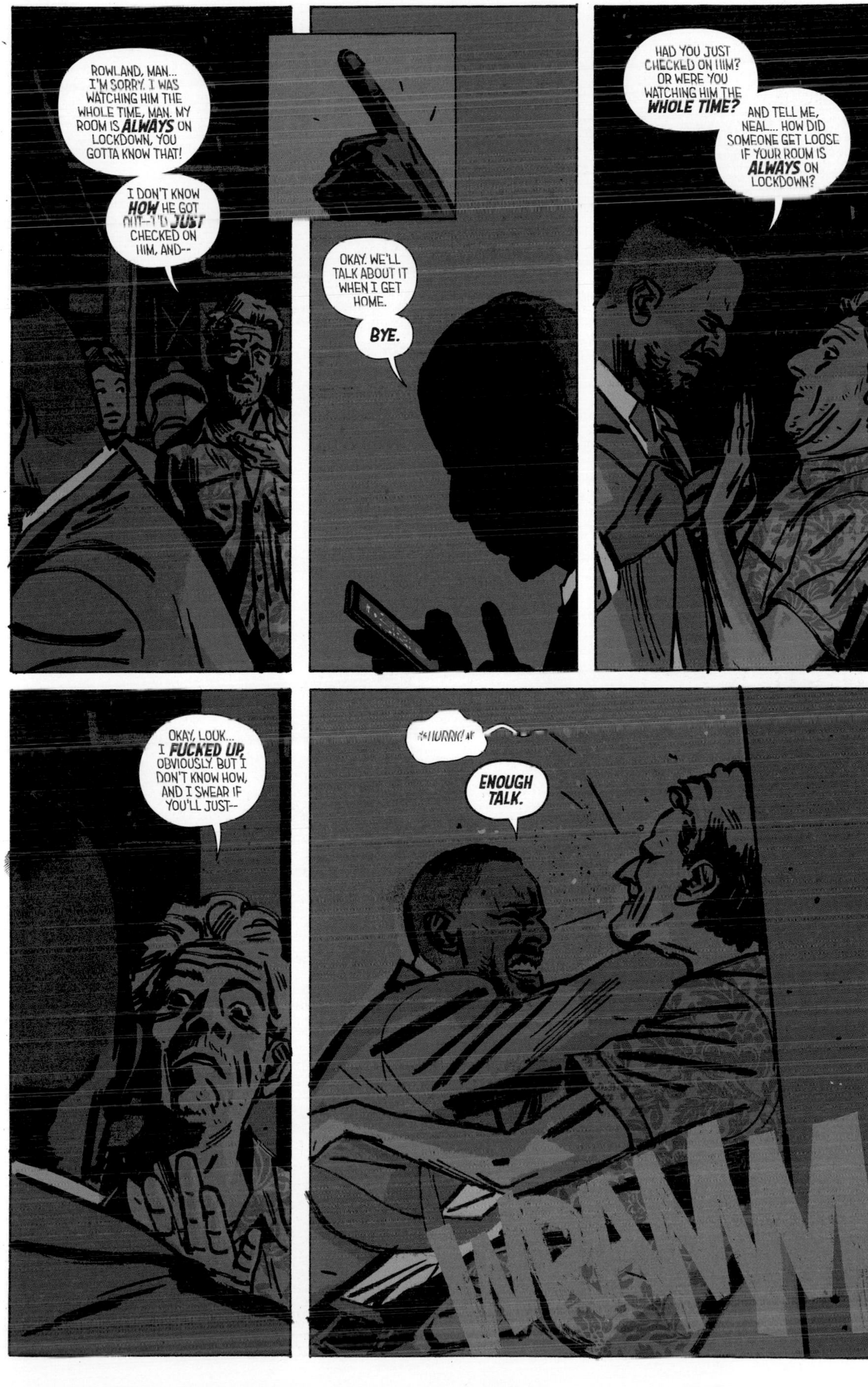
ROWLAND, MAN... I'M SORRY. I WAS WATCHING HIM THE WHOLE TIME, MAN. MY ROOM IS **ALWAYS** ON LOCKDOWN, YOU GOTTA KNOW THAT!
I DON'T KNOW **HOW** HE GOT OUT--I'D **JUST** CHECKED ON HIM, AND--
OKAY. WE'LL TALK ABOUT IT WHEN I GET HOME.
BYE.
HAD YOU JUST CHECKED ON HIM? OR WERE YOU WATCHING HIM THE **WHOLE TIME?**
AND TELL ME, NEAL... HOW DID SOMEONE GET LOOSE IF YOUR ROOM IS **ALWAYS** ON LOCKDOWN?
OKAY, LOOK... I **FUCKED UP**, OBVIOUSLY. BUT I DON'T KNOW HOW, AND I SWEAR IF YOU'LL JUST--
HURRK!
ENOUGH TALK.
WRAMM

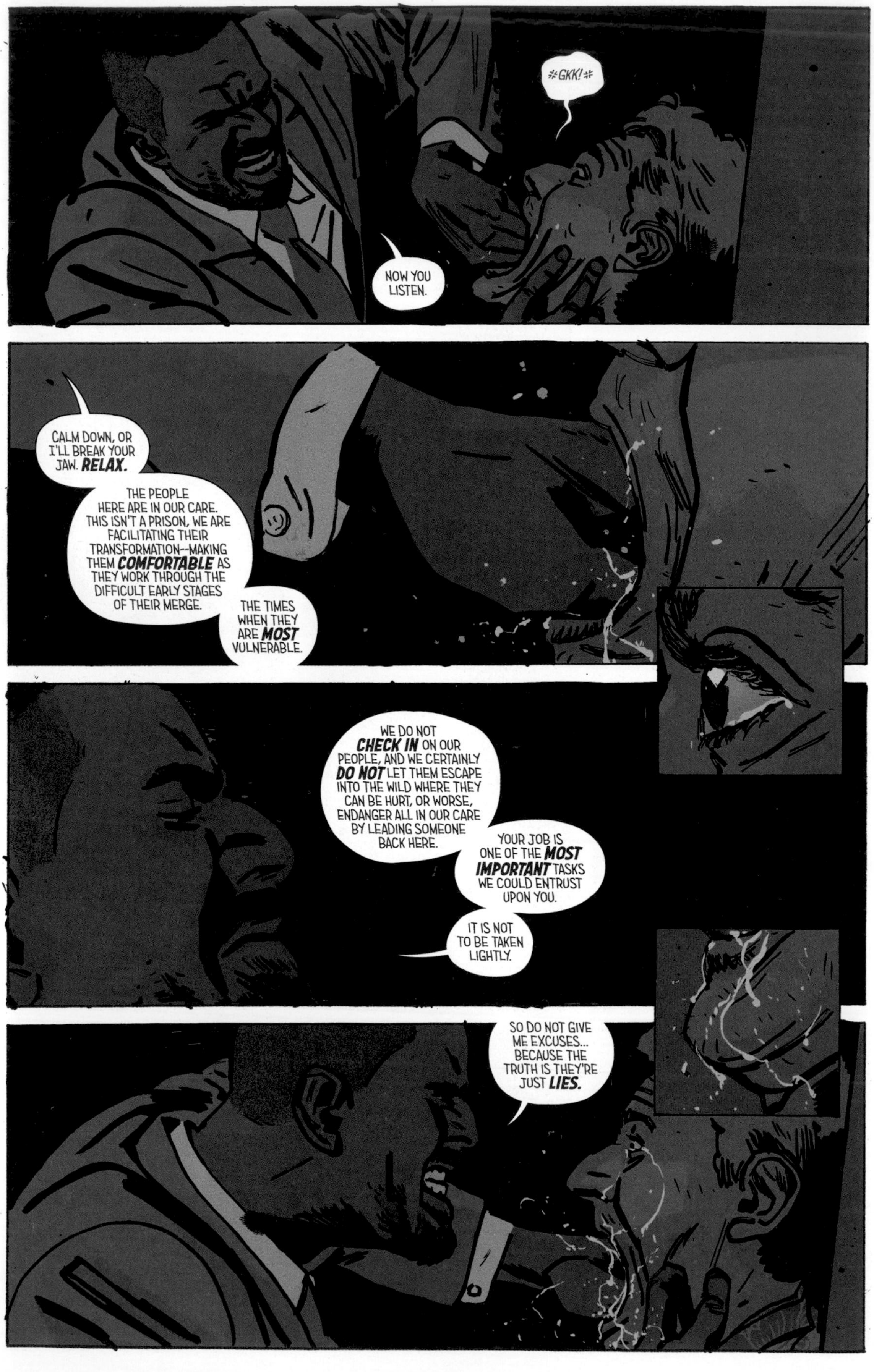
#GKK!#
NOW YOU LISTEN.
CALM DOWN, OR I'LL BREAK YOUR JAW. RELAX.
THE PEOPLE HERE ARE IN OUR CARE. THIS ISN'T A PRISON, WE ARE FACILITATING THEIR TRANSFORMATION--MAKING THEM COMFORTABLE AS THEY WORK THROUGH THE DIFFICULT EARLY STAGES OF THEIR MERGE.
THE TIMES WHEN THEY ARE MOST VULNERABLE.
WE DO NOT CHECK IN ON OUR PEOPLE, AND WE CERTAINLY DO NOT LET THEM ESCAPE INTO THE WILD WHERE THEY CAN BE HURT, OR WORSE, ENDANGER ALL IN OUR CARE BY LEADING SOMEONE BACK HERE.
YOUR JOB IS ONE OF THE MOST IMPORTANT TASKS WE COULD ENTRUST UPON YOU.
IT IS NOT TO BE TAKEN LIGHTLY.
SO DO NOT GIVE ME EXCUSES... BECAUSE THE TRUTH IS THEY'RE JUST LIES.

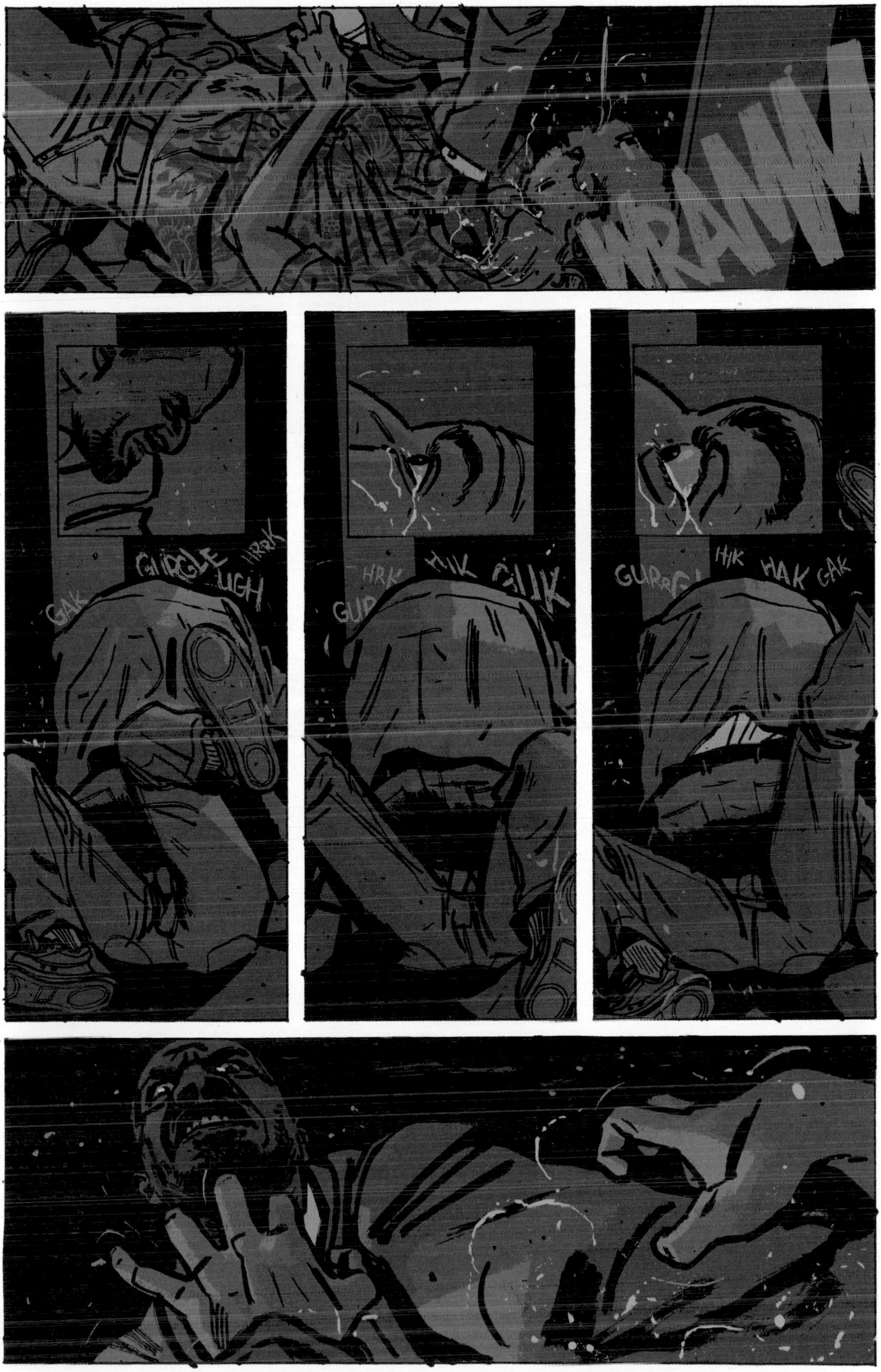
WRAMM
GAK
GURGLE
UGH
HRRK
HRK
GUR
HIK
GURRG
HIK
HAK
GAK

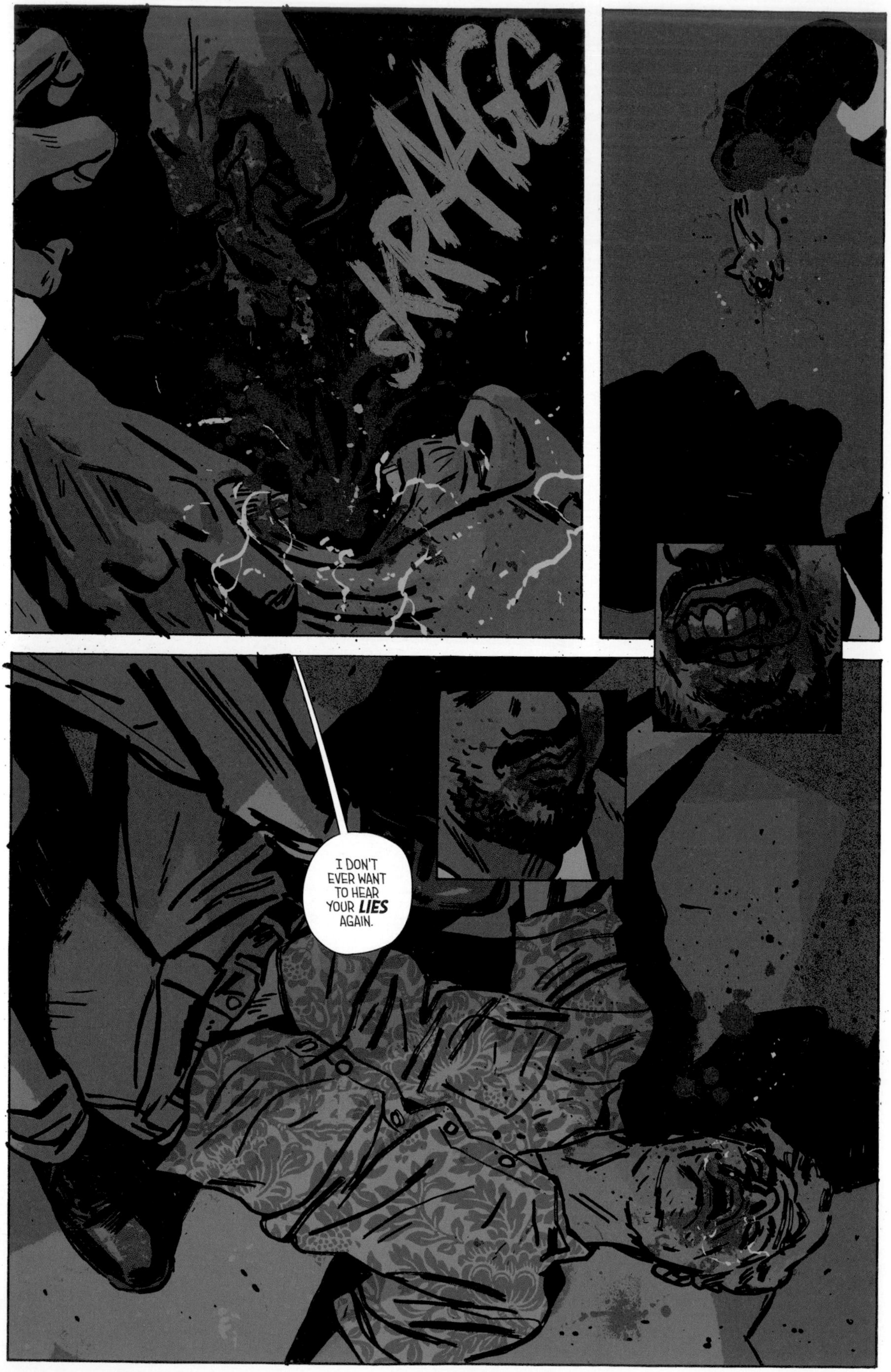
SKRAGG
I DON'T EVER WANT TO HEAR YOUR LIES AGAIN.

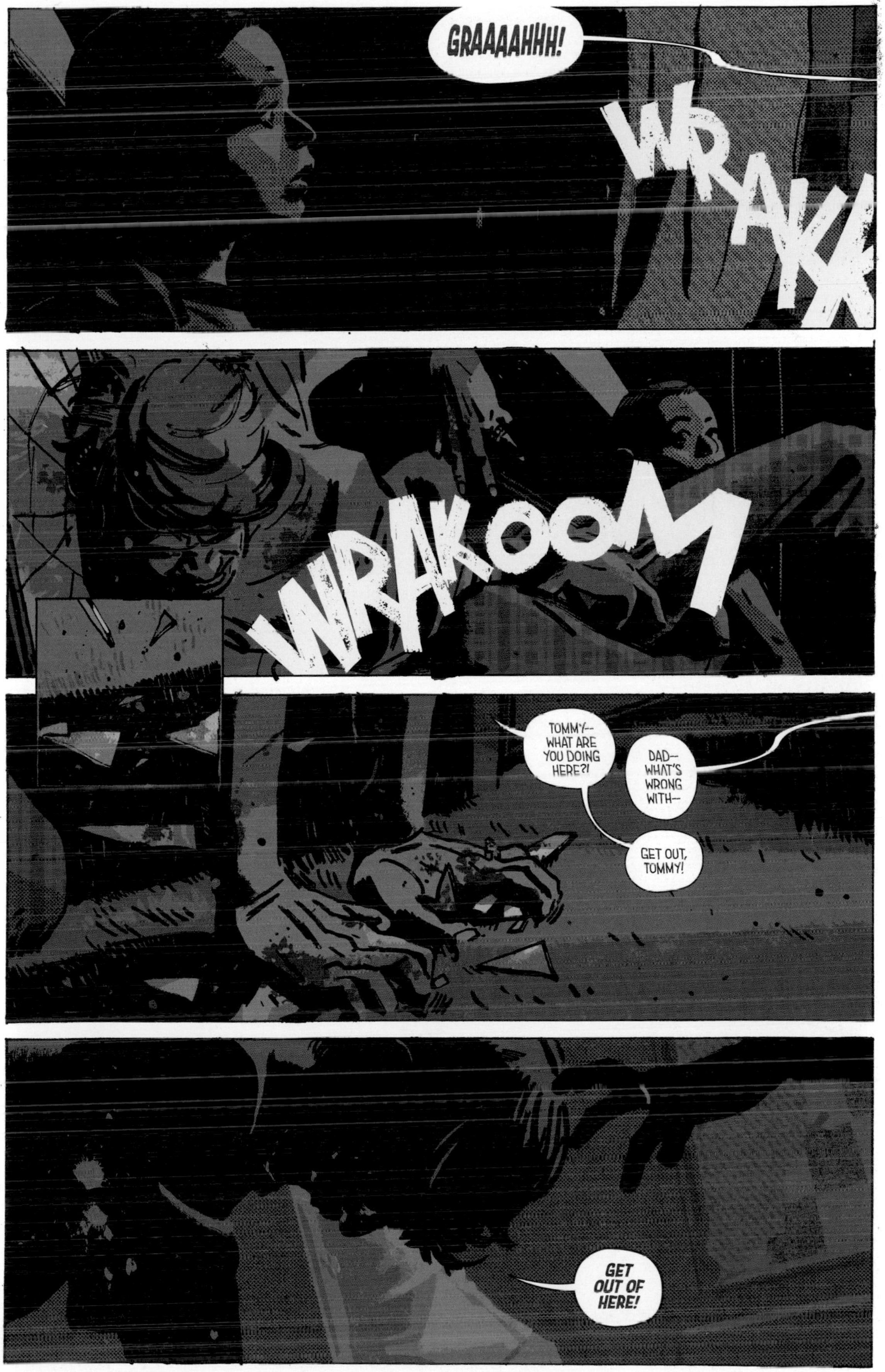
GRAAAAHHH!
WRAKK
WRAKOOM
TOMMY--
WHAT ARE YOU DOING HERE?!
DAD-- WHAT'S WRONG WITH--
GET OUT, TOMMY!
GET OUT OF HERE!

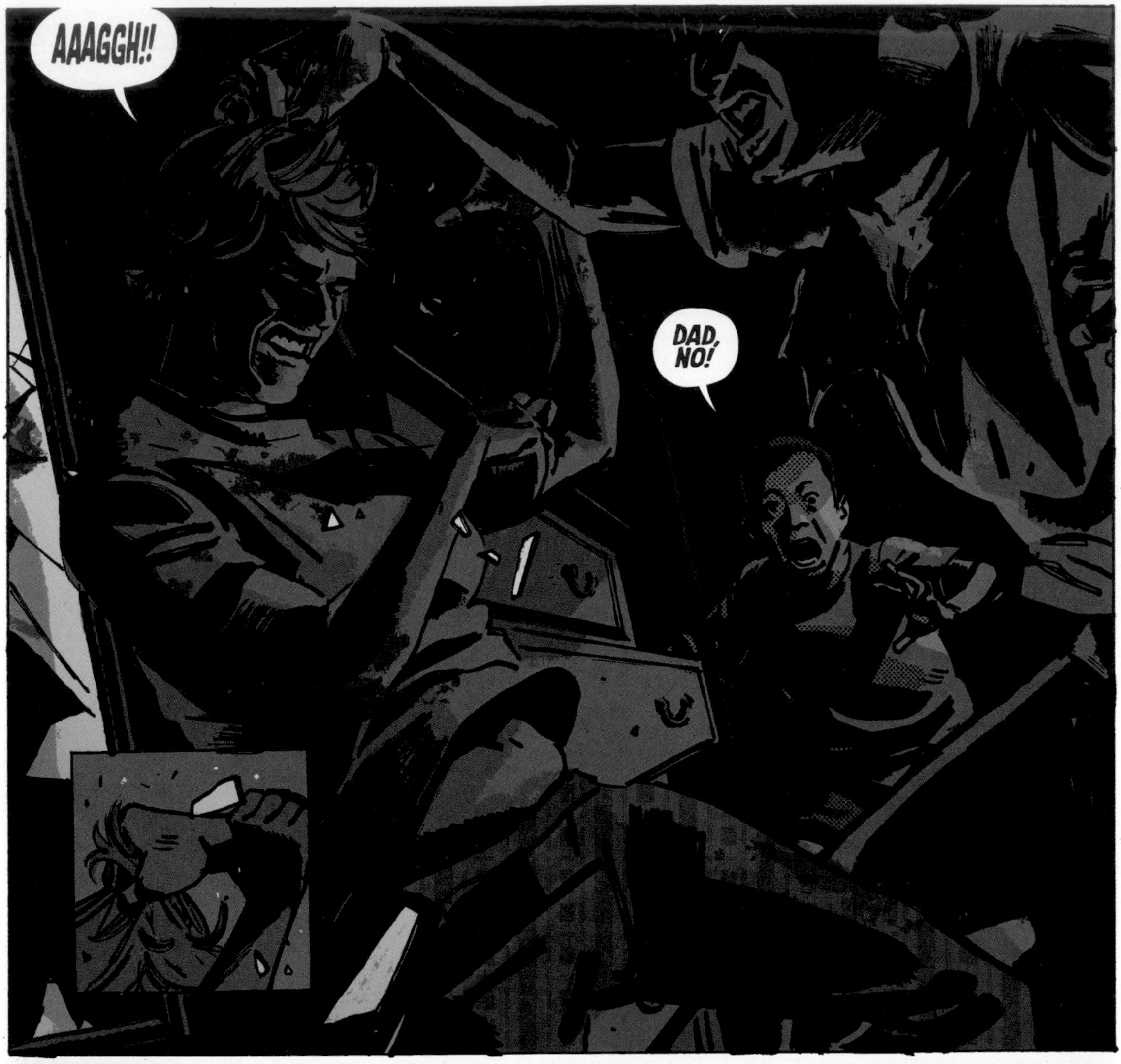
AAAGGH!!
DAD, NO!

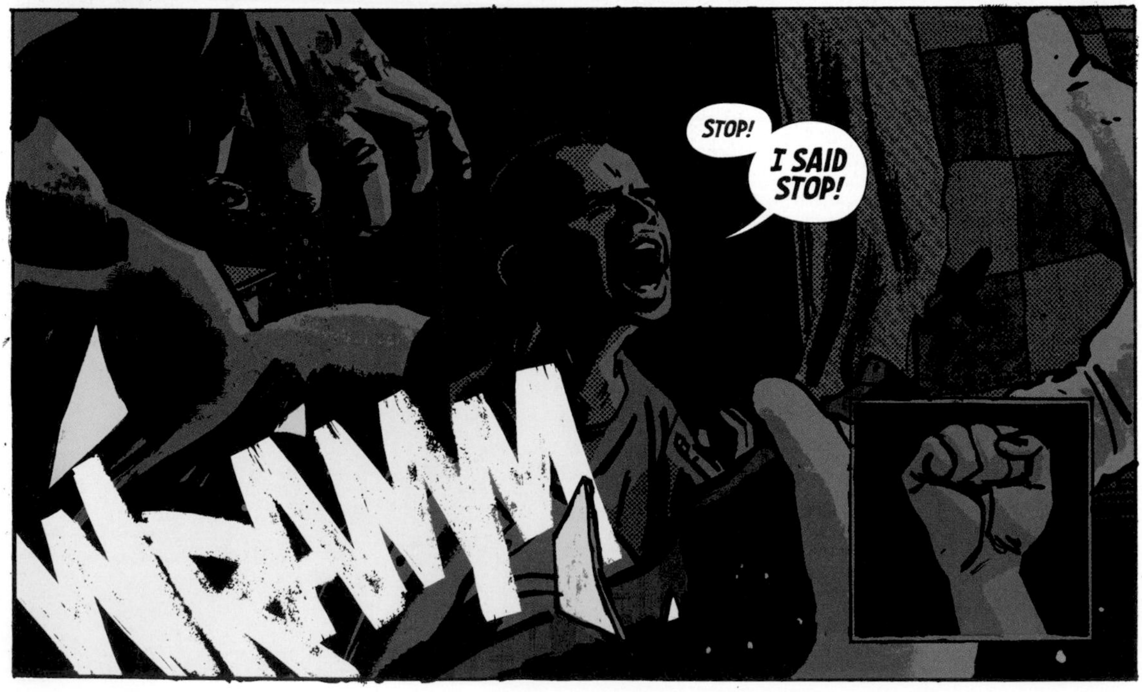
STOP!
I SAID STOP!
WRAMM

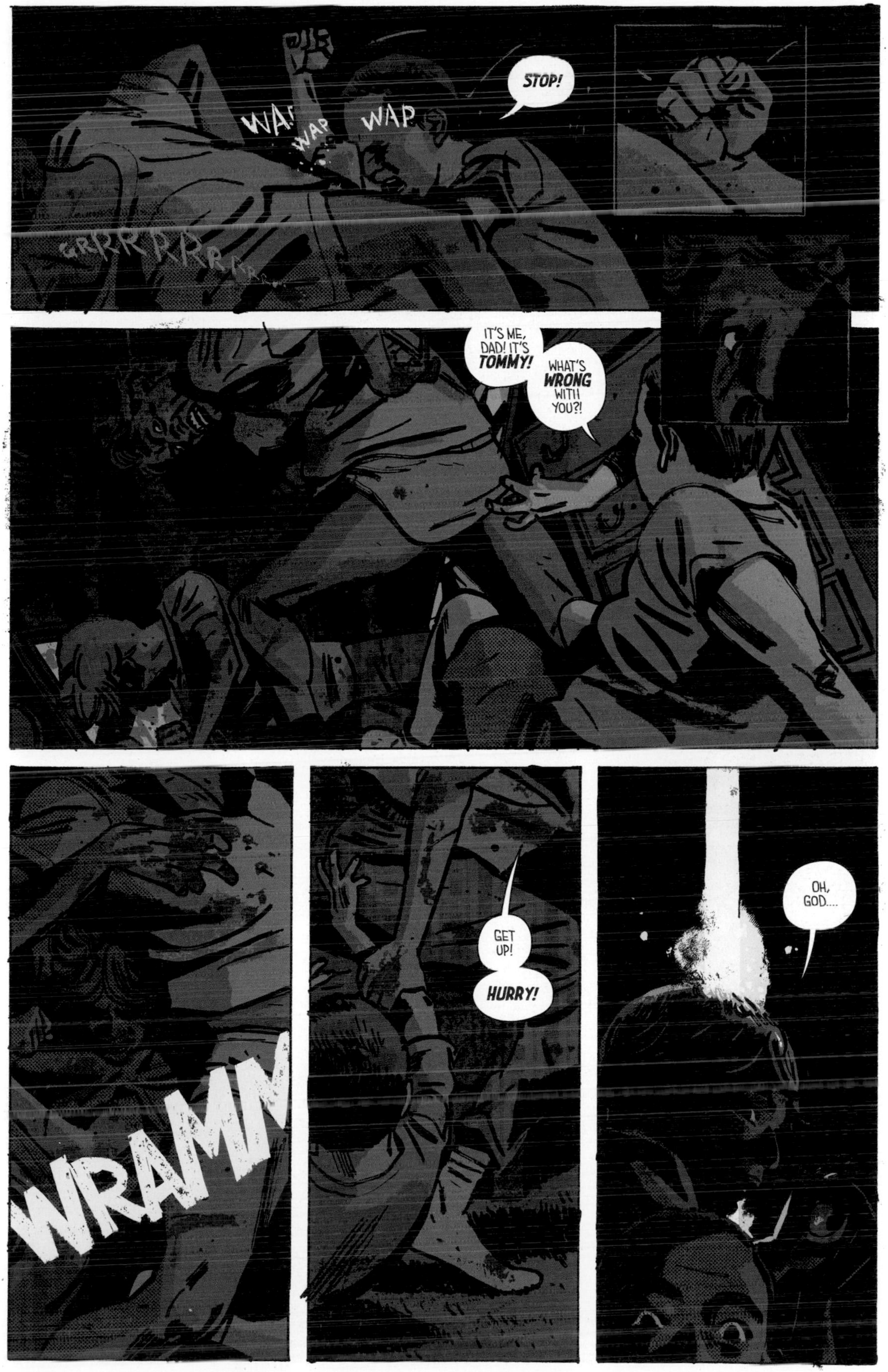
WAP
WAP
WAP
STOP!
GRRRRRRRrrr
IT'S ME, DAD! IT'S TOMMY!
WHAT'S WRONG WITH YOU?!
WRAMM
GET UP!
HURRY!
OH, GOD....

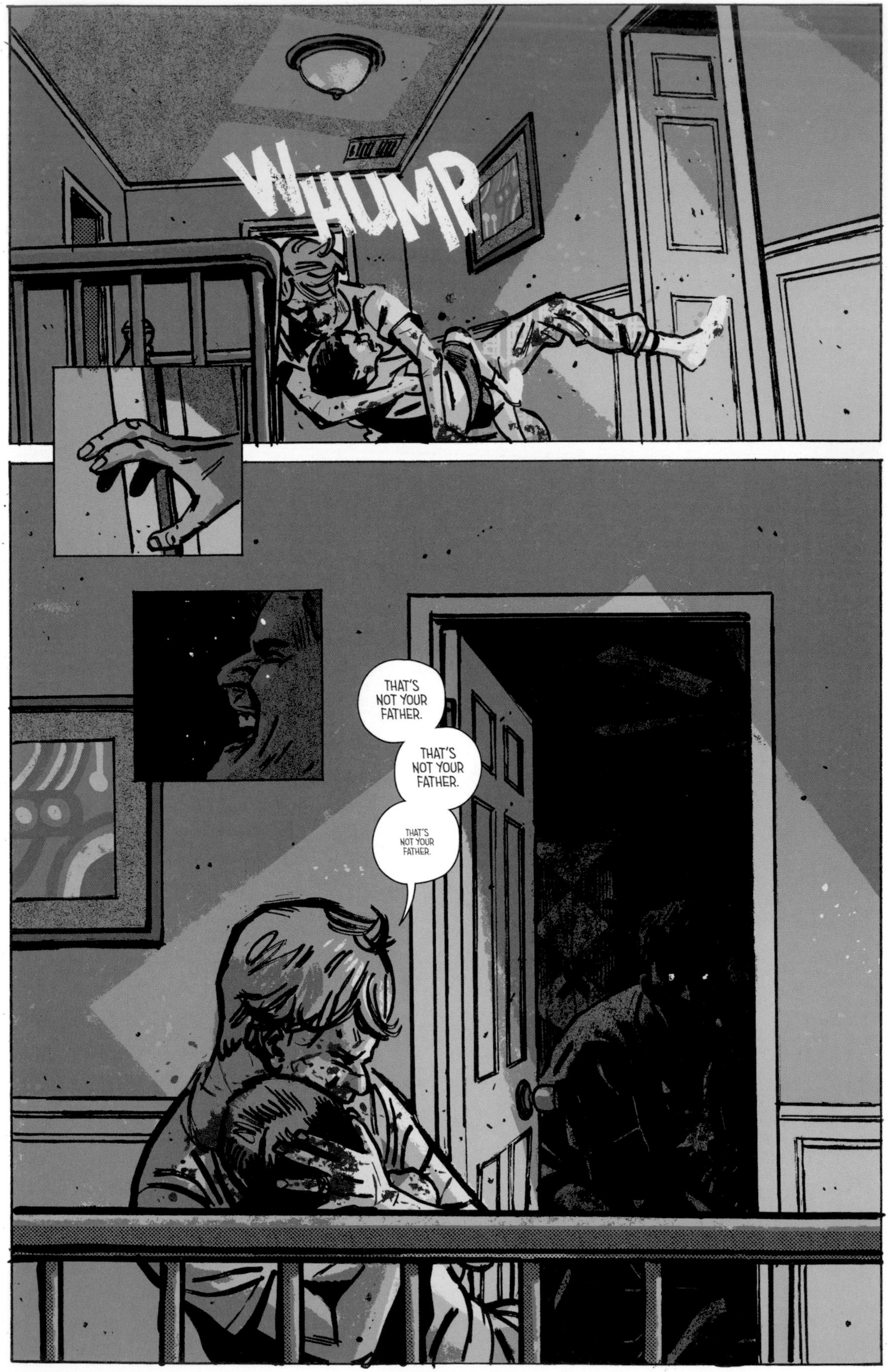
WHUMP
THAT'S NOT YOUR FATHER.
THAT'S NOT YOUR FATHER.
THAT'S NOT YOUR FATHER.

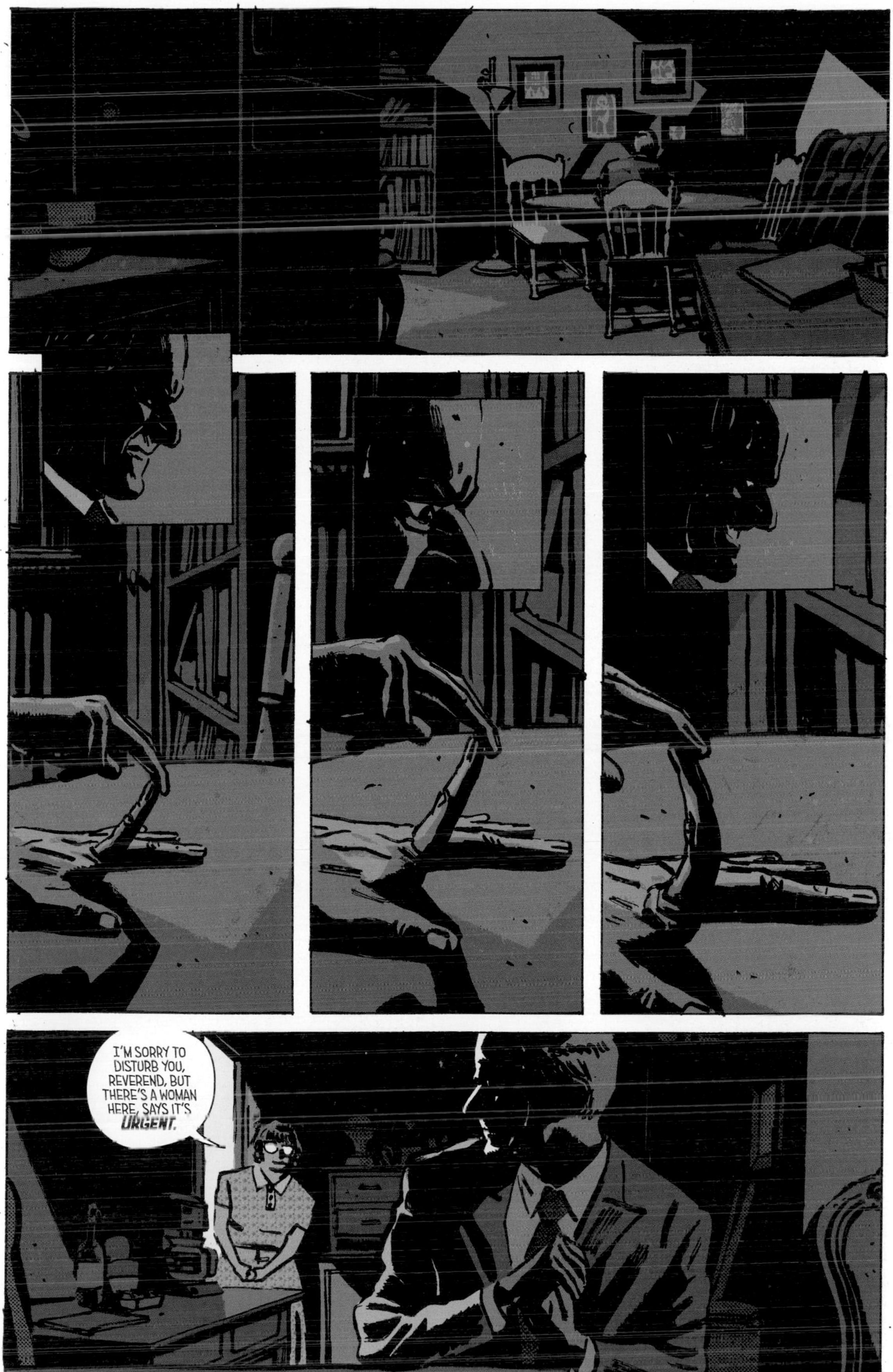
I'M SORRY TO DISTURB YOU, REVEREND, BUT THERE'S A WOMAN HERE, SAYS IT'S URGENT.

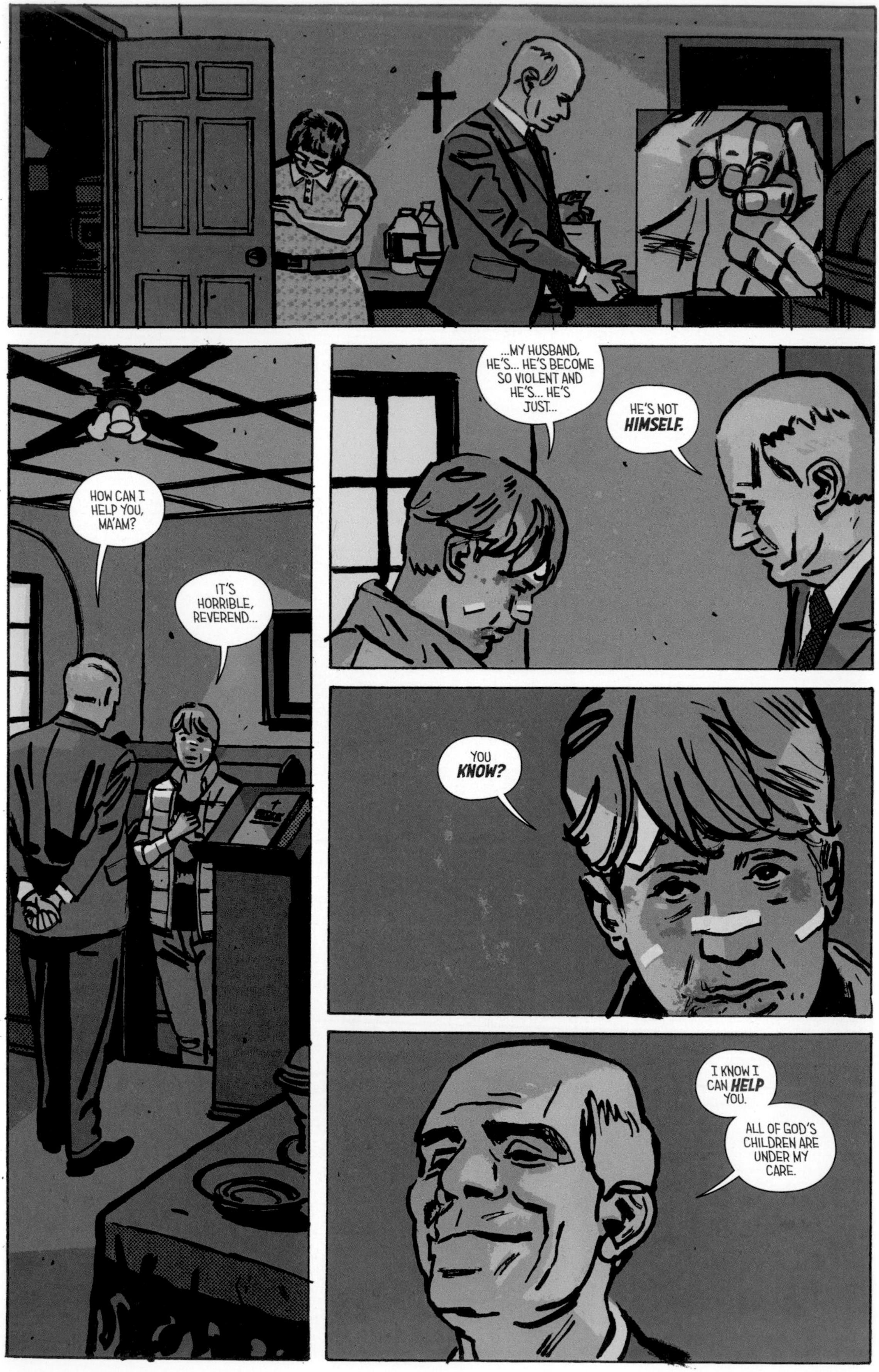
HOW CAN I HELP YOU, MA'AM?
IT'S HORRIBLE, REVEREND...
...MY HUSBAND, HE'S... HE'S BECOME SO VIOLENT AND HE'S... HE'S JUST...
HE'S NOT **HIMSELF.**
YOU **KNOW?**
I KNOW I CAN **HELP** YOU.
ALL OF GOD'S CHILDREN ARE UNDER MY CARE.

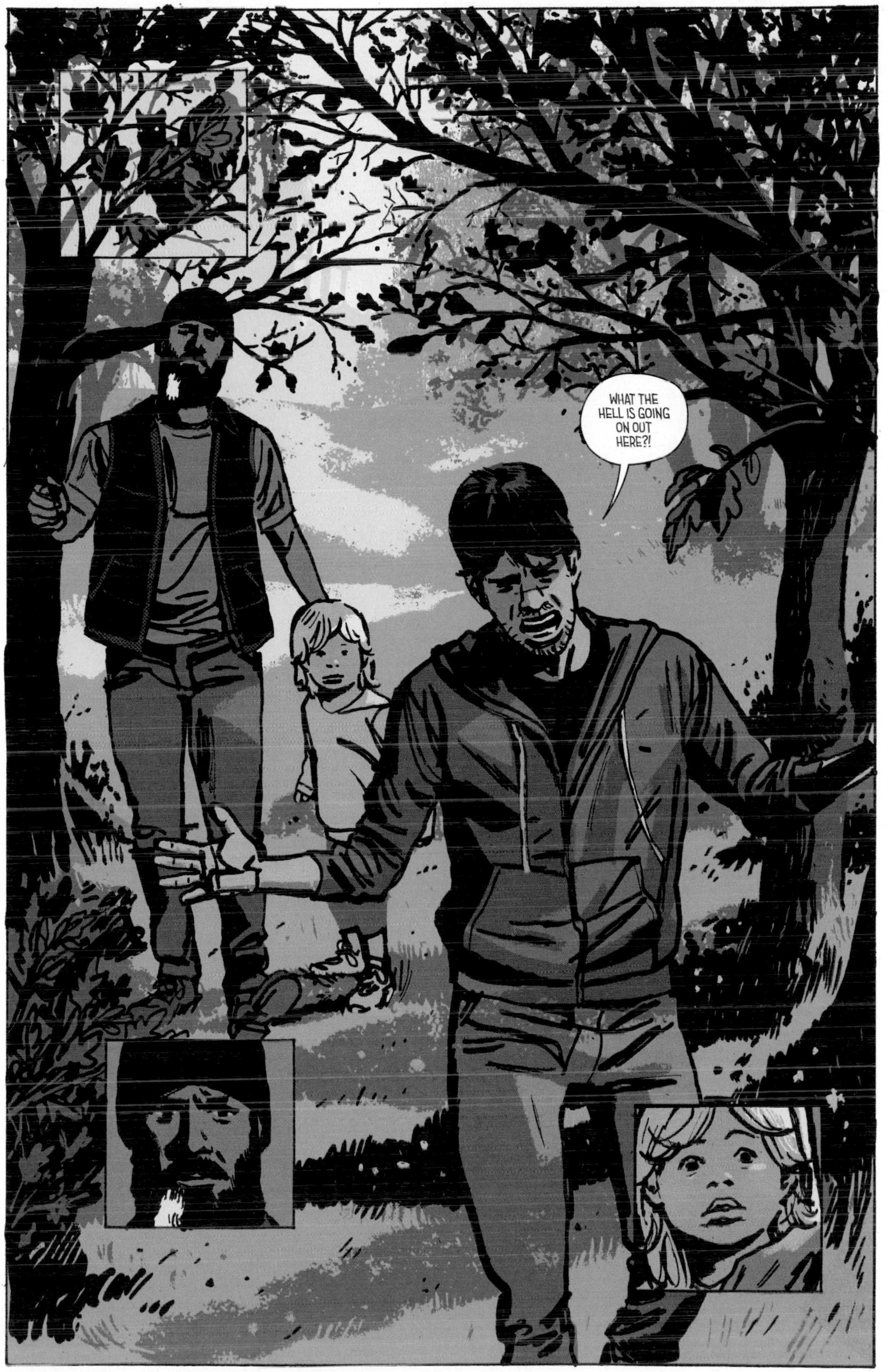
WHAT THE HELL IS GOING ON OUT HERE?!

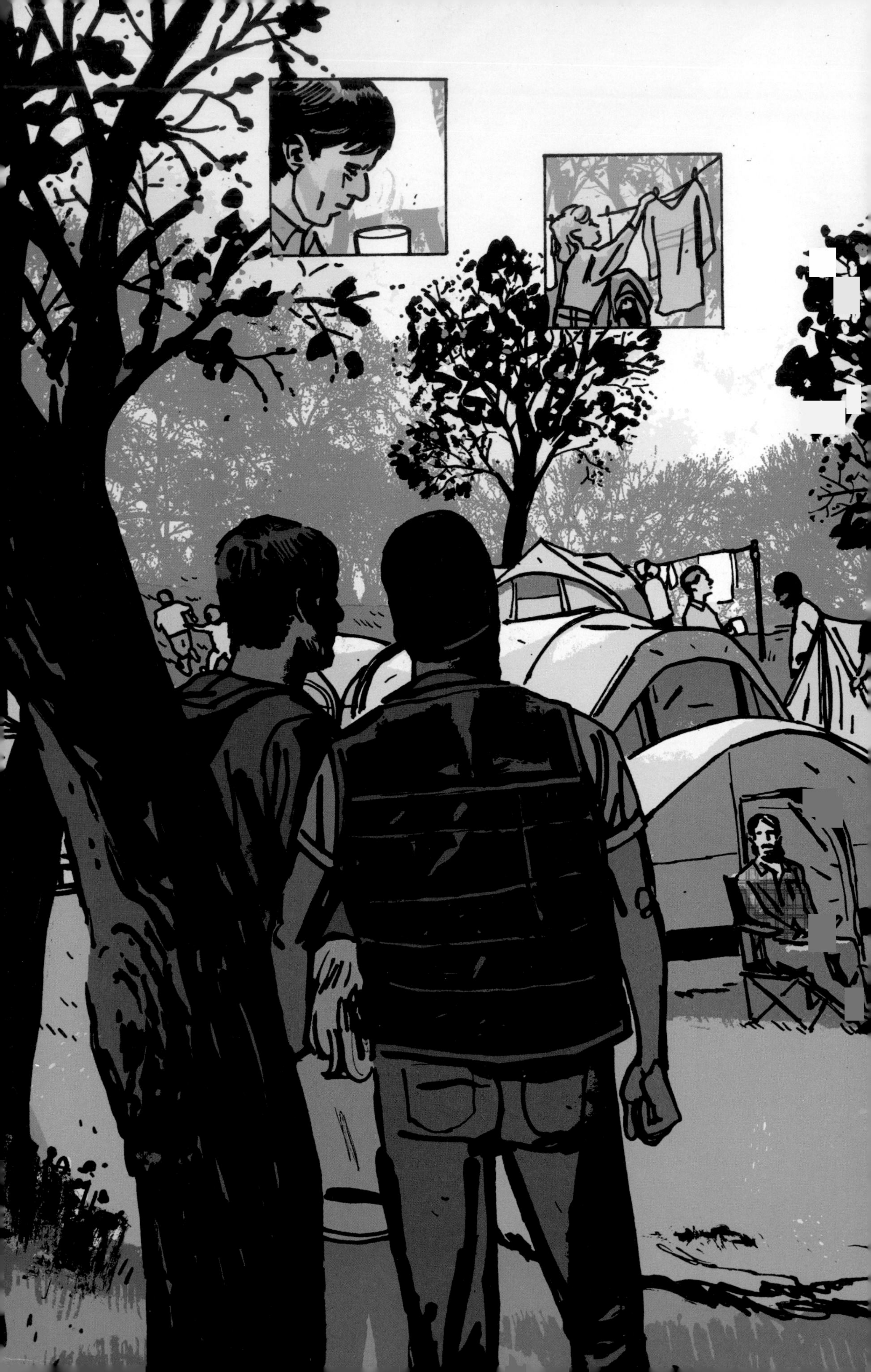

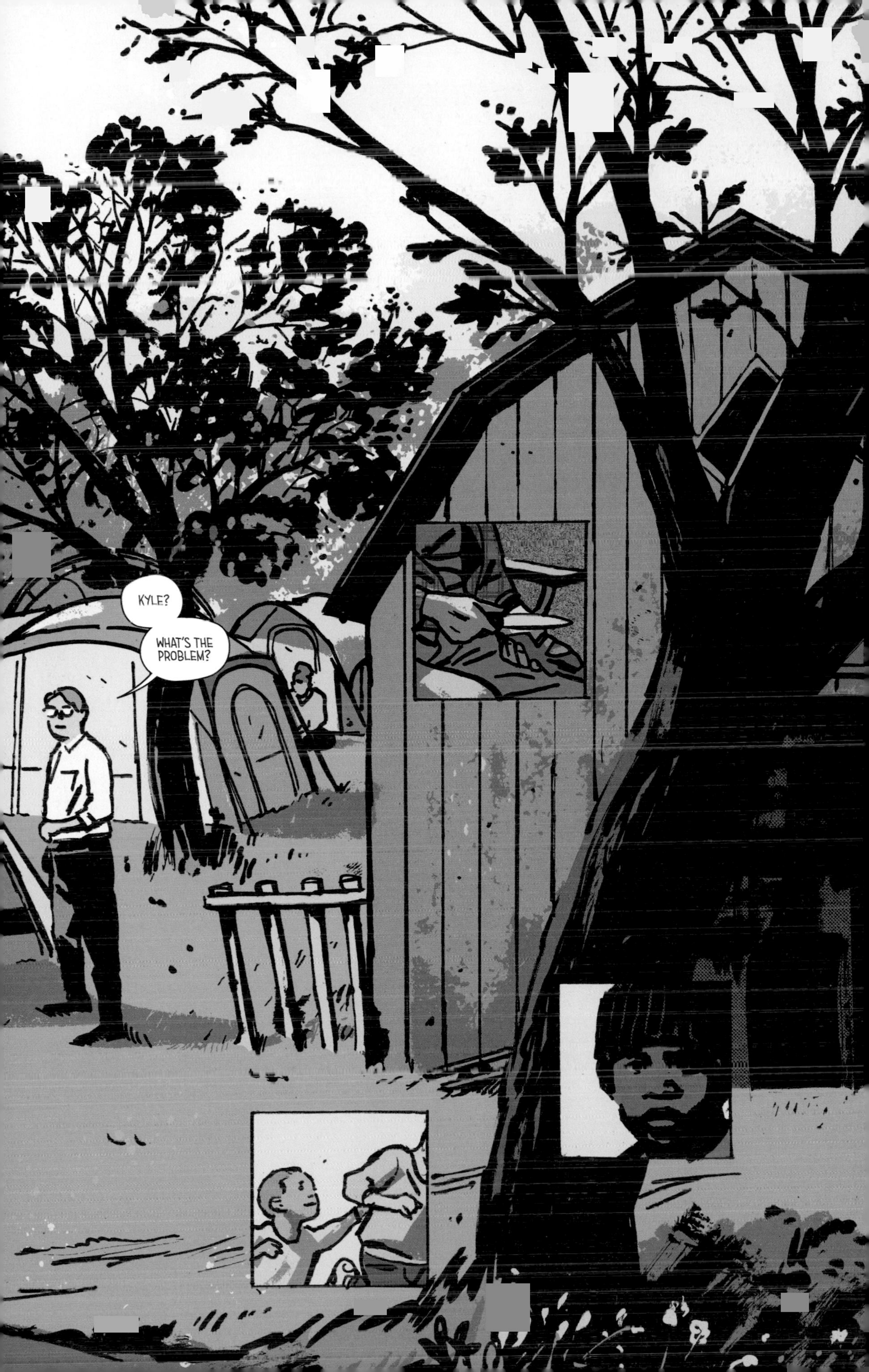
KYLE?
WHAT'S THE PROBLEM?

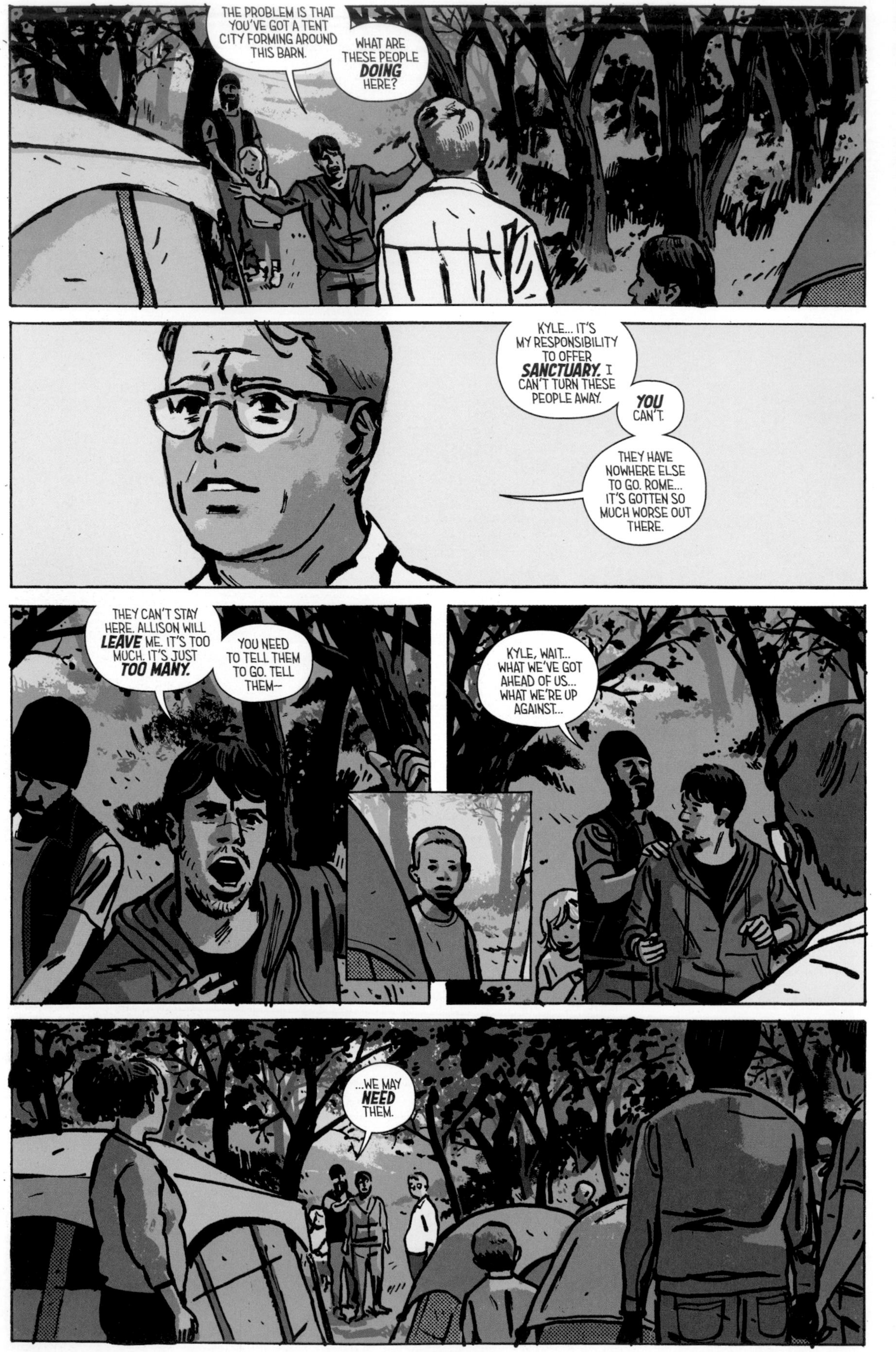
THE PROBLEM IS THAT YOU'VE GOT A TENT CITY FORMING AROUND THIS BARN.
WHAT ARE THESE PEOPLE DOING HERE?
KYLE... IT'S MY RESPONSIBILITY TO OFFER SANCTUARY. I CAN'T TURN THESE PEOPLE AWAY.
YOU CAN'T.
THEY HAVE NOWHERE ELSE TO GO. ROME... IT'S GOTTEN SO MUCH WORSE OUT THERE.
THEY CAN'T STAY HERE. ALLISON WILL LEAVE ME. IT'S TOO MUCH. IT'S JUST TOO MANY.
YOU NEED TO TELL THEM TO GO. TELL THEM--
KYLE, WAIT... WHAT WE'VE GOT AHEAD OF US... WHAT WE'RE UP AGAINST...
...WE MAY NEED THEM.

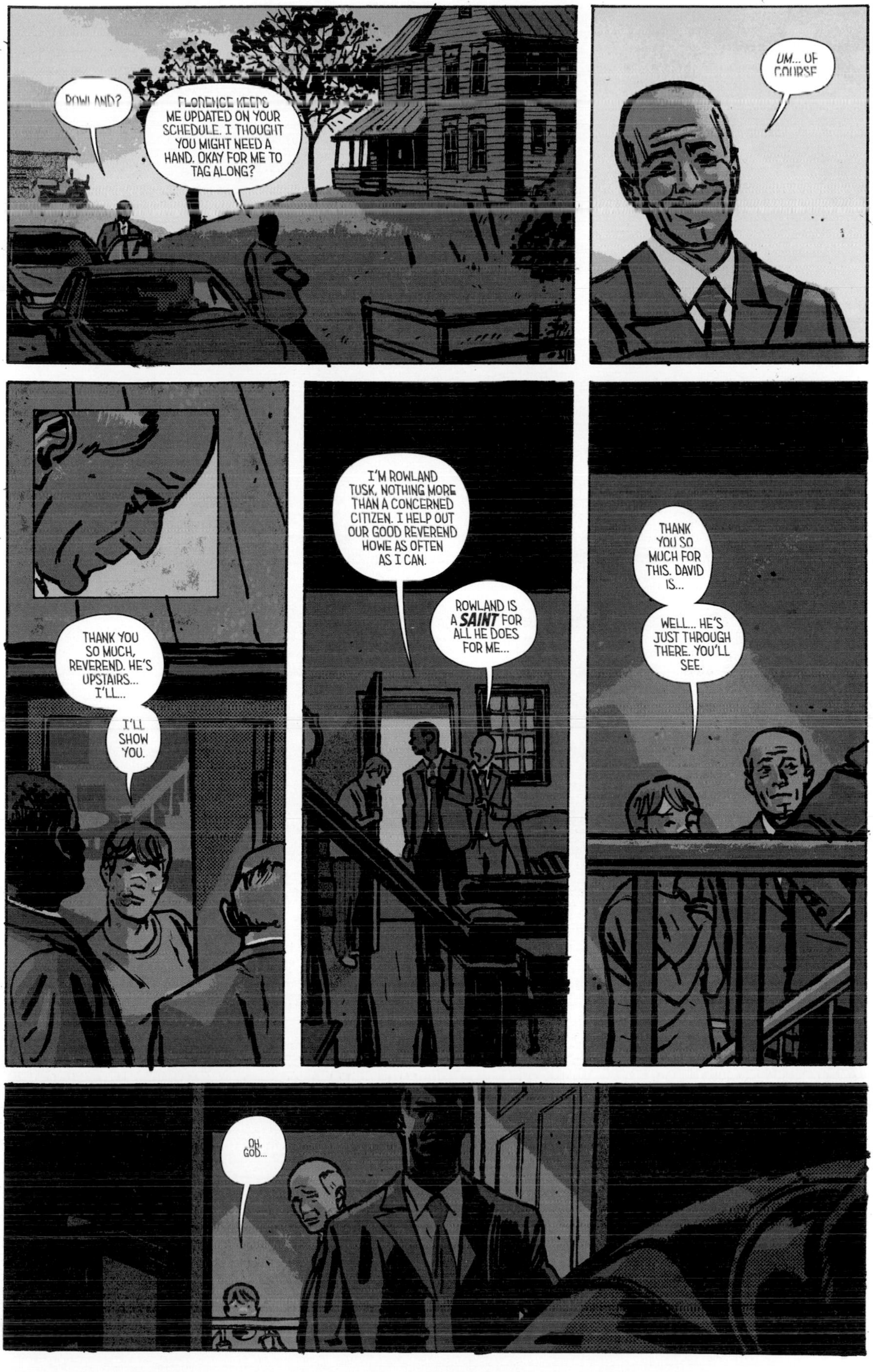
ROWLAND?
FLORENCE KEEPS ME UPDATED ON YOUR SCHEDULE. I THOUGHT YOU MIGHT NEED A HAND. OKAY FOR ME TO TAG ALONG?
UM... OF COURSE
THANK YOU SO MUCH, REVEREND. HE'S UPSTAIRS... I'LL...
I'LL SHOW YOU.
I'M ROWLAND TUSK, NOTHING MORE THAN A CONCERNED CITIZEN. I HELP OUT OUR GOOD REVEREND HOWE AS OFTEN AS I CAN.
ROWLAND IS A SAINT FOR ALL HE DOES FOR ME...
THANK YOU SO MUCH FOR THIS. DAVID IS...
WELL... HE'S JUST THROUGH THERE. YOU'LL SEE.
OH, GOD...

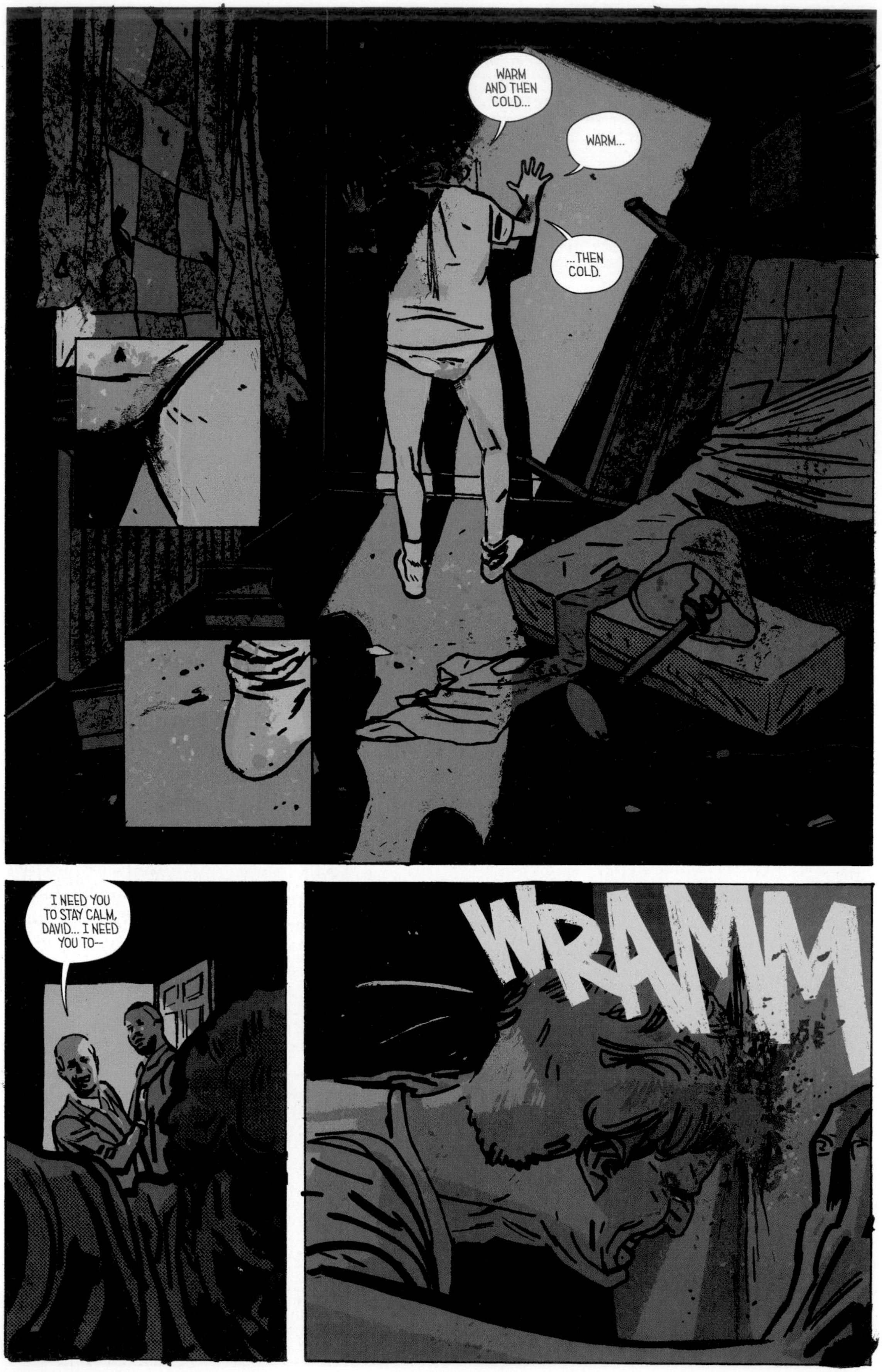
WARM AND THEN COLD...
WARM...
...THEN COLD.
I NEED YOU TO STAY CALM, DAVID... I NEED YOU TO--
WRAMM

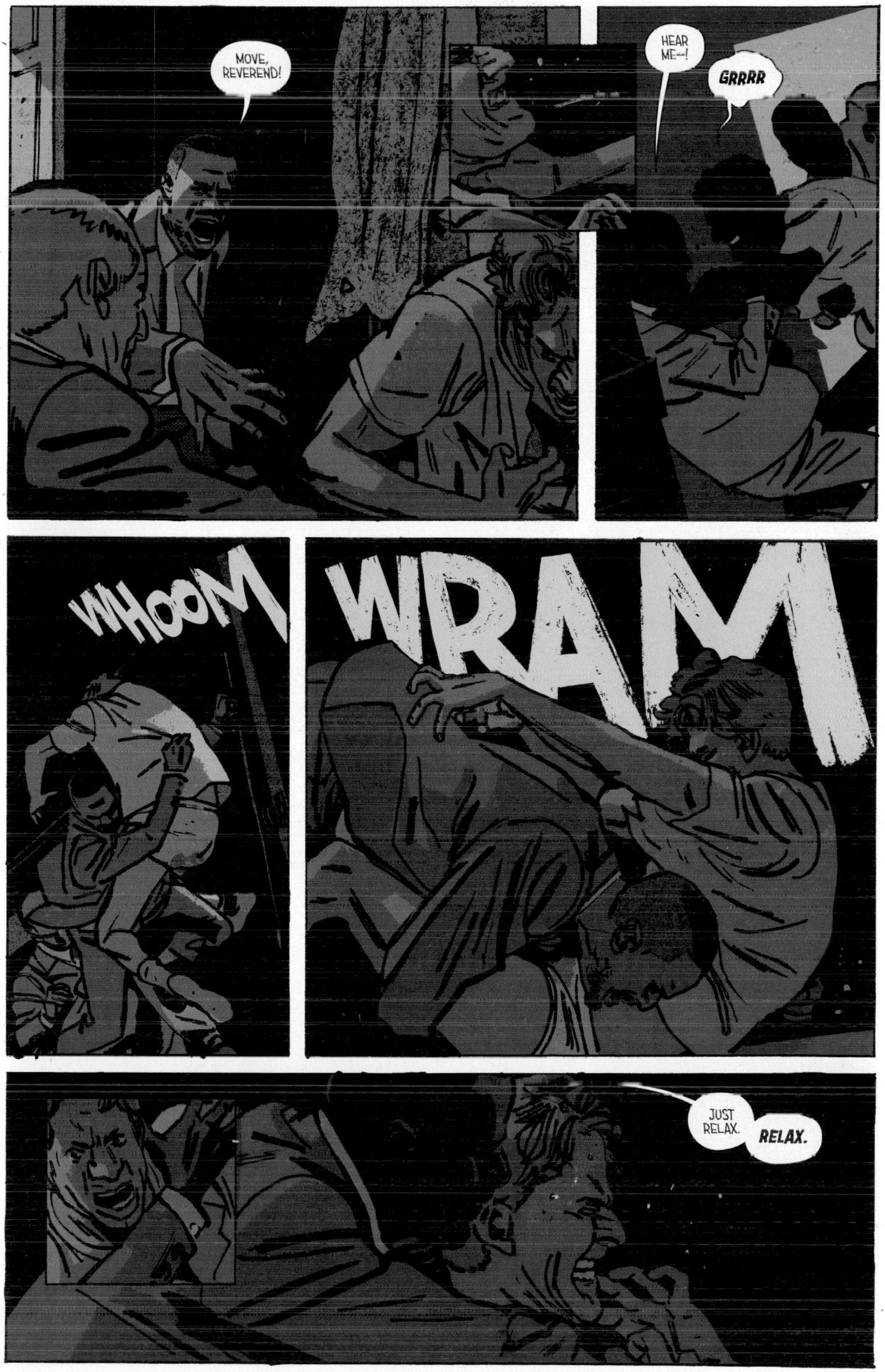
MOVE, REVEREND!
HEAR ME--!
GRRRR
WHOOM
WRAM
JUST RELAX.
RELAX.

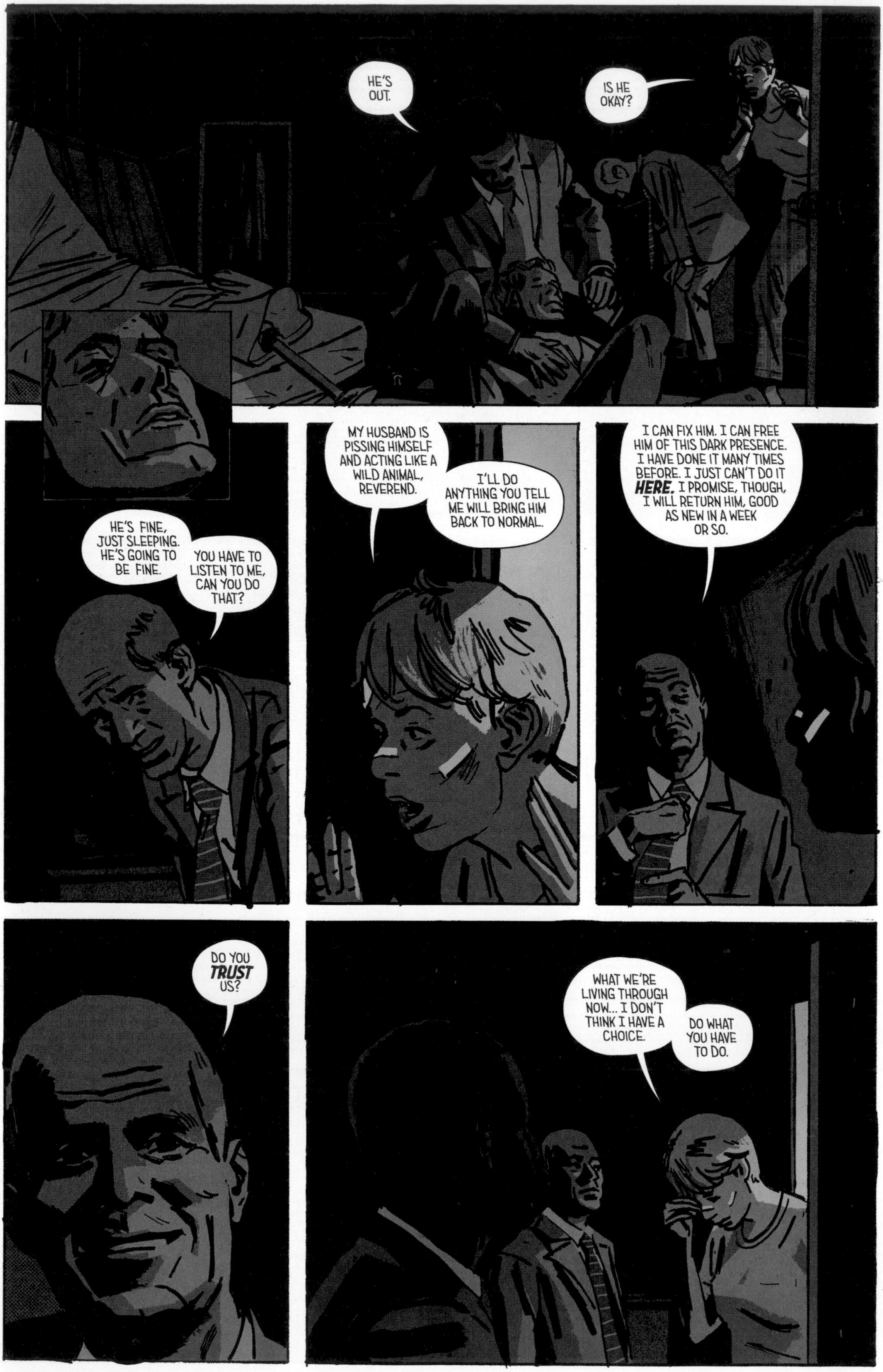
HE'S OUT.
IS HE OKAY?
HE'S FINE, JUST SLEEPING. HE'S GOING TO BE FINE.
YOU HAVE TO LISTEN TO ME, CAN YOU DO THAT?
MY HUSBAND IS PISSING HIMSELF AND ACTING LIKE A WILD ANIMAL, REVEREND.
I'LL DO ANYTHING YOU TELL ME WILL BRING HIM BACK TO NORMAL.
I CAN FIX HIM. I CAN FREE HIM OF THIS DARK PRESENCE. I HAVE DONE IT MANY TIMES BEFORE. I JUST CAN'T DO IT HERE. I PROMISE, THOUGH, I WILL RETURN HIM, GOOD AS NEW IN A WEEK OR SO.
DO YOU TRUST US?
WHAT WE'RE LIVING THROUGH NOW... I DON'T THINK I HAVE A CHOICE.
DO WHAT YOU HAVE TO DO.

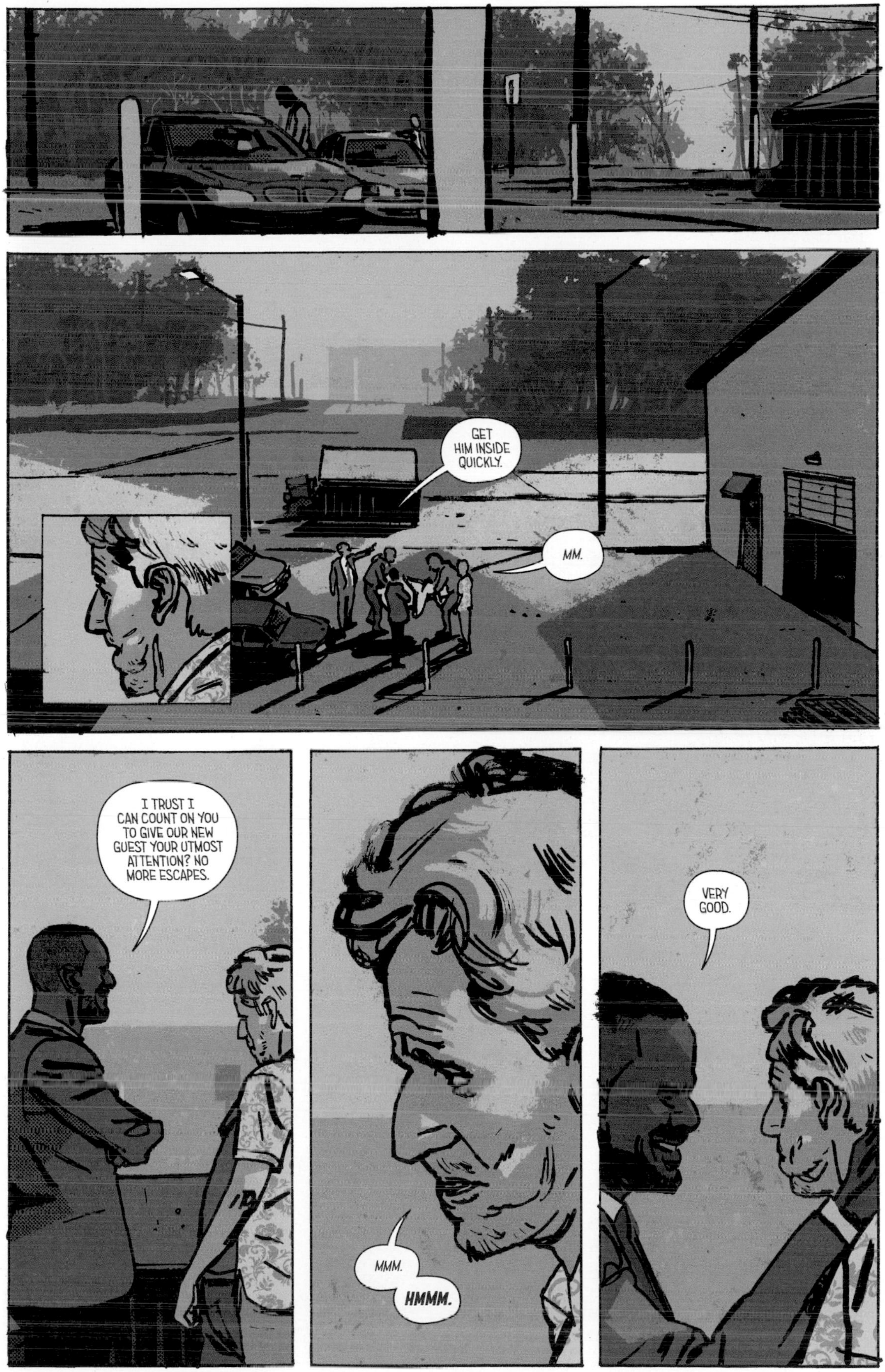
GET HIM INSIDE QUICKLY.
MM.
I TRUST I CAN COUNT ON YOU TO GIVE OUR NEW GUEST YOUR UTMOST ATTENTION? NO MORE ESCAPES.
MMM.
HMMM.
VERY GOOD.

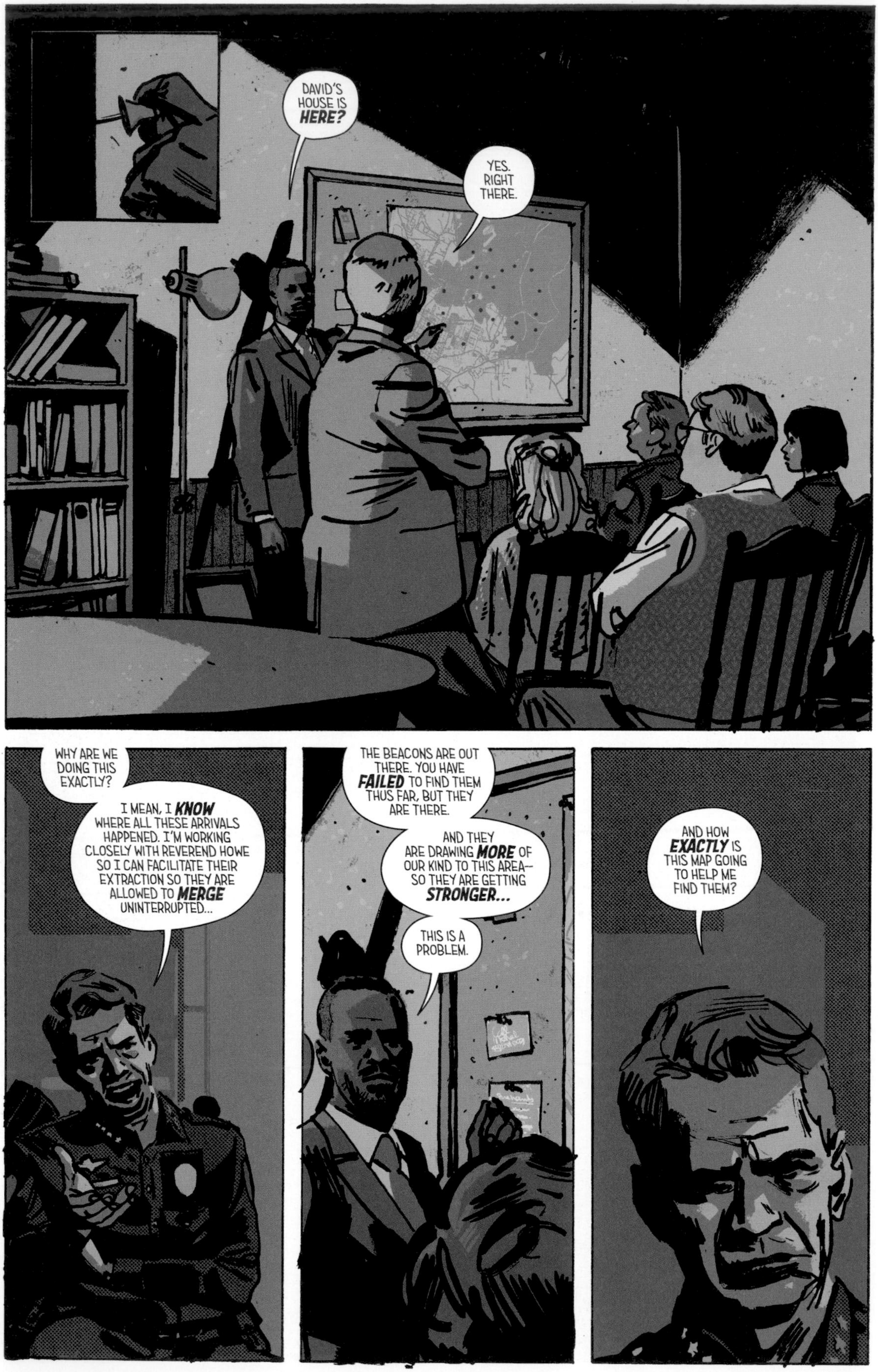
DAVID'S HOUSE IS HERE?
YES. RIGHT THERE.
WHY ARE WE DOING THIS EXACTLY?
I MEAN, I KNOW WHERE ALL THESE ARRIVALS HAPPENED. I'M WORKING CLOSELY WITH REVEREND HOWE SO I CAN FACILITATE THEIR EXTRACTION SO THEY ARE ALLOWED TO MERGE UNINTERRUPTED...
THE BEACONS ARE OUT THERE. YOU HAVE FAILED TO FIND THEM THUS FAR, BUT THEY ARE THERE.
AND THEY ARE DRAWING MORE OF OUR KIND TO THIS AREA-- SO THEY ARE GETTING STRONGER...
THIS IS A PROBLEM.
AND HOW EXACTLY IS THIS MAP GOING TO HELP ME FIND THEM?

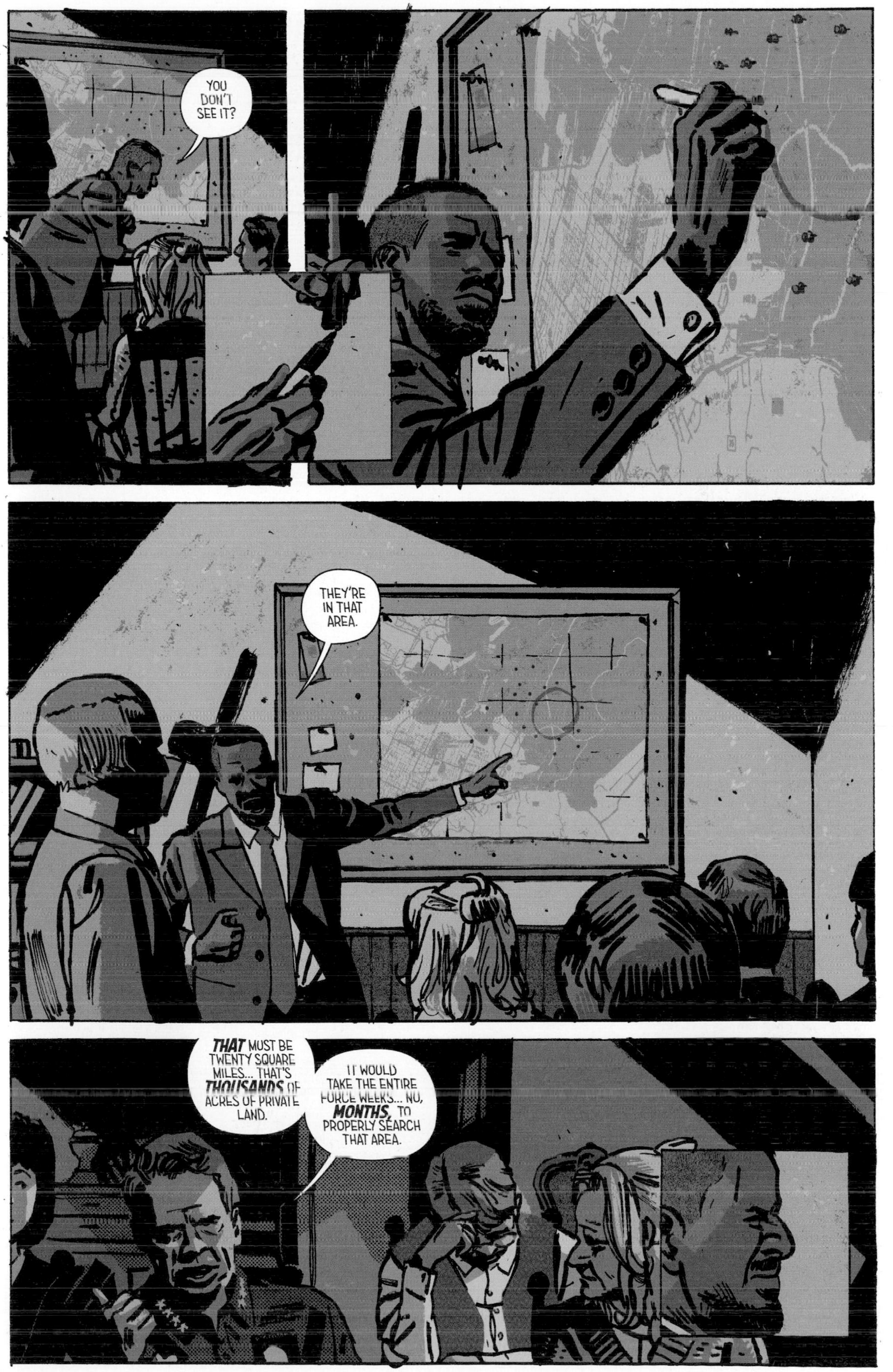
YOU DON'T SEE IT?
THEY'RE IN THAT AREA.
THAT MUST BE TWENTY SQUARE MILES... THAT'S THOUSANDS OF ACRES OF PRIVATE LAND.
IT WOULD TAKE THE ENTIRE FORCE WEEKS... NO, MONTHS, TO PROPERLY SEARCH THAT AREA.

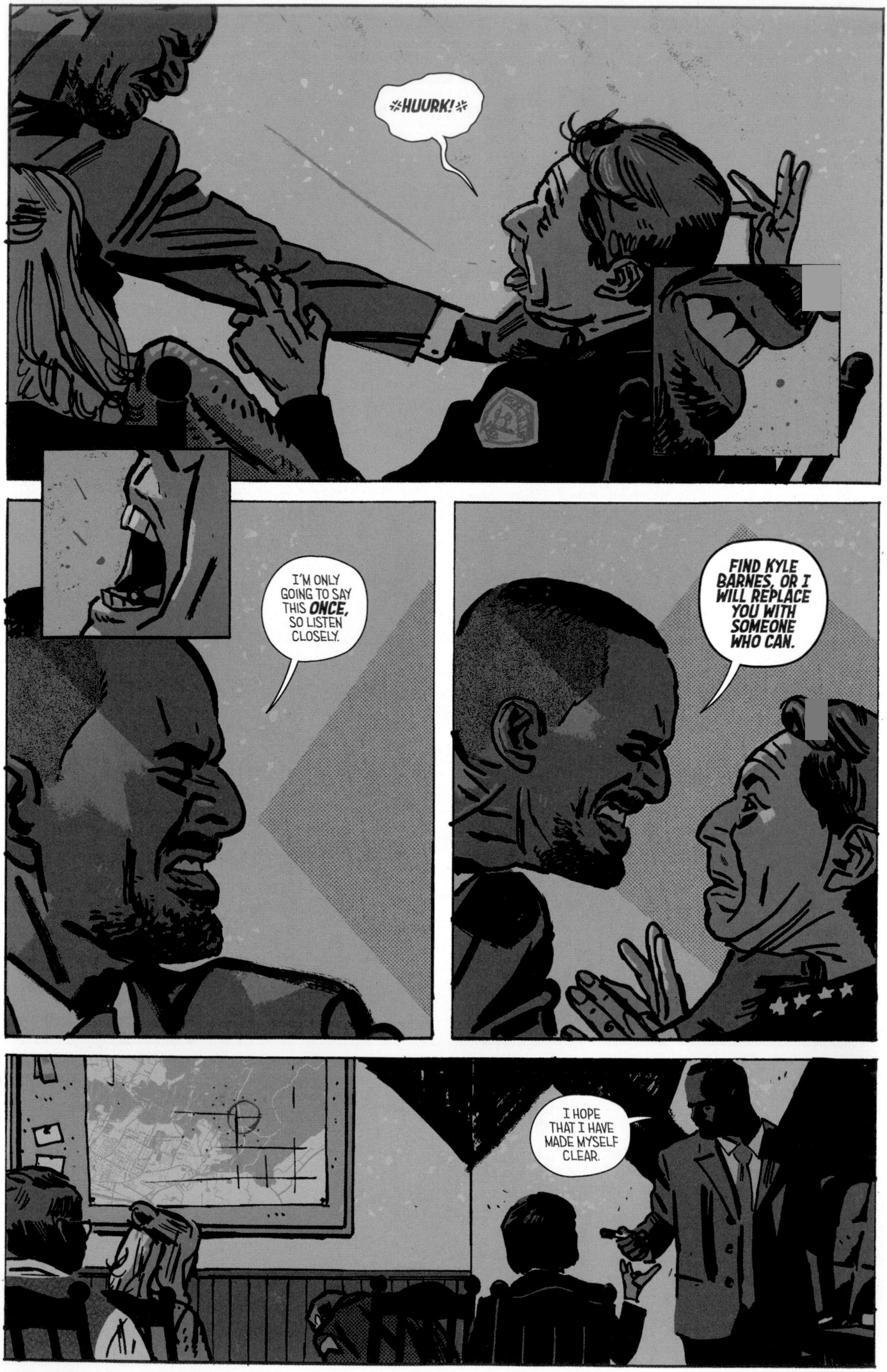
HUURK!
I'M ONLY GOING TO SAY THIS ONCE, SO LISTEN CLOSELY.
FIND KYLE BARNES, OR I WILL REPLACE YOU WITH SOMEONE WHO CAN.
I HOPE THAT I HAVE MADE MYSELF CLEAR.

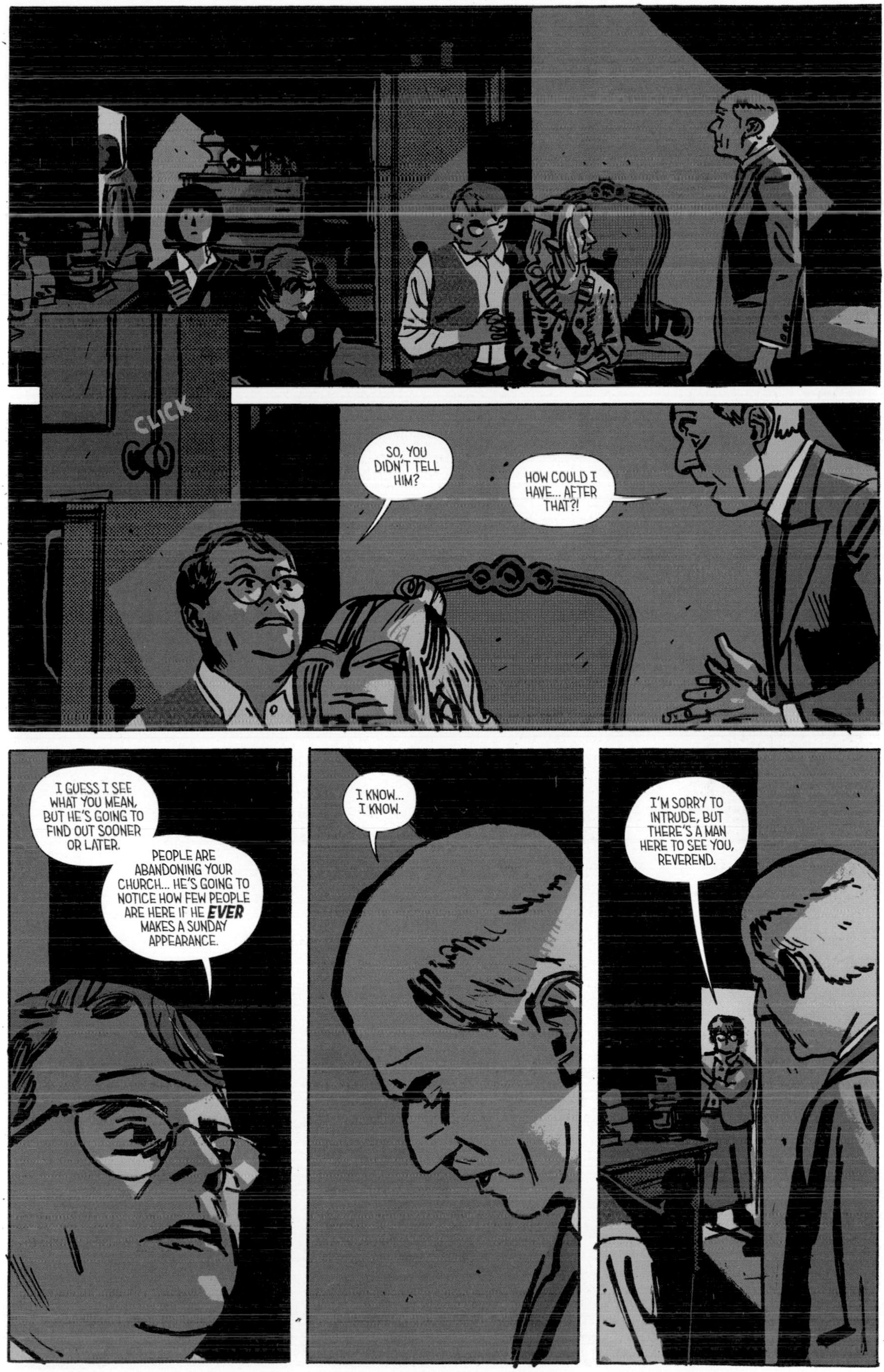
CLICK
SO, YOU DIDN'T TELL HIM?
HOW COULD I HAVE... AFTER THAT?!
I GUESS I SEE WHAT YOU MEAN, BUT HE'S GOING TO FIND OUT SOONER OR LATER.
PEOPLE ARE ABANDONING YOUR CHURCH... HE'S GOING TO NOTICE HOW FEW PEOPLE ARE HERE IF HE EVER MAKES A SUNDAY APPEARANCE.
I KNOW... I KNOW.
I'M SORRY TO INTRUDE, BUT THERE'S A MAN HERE TO SEE YOU, REVEREND.

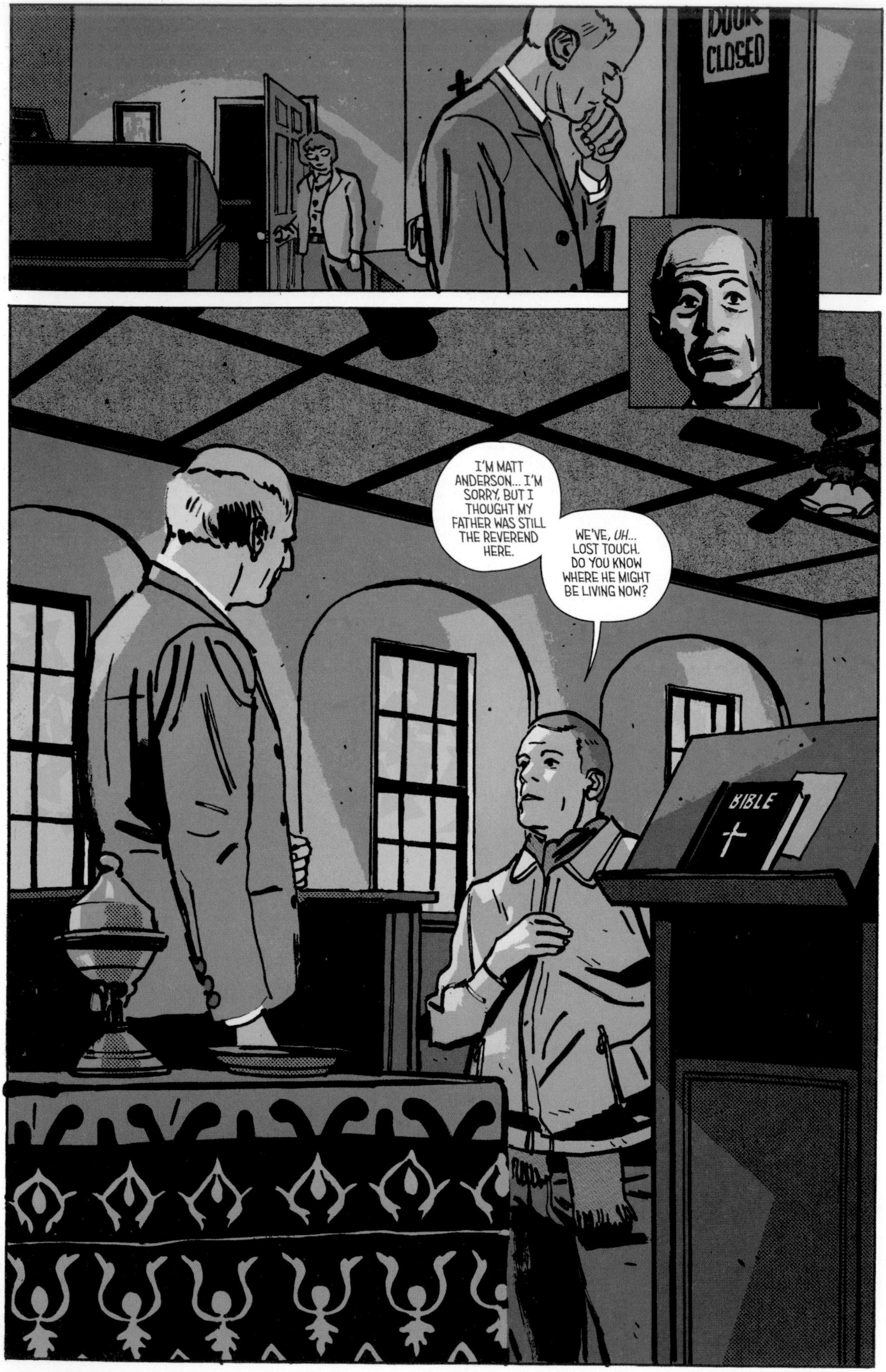
DOOR CLOSED
I'M MATT ANDERSON... I'M SORRY, BUT I THOUGHT MY FATHER WAS STILL THE REVEREND HERE.
WE'VE, UH... LOST TOUCH. DO YOU KNOW WHERE HE MIGHT BE LIVING NOW?
BIBLE

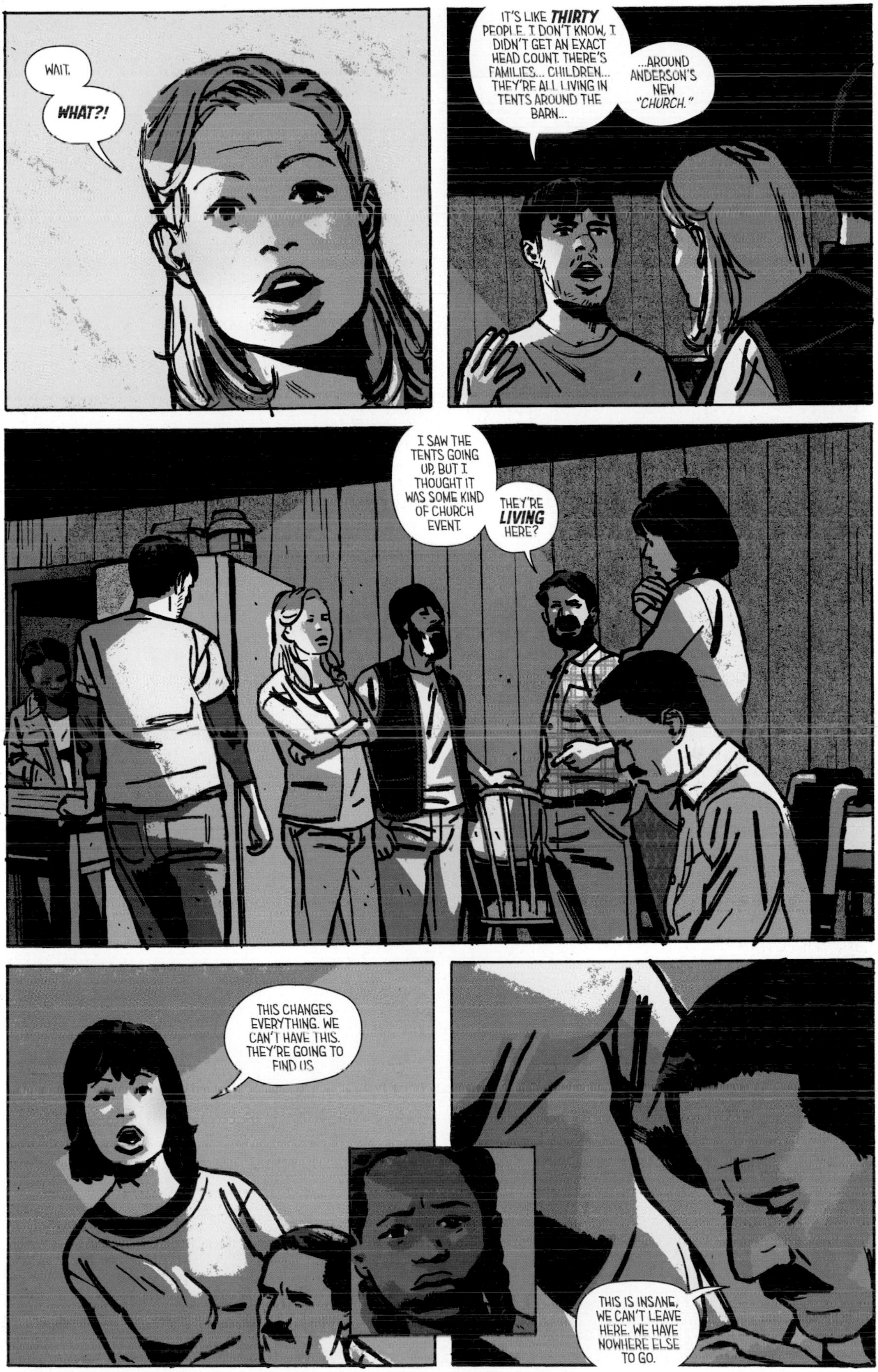
WAIT.
WHAT?!
IT'S LIKE THIRTY PEOPLE. I DON'T KNOW, I DIDN'T GET AN EXACT HEAD COUNT. THERE'S FAMILIES... CHILDREN... THEY'RE ALL LIVING IN TENTS AROUND THE BARN...
...AROUND ANDERSON'S NEW "CHURCH."
I SAW THE TENTS GOING UP, BUT I THOUGHT IT WAS SOME KIND OF CHURCH EVENT.
THEY'RE LIVING HERE?
THIS CHANGES EVERYTHING. WE CAN'T HAVE THIS. THEY'RE GOING TO FIND US
THIS IS INSANE, WE CAN'T LEAVE HERE. WE HAVE NOWHERE ELSE TO GO.

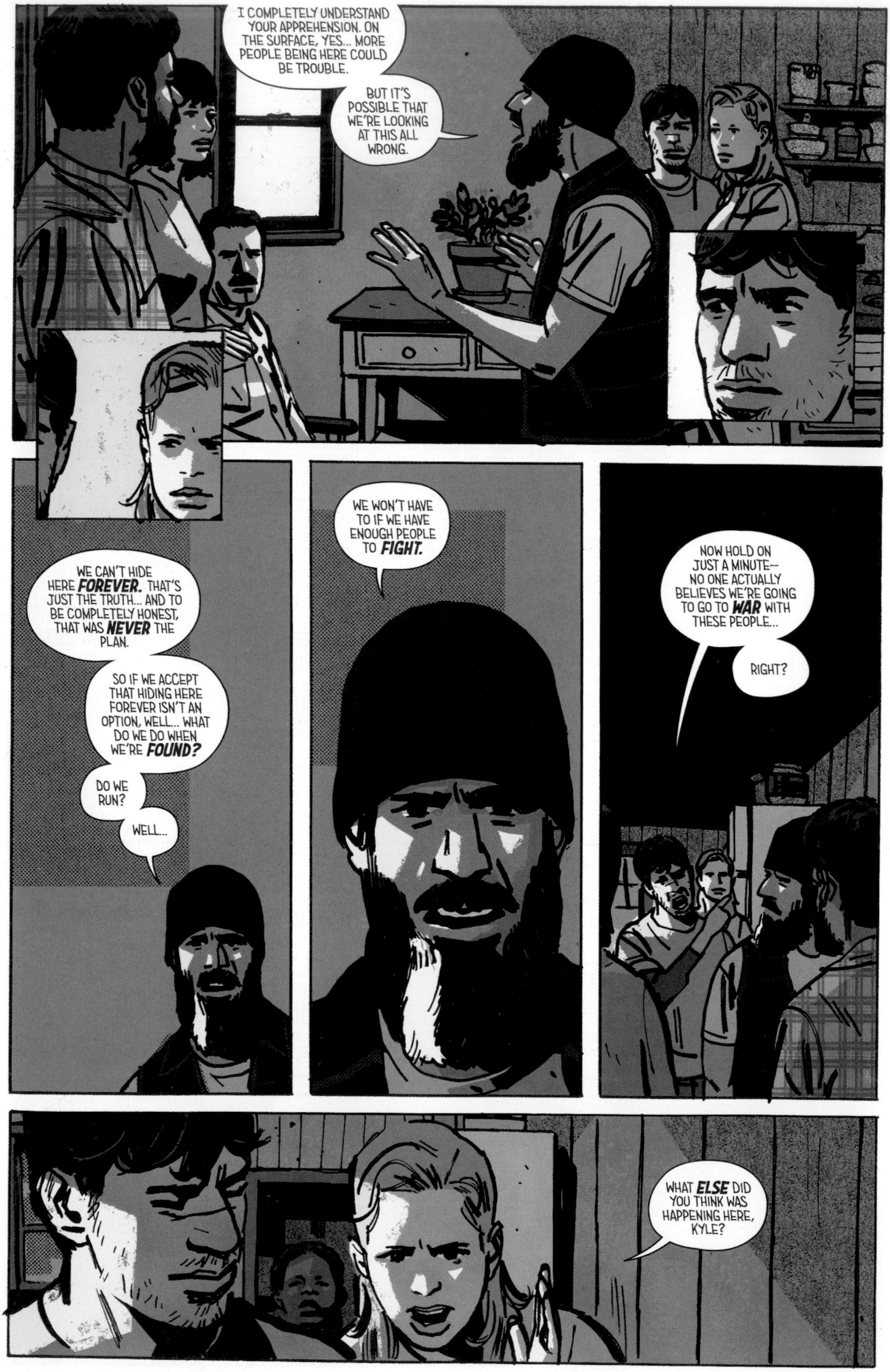
I COMPLETELY UNDERSTAND YOUR APPREHENSION. ON THE SURFACE, YES... MORE PEOPLE BEING HERE COULD BE TROUBLE.
BUT IT'S POSSIBLE THAT WE'RE LOOKING AT THIS ALL WRONG.
WE CAN'T HIDE HERE FOREVER. THAT'S JUST THE TRUTH... AND TO BE COMPLETELY HONEST, THAT WAS NEVER THE PLAN.
SO IF WE ACCEPT THAT HIDING HERE FOREVER ISN'T AN OPTION, WELL... WHAT DO WE DO WHEN WE'RE FOUND?
DO WE RUN?
WELL...
WE WON'T HAVE TO IF WE HAVE ENOUGH PEOPLE TO FIGHT.
NOW HOLD ON JUST A MINUTE-- NO ONE ACTUALLY BELIEVES WE'RE GOING TO GO TO WAR WITH THESE PEOPLE...
RIGHT?
WHAT ELSE DID YOU THINK WAS HAPPENING HERE, KYLE?

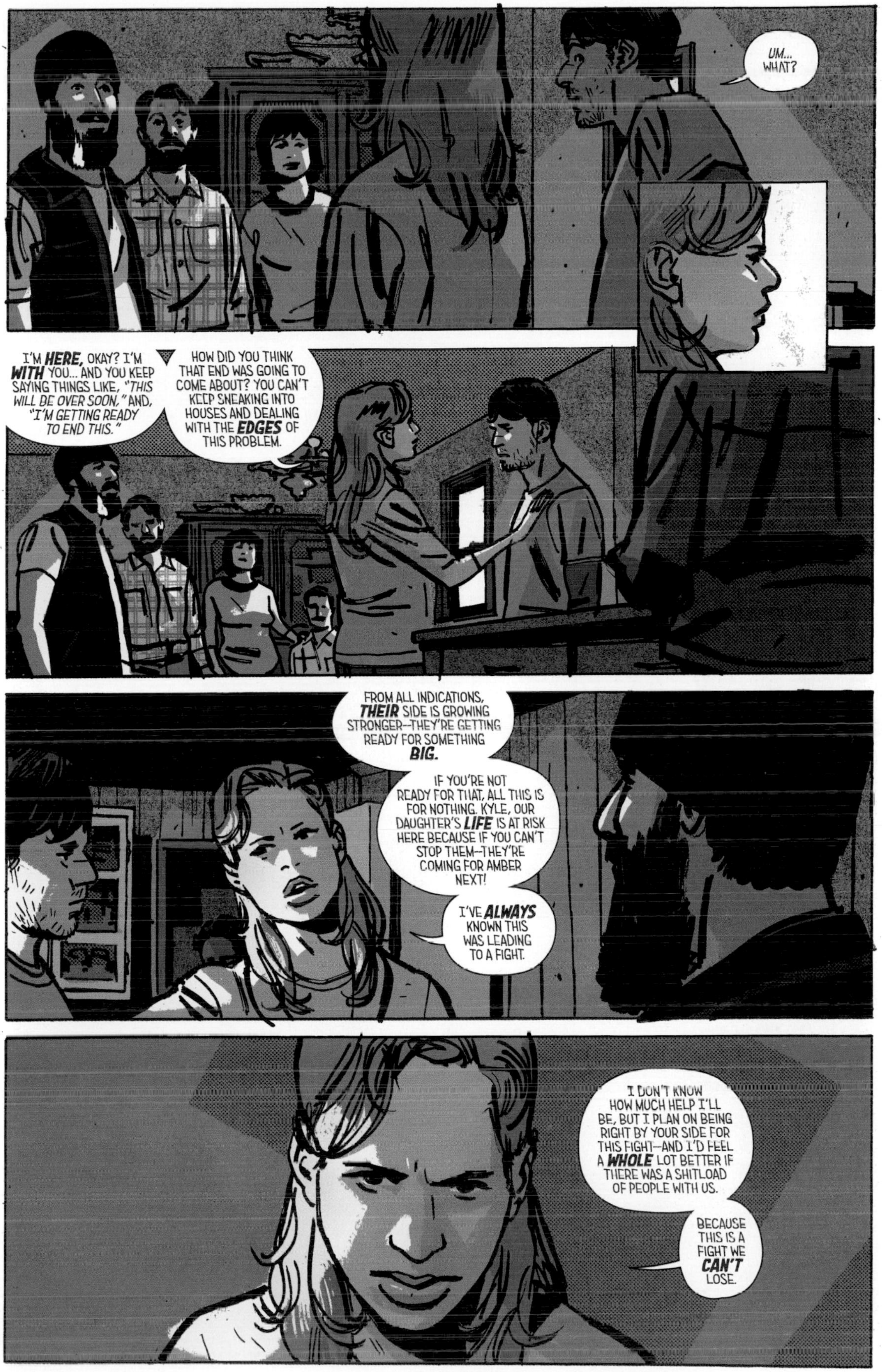
UM... WHAT?
I'M HERE, OKAY? I'M WITH YOU... AND YOU KEEP SAYING THINGS LIKE, "THIS WILL BE OVER SOON," AND, "I'M GETTING READY TO END THIS."
HOW DID YOU THINK THAT END WAS GOING TO COME ABOUT? YOU CAN'T KEEP SNEAKING INTO HOUSES AND DEALING WITH THE EDGES OF THIS PROBLEM.
FROM ALL INDICATIONS, THEIR SIDE IS GROWING STRONGER--THEY'RE GETTING READY FOR SOMETHING BIG.
IF YOU'RE NOT READY FOR THAT, ALL THIS IS FOR NOTHING. KYLE, OUR DAUGHTER'S LIFE IS AT RISK HERE BECAUSE IF YOU CAN'T STOP THEM--THEY'RE COMING FOR AMBER NEXT!
I'VE ALWAYS KNOWN THIS WAS LEADING TO A FIGHT.
I DON'T KNOW HOW MUCH HELP I'LL BE, BUT I PLAN ON BEING RIGHT BY YOUR SIDE FOR THIS FIGHT--AND I'D FEEL A WHOLE LOT BETTER IF THERE WAS A SHITLOAD OF PEOPLE WITH US.
BECAUSE THIS IS A FIGHT WE CAN'T LOSE.

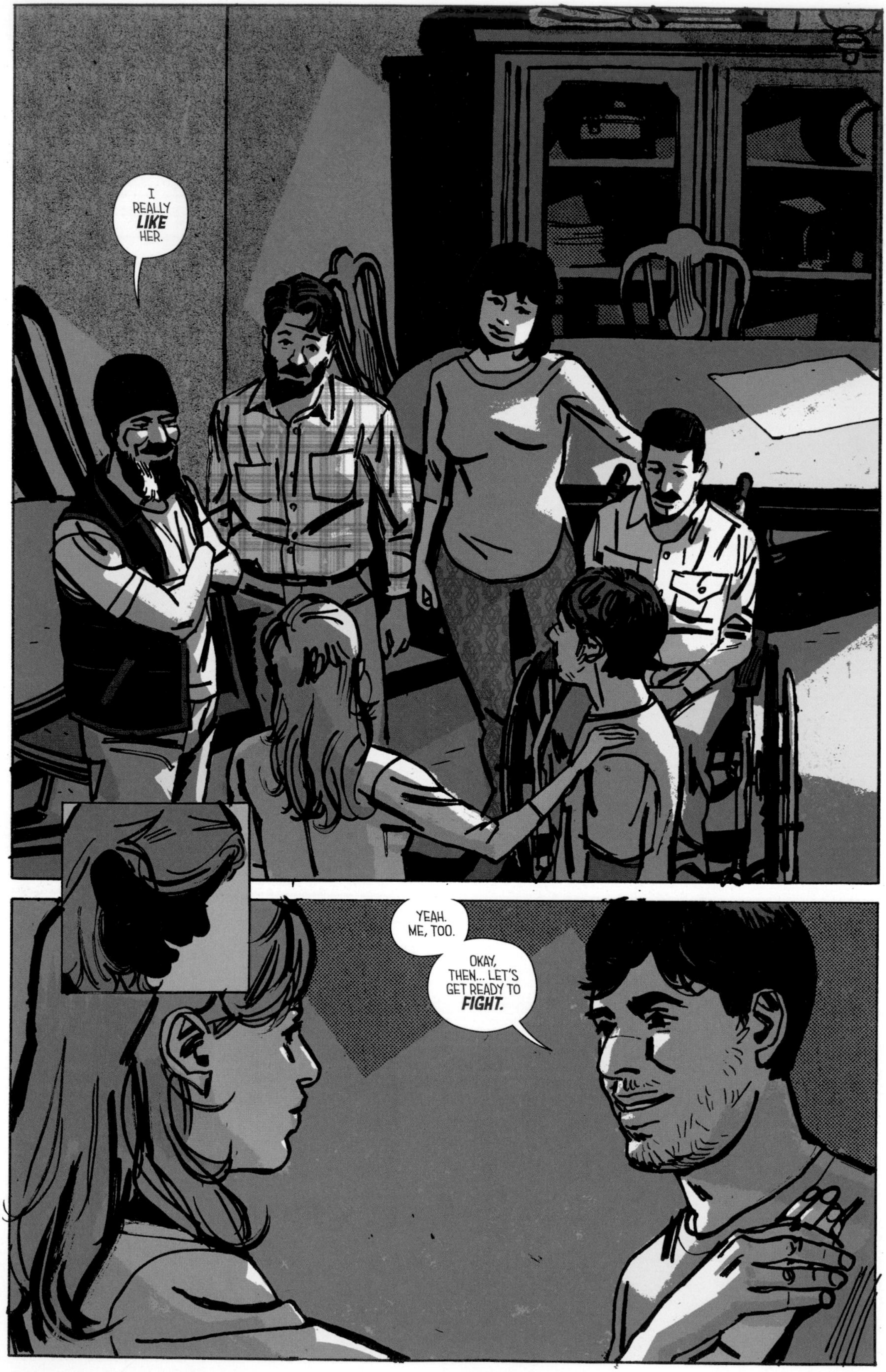
I REALLY LIKE HER.
YEAH. ME, TOO.
OKAY, THEN... LET'S GET READY TO FIGHT.

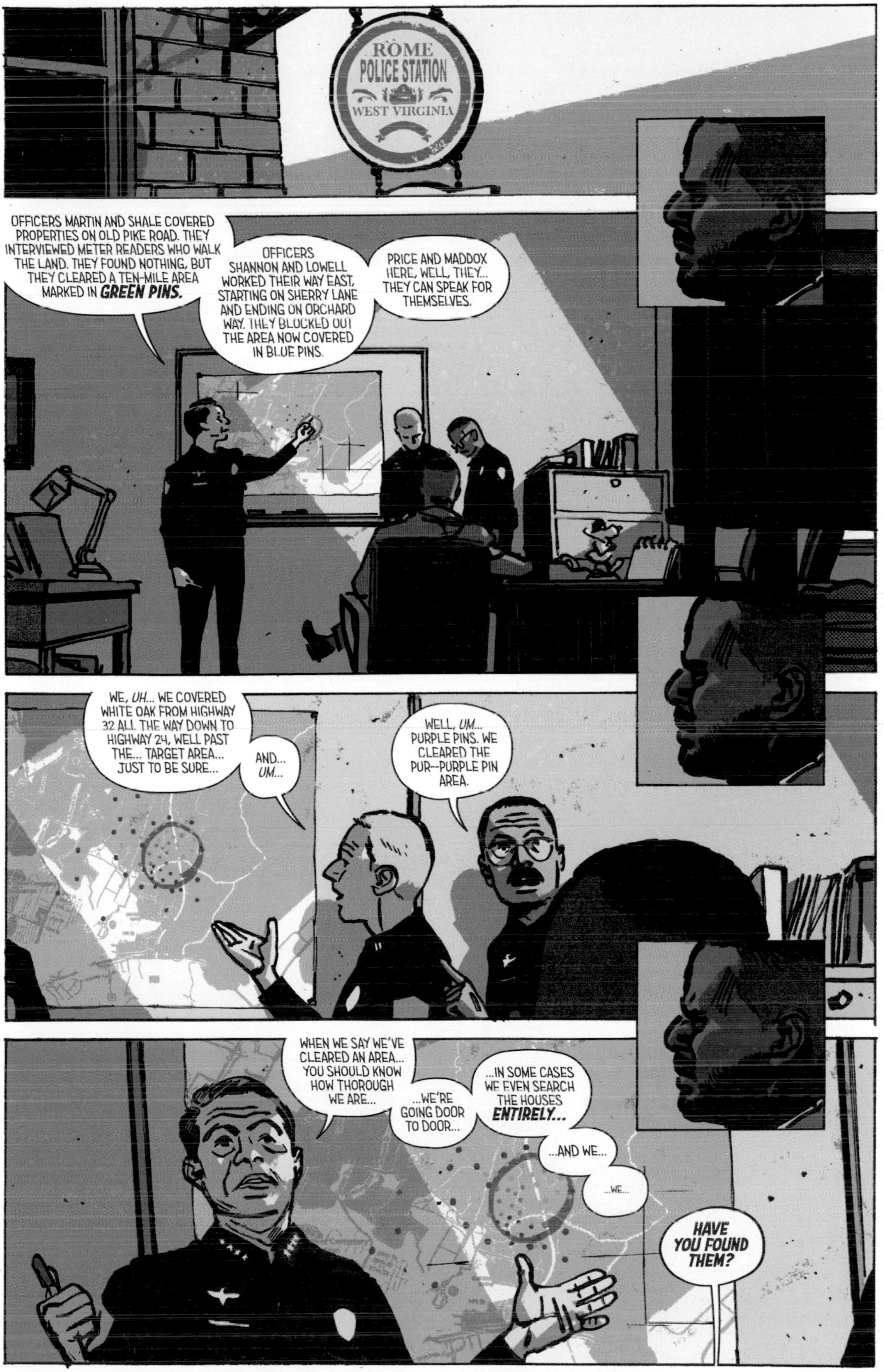
ROME
POLICE STATION
WEST VIRGINIA
OFFICERS MARTIN AND SHALE COVERED PROPERTIES ON OLD PIKE ROAD. THEY INTERVIEWED METER READERS WHO WALK THE LAND. THEY FOUND NOTHING, BUT THEY CLEARED A TEN-MILE AREA MARKED IN GREEN PINS.
OFFICERS SHANNON AND LOWELL WORKED THEIR WAY EAST, STARTING ON SHERRY LANE AND ENDING ON ORCHARD WAY. THEY BLOCKED OUT THE AREA NOW COVERED IN BLUE PINS.
PRICE AND MADDOX HERE, WELL, THEY... THEY CAN SPEAK FOR THEMSELVES.
WE, UH... WE COVERED WHITE OAK FROM HIGHWAY 32 ALL THE WAY DOWN TO HIGHWAY 24, WELL PAST THE... TARGET AREA... JUST TO BE SURE...
AND... UM...
WELL, UM... PURPLE PINS. WE CLEARED THE PUR--PURPLE PIN AREA.
WHEN WE SAY WE'VE CLEARED AN AREA... YOU SHOULD KNOW HOW THOROUGH WE ARE...
...WE'RE GOING DOOR TO DOOR...
...IN SOME CASES WE EVEN SEARCH THE HOUSES ENTIRELY...
...AND WE...
...WE...
HAVE YOU FOUND THEM?

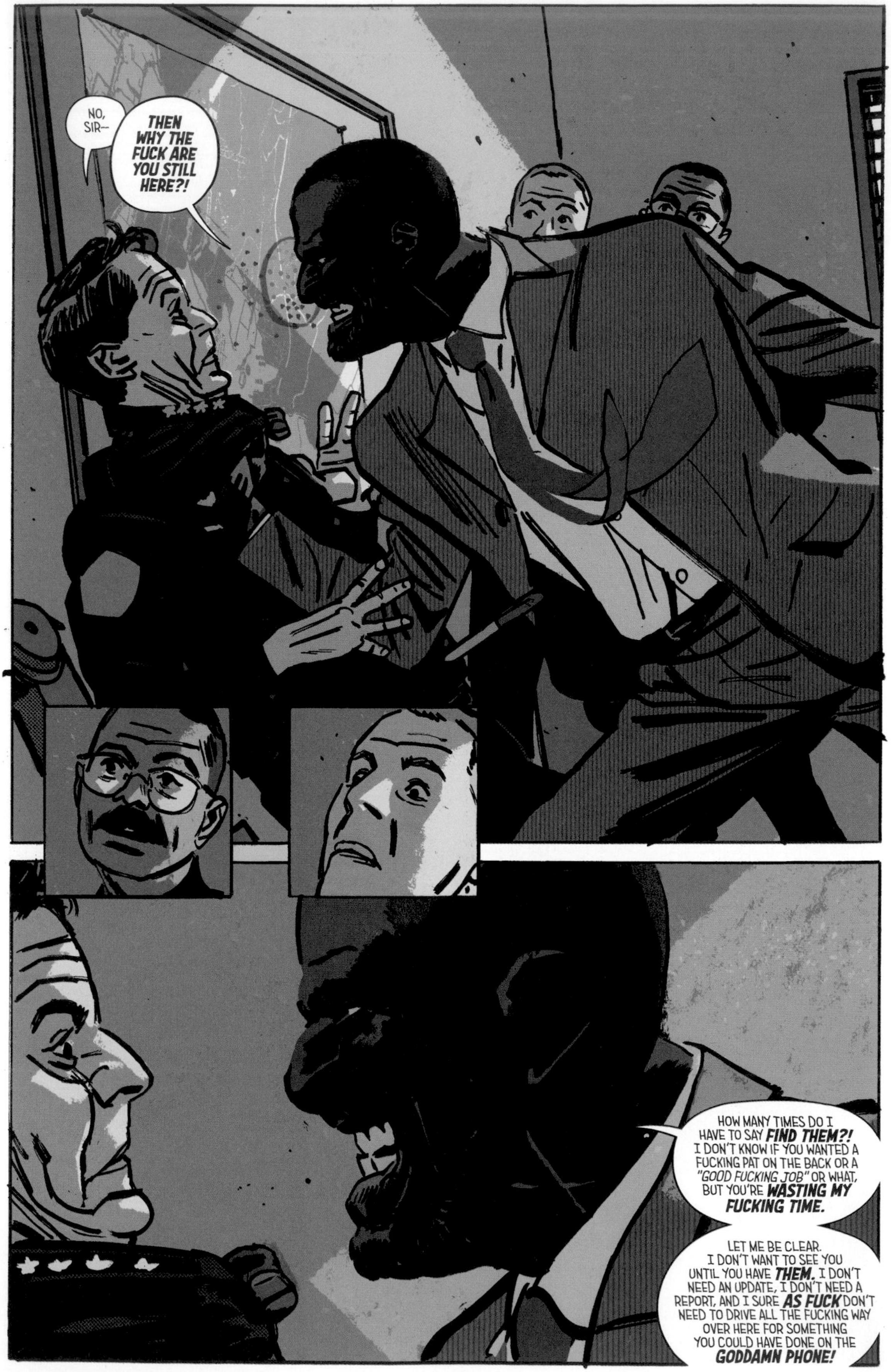

NO, SIR--
THEN WHY THE FUCK ARE YOU STILL HERE?!
HOW MANY TIMES DO I HAVE TO SAY FIND THEM?! I DON'T KNOW IF YOU WANTED A FUCKING PAT ON THE BACK OR A "GOOD FUCKING JOB" OR WHAT, BUT YOU'RE WASTING MY FUCKING TIME.
LET ME BE CLEAR. I DON'T WANT TO SEE YOU UNTIL YOU HAVE THEM. I DON'T NEED AN UPDATE, I DON'T NEED A REPORT, AND I SURE AS FUCK DON'T NEED TO DRIVE ALL THE FUCKING WAY OVER HERE FOR SOMETHING YOU COULD HAVE DONE ON THE GODDAMN PHONE!

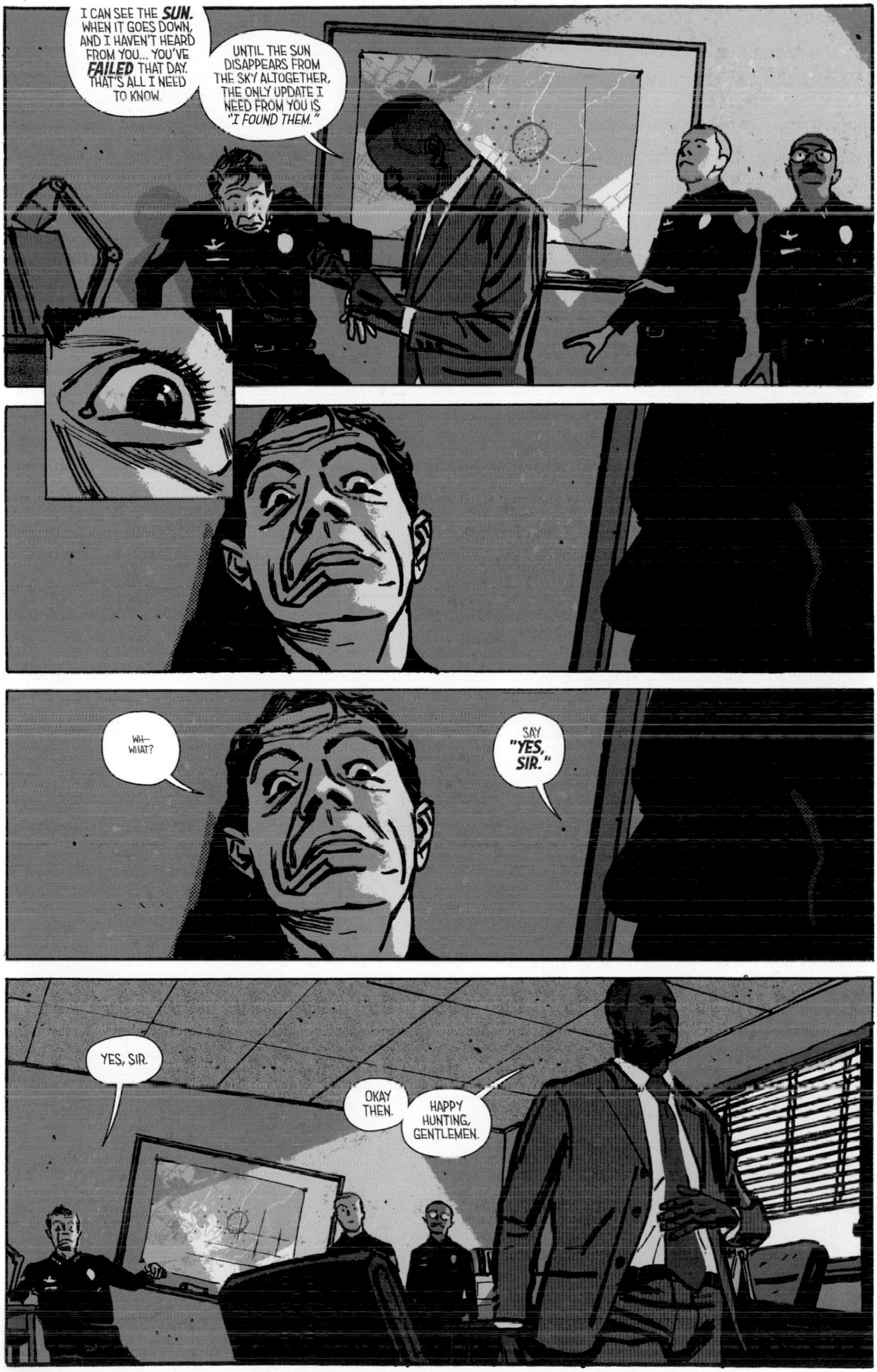
I CAN SEE THE SUN. WHEN IT GOES DOWN, AND I HAVEN'T HEARD FROM YOU... YOU'VE FAILED THAT DAY. THAT'S ALL I NEED TO KNOW.
UNTIL THE SUN DISAPPEARS FROM THE SKY ALTOGETHER, THE ONLY UPDATE I NEED FROM YOU IS "I FOUND THEM."
WH— WHAT?
SAY "YES, SIR."
YES, SIR.
OKAY THEN.
HAPPY HUNTING, GENTLEMEN.

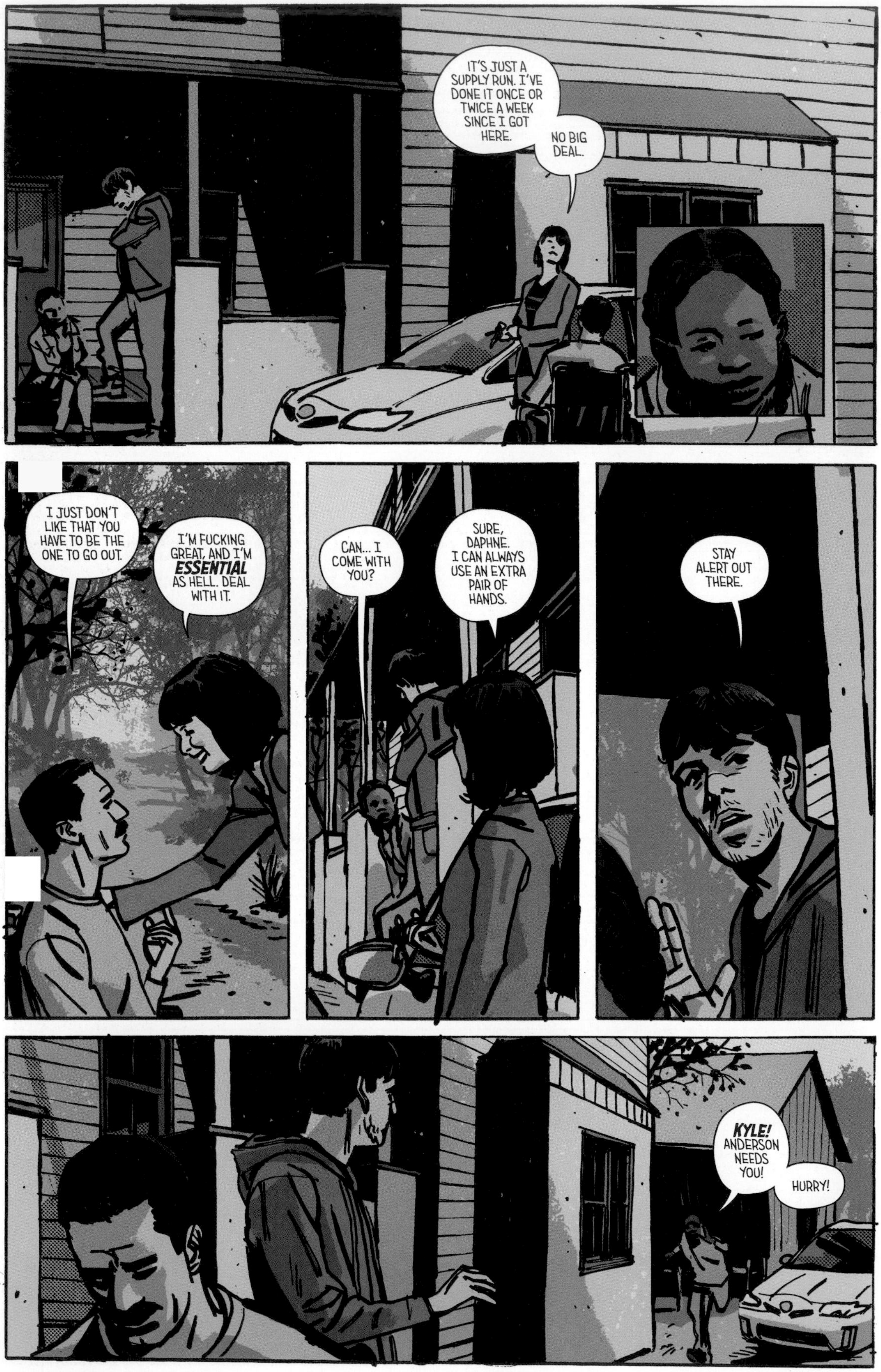
IT'S JUST A SUPPLY RUN. I'VE DONE IT ONCE OR TWICE A WEEK SINCE I GOT HERE.
NO BIG DEAL.
I JUST DON'T LIKE THAT YOU HAVE TO BE THE ONE TO GO OUT.
I'M FUCKING GREAT, AND I'M ESSENTIAL AS HELL. DEAL WITH IT.
CAN... I COME WITH YOU?
SURE, DAPHNE. I CAN ALWAYS USE AN EXTRA PAIR OF HANDS.
STAY ALERT OUT THERE.
KYLE! ANDERSON NEEDS YOU!
HURRY!

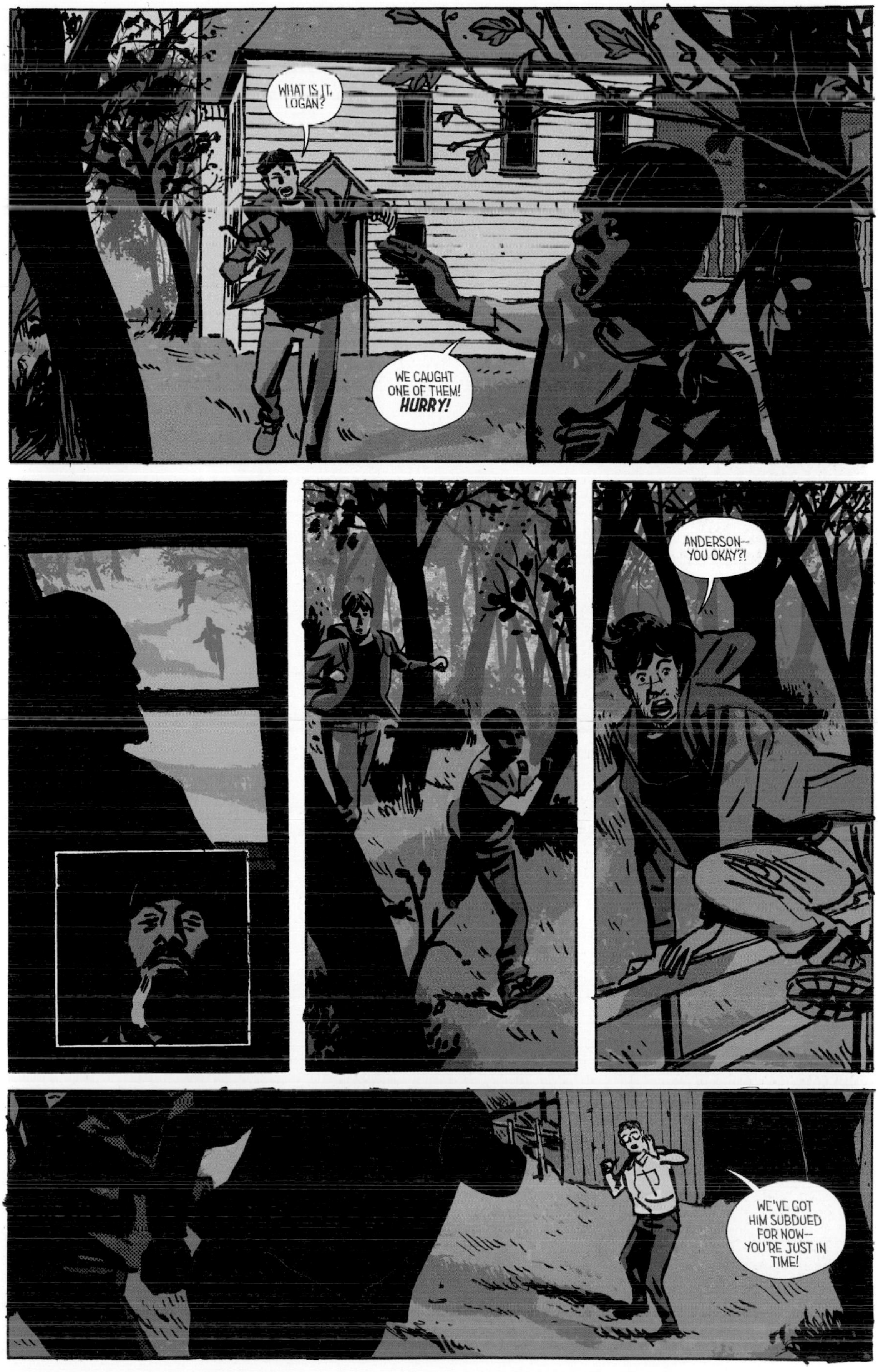
WHAT IS IT, LOGAN?
WE CAUGHT ONE OF THEM! **HURRY!**
ANDERSON-- YOU OKAY?!
WE'VE GOT HIM SUBDUED FOR NOW-- YOU'RE JUST IN TIME!

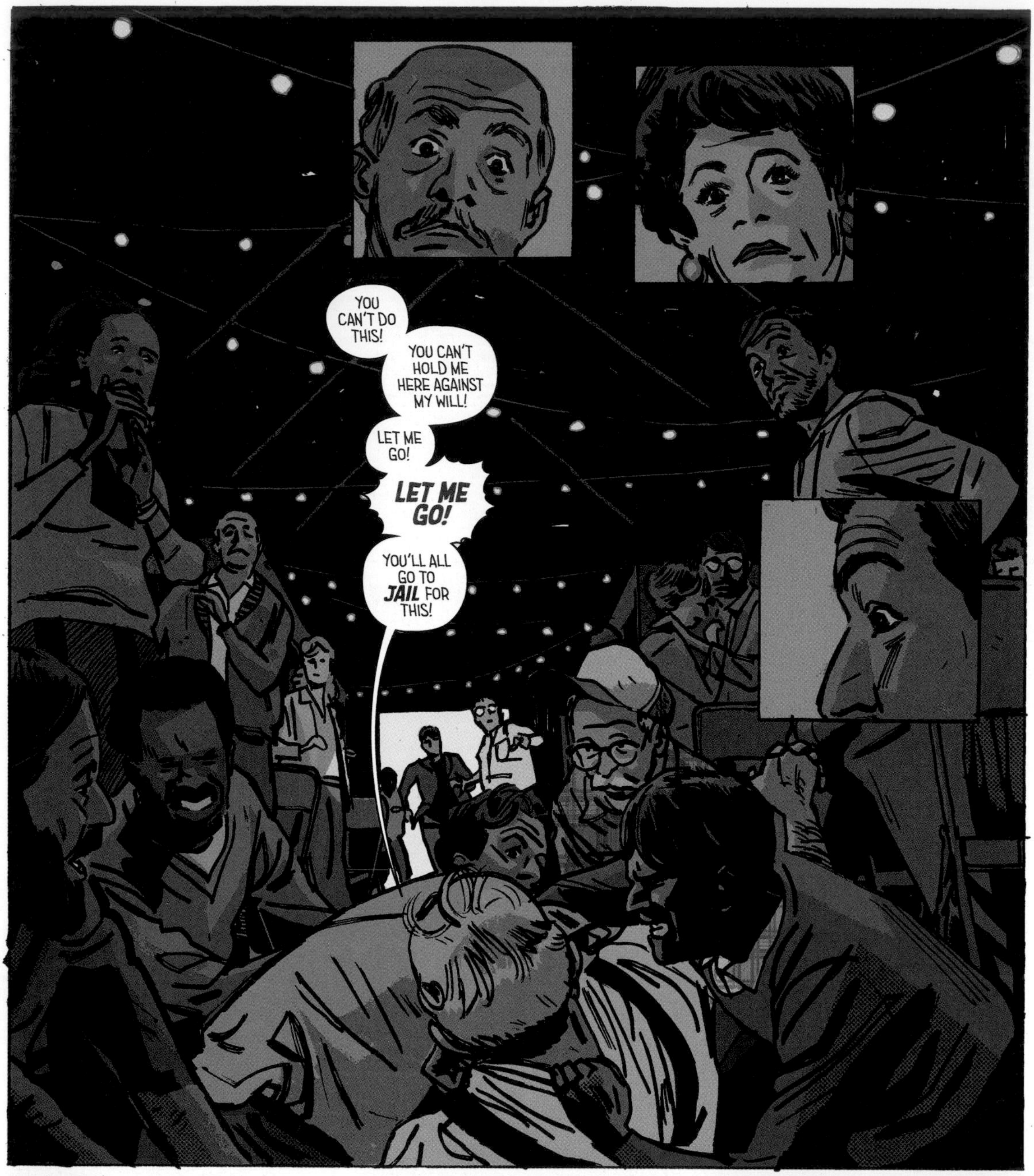
YOU CAN'T DO THIS!
YOU CAN'T HOLD ME HERE AGAINST MY WILL!
LET ME GO!
LET ME GO!
YOU'LL ALL GO TO JAIL FOR THIS!

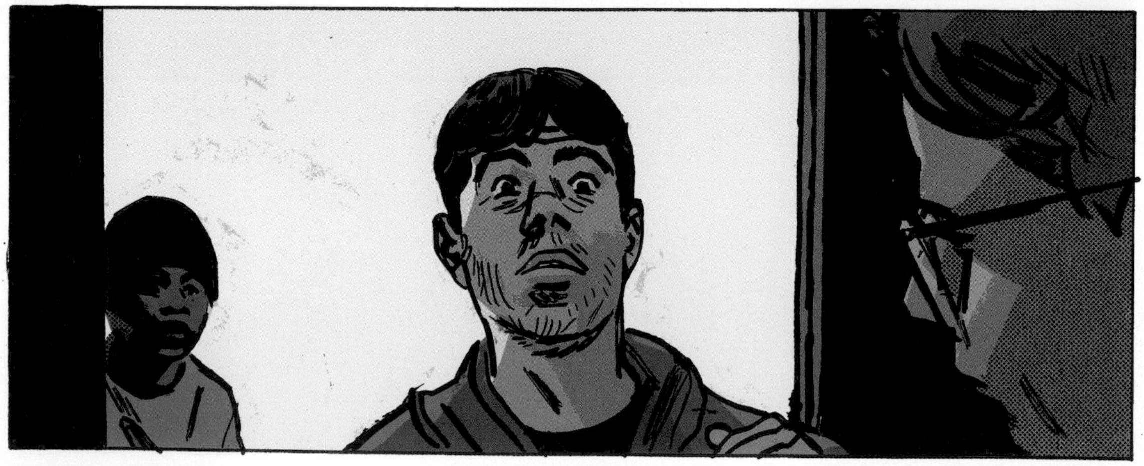

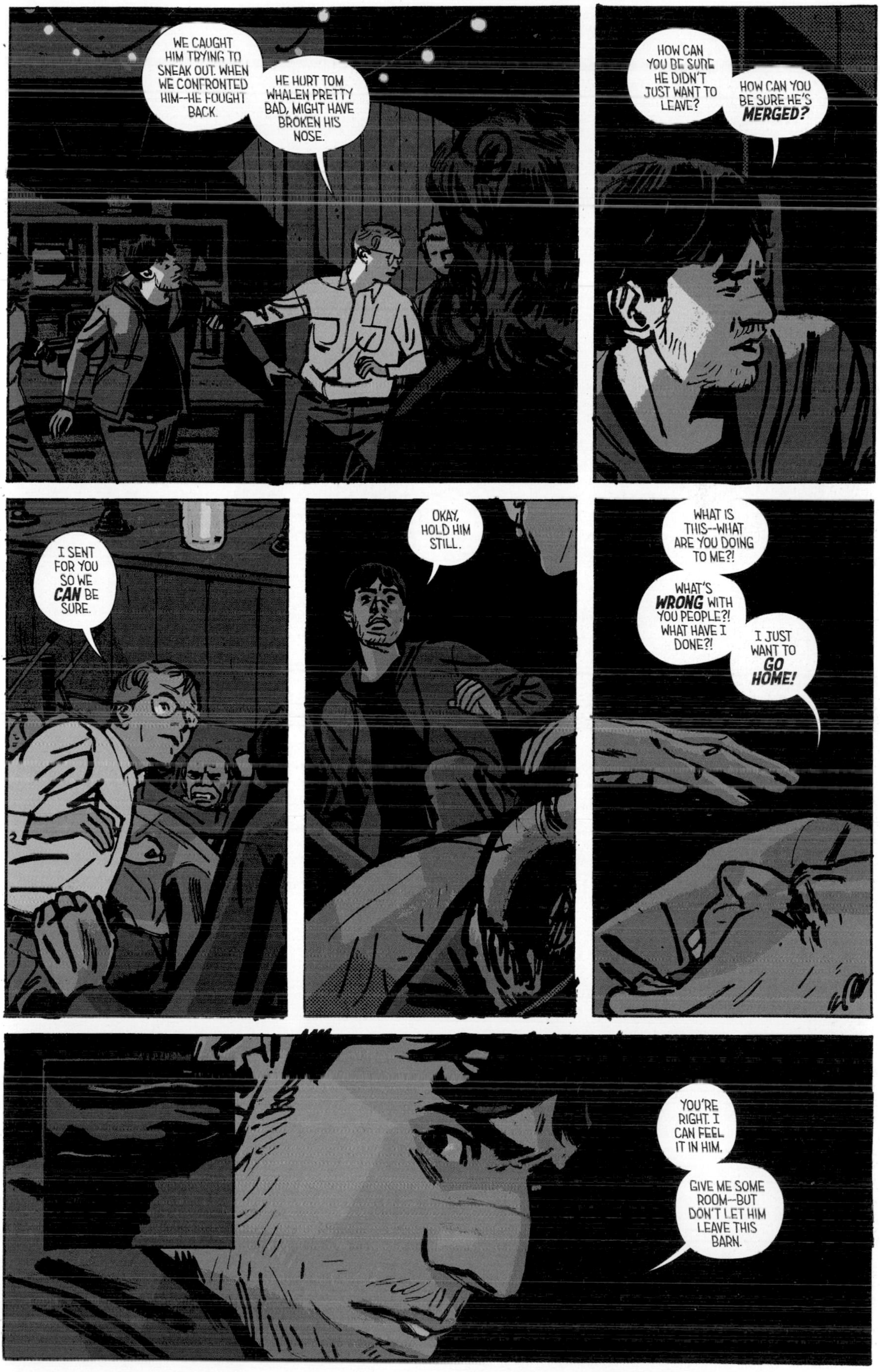
WE CAUGHT HIM TRYING TO SNEAK OUT. WHEN WE CONFRONTED HIM--HE FOUGHT BACK.
HE HURT TOM WHALEN PRETTY BAD, MIGHT HAVE BROKEN HIS NOSE.
HOW CAN YOU BE SURE HE DIDN'T JUST WANT TO LEAVE?
HOW CAN YOU BE SURE HE'S MERGED?
I SENT FOR YOU SO WE CAN BE SURE.
OKAY, HOLD HIM STILL.
WHAT IS THIS--WHAT ARE YOU DOING TO ME?!
WHAT'S WRONG WITH YOU PEOPLE?! WHAT HAVE I DONE?!
I JUST WANT TO GO HOME!
YOU'RE RIGHT. I CAN FEEL IT IN HIM.
GIVE ME SOME ROOM--BUT DON'T LET HIM LEAVE THIS BARN.

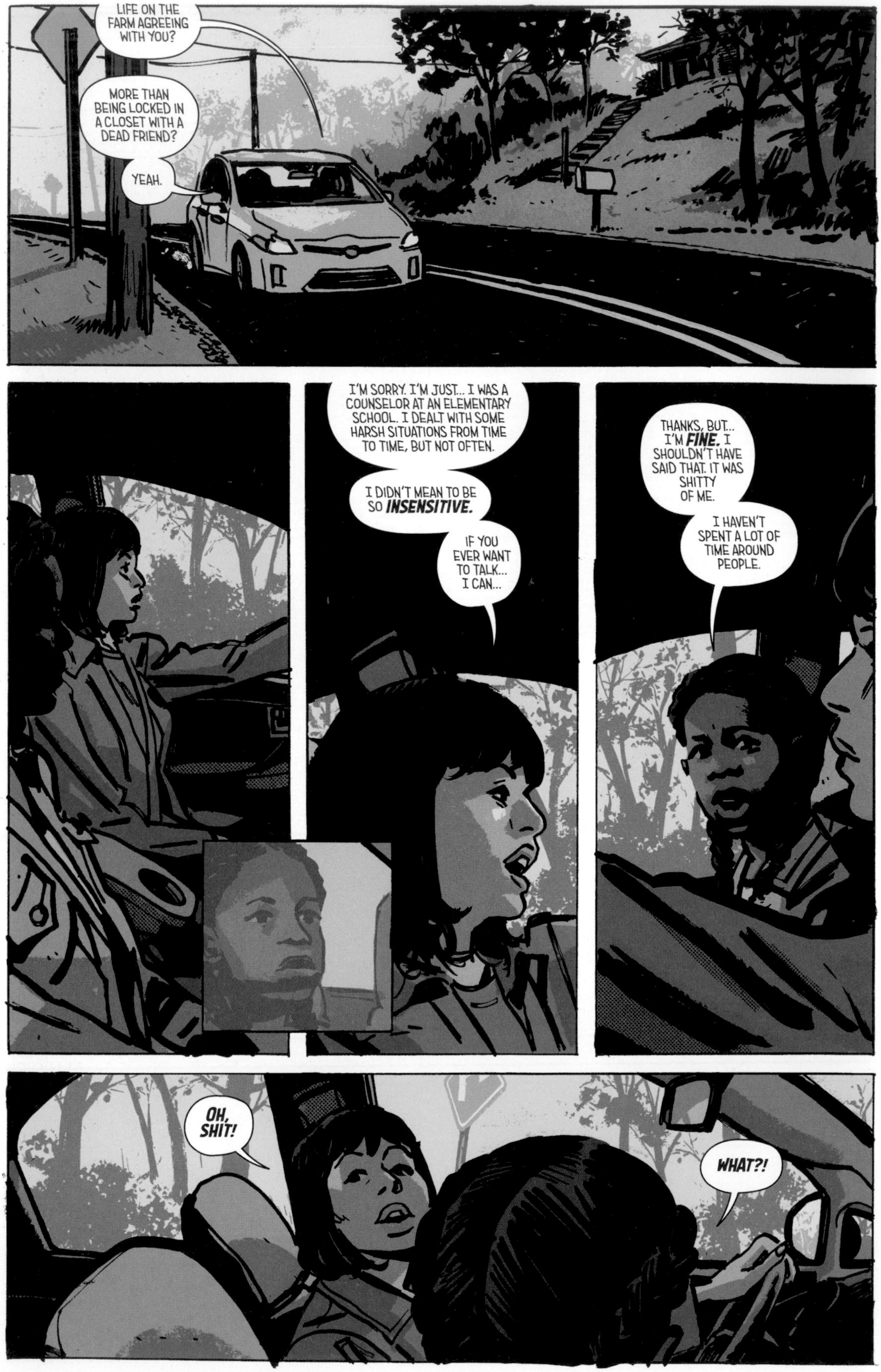
LIFE ON THE FARM AGREEING WITH YOU?
MORE THAN BEING LOCKED IN A CLOSET WITH A DEAD FRIEND?
YEAH.
I'M SORRY. I'M JUST... I WAS A COUNSELOR AT AN ELEMENTARY SCHOOL. I DEALT WITH SOME HARSH SITUATIONS FROM TIME TO TIME, BUT NOT OFTEN.
I DIDN'T MEAN TO BE SO INSENSITIVE.
IF YOU EVER WANT TO TALK... I CAN...
THANKS, BUT... I'M FINE. I SHOULDN'T HAVE SAID THAT. IT WAS SHITTY OF ME.
I HAVEN'T SPENT A LOT OF TIME AROUND PEOPLE.
OH, SHIT!
WHAT?!

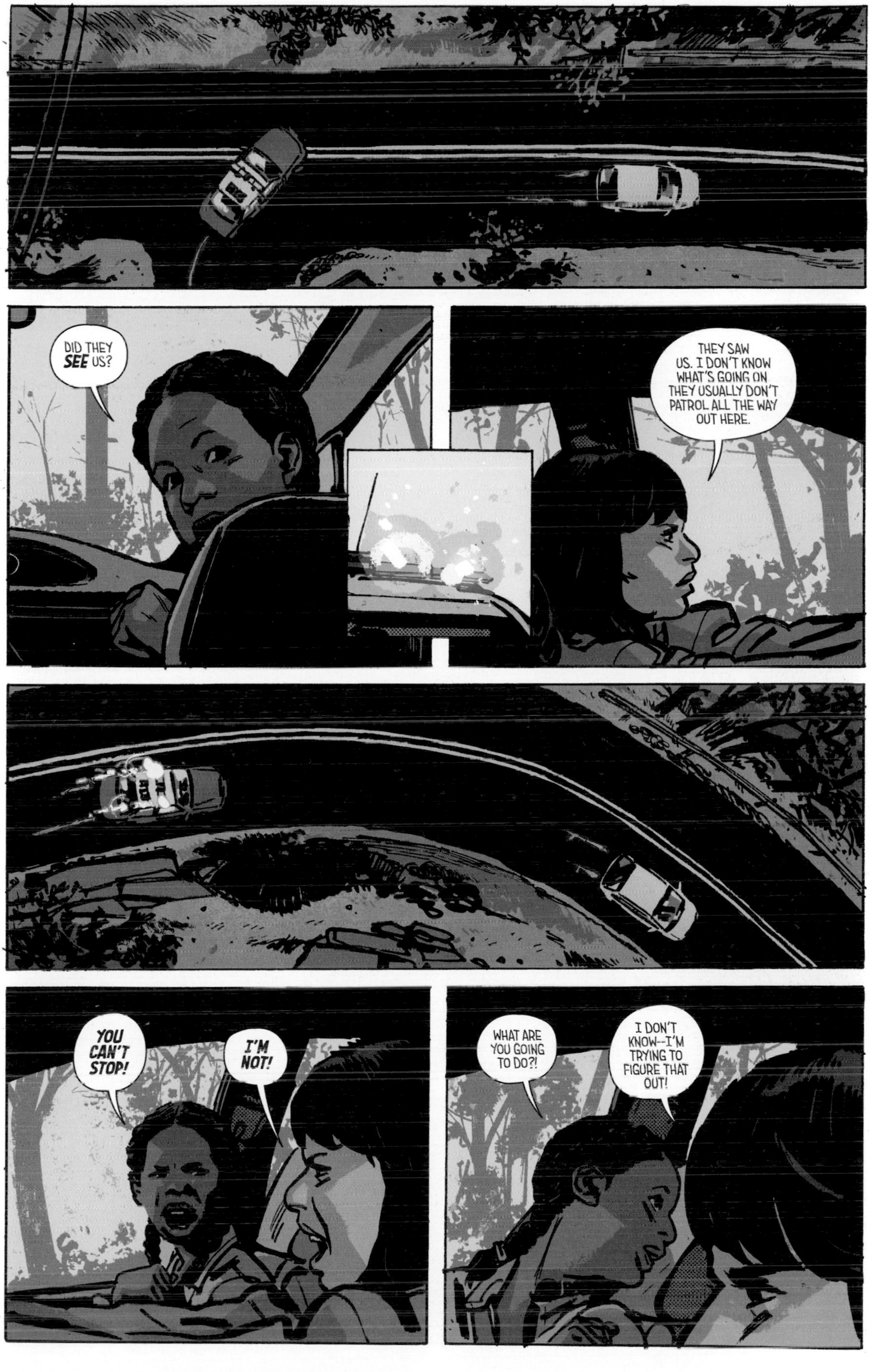
DID THEY SEE US?
THEY SAW US. I DON'T KNOW WHAT'S GOING ON THEY USUALLY DON'T PATROL ALL THE WAY OUT HERE.
YOU CAN'T STOP!
I'M NOT!
WHAT ARE YOU GOING TO DO?!
I DON'T KNOW--I'M TRYING TO FIGURE THAT OUT!

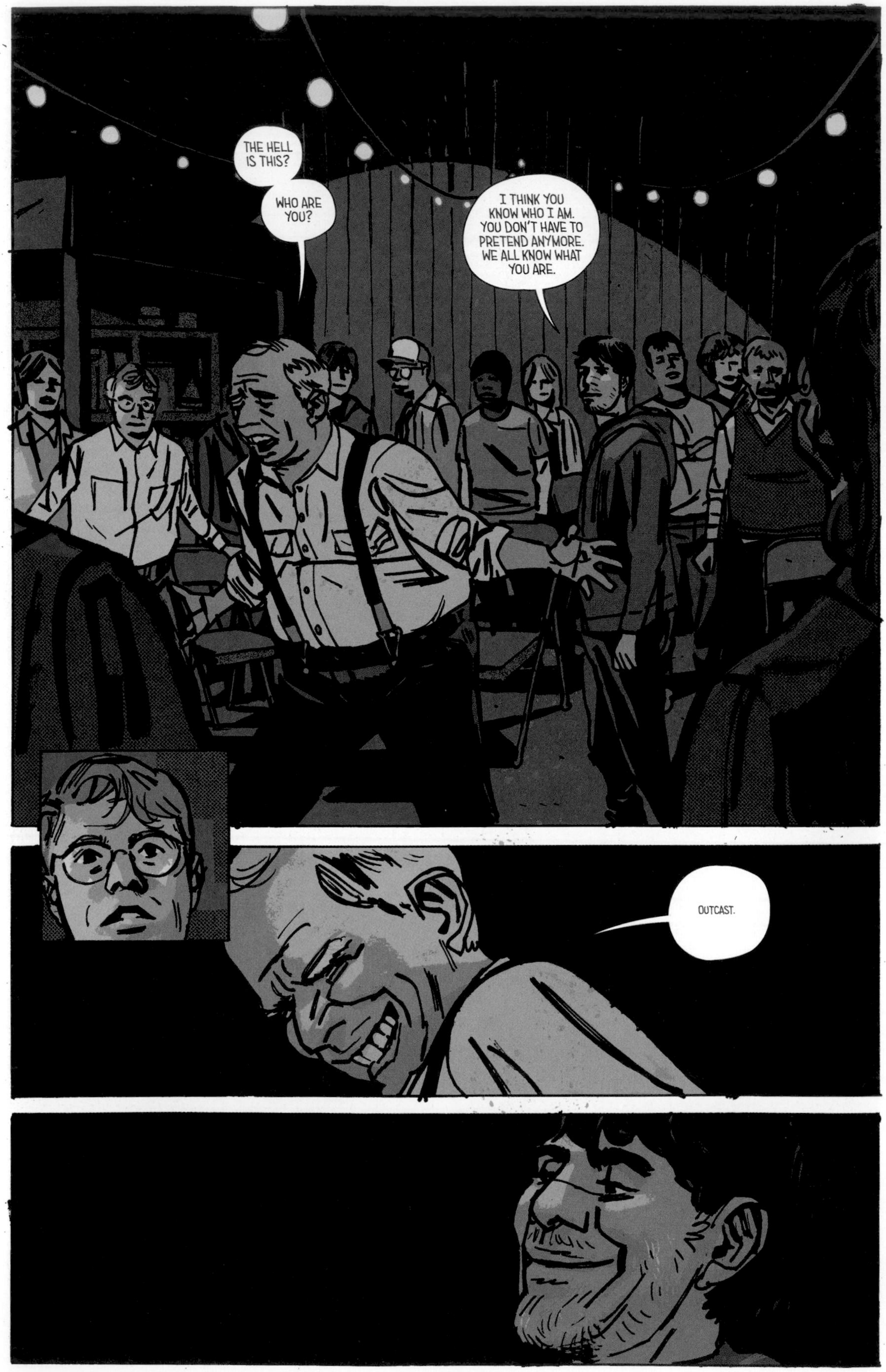
THE HELL IS THIS?
WHO ARE YOU?
I THINK YOU KNOW WHO I AM. YOU DON'T HAVE TO PRETEND ANYMORE. WE ALL KNOW WHAT YOU ARE.
OUTCAST.

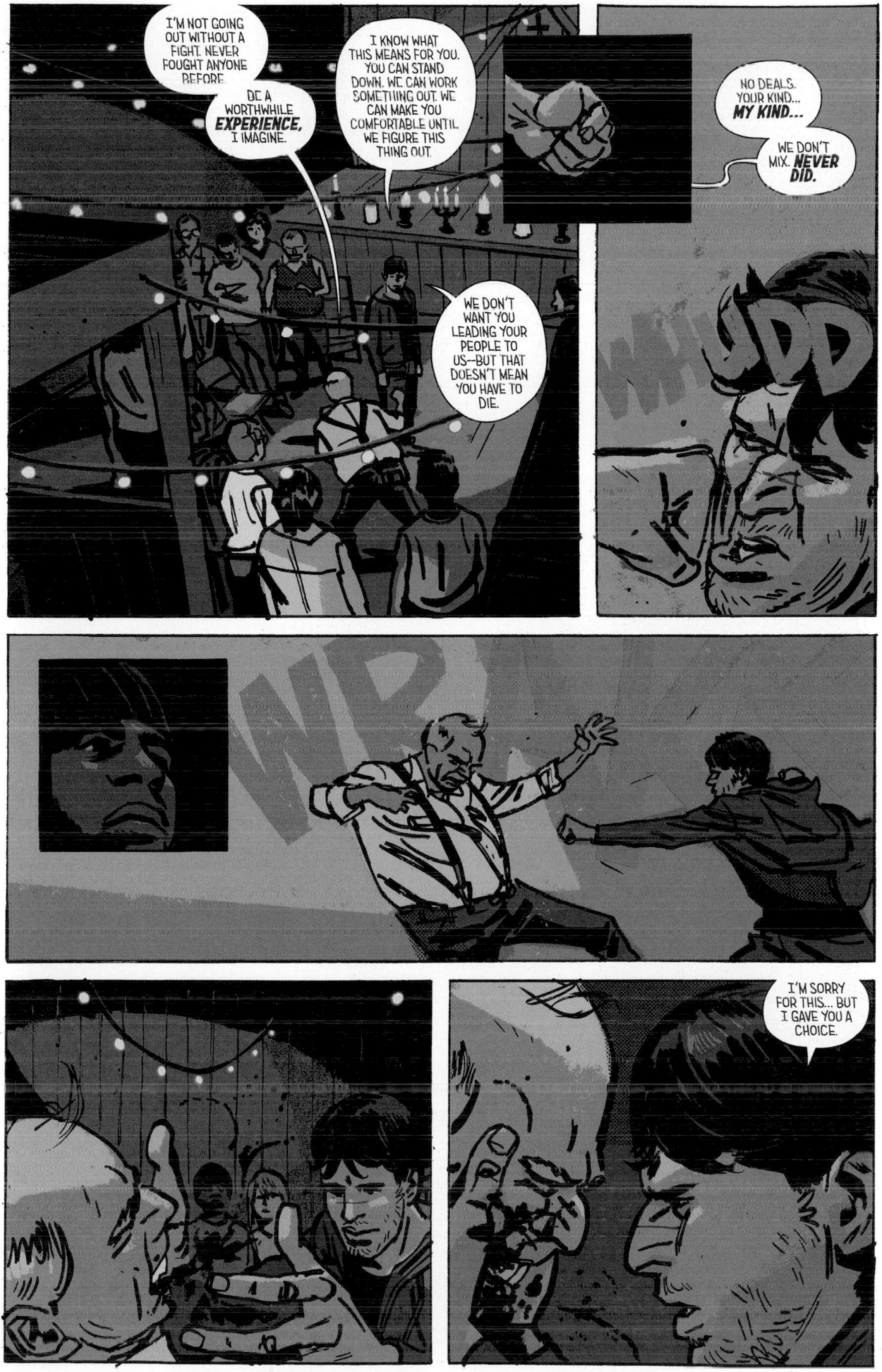
I'M NOT GOING OUT WITHOUT A FIGHT. NEVER FOUGHT ANYONE BEFORE.
BE A WORTHWHILE **EXPERIENCE,** I IMAGINE.
I KNOW WHAT THIS MEANS FOR YOU. YOU CAN STAND DOWN. WE CAN WORK SOMETHING OUT. WE CAN MAKE YOU COMFORTABLE UNTIL WE FIGURE THIS THING OUT.
WE DON'T WANT YOU LEADING YOUR PEOPLE TO US--BUT THAT DOESN'T MEAN YOU HAVE TO DIE.
NO DEALS. YOUR KIND... **MY KIND...**
WE DON'T MIX. **NEVER DID.**
WHUDD
WR
I'M SORRY FOR THIS... BUT I GAVE YOU A CHOICE.

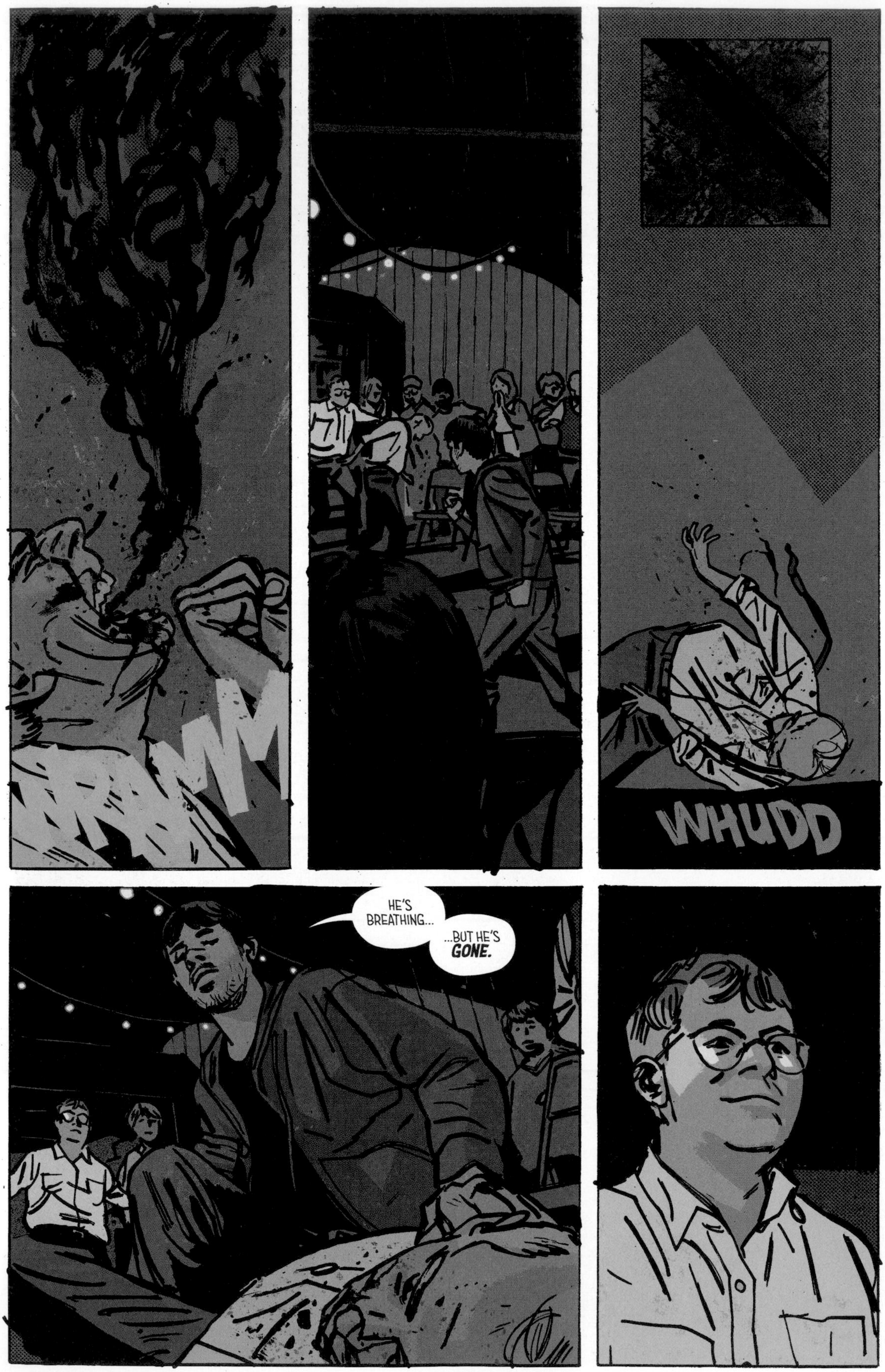

BRAMM
WHUDD
HE'S BREATHING...
...BUT HE'S **GONE.**

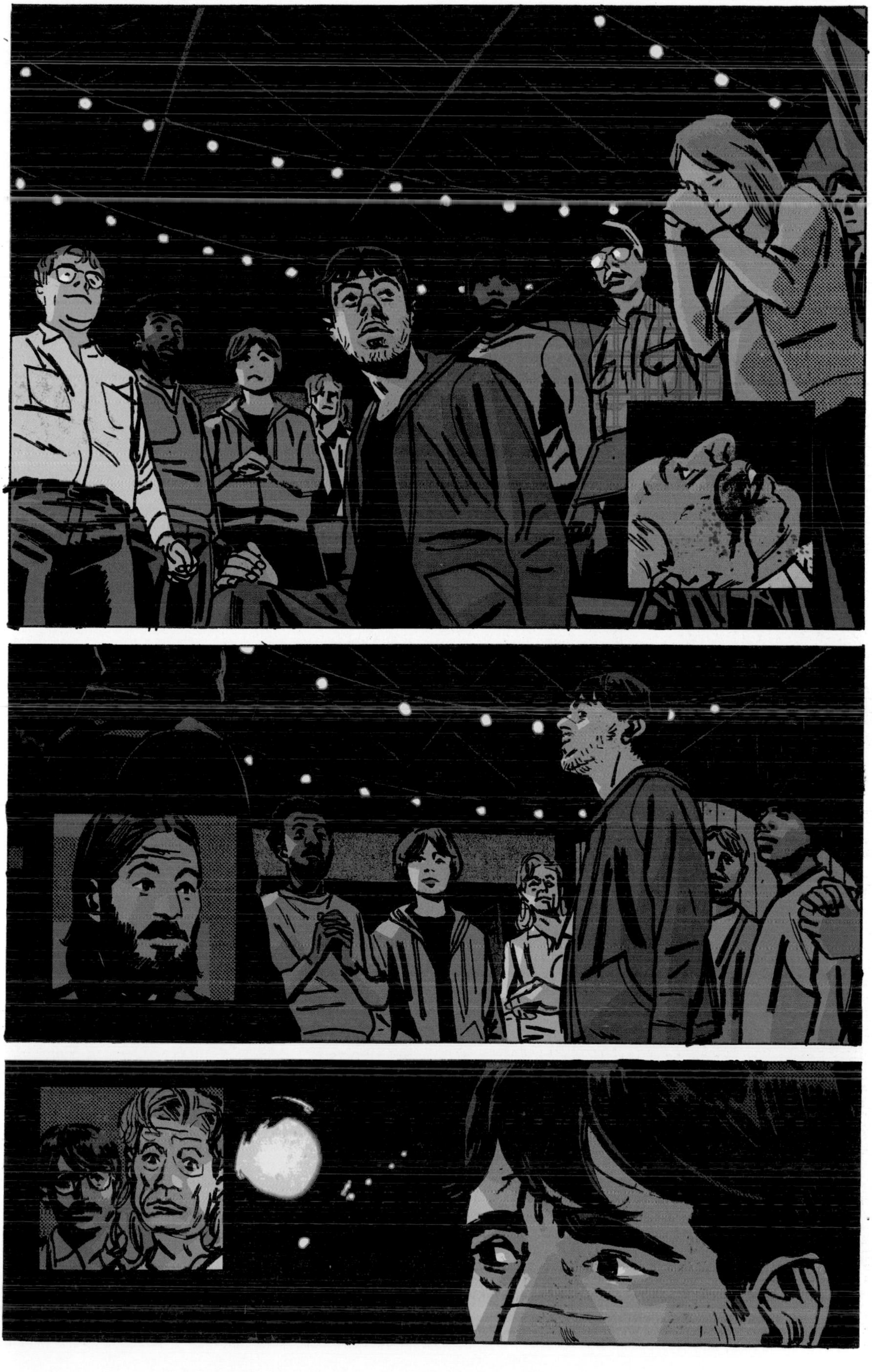

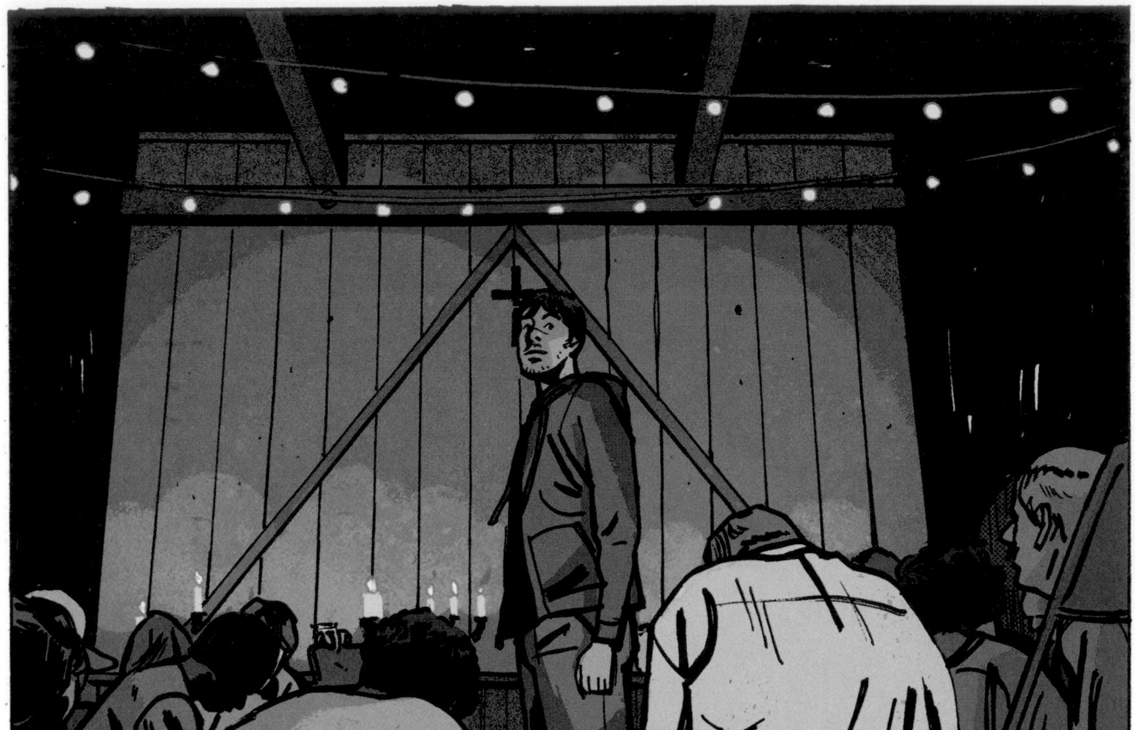

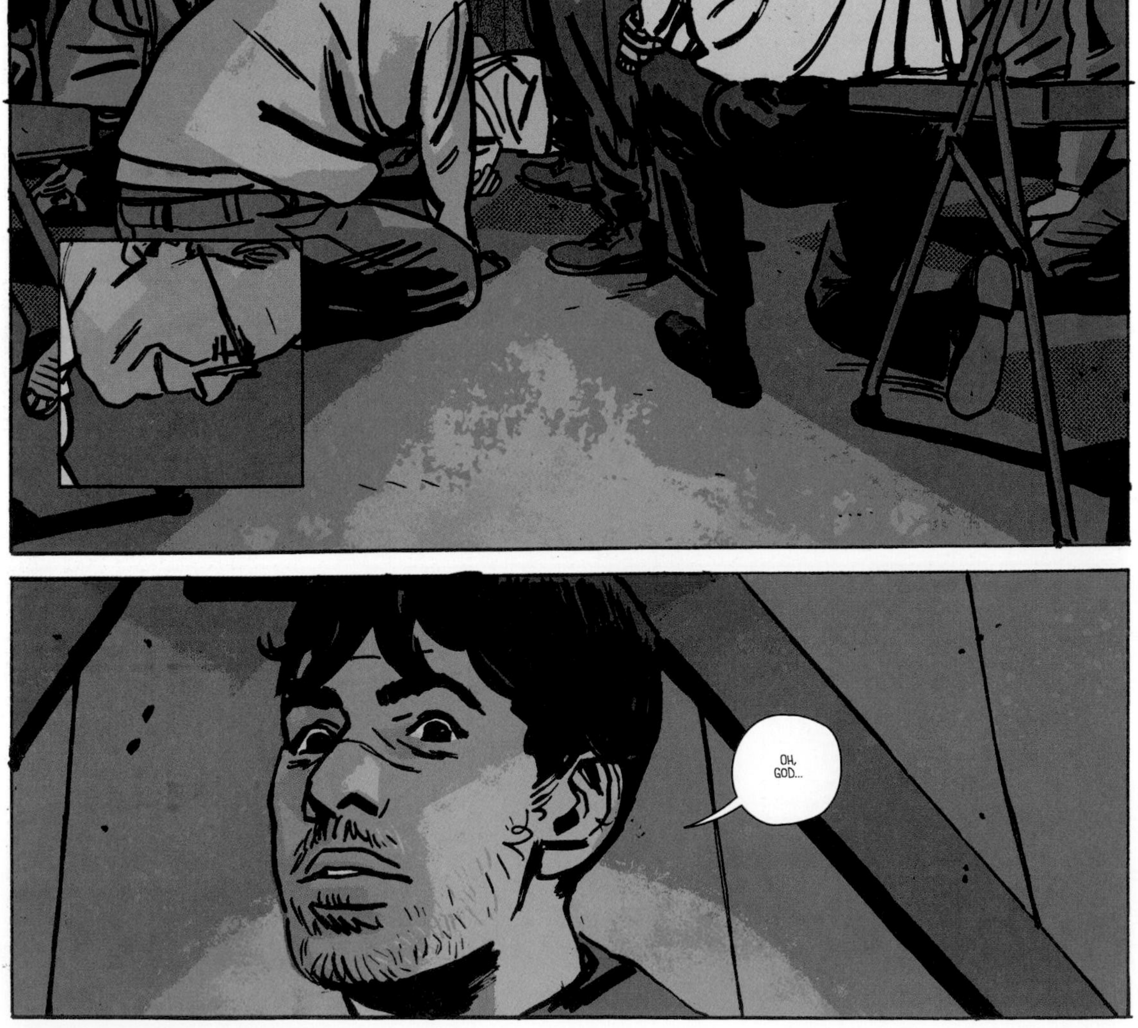
OH, GOD...

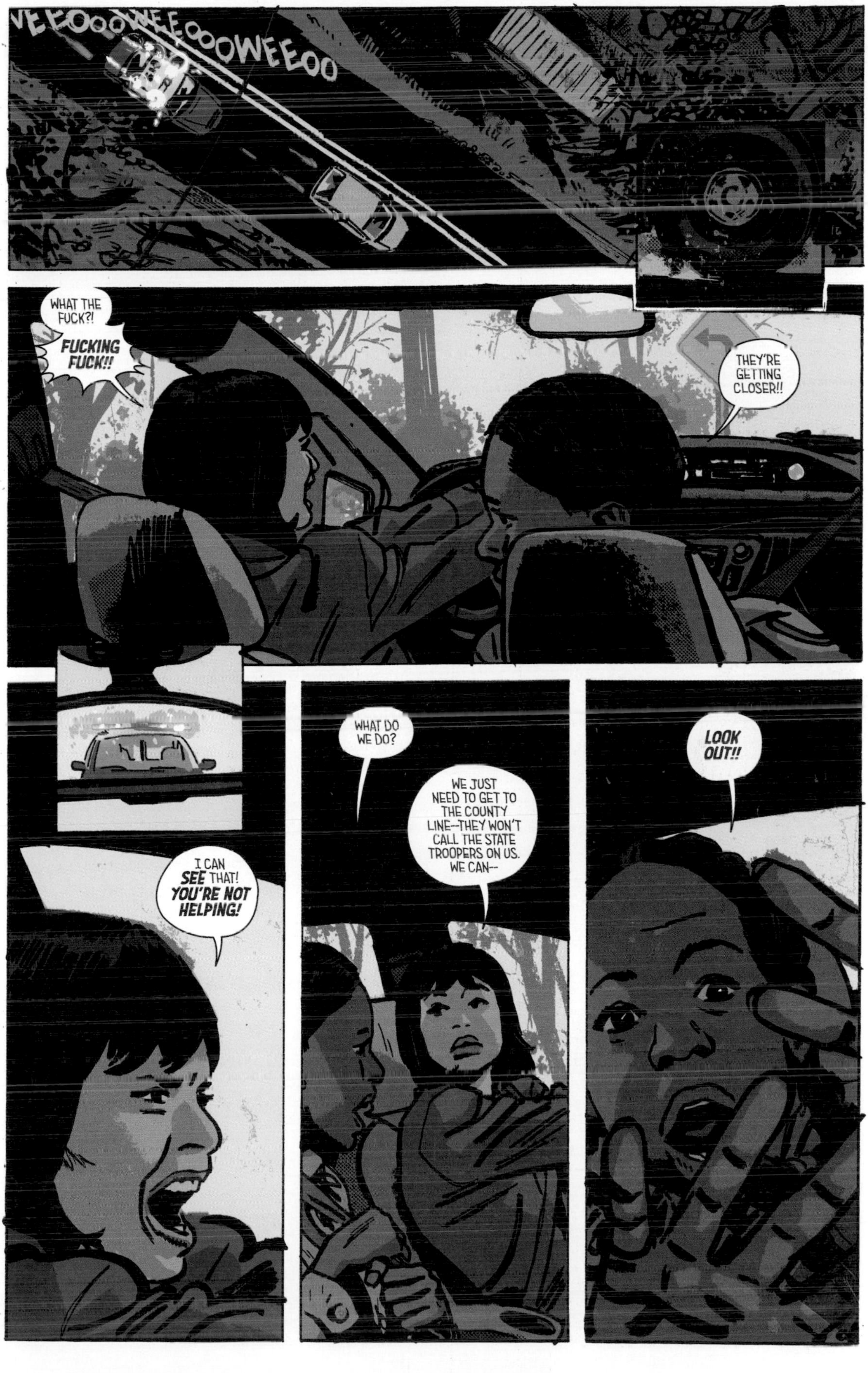
WEEOOOWEEOOOWEEOO
WHAT THE FUCK?!
FUCKING FUCK!!
THEY'RE GETTING CLOSER!!
I CAN SEE THAT! YOU'RE NOT HELPING!
WHAT DO WE DO?
WE JUST NEED TO GET TO THE COUNTY LINE--THEY WON'T CALL THE STATE TROOPERS ON US. WE CAN--
LOOK OUT!!

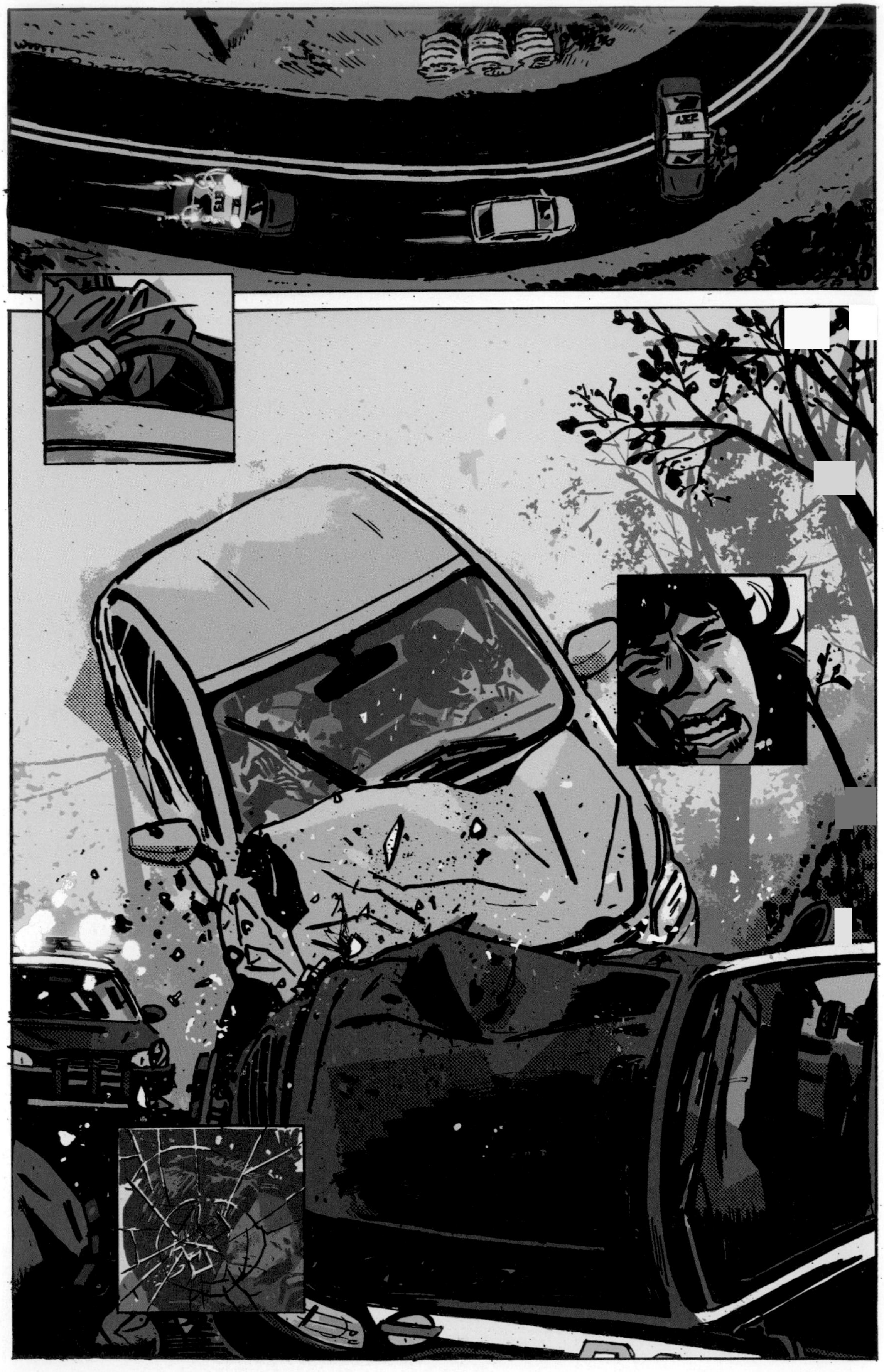

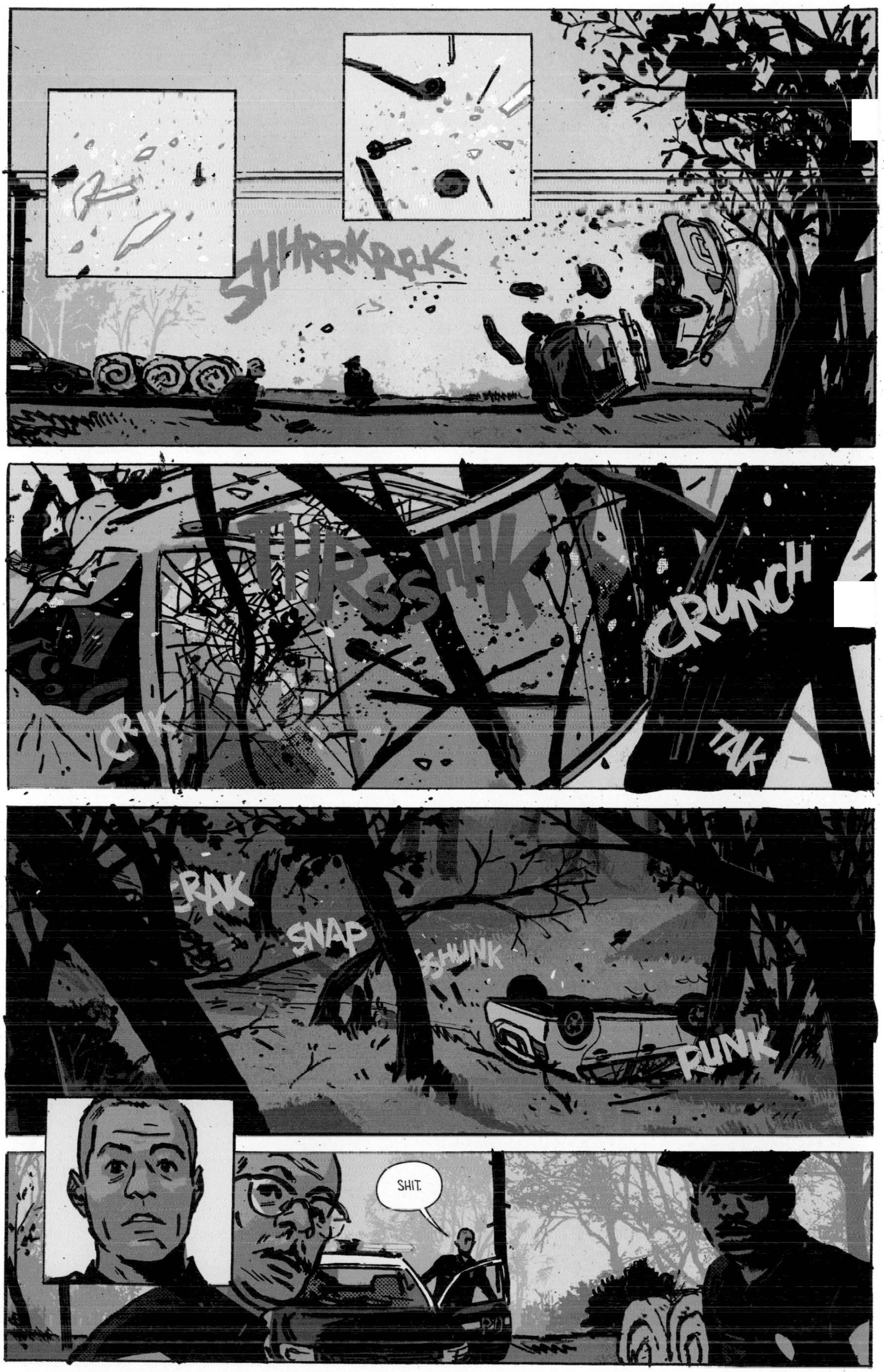
SHHRRKRRK
THRSSHHK
CRUNCH
CRIK
TAK
CRAK
SNAP
SHUNK
RUNK
SHIT.

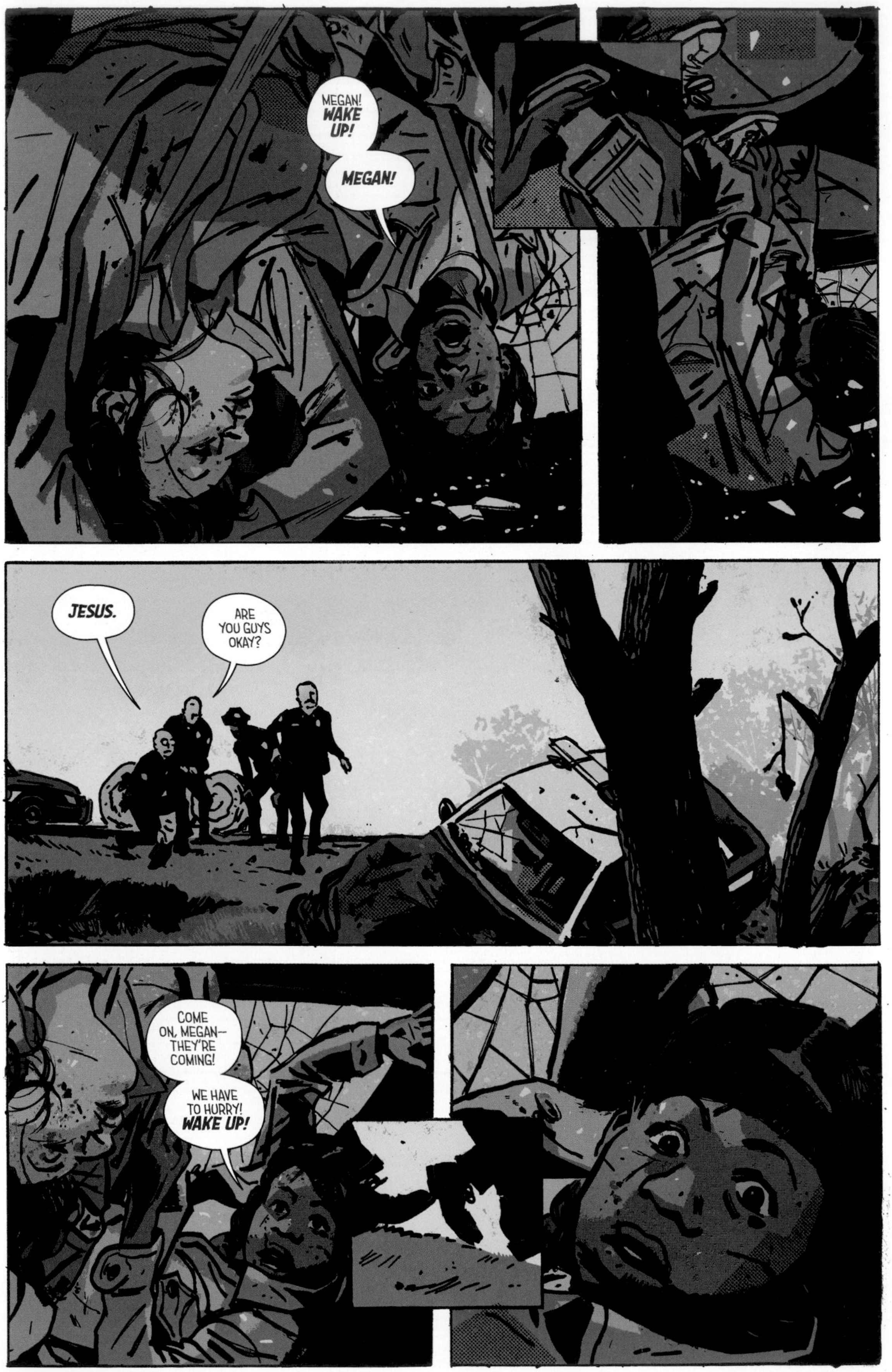
MEGAN! WAKE UP!
MEGAN!
JESUS.
ARE YOU GUYS OKAY?
COME ON, MEGAN— THEY'RE COMING!
WE HAVE TO HURRY! WAKE UP!

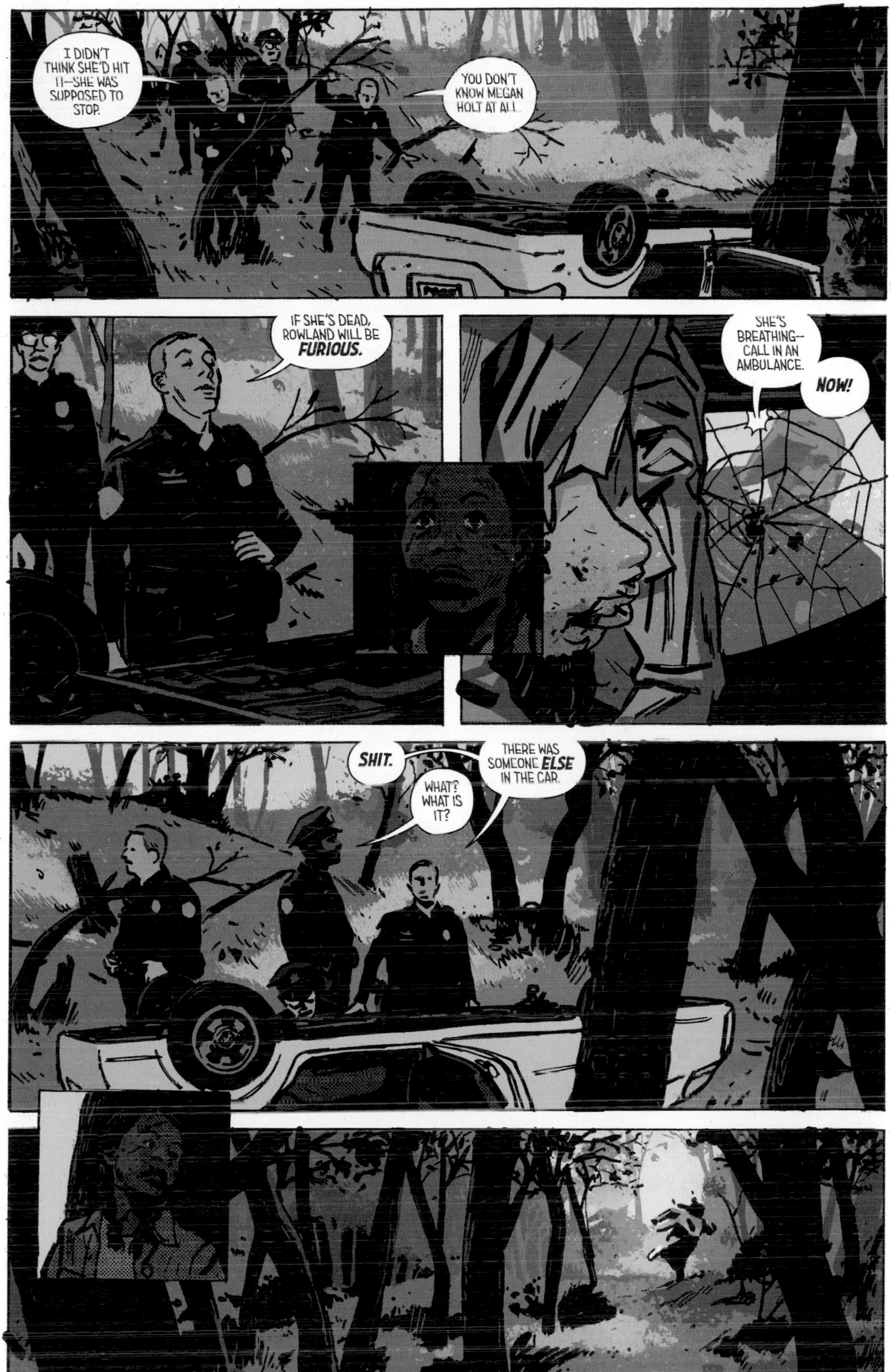

I DIDN'T THINK SHE'D HIT IT--SHE WAS SUPPOSED TO STOP.
YOU DON'T KNOW MEGAN HOLT AT ALL.
IF SHE'S DEAD, ROWLAND WILL BE FURIOUS.
SHE'S BREATHING-- CALL IN AN AMBULANCE.
NOW!
SHIT.
THERE WAS SOMEONE ELSE IN THE CAR.
WHAT? WHAT IS IT?

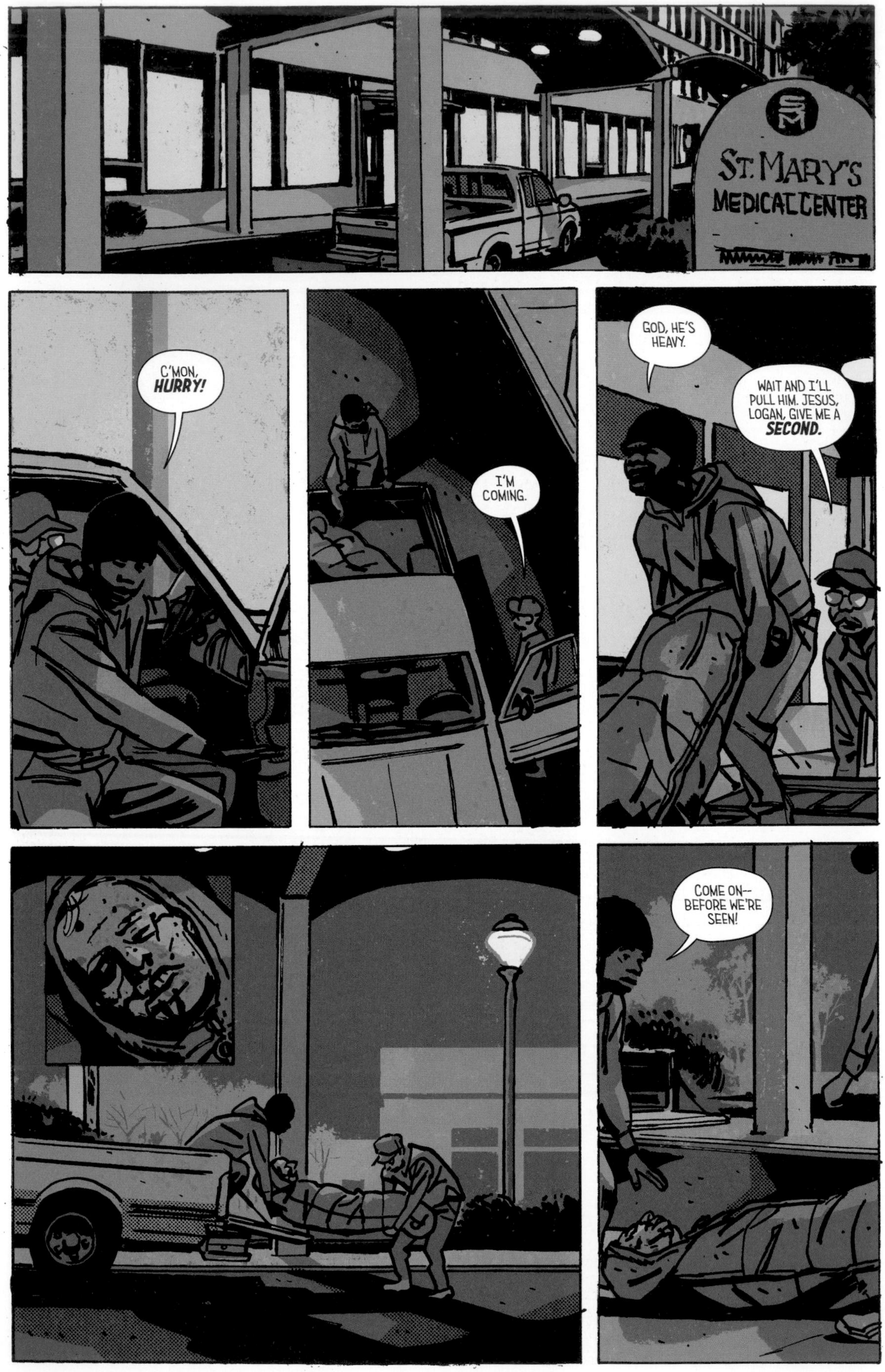
ST. MARY'S
MEDICAL CENTER
C'MON, HURRY!
I'M COMING.
GOD, HE'S HEAVY.
WAIT AND I'LL PULL HIM. JESUS, LOGAN, GIVE ME A SECOND.
COME ON-- BEFORE WE'RE SEEN!

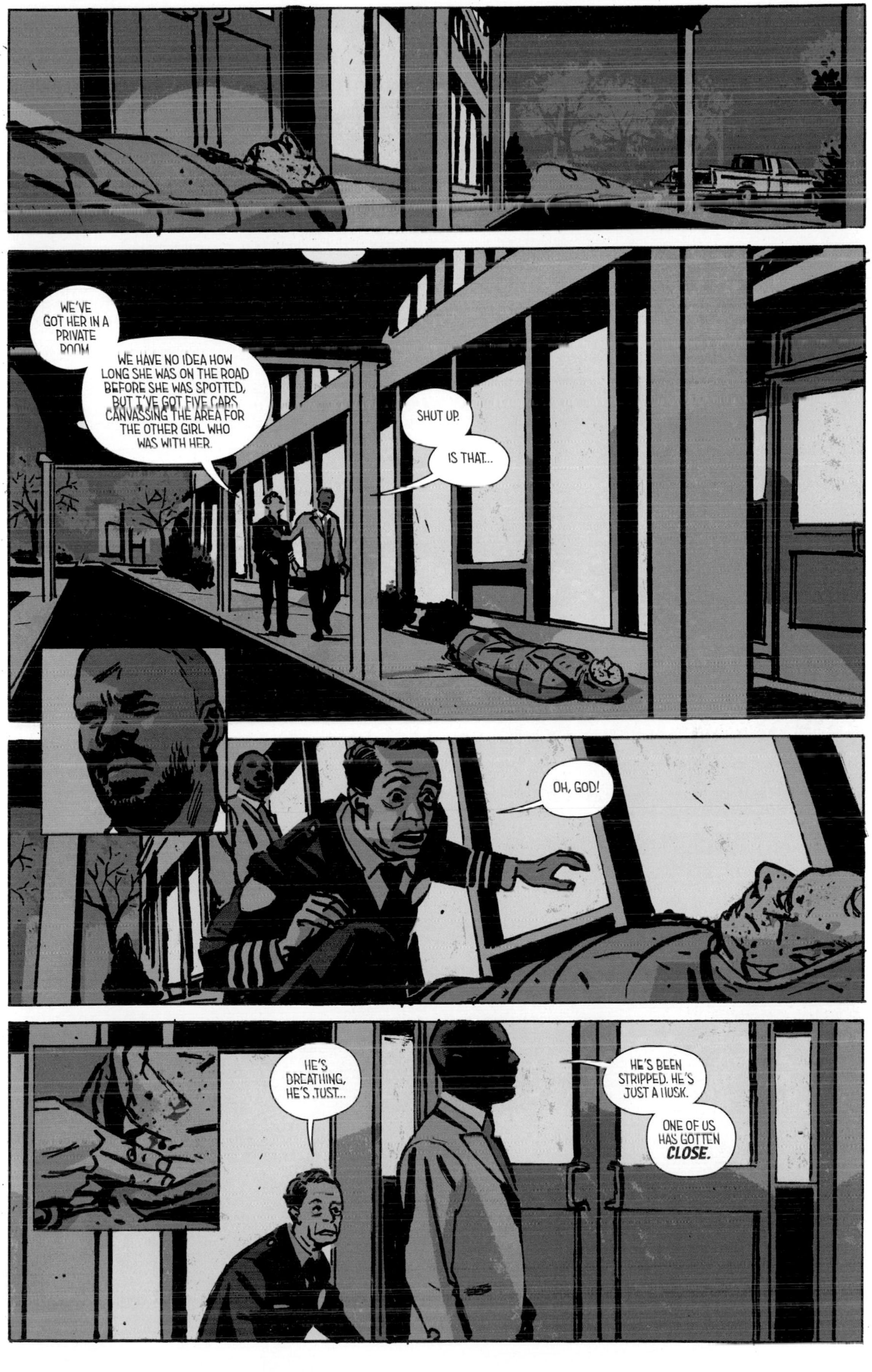
WE'VE GOT HER IN A PRIVATE ROOM.
WE HAVE NO IDEA HOW LONG SHE WAS ON THE ROAD BEFORE SHE WAS SPOTTED, BUT I'VE GOT FIVE CARS CANVASSING THE AREA FOR THE OTHER GIRL WHO WAS WITH HER.
SHUT UP.
IS THAT...
OH, GOD!
HE'S BREATHING, HE'S JUST...
HE'S BEEN STRIPPED. HE'S JUST A HUSK.
ONE OF US HAS GOTTEN CLOSE.

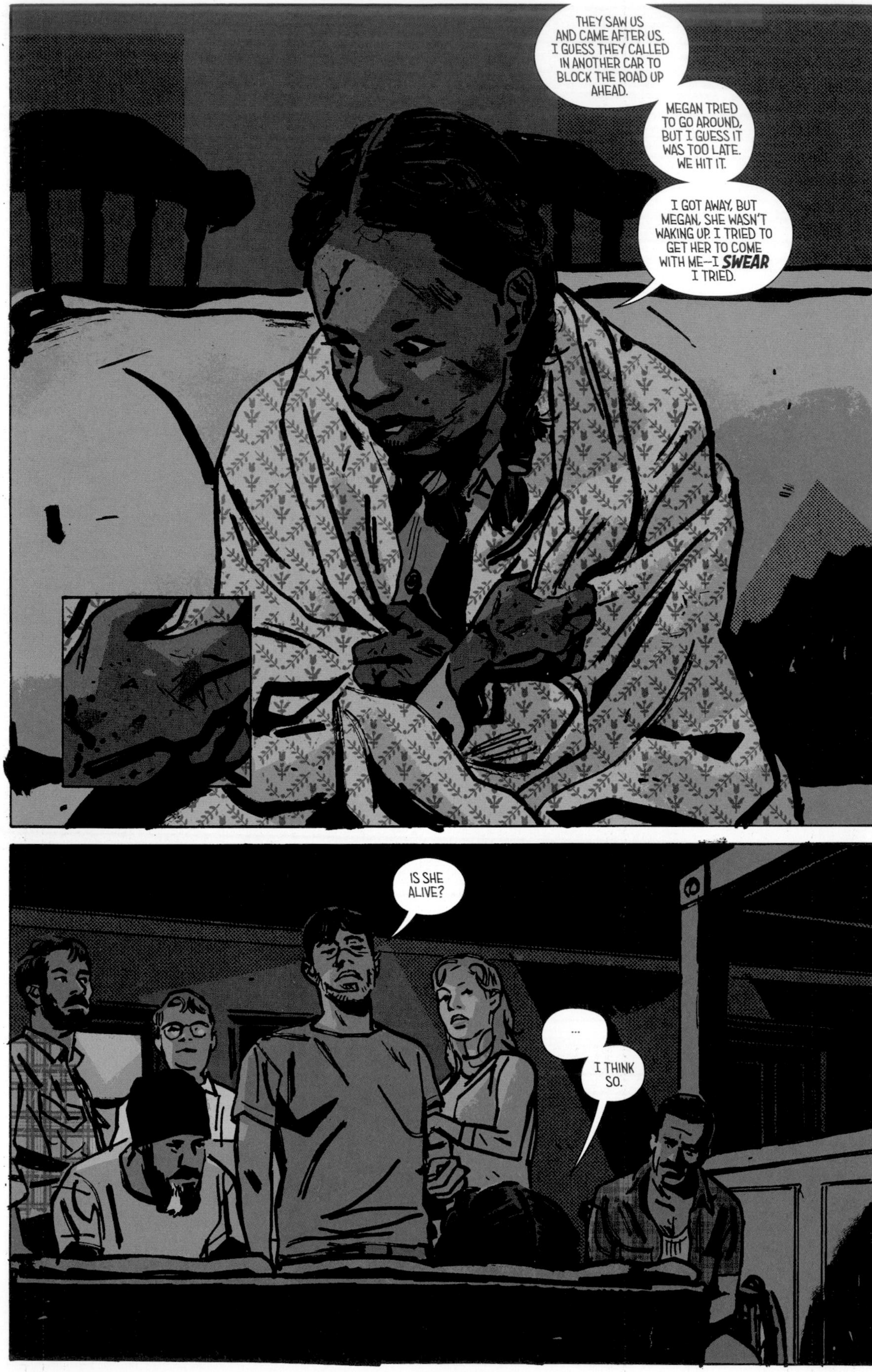
THEY SAW US AND CAME AFTER US. I GUESS THEY CALLED IN ANOTHER CAR TO BLOCK THE ROAD UP AHEAD.
MEGAN TRIED TO GO AROUND, BUT I GUESS IT WAS TOO LATE. WE HIT IT.
I GOT AWAY, BUT MEGAN, SHE WASN'T WAKING UP. I TRIED TO GET HER TO COME WITH ME--I SWEAR I TRIED.
IS SHE ALIVE?
...
I THINK SO.

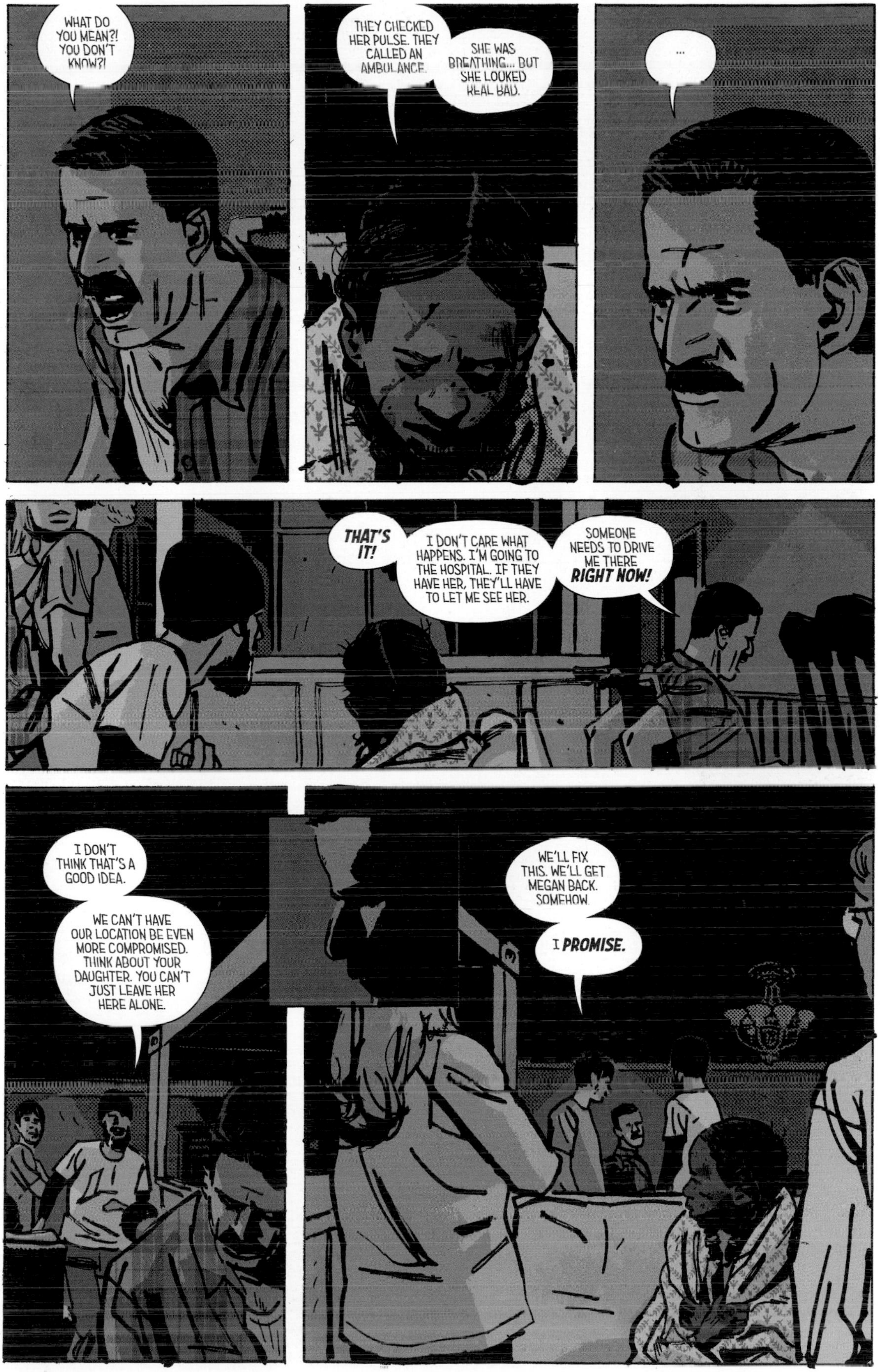
WHAT DO YOU MEAN?! YOU DON'T KNOW?!
THEY CHECKED HER PULSE. THEY CALLED AN AMBULANCE.
SHE WAS BREATHING... BUT SHE LOOKED REAL BAD.
...
THAT'S IT!
I DON'T CARE WHAT HAPPENS. I'M GOING TO THE HOSPITAL. IF THEY HAVE HER, THEY'LL HAVE TO LET ME SEE HER.
SOMEONE NEEDS TO DRIVE ME THERE RIGHT NOW!
I DON'T THINK THAT'S A GOOD IDEA.
WE CAN'T HAVE OUR LOCATION BE EVEN MORE COMPROMISED. THINK ABOUT YOUR DAUGHTER. YOU CAN'T JUST LEAVE HER HERE ALONE.
WE'LL FIX THIS. WE'LL GET MEGAN BACK. SOMEHOW.
I PROMISE.

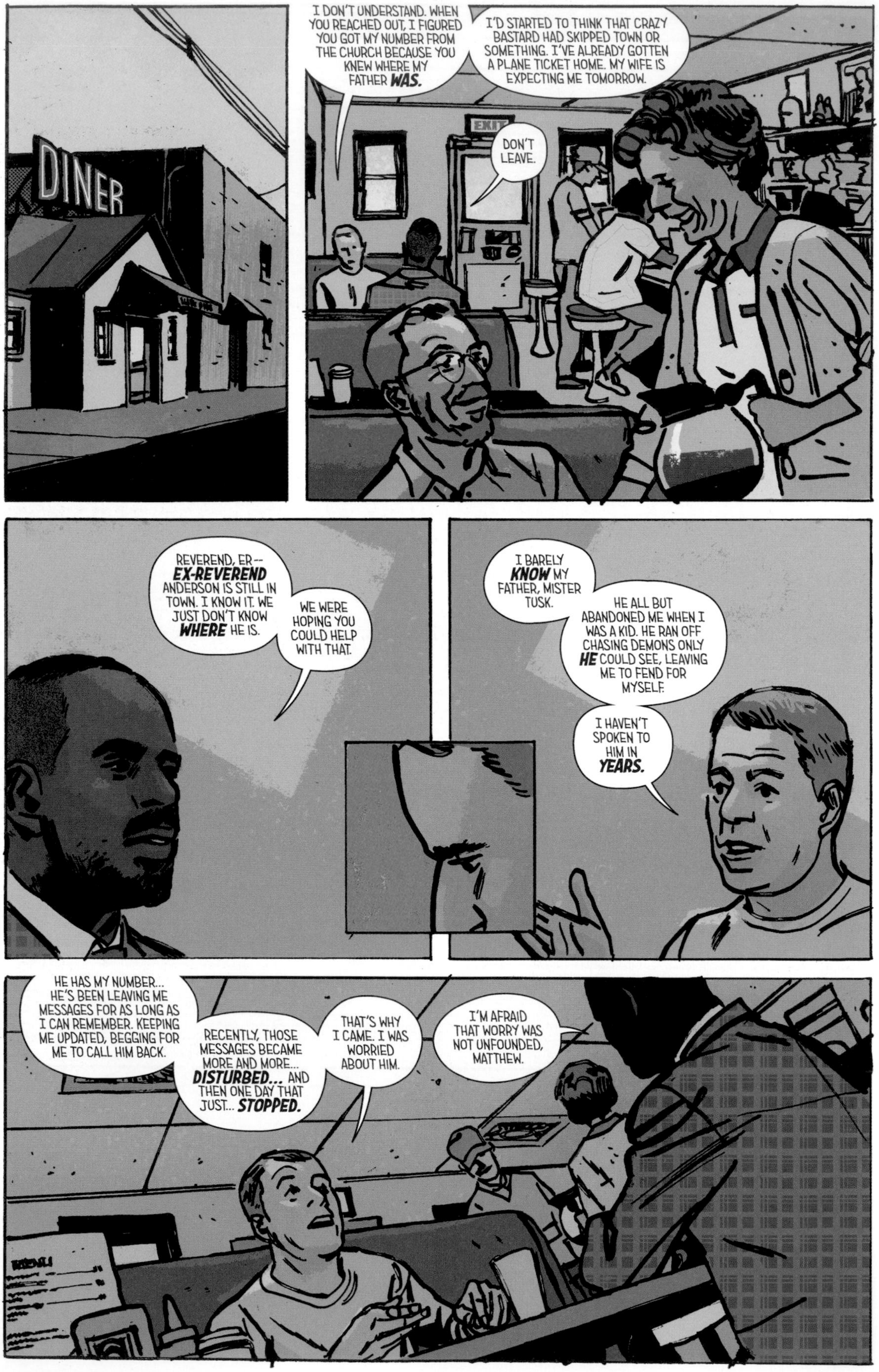
DINER
I DON'T UNDERSTAND. WHEN YOU REACHED OUT, I FIGURED YOU GOT MY NUMBER FROM THE CHURCH BECAUSE YOU KNEW WHERE MY FATHER WAS.
I'D STARTED TO THINK THAT CRAZY BASTARD HAD SKIPPED TOWN OR SOMETHING. I'VE ALREADY GOTTEN A PLANE TICKET HOME. MY WIFE IS EXPECTING ME TOMORROW.
EXIT
DON'T LEAVE.
REVEREND, ER-- EX-REVEREND ANDERSON IS STILL IN TOWN. I KNOW IT. WE JUST DON'T KNOW WHERE HE IS.
WE WERE HOPING YOU COULD HELP WITH THAT.
I BARELY KNOW MY FATHER, MISTER TUSK.
HE ALL BUT ABANDONED ME WHEN I WAS A KID. HE RAN OFF CHASING DEMONS ONLY HE COULD SEE, LEAVING ME TO FEND FOR MYSELF.
I HAVEN'T SPOKEN TO HIM IN YEARS.
HE HAS MY NUMBER... HE'S BEEN LEAVING ME MESSAGES FOR AS LONG AS I CAN REMEMBER. KEEPING ME UPDATED, BEGGING FOR ME TO CALL HIM BACK.
RECENTLY, THOSE MESSAGES BECAME MORE AND MORE... DISTURBED... AND THEN ONE DAY THAT JUST... STOPPED.
THAT'S WHY I CAME. I WAS WORRIED ABOUT HIM.
I'M AFRAID THAT WORRY WAS NOT UNFOUNDED, MATTHEW.

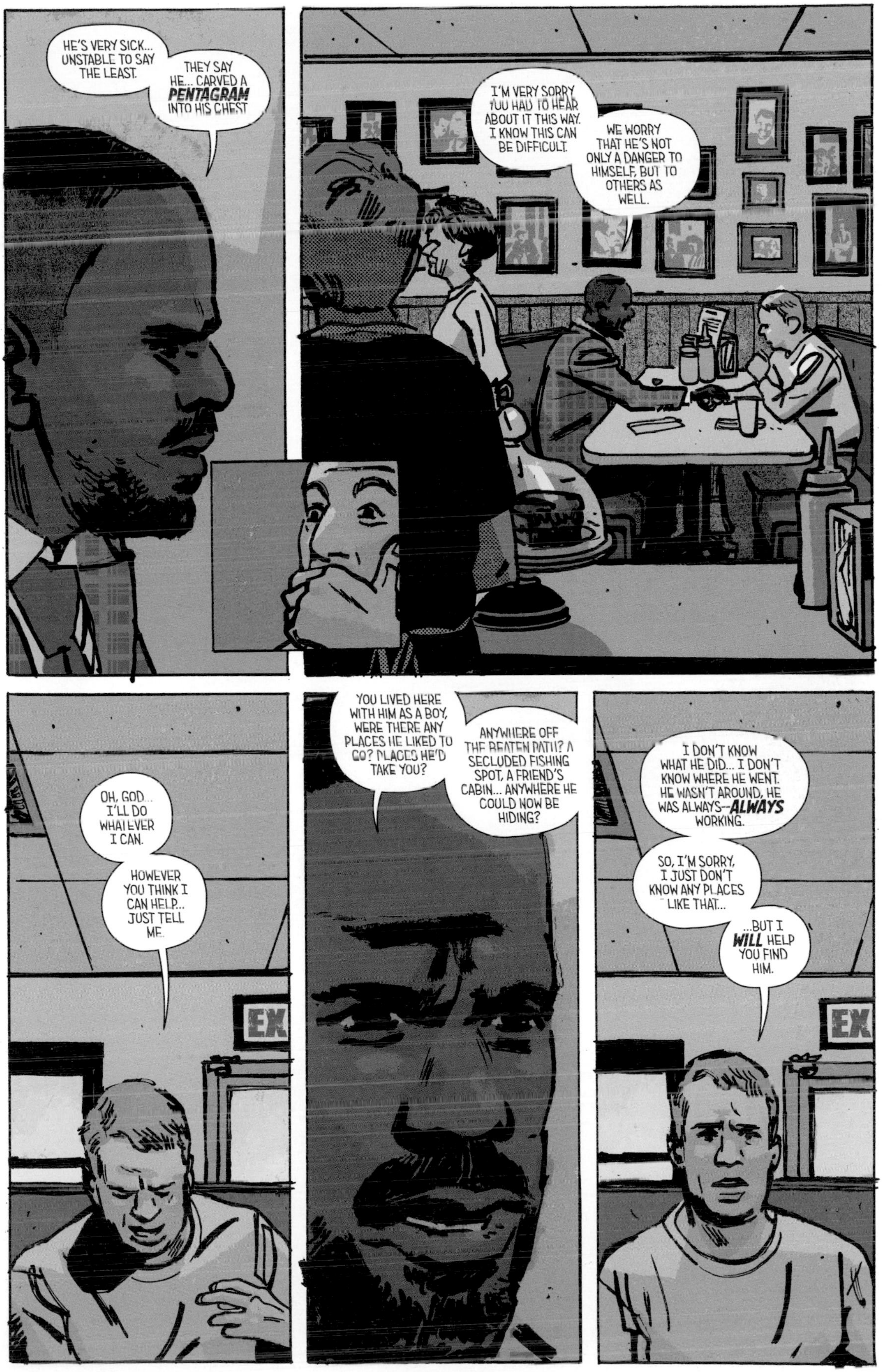
HE'S VERY SICK... UNSTABLE TO SAY THE LEAST.
THEY SAY HE... CARVED A PENTAGRAM INTO HIS CHEST.
I'M VERY SORRY YOU HAD TO HEAR ABOUT IT THIS WAY. I KNOW THIS CAN BE DIFFICULT.
WE WORRY THAT HE'S NOT ONLY A DANGER TO HIMSELF, BUT TO OTHERS AS WELL.
OH, GOD... I'LL DO WHATEVER I CAN.
HOWEVER YOU THINK I CAN HELP... JUST TELL ME.
YOU LIVED HERE WITH HIM AS A BOY, WERE THERE ANY PLACES HE LIKED TO GO? PLACES HE'D TAKE YOU?
ANYWHERE OFF THE BEATEN PATH? A SECLUDED FISHING SPOT, A FRIEND'S CABIN... ANYWHERE HE COULD NOW BE HIDING?
I DON'T KNOW WHAT HE DID... I DON'T KNOW WHERE HE WENT. HE WASN'T AROUND, HE WAS ALWAYS--ALWAYS WORKING.
SO, I'M SORRY, I JUST DON'T KNOW ANY PLACES LIKE THAT...
...BUT I WILL HELP YOU FIND HIM.

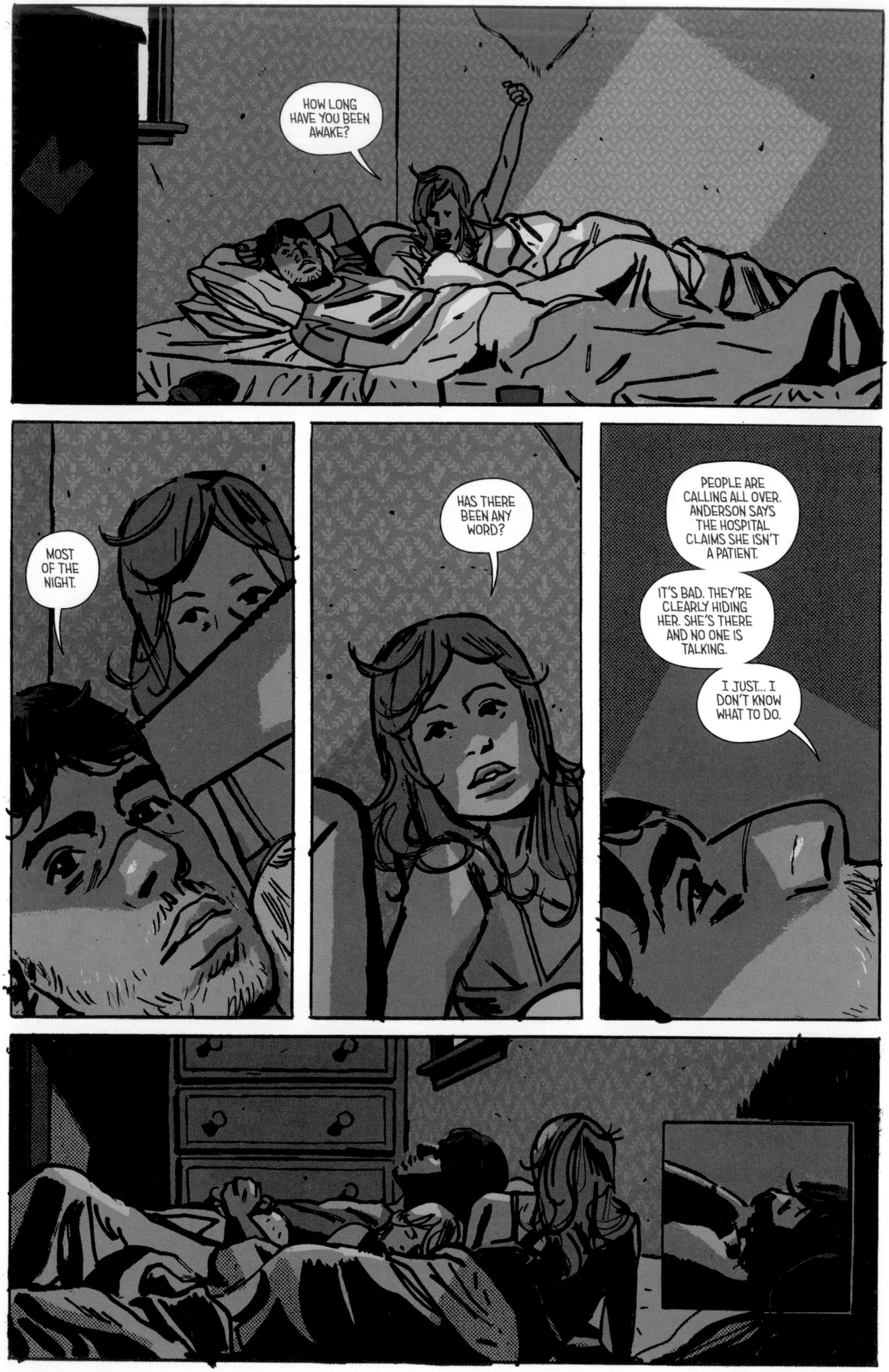
HOW LONG HAVE YOU BEEN AWAKE?
MOST OF THE NIGHT.
HAS THERE BEEN ANY WORD?
PEOPLE ARE CALLING ALL OVER. ANDERSON SAYS THE HOSPITAL CLAIMS SHE ISN'T A PATIENT.
IT'S BAD. THEY'RE CLEARLY HIDING HER. SHE'S THERE AND NO ONE IS TALKING.
I JUST... I DON'T KNOW WHAT TO DO.

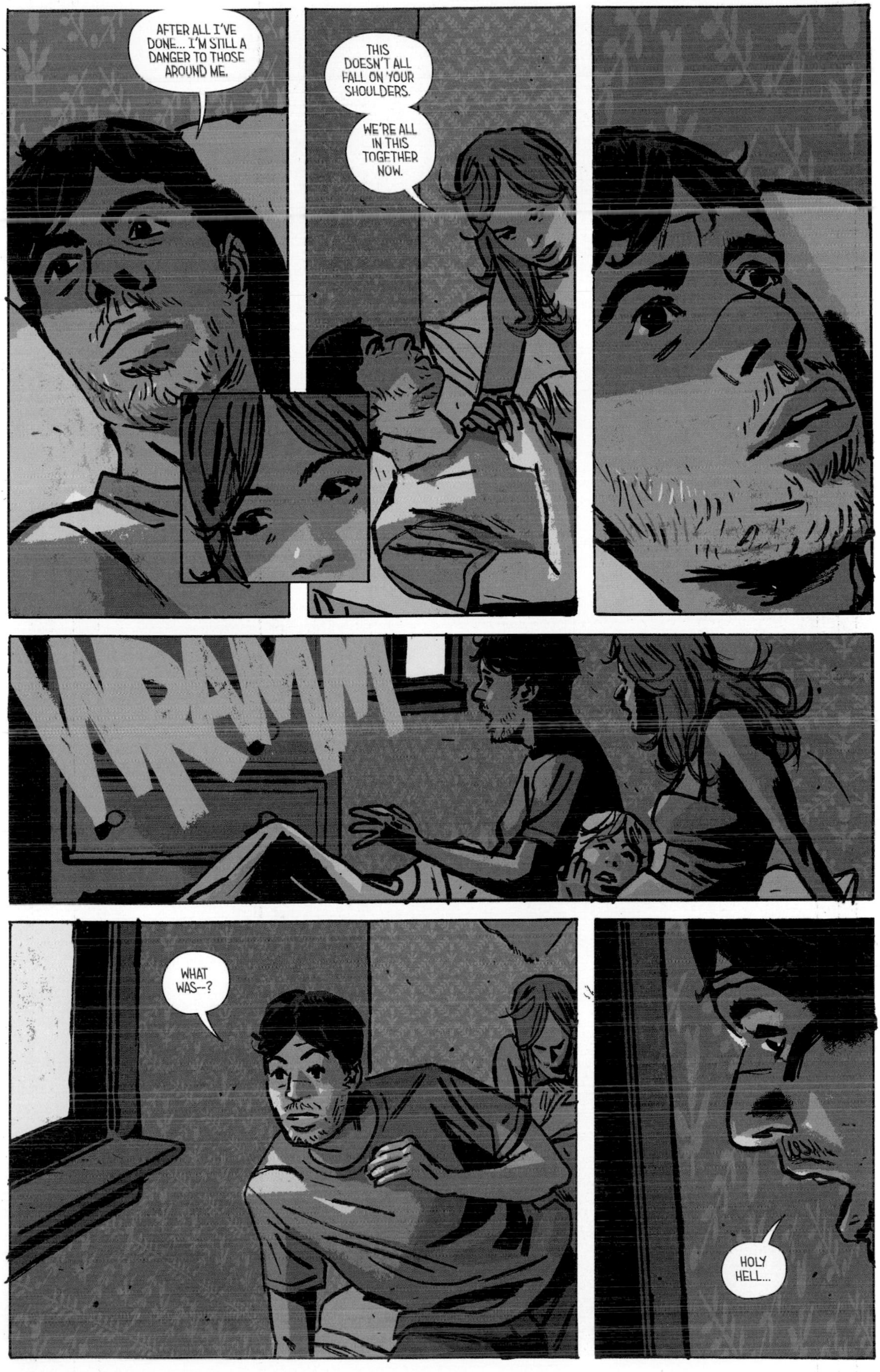
AFTER ALL I'VE DONE... I'M STILL A DANGER TO THOSE AROUND ME.
THIS DOESN'T ALL FALL ON YOUR SHOULDERS.
WE'RE ALL IN THIS TOGETHER NOW.
VRAMM
WHAT WAS--?
HOLY HELL...

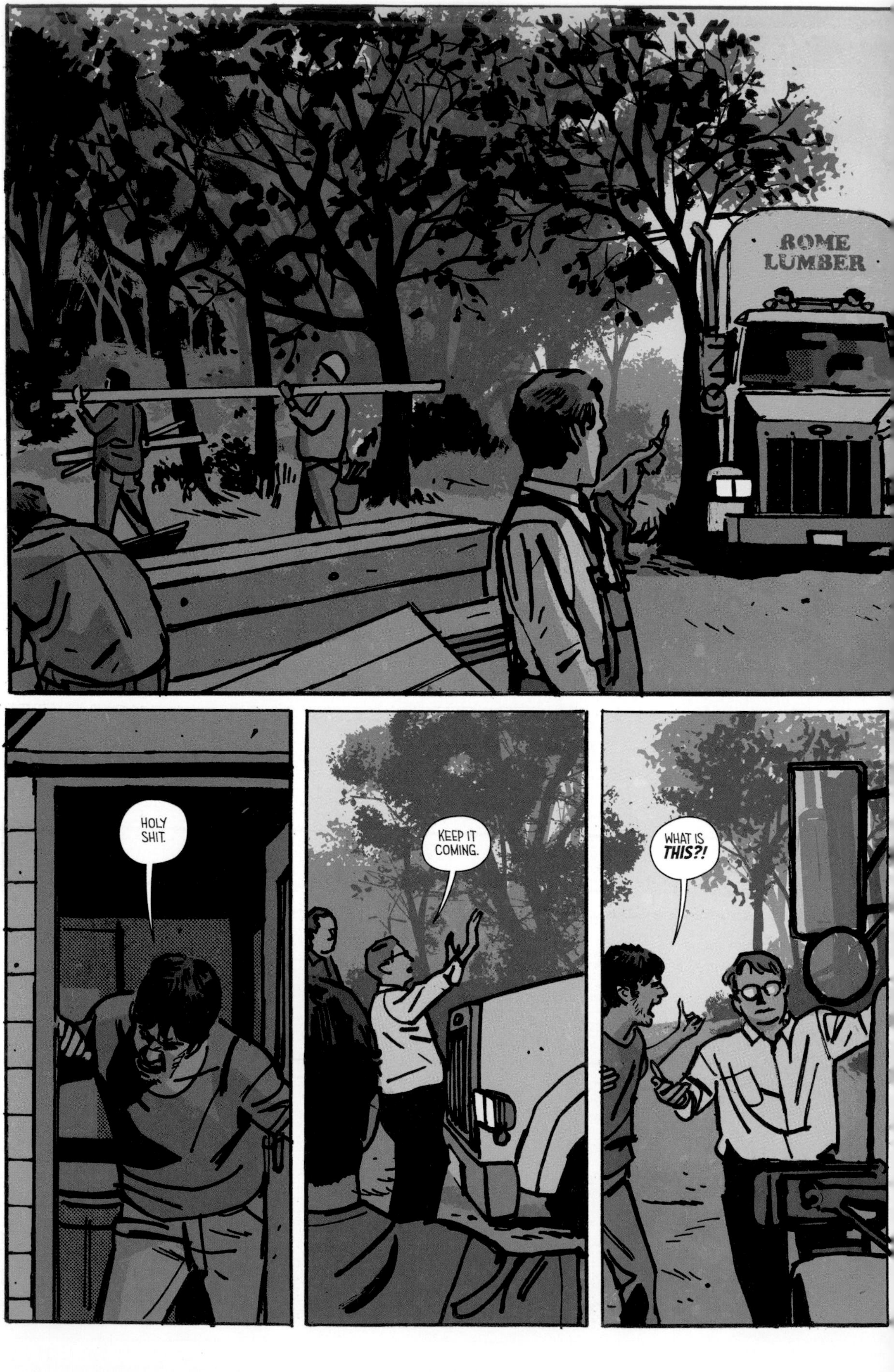
ROME
LUMBER
HOLY SHIT.
KEEP IT COMING.
WHAT IS THIS?!

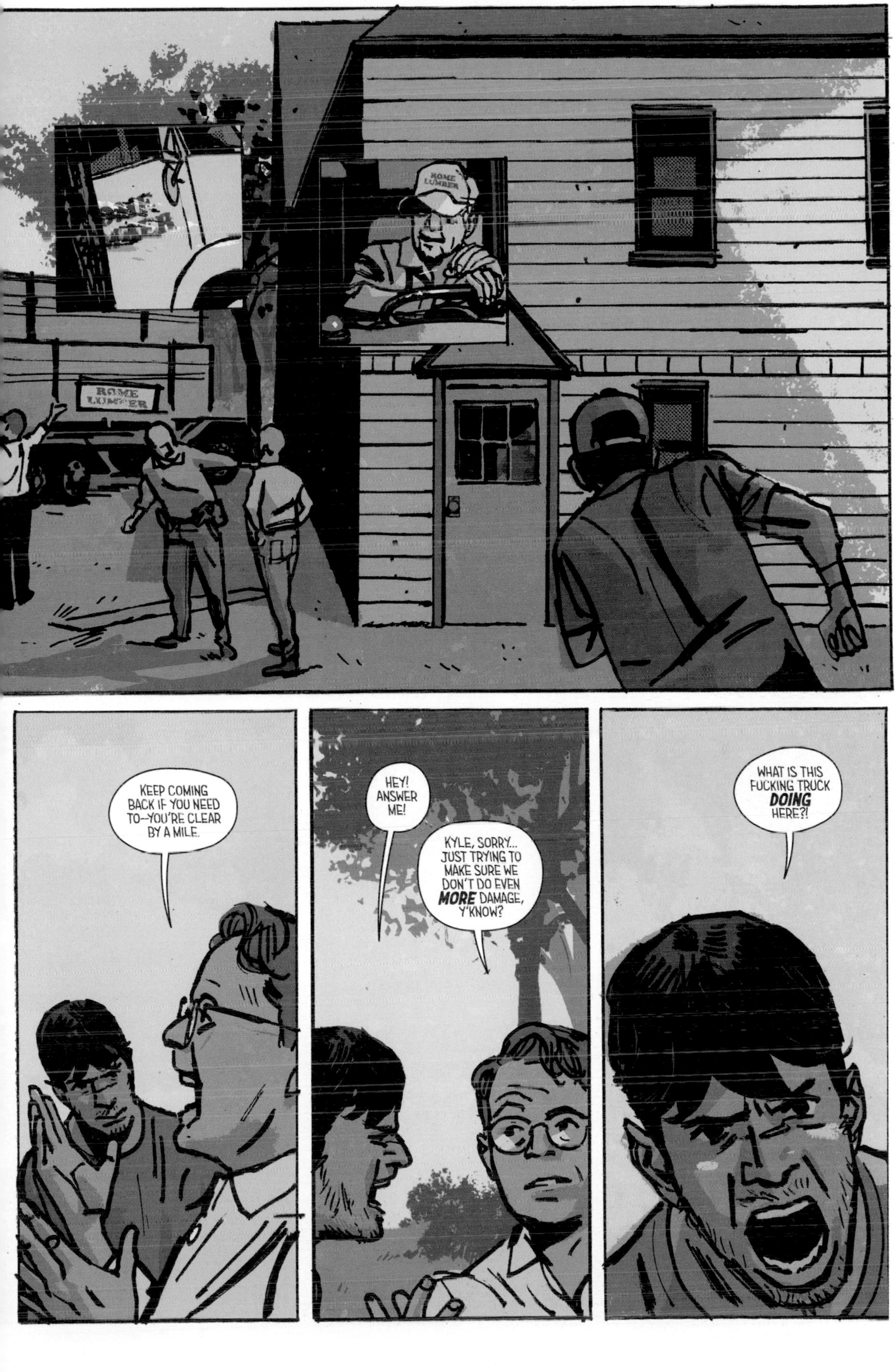
ROME LUMBER
KEEP COMING BACK IF YOU NEED TO--YOU'RE CLEAR BY A MILE.
HEY! ANSWER ME!
KYLE, SORRY... JUST TRYING TO MAKE SURE WE DON'T DO EVEN MORE DAMAGE, Y'KNOW?
WHAT IS THIS FUCKING TRUCK DOING HERE?!

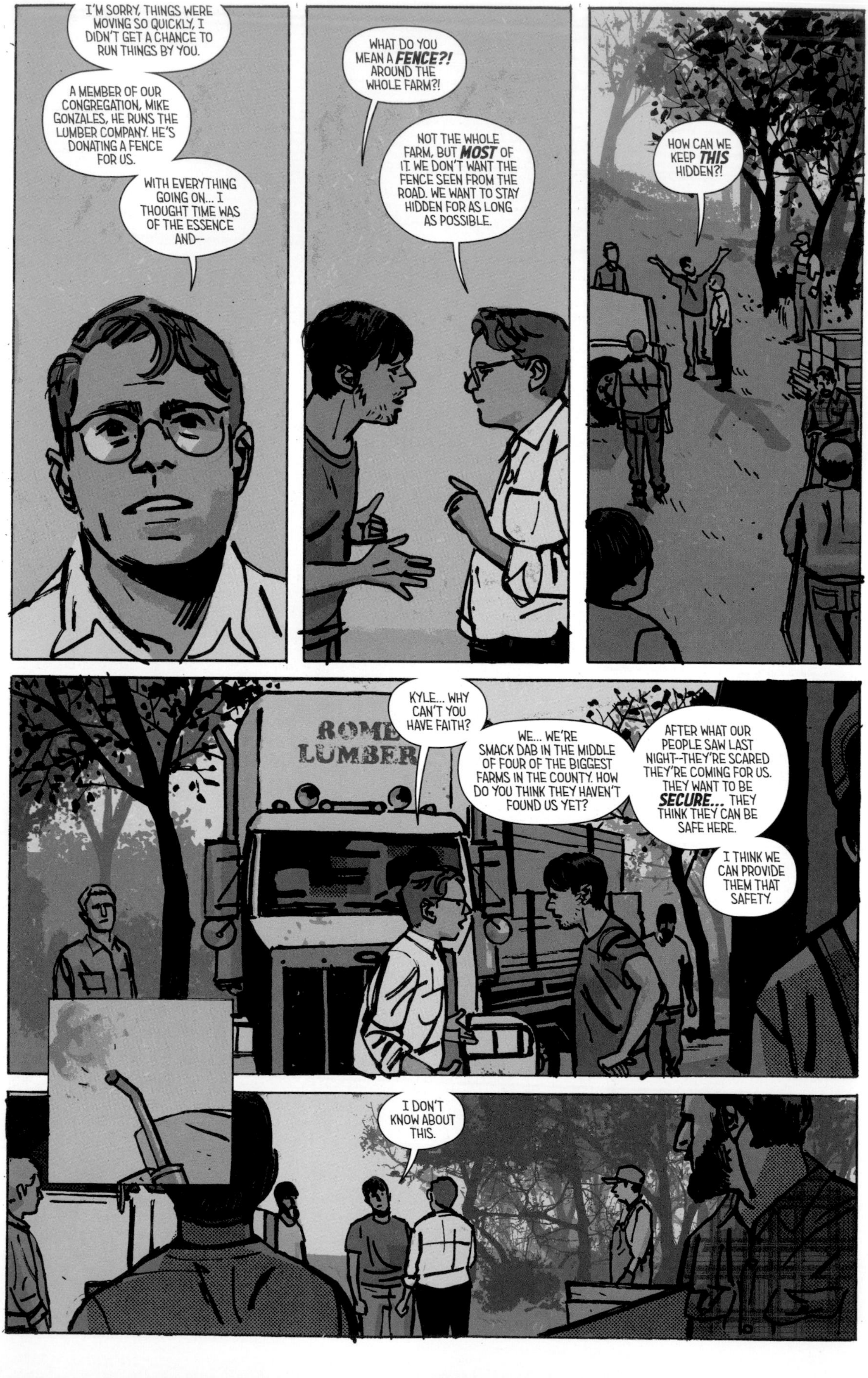
I'M SORRY, THINGS WERE MOVING SO QUICKLY, I DIDN'T GET A CHANCE TO RUN THINGS BY YOU.
A MEMBER OF OUR CONGREGATION, MIKE GONZALES, HE RUNS THE LUMBER COMPANY. HE'S DONATING A FENCE FOR US.
WITH EVERYTHING GOING ON... I THOUGHT TIME WAS OF THE ESSENCE AND--
WHAT DO YOU MEAN A FENCE?! AROUND THE WHOLE FARM?!
NOT THE WHOLE FARM, BUT MOST OF IT. WE DON'T WANT THE FENCE SEEN FROM THE ROAD. WE WANT TO STAY HIDDEN FOR AS LONG AS POSSIBLE.
HOW CAN WE KEEP THIS HIDDEN?!
ROME
LUMBER
KYLE... WHY CAN'T YOU HAVE FAITH?
WE... WE'RE SMACK DAB IN THE MIDDLE OF FOUR OF THE BIGGEST FARMS IN THE COUNTY. HOW DO YOU THINK THEY HAVEN'T FOUND US YET?
AFTER WHAT OUR PEOPLE SAW LAST NIGHT--THEY'RE SCARED THEY'RE COMING FOR US. THEY WANT TO BE SECURE... THEY THINK THEY CAN BE SAFE HERE.
I THINK WE CAN PROVIDE THEM THAT SAFETY.
I DON'T KNOW ABOUT THIS.

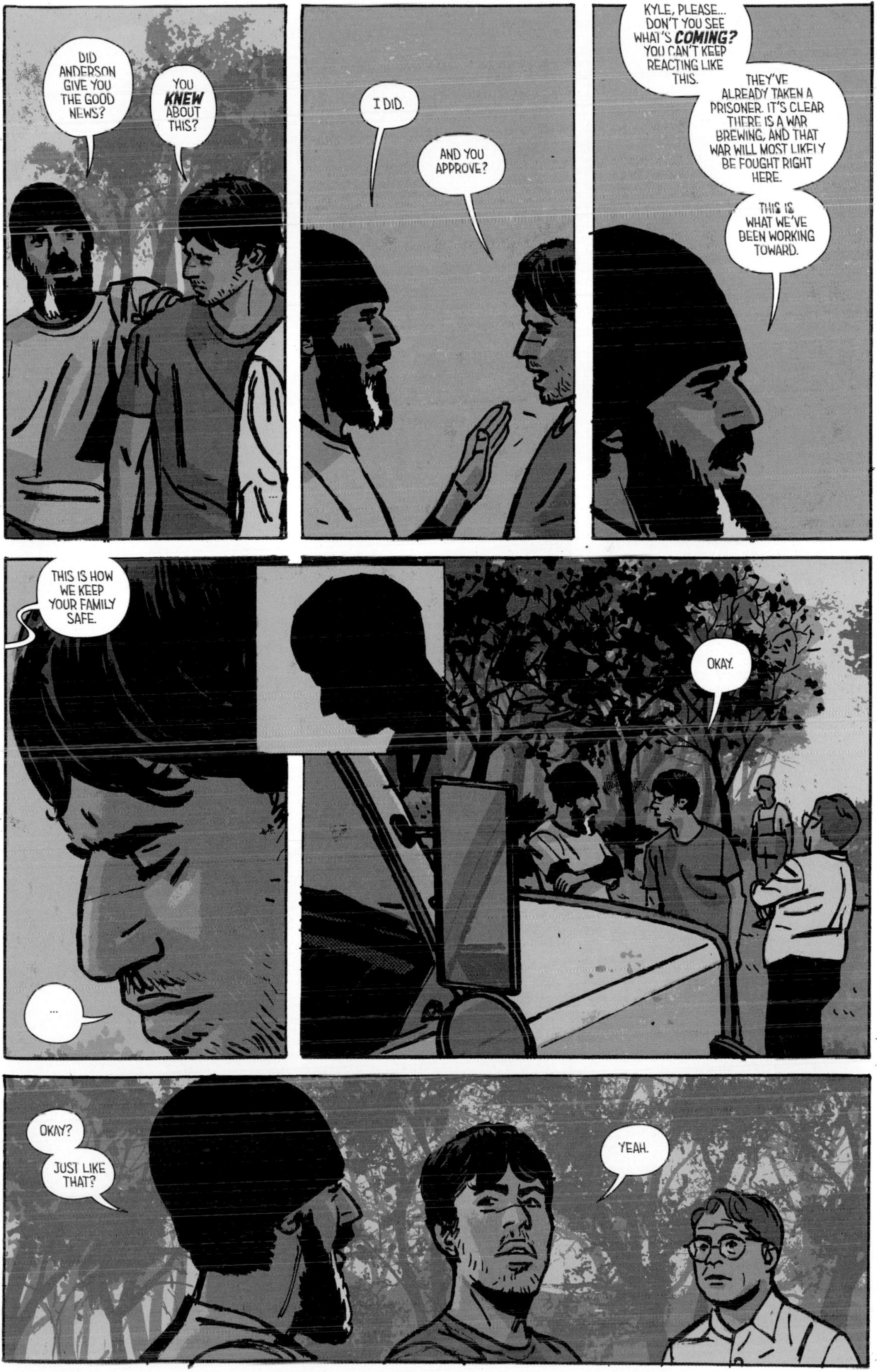

DID ANDERSON GIVE YOU THE GOOD NEWS?
YOU KNEW ABOUT THIS?
I DID.
AND YOU APPROVE?
KYLE, PLEASE... DON'T YOU SEE WHAT'S COMING? YOU CAN'T KEEP REACTING LIKE THIS.
THEY'VE ALREADY TAKEN A PRISONER. IT'S CLEAR THERE IS A WAR BREWING, AND THAT WAR WILL MOST LIKELY BE FOUGHT RIGHT HERE.
THIS IS WHAT WE'VE BEEN WORKING TOWARD.
THIS IS HOW WE KEEP YOUR FAMILY SAFE.
...
OKAY.
OKAY?
JUST LIKE THAT?
YEAH.

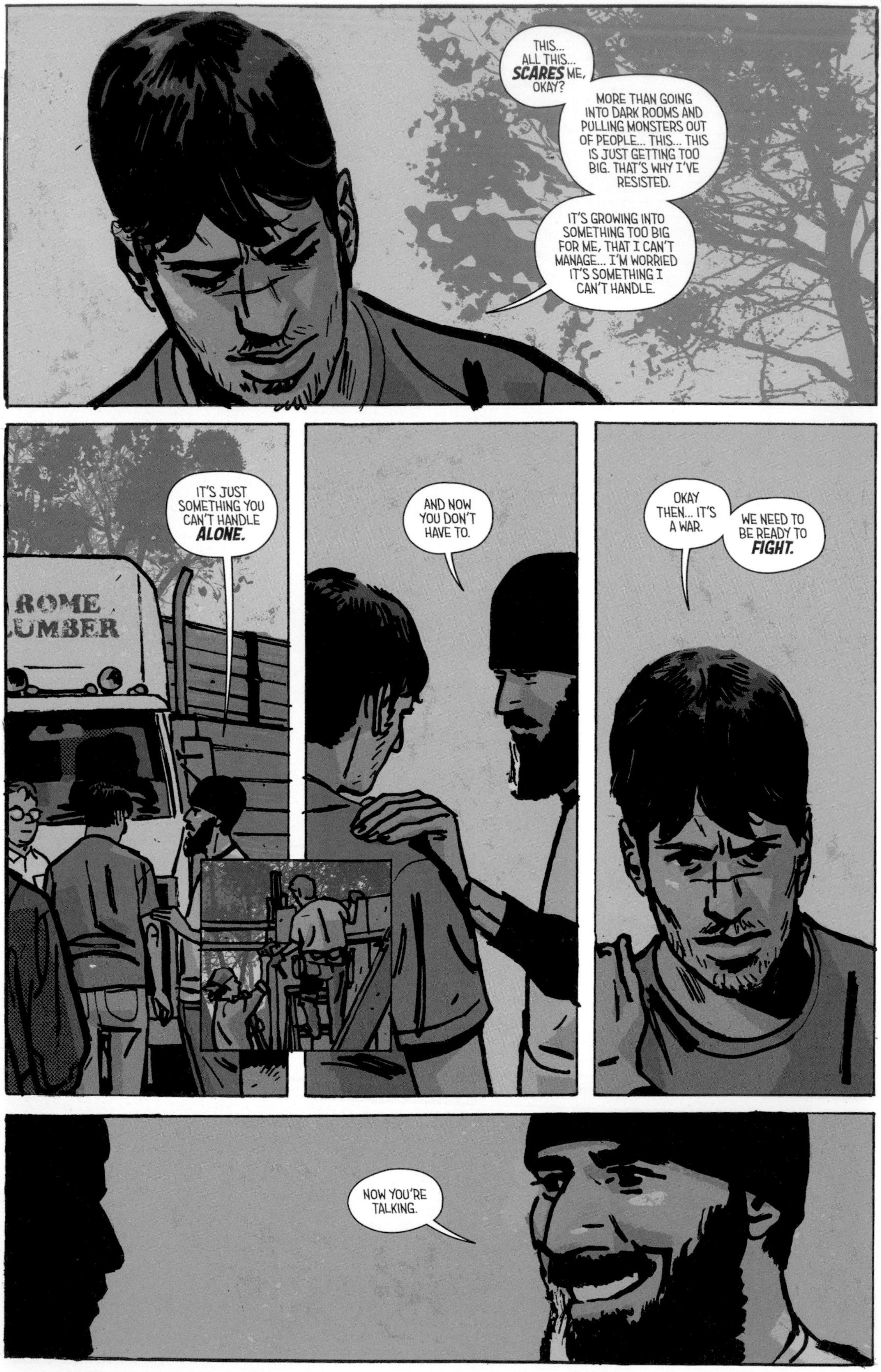
THIS... ALL THIS... SCARES ME, OKAY?
MORE THAN GOING INTO DARK ROOMS AND PULLING MONSTERS OUT OF PEOPLE... THIS... THIS IS JUST GETTING TOO BIG. THAT'S WHY I'VE RESISTED.
IT'S GROWING INTO SOMETHING TOO BIG FOR ME, THAT I CAN'T MANAGE... I'M WORRIED IT'S SOMETHING I CAN'T HANDLE.
IT'S JUST SOMETHING YOU CAN'T HANDLE ALONE.
ROME LUMBER
AND NOW YOU DON'T HAVE TO.
OKAY THEN... IT'S A WAR.
WE NEED TO BE READY TO FIGHT.
NOW YOU'RE TALKING.

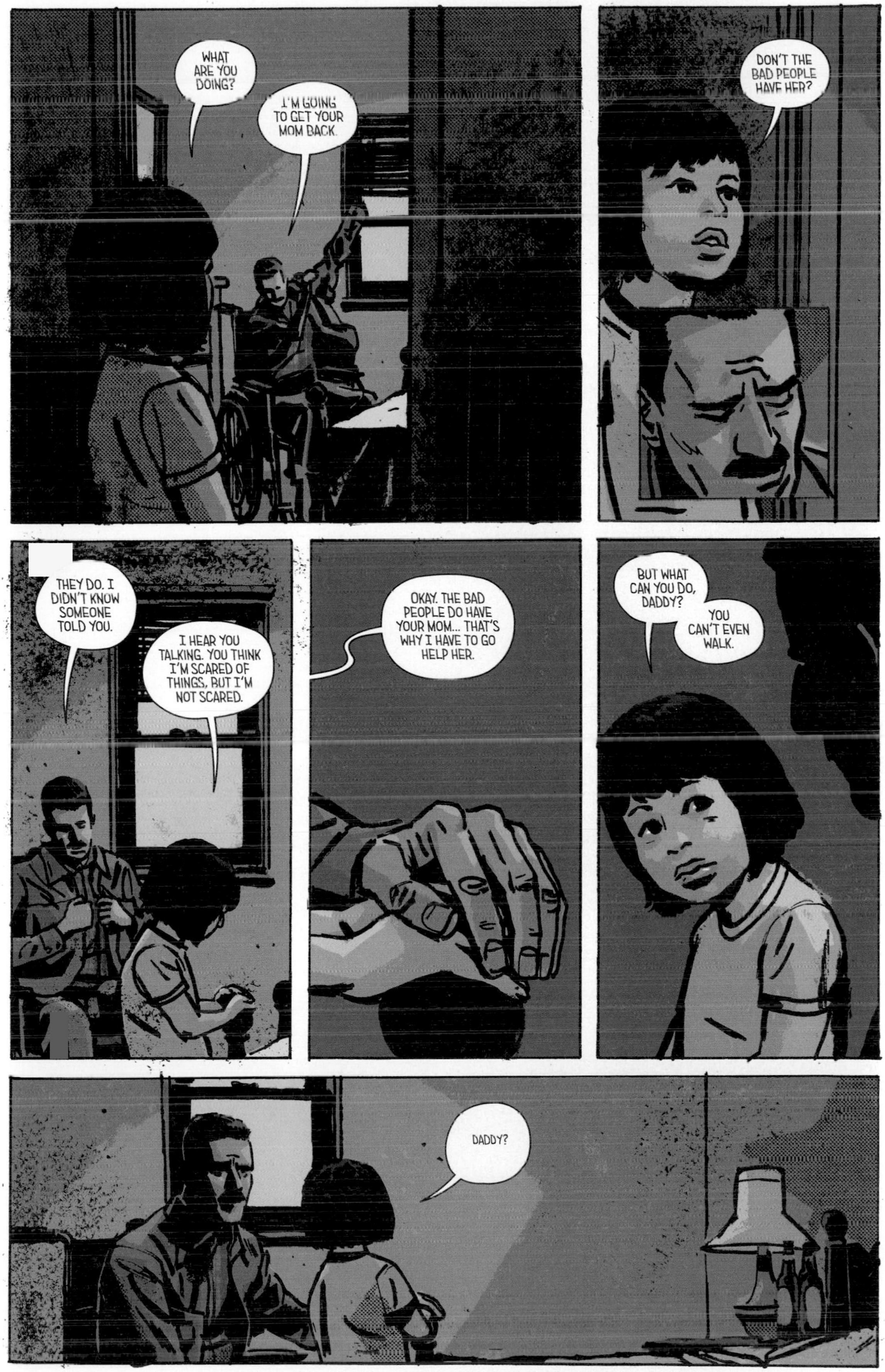
WHAT ARE YOU DOING?
I'M GOING TO GET YOUR MOM BACK.
DON'T THE BAD PEOPLE HAVE HER?
THEY DO. I DIDN'T KNOW SOMEONE TOLD YOU.
I HEAR YOU TALKING. YOU THINK I'M SCARED OF THINGS, BUT I'M NOT SCARED.
OKAY. THE BAD PEOPLE DO HAVE YOUR MOM... THAT'S WHY I HAVE TO GO HELP HER.
BUT WHAT CAN YOU DO, DADDY?
YOU CAN'T EVEN WALK.
DADDY?

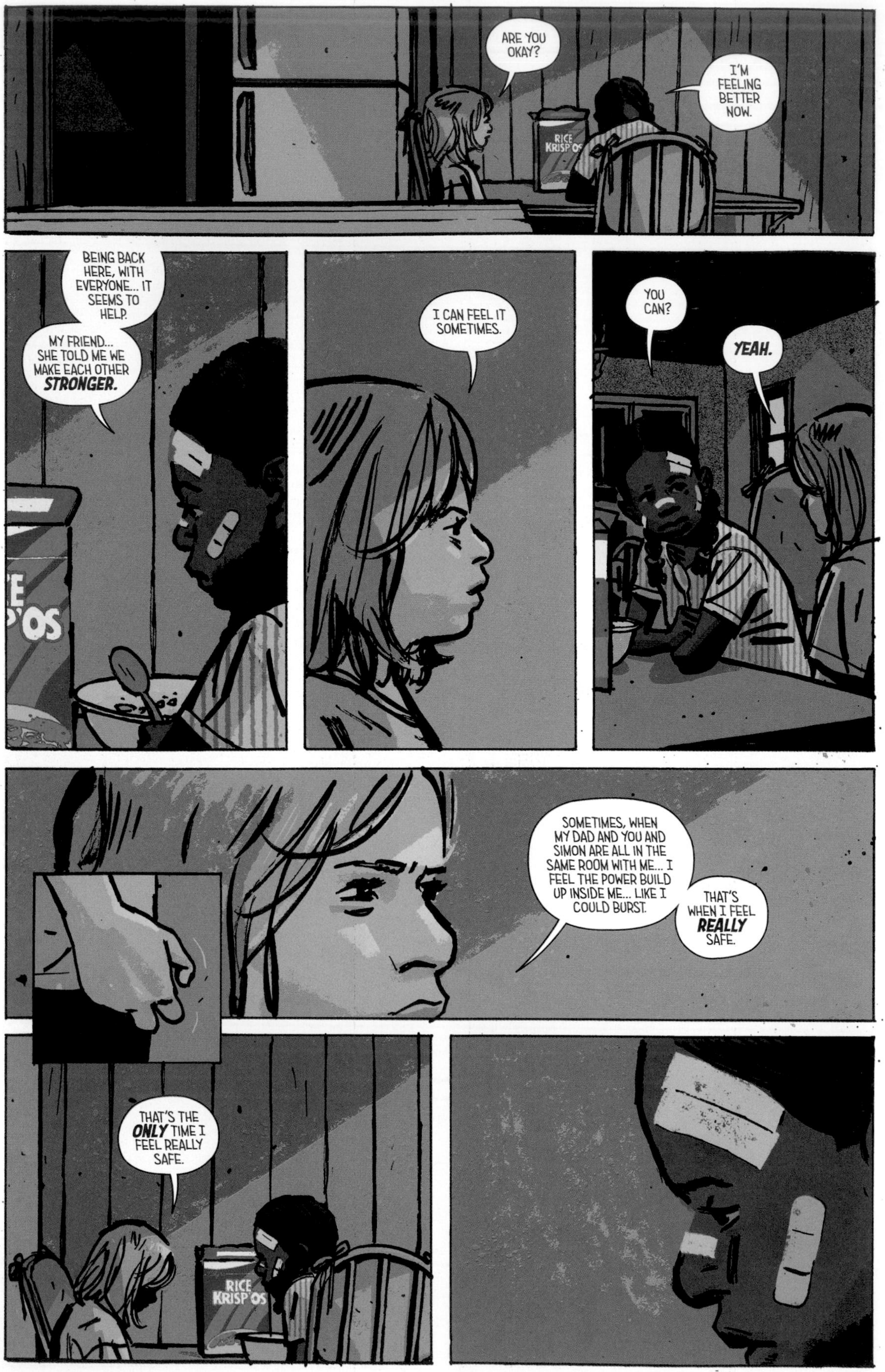
ARE YOU OKAY?
I'M FEELING BETTER NOW.
BEING BACK HERE, WITH EVERYONE... IT SEEMS TO HELP.
MY FRIEND... SHE TOLD ME WE MAKE EACH OTHER **STRONGER.**
I CAN FEEL IT SOMETIMES.
YOU CAN?
YEAH.
SOMETIMES, WHEN MY DAD AND YOU AND SIMON ARE ALL IN THE SAME ROOM WITH ME... I FEEL THE POWER BUILD UP INSIDE ME... LIKE I COULD BURST.
THAT'S WHEN I FEEL **REALLY** SAFE.
THAT'S THE **ONLY** TIME I FEEL REALLY SAFE.

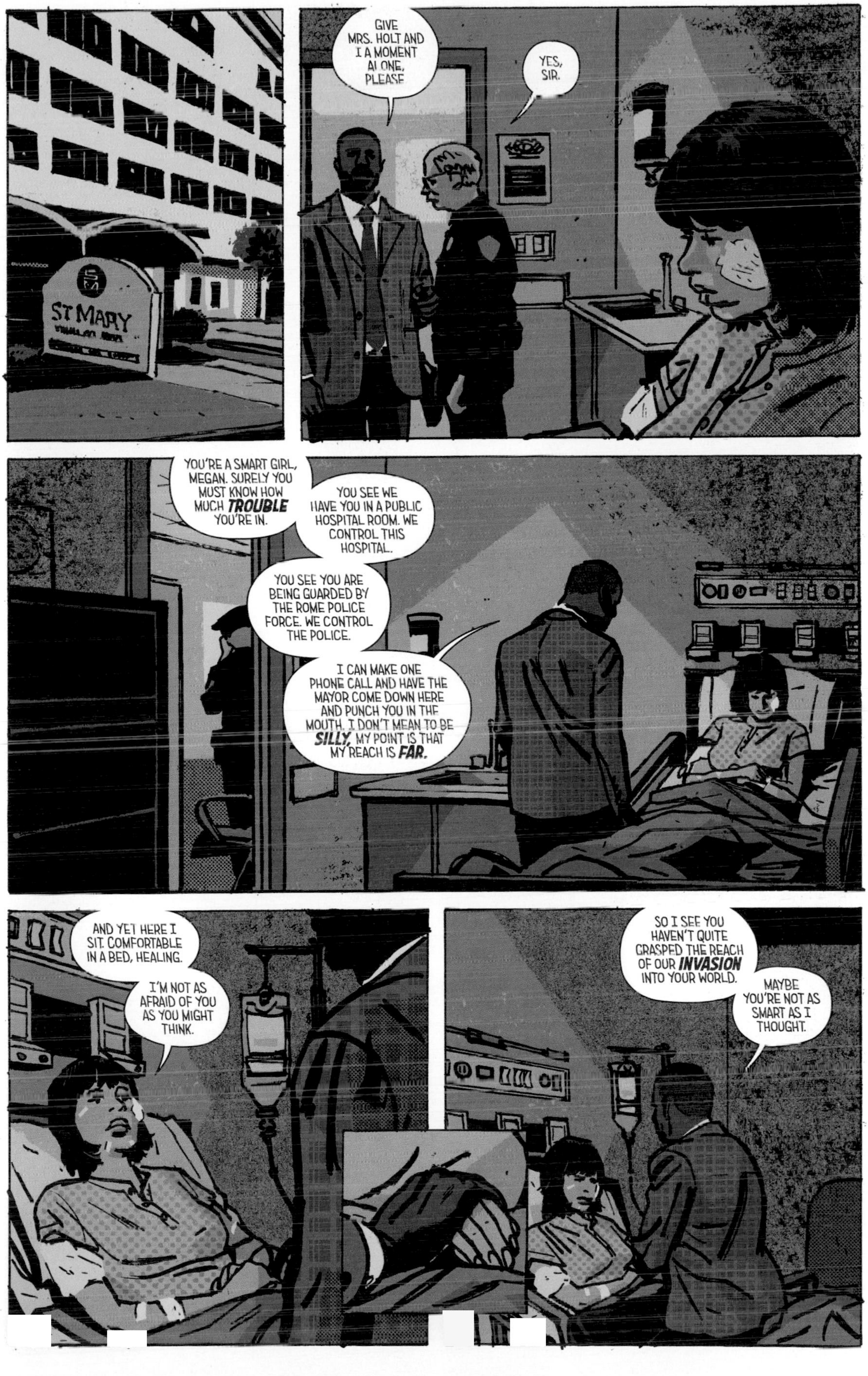
ST MARY
GIVE MRS. HOLT AND I A MOMENT ALONE, PLEASE
YES, SIR.
YOU'RE A SMART GIRL, MEGAN. SURELY YOU MUST KNOW HOW MUCH **TROUBLE** YOU'RE IN.
YOU SEE WE HAVE YOU IN A PUBLIC HOSPITAL ROOM. WE CONTROL THIS HOSPITAL.
YOU SEE YOU ARE BEING GUARDED BY THE ROME POLICE FORCE. WE CONTROL THE POLICE.
I CAN MAKE ONE PHONE CALL AND HAVE THE MAYOR COME DOWN HERE AND PUNCH YOU IN THE MOUTH. I DON'T MEAN TO BE **SILLY,** MY POINT IS THAT MY REACH IS **FAR.**
AND YET HERE I SIT. COMFORTABLE IN A BED, HEALING.
I'M NOT AS AFRAID OF YOU AS YOU MIGHT THINK.
SO I SEE YOU HAVEN'T QUITE GRASPED THE REACH OF OUR **INVASION** INTO YOUR WORLD.
MAYBE YOU'RE NOT AS SMART AS I THOUGHT.

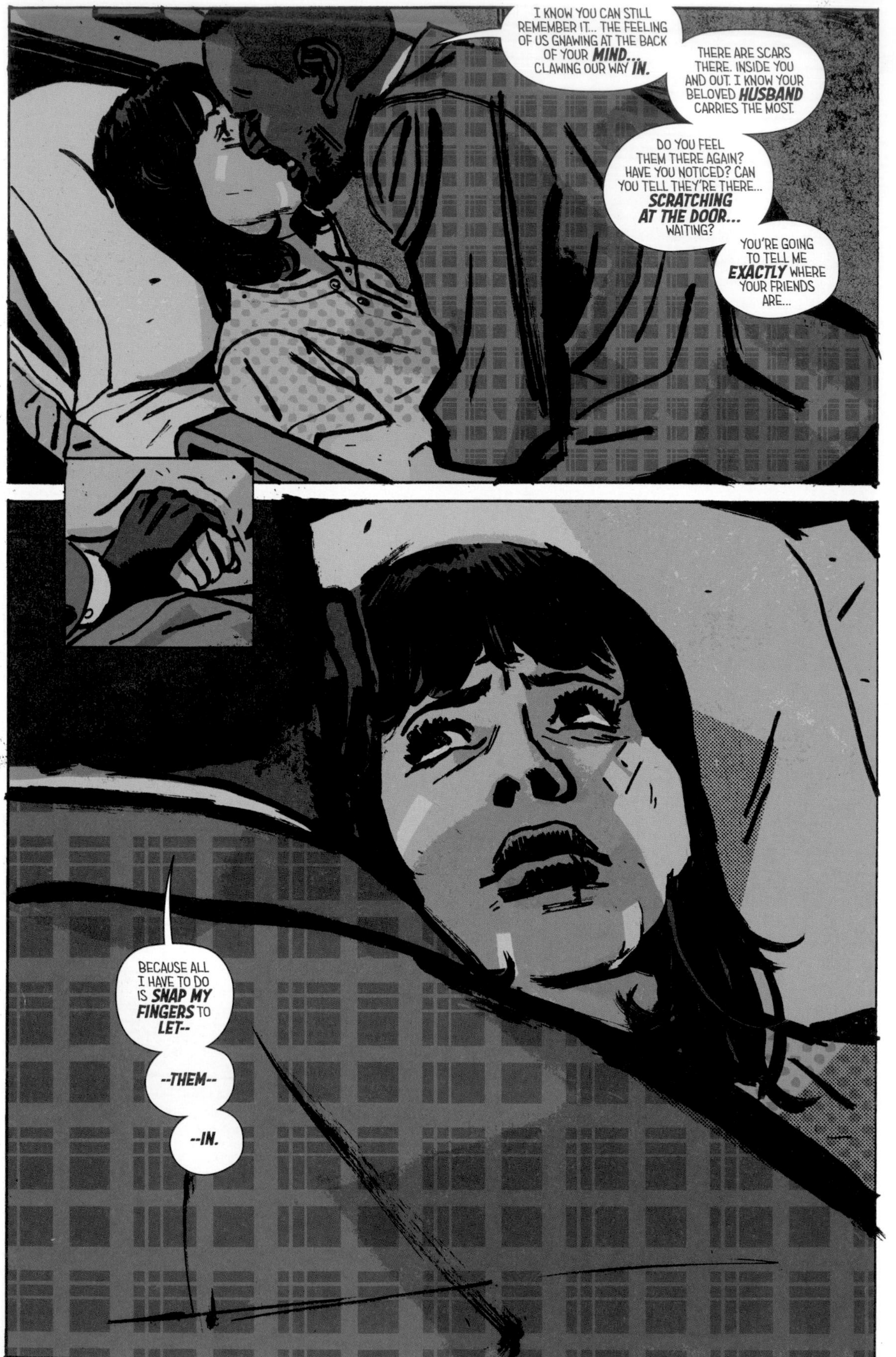
I KNOW YOU CAN STILL REMEMBER IT... THE FEELING OF US GNAWING AT THE BACK OF YOUR **MIND...** CLAWING OUR WAY **IN.**
THERE ARE SCARS THERE. INSIDE YOU AND OUT. I KNOW YOUR BELOVED **HUSBAND** CARRIES THE MOST.
DO YOU FEEL THEM THERE AGAIN? HAVE YOU NOTICED? CAN YOU TELL THEY'RE THERE... **SCRATCHING AT THE DOOR...** WAITING?
YOU'RE GOING TO TELL ME **EXACTLY** WHERE YOUR FRIENDS ARE...
BECAUSE ALL I HAVE TO DO IS **SNAP MY FINGERS** TO **LET--**
--THEM--
--IN.

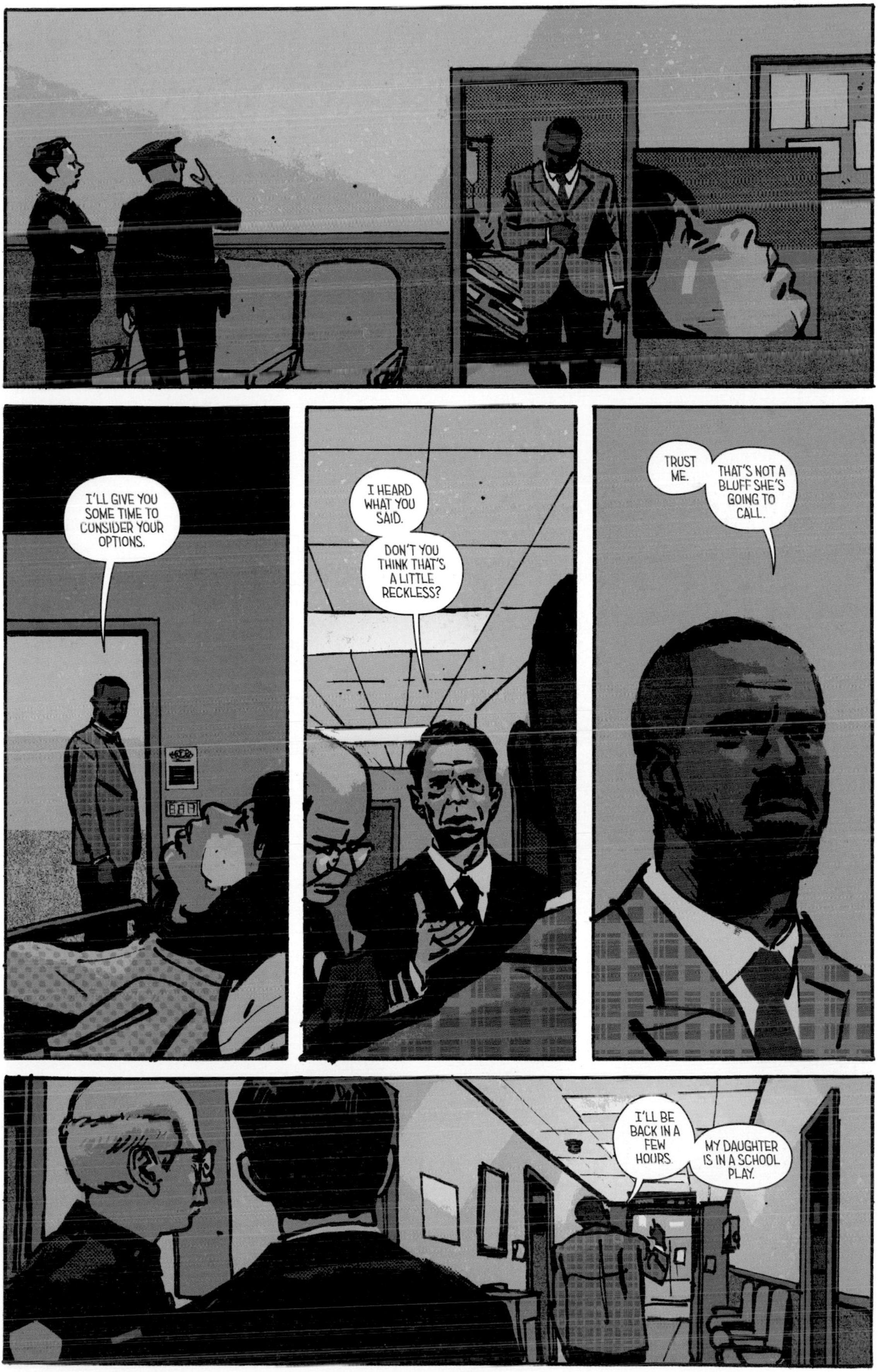
I'LL GIVE YOU SOME TIME TO CONSIDER YOUR OPTIONS.
I HEARD WHAT YOU SAID.
DON'T YOU THINK THAT'S A LITTLE RECKLESS?
TRUST ME.
THAT'S NOT A BLUFF SHE'S GOING TO CALL.
I'LL BE BACK IN A FEW HOURS.
MY DAUGHTER IS IN A SCHOOL PLAY.

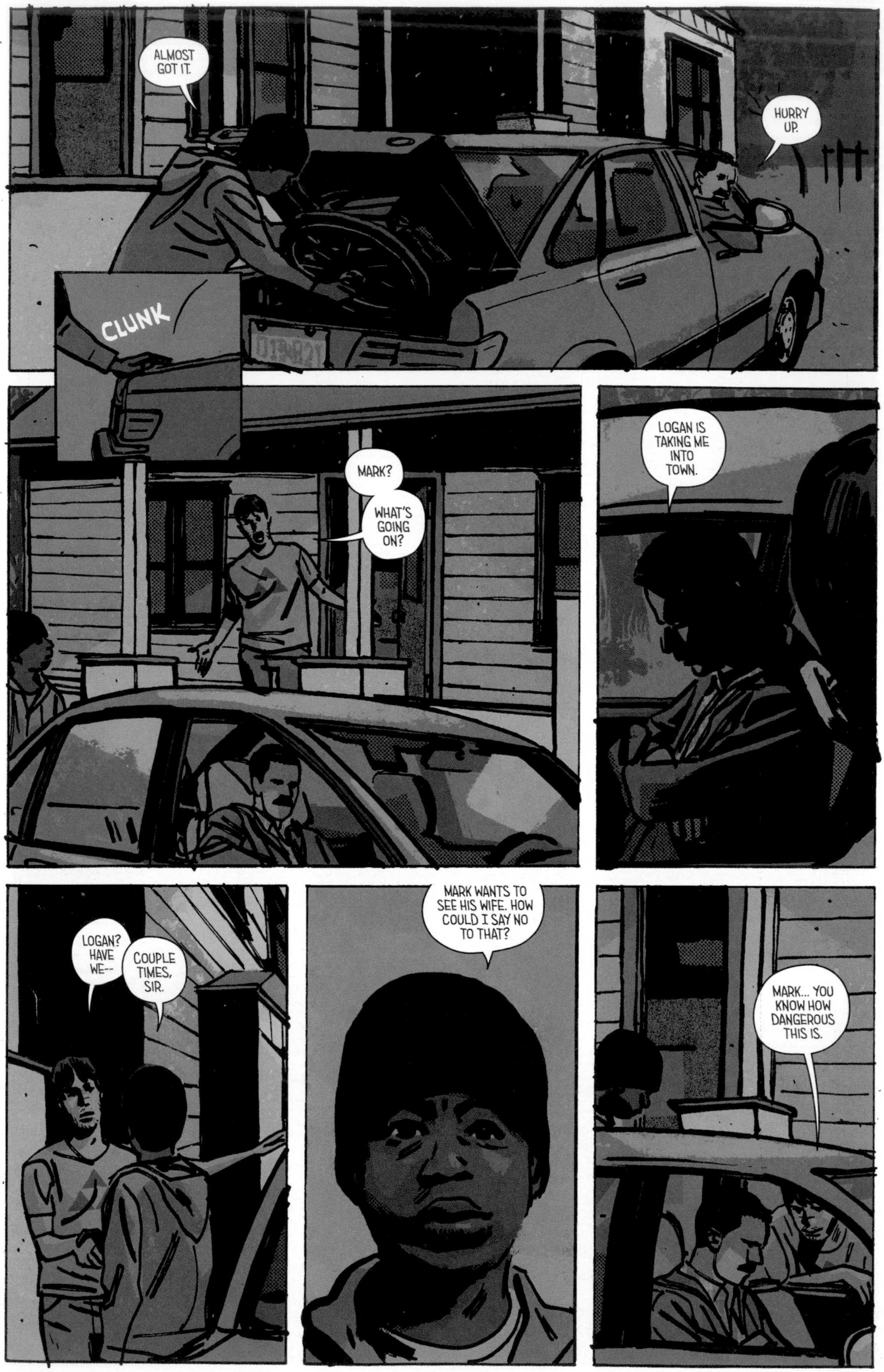
ALMOST GOT IT.
HURRY UP.
CLUNK
MARK?
WHAT'S GOING ON?
LOGAN IS TAKING ME INTO TOWN.
LOGAN? HAVE WE--
COUPLE TIMES, SIR.
MARK WANTS TO SEE HIS WIFE. HOW COULD I SAY NO TO THAT?
MARK... YOU KNOW HOW DANGEROUS THIS IS.

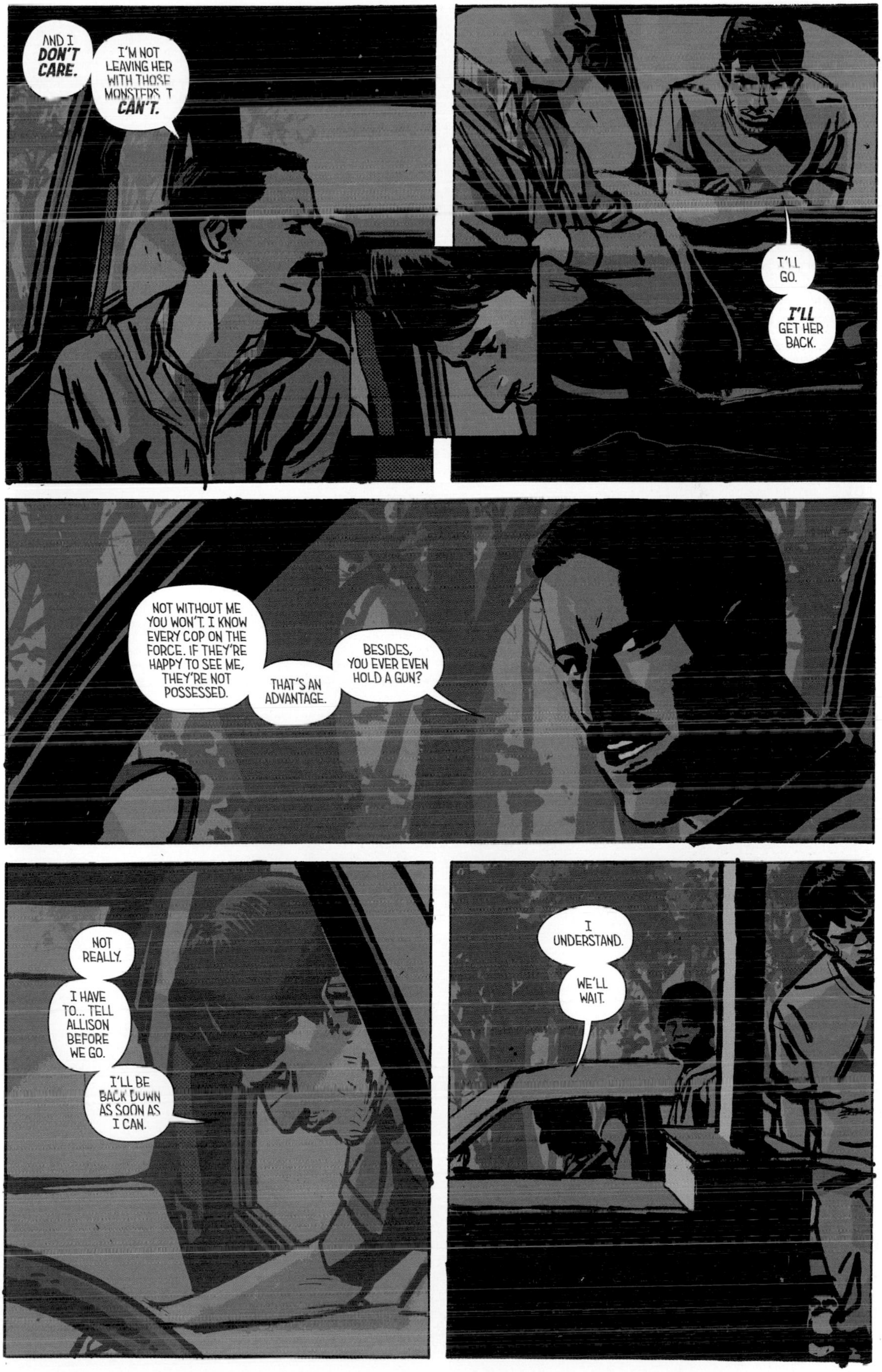
AND I DON'T CARE.
I'M NOT LEAVING HER WITH THOSE MONSTERS. I CAN'T.
I'LL GO.
I'LL GET HER BACK.
NOT WITHOUT ME YOU WON'T. I KNOW EVERY COP ON THE FORCE. IF THEY'RE HAPPY TO SEE ME, THEY'RE NOT POSSESSED.
THAT'S AN ADVANTAGE.
BESIDES, YOU EVER EVEN HOLD A GUN?
NOT REALLY.
I HAVE TO... TELL ALLISON BEFORE WE GO.
I'LL BE BACK DOWN AS SOON AS I CAN.
I UNDERSTAND.
WE'LL WAIT.

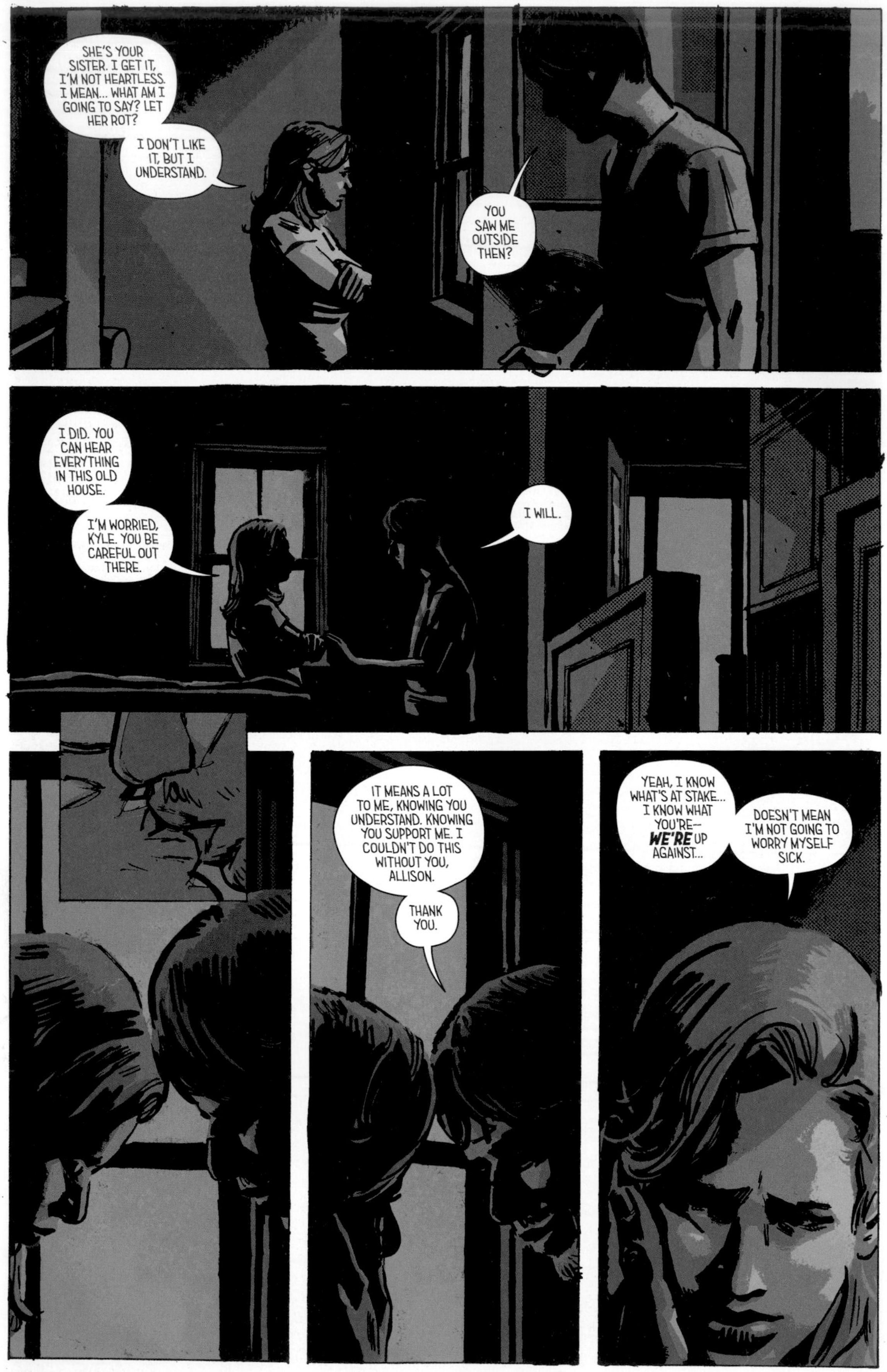
SHE'S YOUR SISTER. I GET IT, I'M NOT HEARTLESS. I MEAN... WHAT AM I GOING TO SAY? LET HER ROT?
I DON'T LIKE IT, BUT I UNDERSTAND.
YOU SAW ME OUTSIDE THEN?
I DID. YOU CAN HEAR EVERYTHING IN THIS OLD HOUSE.
I'M WORRIED, KYLE. YOU BE CAREFUL OUT THERE.
I WILL.
IT MEANS A LOT TO ME, KNOWING YOU UNDERSTAND. KNOWING YOU SUPPORT ME. I COULDN'T DO THIS WITHOUT YOU, ALLISON.
THANK YOU.
YEAH, I KNOW WHAT'S AT STAKE... I KNOW WHAT YOU'RE-- **WE'RE** UP AGAINST...
DOESN'T MEAN I'M NOT GOING TO WORRY MYSELF SICK.

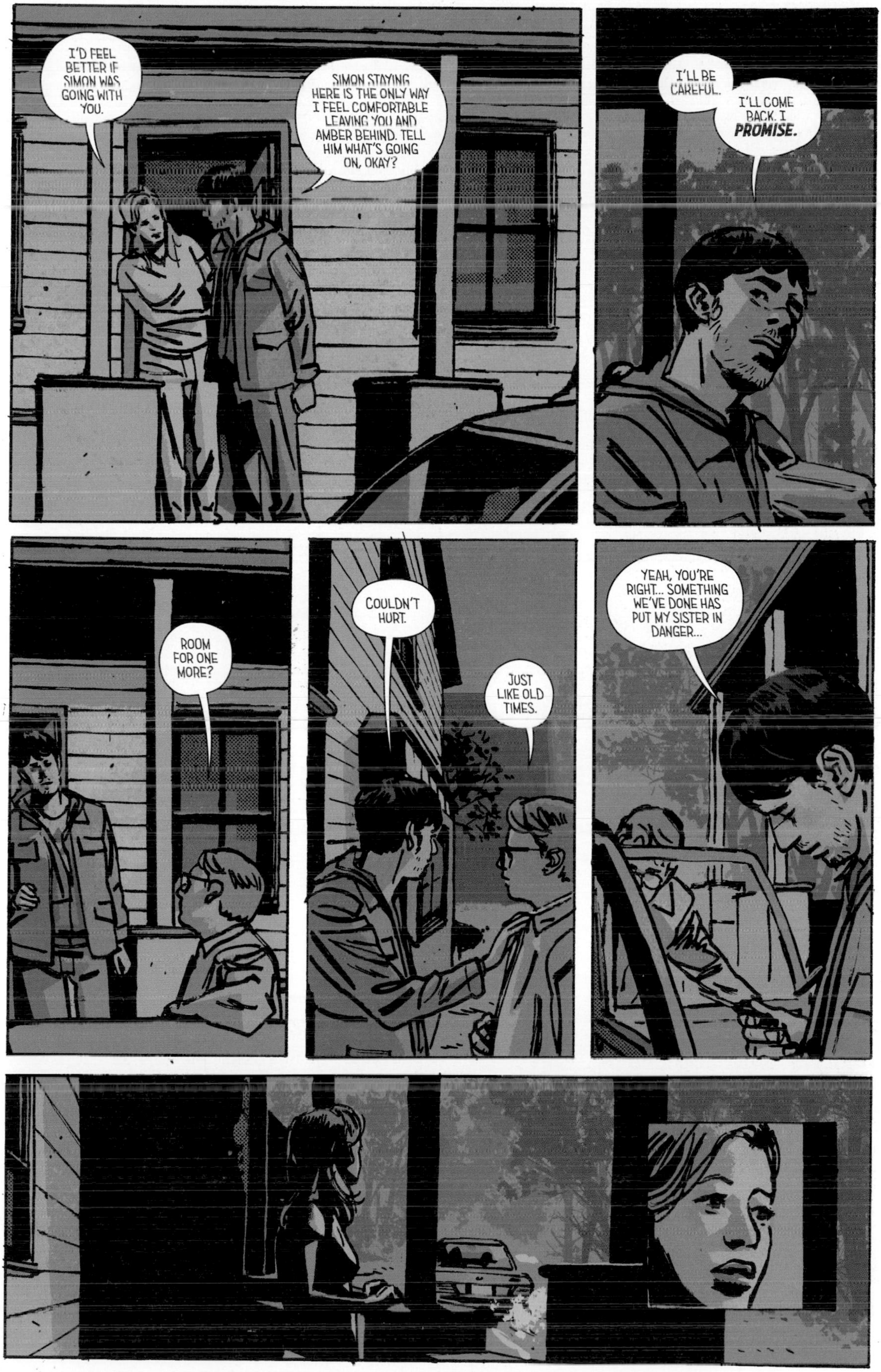
I'D FEEL BETTER IF SIMON WAS GOING WITH YOU.
SIMON STAYING HERE IS THE ONLY WAY I FEEL COMFORTABLE LEAVING YOU AND AMBER BEHIND. TELL HIM WHAT'S GOING ON, OKAY?
I'LL BE CAREFUL.
I'LL COME BACK. I PROMISE.
ROOM FOR ONE MORE?
COULDN'T HURT.
JUST LIKE OLD TIMES.
YEAH, YOU'RE RIGHT... SOMETHING WE'VE DONE HAS PUT MY SISTER IN DANGER...

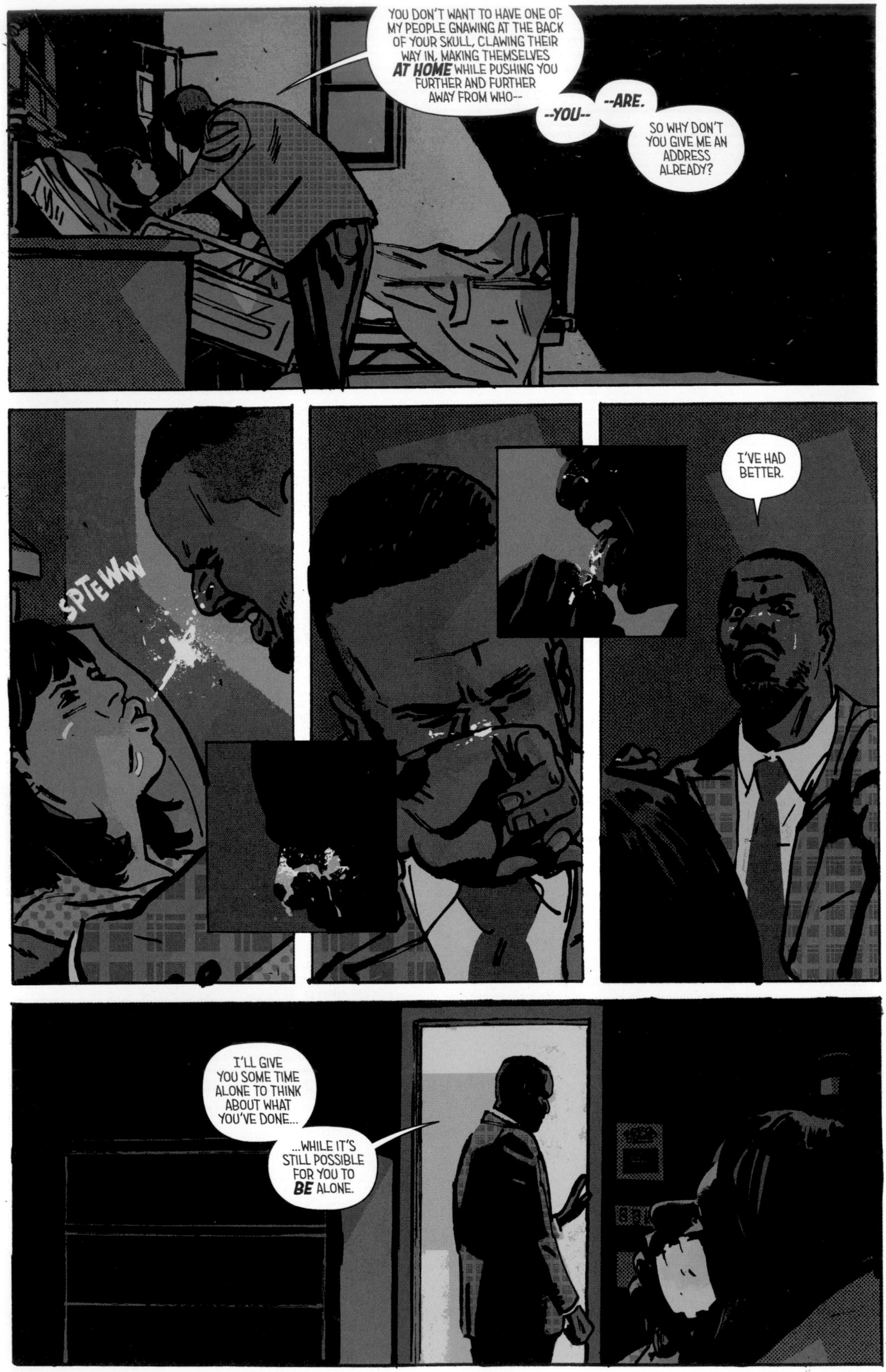
YOU DON'T WANT TO HAVE ONE OF MY PEOPLE GNAWING AT THE BACK OF YOUR SKULL, CLAWING THEIR WAY IN, MAKING THEMSELVES **AT HOME** WHILE PUSHING YOU FURTHER AND FURTHER AWAY FROM WHO--
--YOU--
--ARE.
SO WHY DON'T YOU GIVE ME AN ADDRESS ALREADY?
SPTEWW
I'VE HAD BETTER.
I'LL GIVE YOU SOME TIME ALONE TO THINK ABOUT WHAT YOU'VE DONE...
...WHILE IT'S STILL POSSIBLE FOR YOU TO **BE** ALONE.

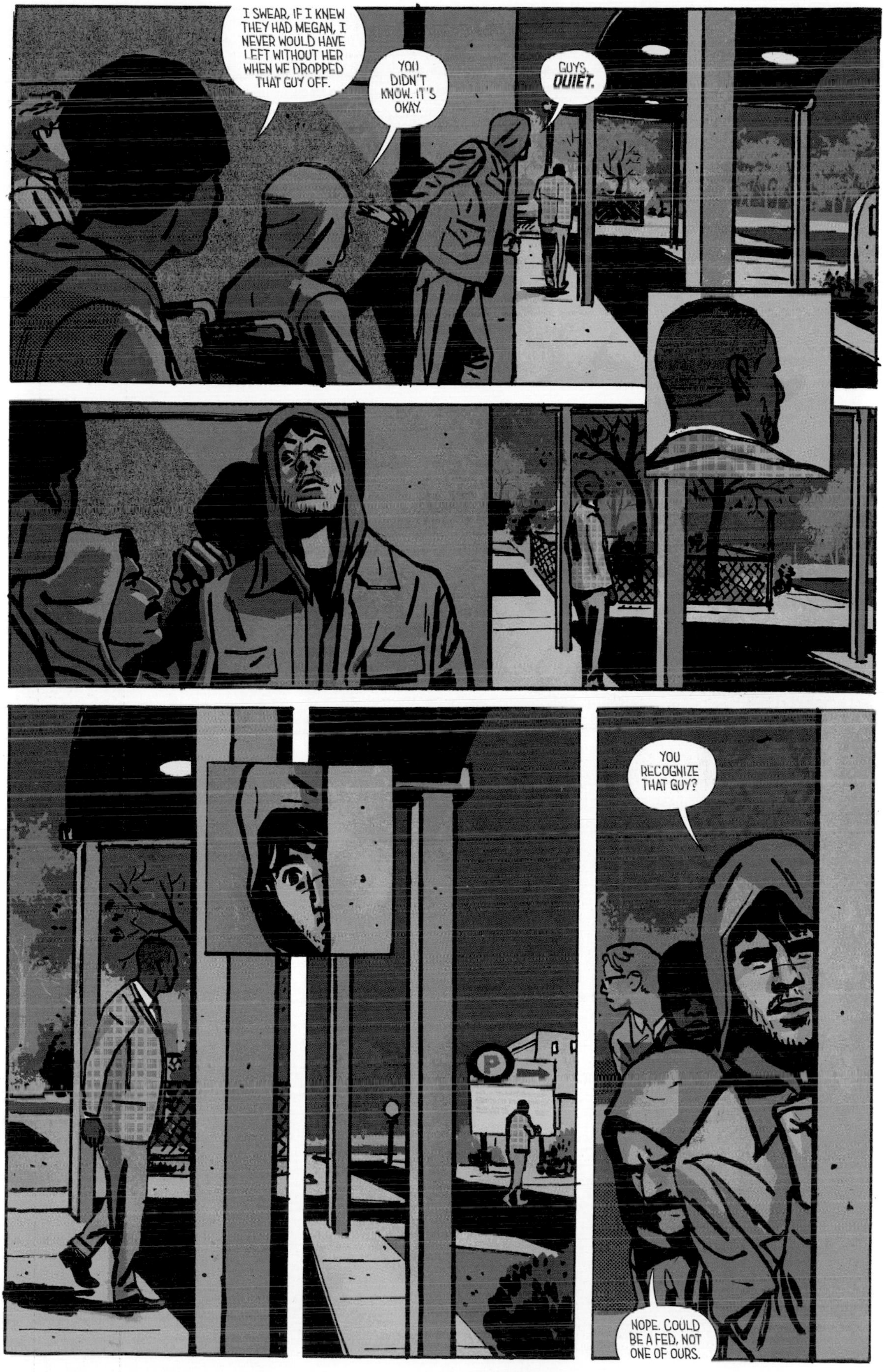
I SWEAR, IF I KNEW THEY HAD MEGAN, I NEVER WOULD HAVE LEFT WITHOUT HER WHEN WE DROPPED THAT GUY OFF.
YOU DIDN'T KNOW. IT'S OKAY.
GUYS. QUIET.
YOU RECOGNIZE THAT GUY?
NOPE. COULD BE A FED, NOT ONE OF OURS.

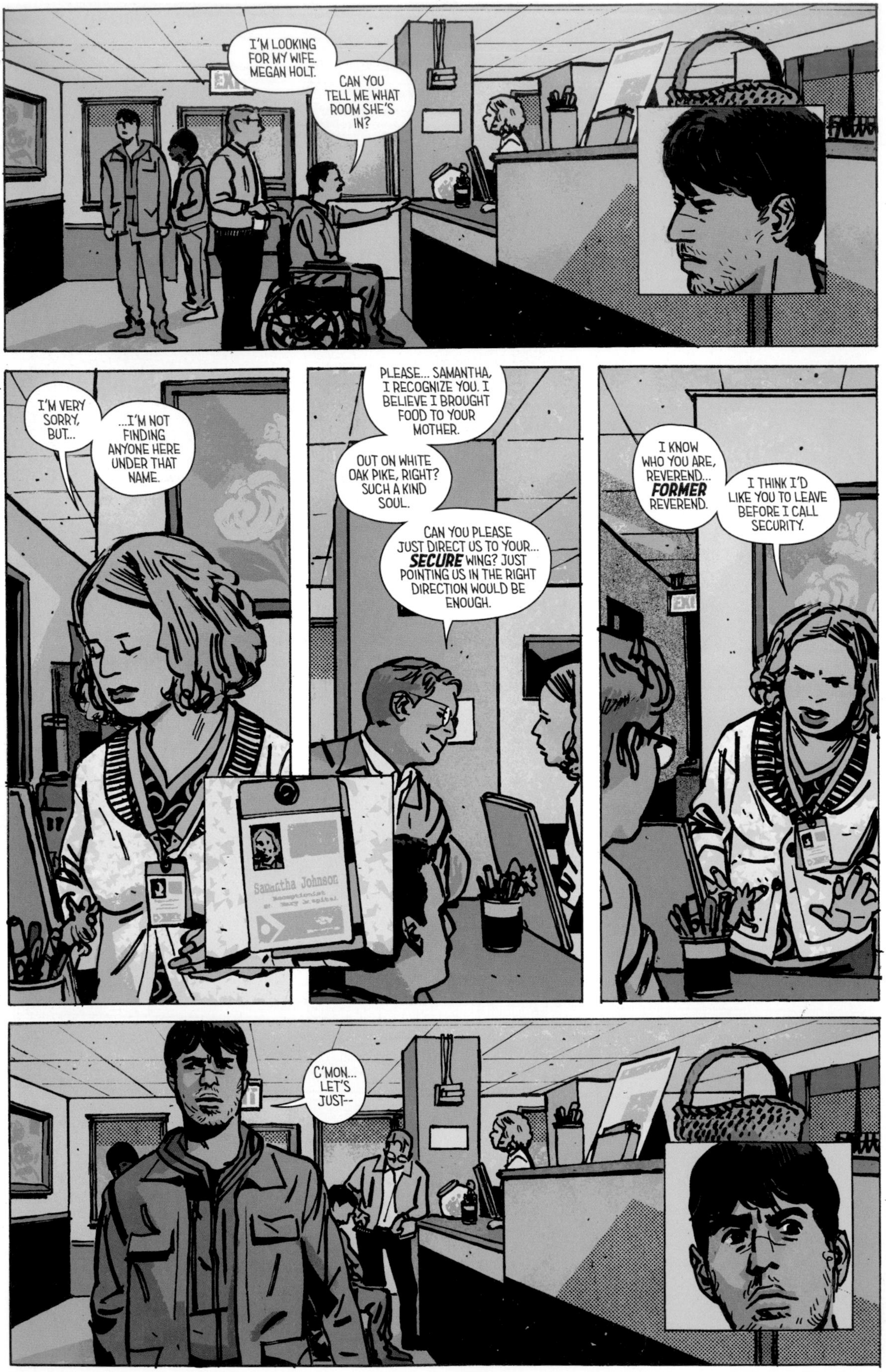
I'M LOOKING FOR MY WIFE. MEGAN HOLT.
CAN YOU TELL ME WHAT ROOM SHE'S IN?
I'M VERY SORRY, BUT...
...I'M NOT FINDING ANYONE HERE UNDER THAT NAME.
Samantha Johnson
PLEASE... SAMANTHA, I RECOGNIZE YOU. I BELIEVE I BROUGHT FOOD TO YOUR MOTHER.
OUT ON WHITE OAK PIKE, RIGHT? SUCH A KIND SOUL.
CAN YOU PLEASE JUST DIRECT US TO YOUR... SECURE WING? JUST POINTING US IN THE RIGHT DIRECTION WOULD BE ENOUGH.
I KNOW WHO YOU ARE, REVEREND... FORMER REVEREND.
I THINK I'D LIKE YOU TO LEAVE BEFORE I CALL SECURITY.
C'MON... LET'S JUST--

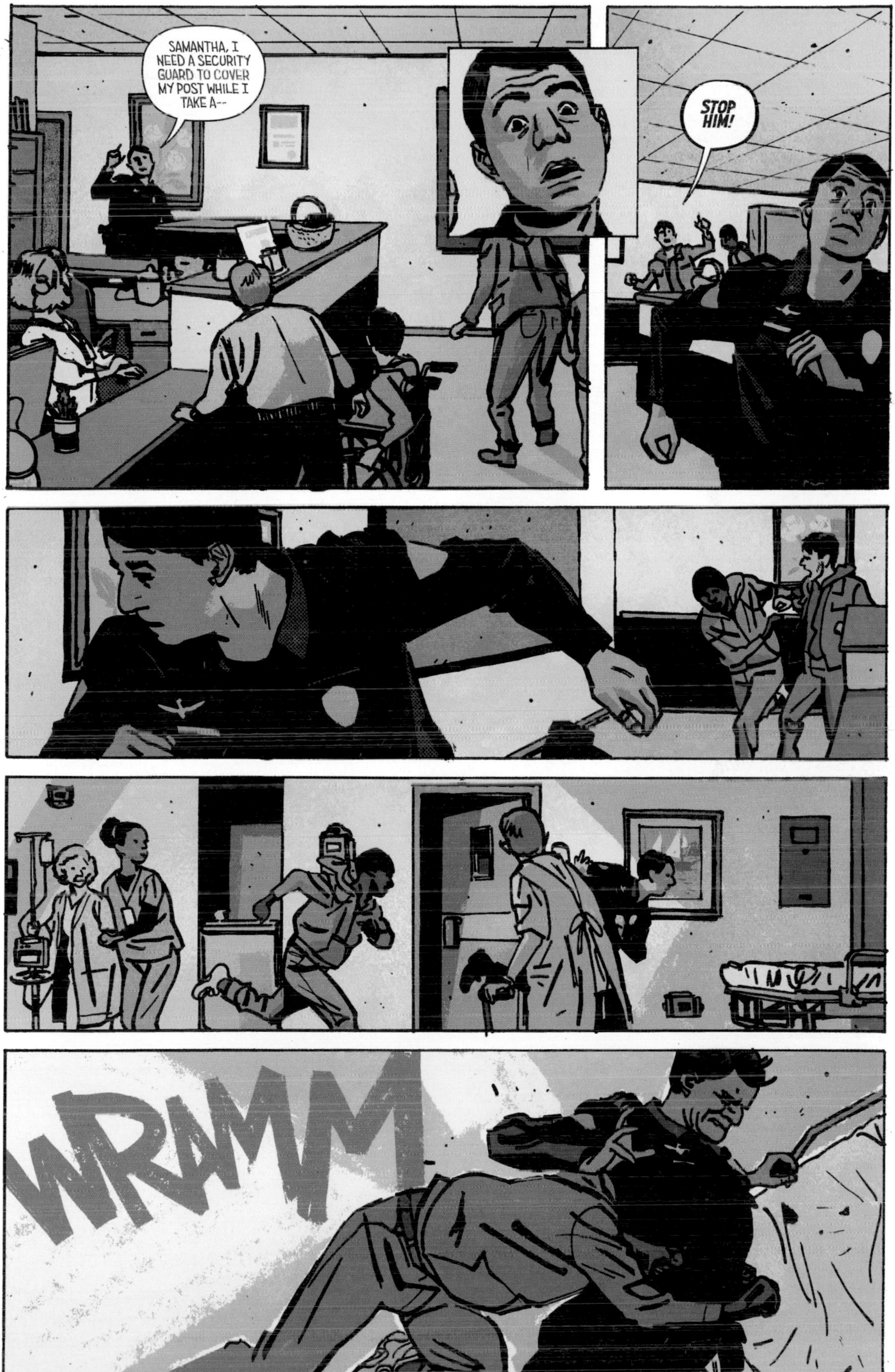
SAMANTHA, I NEED A SECURITY GUARD TO COVER MY POST WHILE I TAKE A--
STOP HIM!
WRAMM

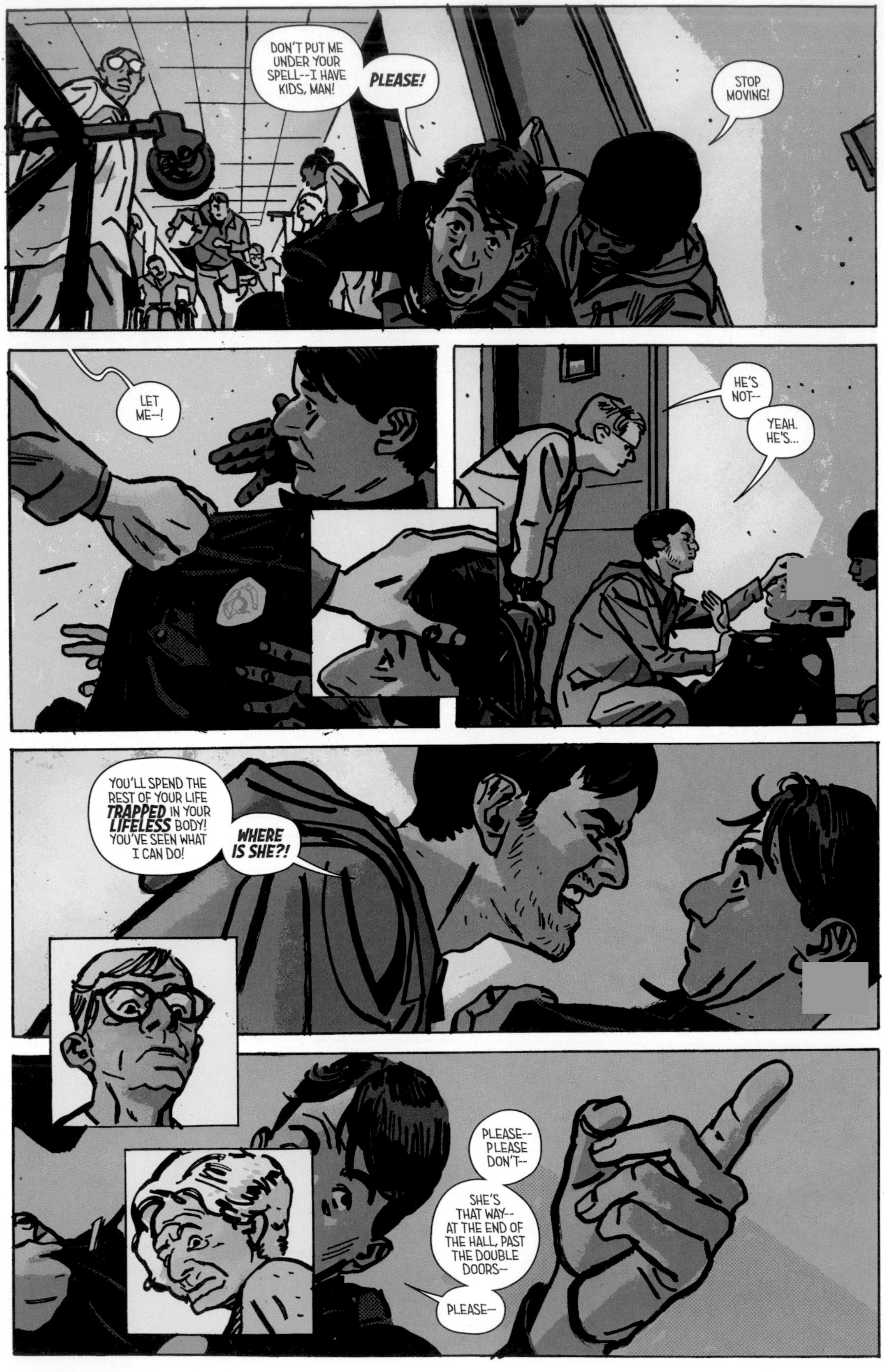
DON'T PUT ME UNDER YOUR SPELL--I HAVE KIDS, MAN!
PLEASE!
STOP MOVING!
LET ME--!
HE'S NOT--
YEAH. HE'S...
YOU'LL SPEND THE REST OF YOUR LIFE TRAPPED IN YOUR LIFELESS BODY! YOU'VE SEEN WHAT I CAN DO!
WHERE IS SHE?!
PLEASE-- PLEASE DON'T--
SHE'S THAT WAY-- AT THE END OF THE HALL, PAST THE DOUBLE DOORS--
PLEASE--

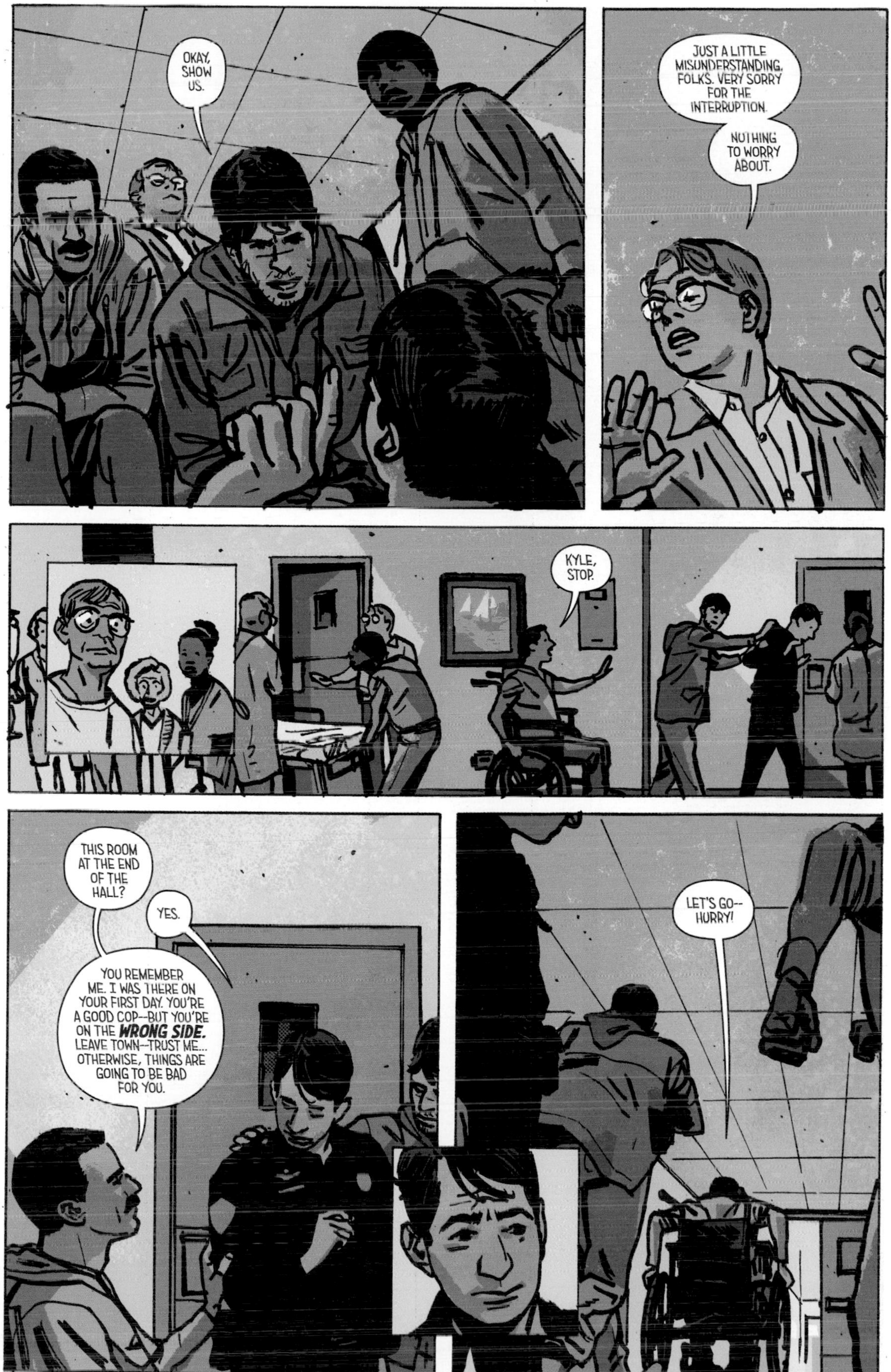
OKAY, SHOW US.
JUST A LITTLE MISUNDERSTANDING, FOLKS. VERY SORRY FOR THE INTERRUPTION.
NOTHING TO WORRY ABOUT.
KYLE, STOP.
THIS ROOM AT THE END OF THE HALL?
YES.
YOU REMEMBER ME. I WAS THERE ON YOUR FIRST DAY. YOU'RE A GOOD COP--BUT YOU'RE ON THE **WRONG SIDE.** LEAVE TOWN--TRUST ME... OTHERWISE, THINGS ARE GOING TO BE BAD FOR YOU.
LET'S GO--HURRY!

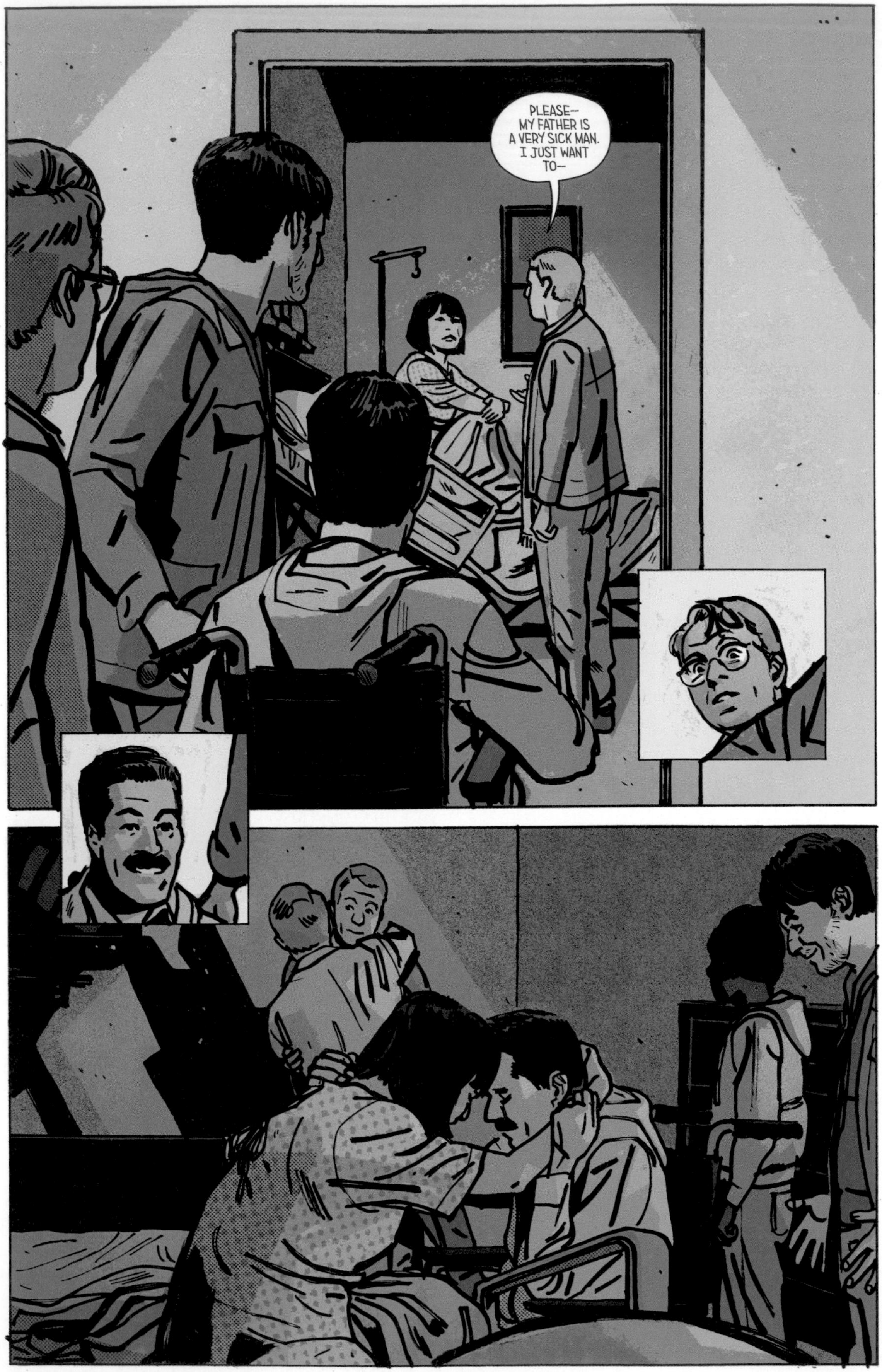
PLEASE-- MY FATHER IS A VERY SICK MAN. I JUST WANT TO--

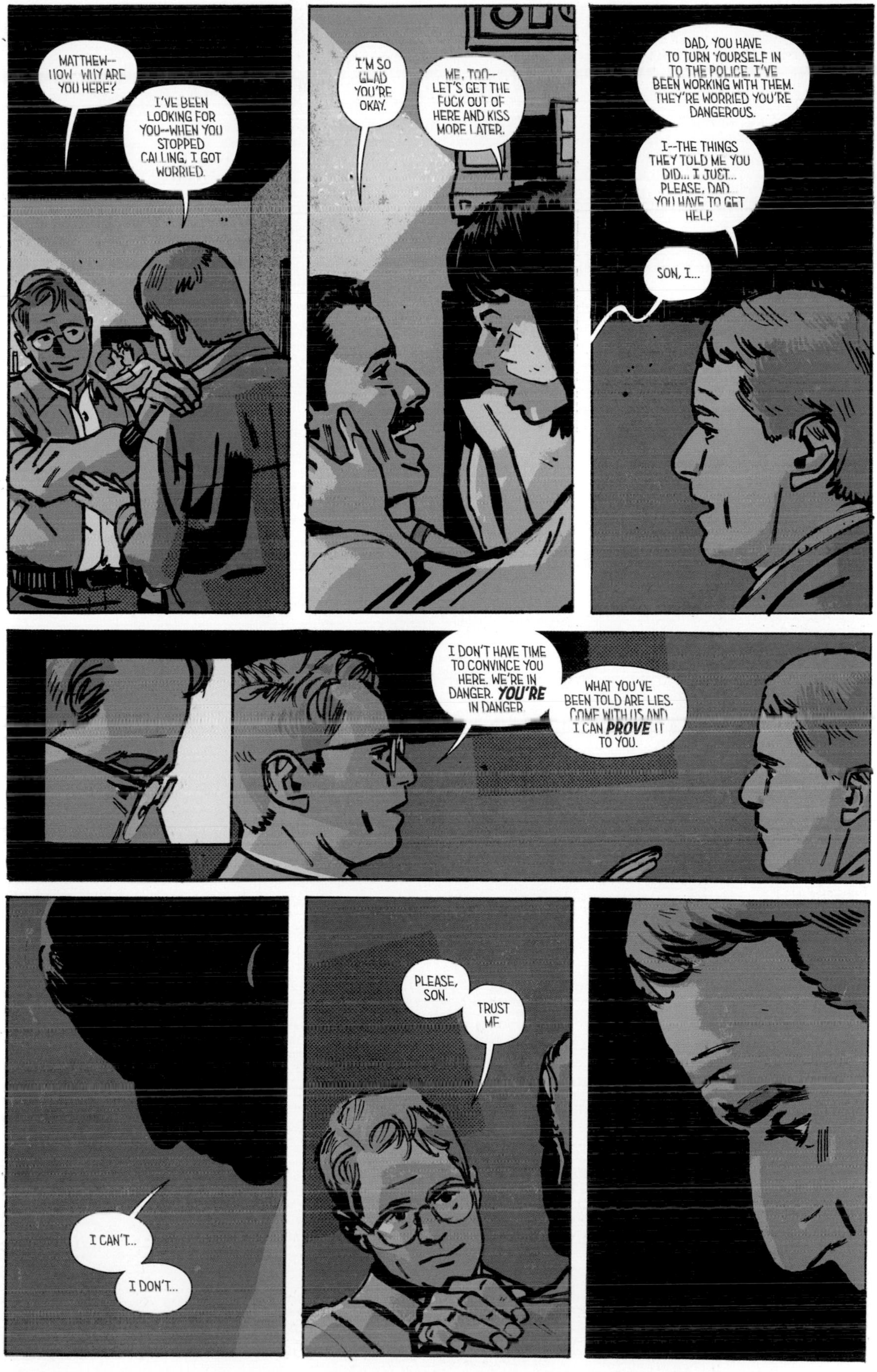
MATTHEW-- HOW-- WHY ARE YOU HERE?
I'VE BEEN LOOKING FOR YOU--WHEN YOU STOPPED CALLING, I GOT WORRIED.
I'M SO GLAD YOU'RE OKAY.
ME, TOO-- LET'S GET THE FUCK OUT OF HERE AND KISS MORE LATER.
DAD, YOU HAVE TO TURN YOURSELF IN TO THE POLICE. I'VE BEEN WORKING WITH THEM. THEY'RE WORRIED YOU'RE DANGEROUS.
I--THE THINGS THEY TOLD ME YOU DID... I JUST... PLEASE, DAD. YOU HAVE TO GET HELP.
SON, I...
I DON'T HAVE TIME TO CONVINCE YOU HERE. WE'RE IN DANGER. YOU'RE IN DANGER.
WHAT YOU'VE BEEN TOLD ARE LIES. COME WITH US AND I CAN PROVE IT TO YOU.
I CAN'T...
I DON'T...
PLEASE, SON.
TRUST ME.

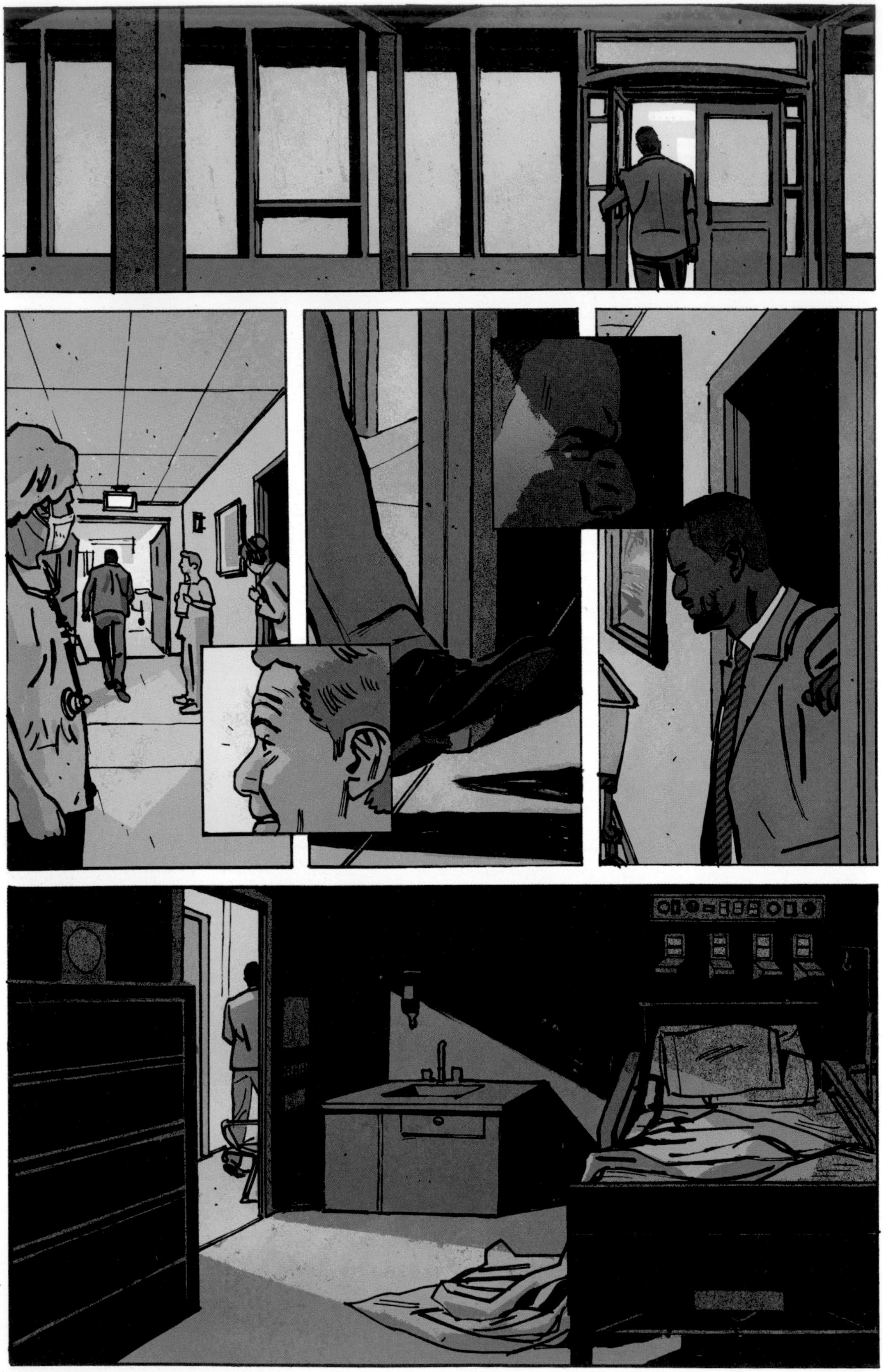

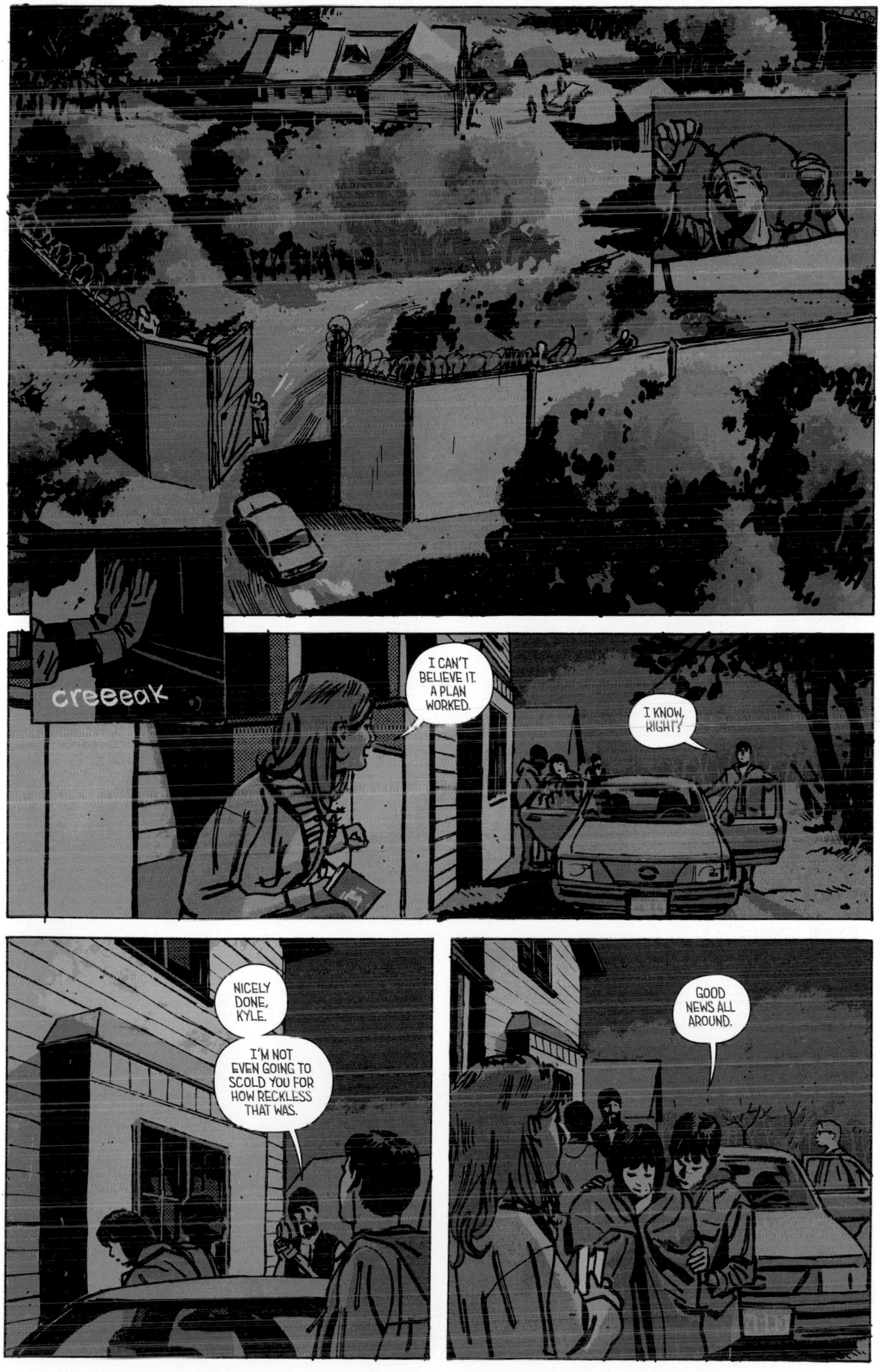
creeeak
I CAN'T BELIEVE IT. A PLAN WORKED.
I KNOW, RIGHT?
NICELY DONE, KYLE.
I'M NOT EVEN GOING TO SCOLD YOU FOR HOW RECKLESS THAT WAS.
GOOD NEWS ALL AROUND.

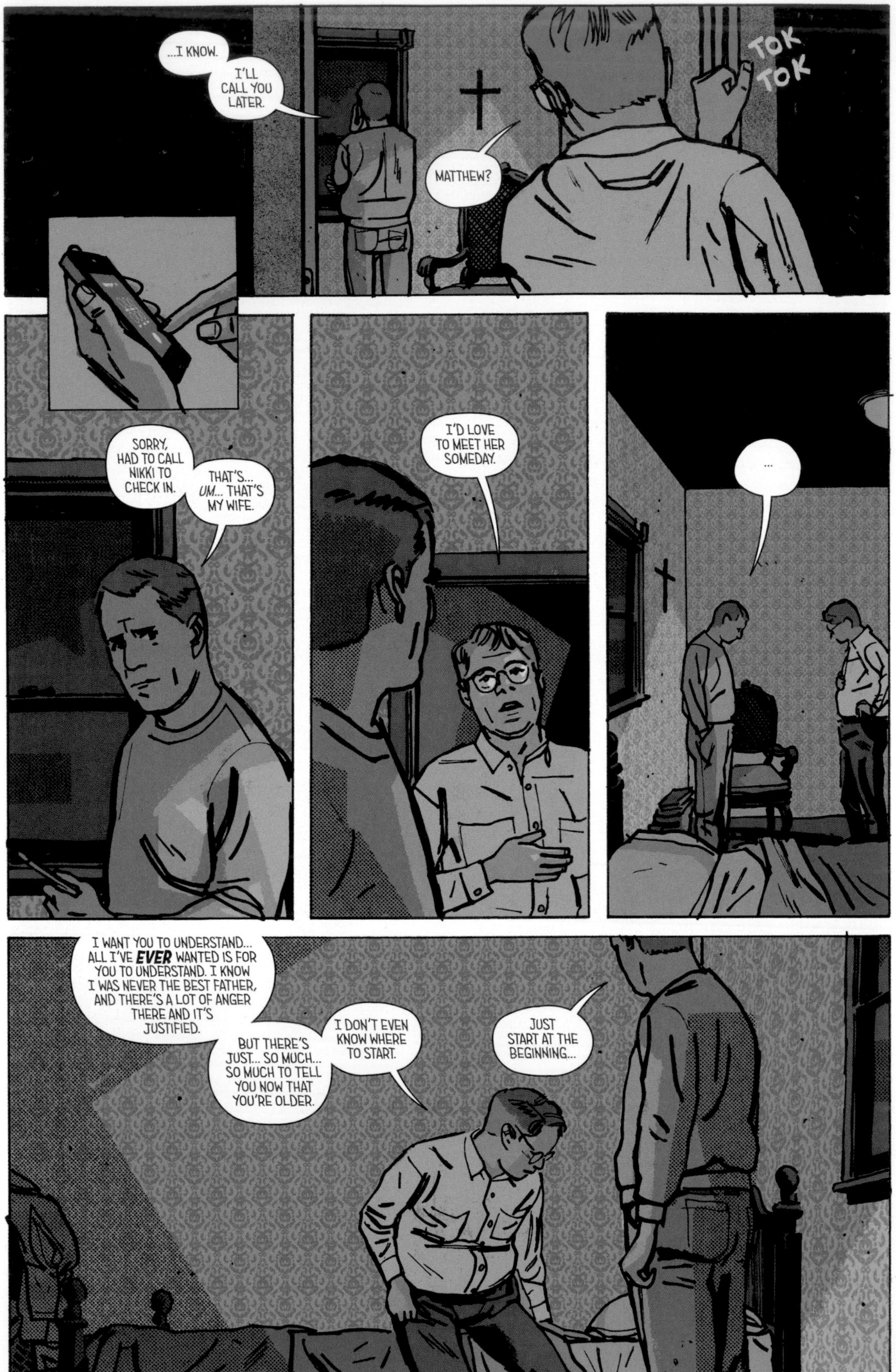
...I KNOW.
I'LL CALL YOU LATER.
MATTHEW?
TOK TOK
SORRY, HAD TO CALL NIKKI TO CHECK IN.
THAT'S... *UM*... THAT'S MY WIFE.
I'D LOVE TO MEET HER SOMEDAY.
...
I WANT YOU TO UNDERSTAND... ALL I'VE **EVER** WANTED IS FOR YOU TO UNDERSTAND. I KNOW I WAS NEVER THE BEST FATHER, AND THERE'S A LOT OF ANGER THERE AND IT'S JUSTIFIED.
BUT THERE'S JUST... SO MUCH... SO MUCH TO TELL YOU NOW THAT YOU'RE OLDER.
I DON'T EVEN KNOW WHERE TO START.
JUST START AT THE BEGINNING...

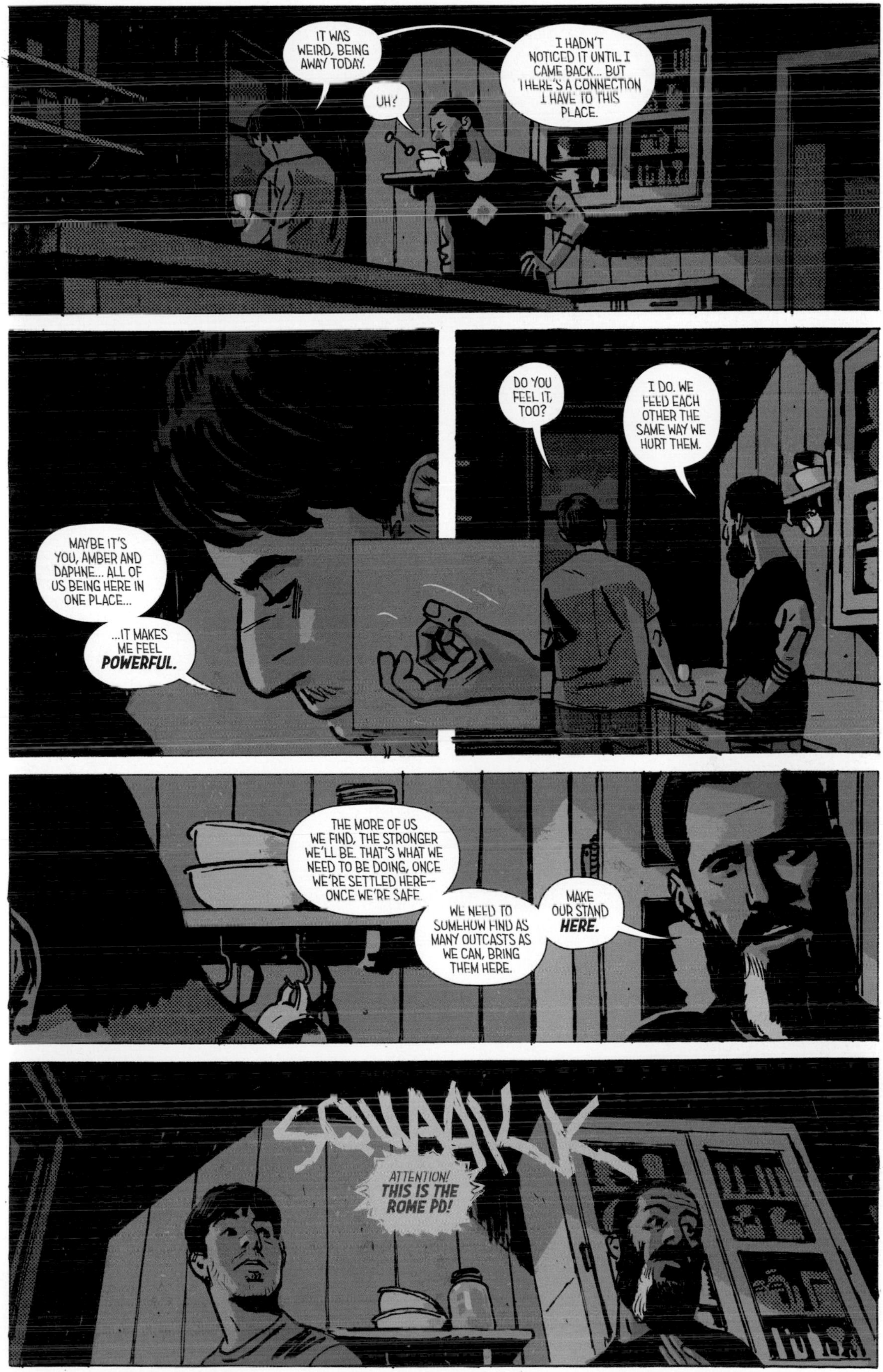

IT WAS WEIRD, BEING AWAY TODAY.
UH?
I HADN'T NOTICED IT UNTIL I CAME BACK... BUT THERE'S A CONNECTION I HAVE TO THIS PLACE.
MAYBE IT'S YOU, AMBER AND DAPHNE... ALL OF US BEING HERE IN ONE PLACE...
...IT MAKES ME FEEL **POWERFUL.**
DO YOU FEEL IT, TOO?
I DO. WE FEED EACH OTHER THE SAME WAY WE HURT THEM.
THE MORE OF US WE FIND, THE STRONGER WE'LL BE. THAT'S WHAT WE NEED TO BE DOING, ONCE WE'RE SETTLED HERE-- ONCE WE'RE SAFE.
WE NEED TO SOMEHOW FIND AS MANY OUTCASTS AS WE CAN, BRING THEM HERE.
MAKE OUR STAND **HERE.**
SQUAAK
ATTENTION! ***THIS IS THE ROME PD!***

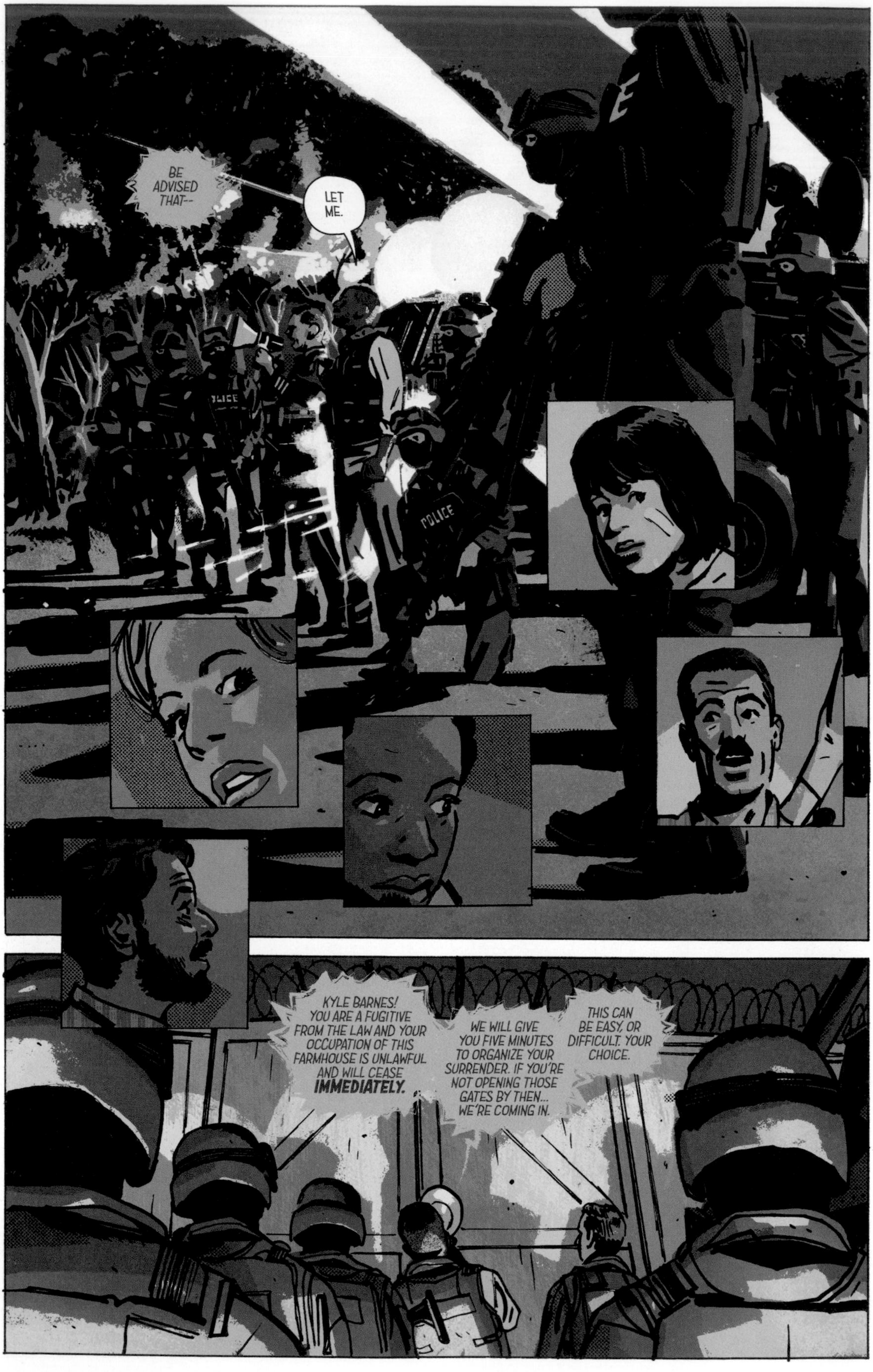
BE ADVISED THAT--
LET ME.
POLICE
POLICE
KYLE BARNES! YOU ARE A FUGITIVE FROM THE LAW AND YOUR OCCUPATION OF THIS FARMHOUSE IS UNLAWFUL AND WILL CEASE **IMMEDIATELY.**
WE WILL GIVE YOU FIVE MINUTES TO ORGANIZE YOUR SURRENDER. IF YOU'RE NOT OPENING THOSE GATES BY THEN... WE'RE COMING IN.
THIS CAN BE EASY, OR DIFFICULT. YOUR CHOICE.

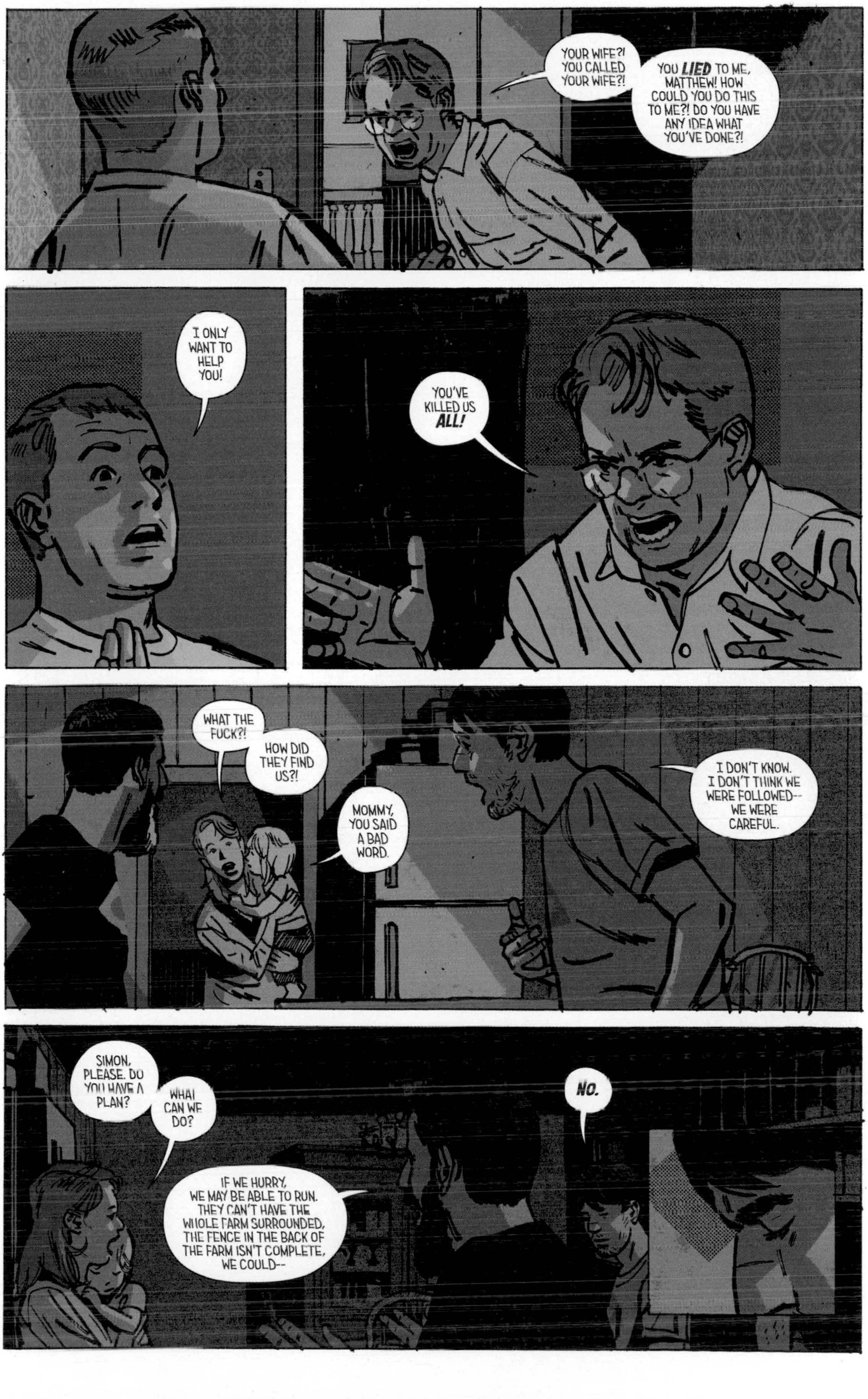
YOUR WIFE?! YOU CALLED YOUR WIFE?!
YOU **LIED** TO ME, MATTHEW! HOW COULD YOU DO THIS TO ME?! DO YOU HAVE ANY IDEA WHAT YOU'VE DONE?!
I ONLY WANT TO HELP YOU!
YOU'VE KILLED US **ALL!**
WHAT THE FUCK?!
HOW DID THEY FIND US?!
MOMMY, YOU SAID A BAD WORD.
I DON'T KNOW. I DON'T THINK WE WERE FOLLOWED-- WE WERE CAREFUL.
SIMON, PLEASE. DO YOU HAVE A PLAN?
WHAT CAN WE DO?
IF WE HURRY, WE MAY BE ABLE TO RUN. THEY CAN'T HAVE THE WHOLE FARM SURROUNDED, THE FENCE IN THE BACK OF THE FARM ISN'T COMPLETE, WE COULD--
NO.

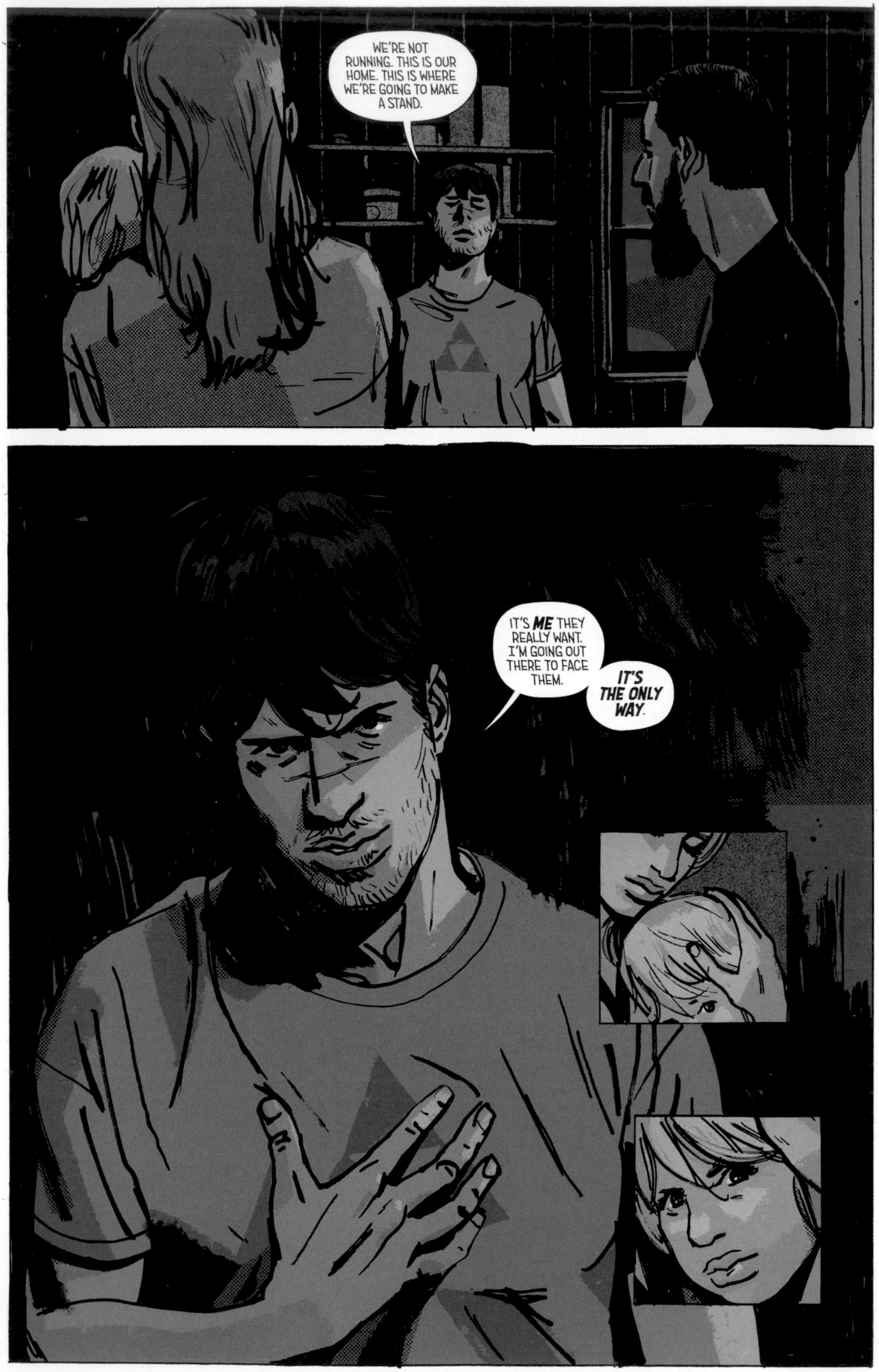
WE'RE NOT RUNNING. THIS IS OUR HOME. THIS IS WHERE WE'RE GOING TO MAKE A STAND.
IT'S **ME** THEY REALLY WANT. I'M GOING OUT THERE TO FACE THEM.
IT'S THE ONLY WAY.

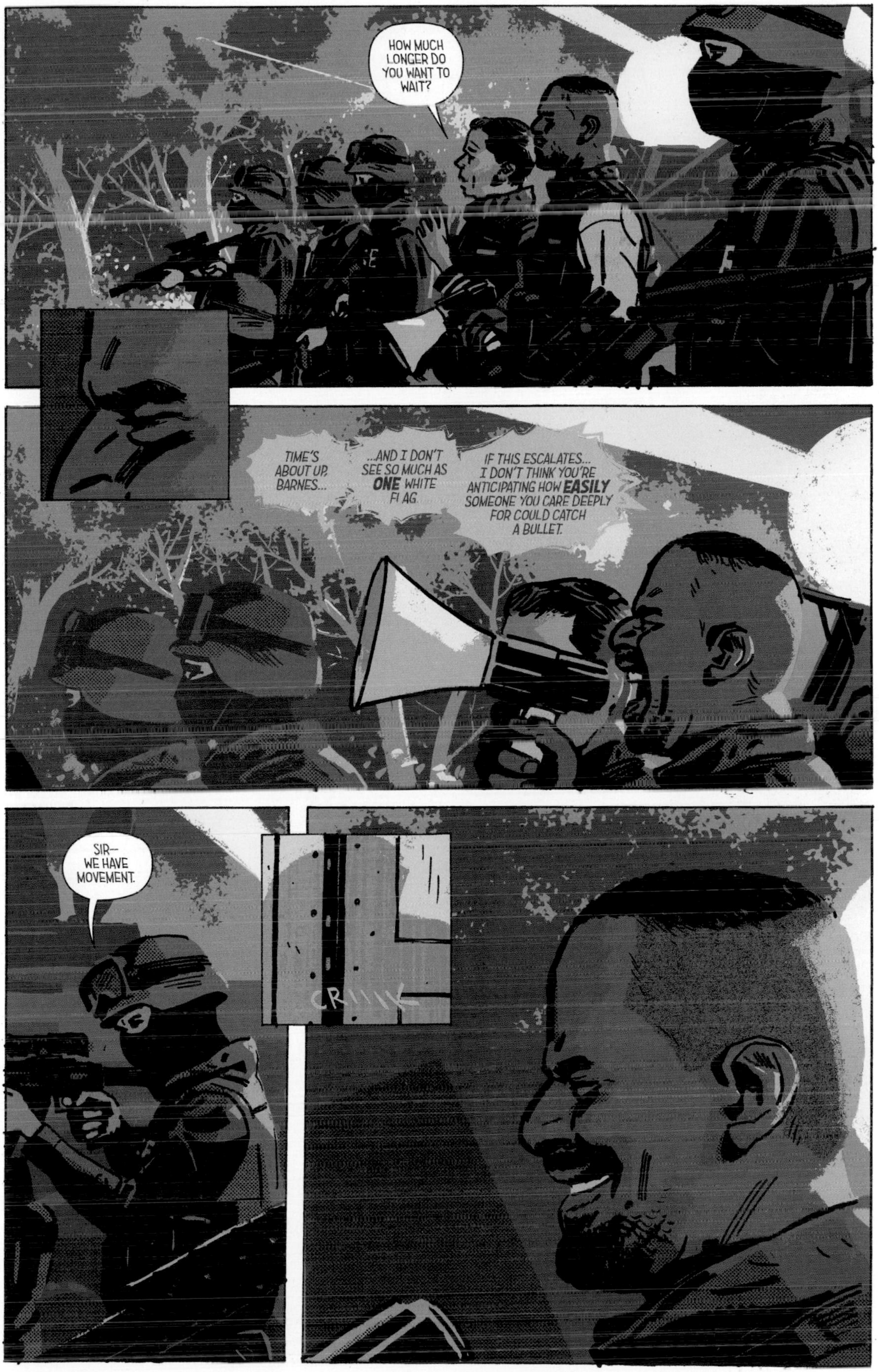
HOW MUCH LONGER DO YOU WANT TO WAIT?
TIME'S ABOUT UP, BARNES...
...AND I DON'T SEE SO MUCH AS ONE WHITE FLAG.
IF THIS ESCALATES... I DON'T THINK YOU'RE ANTICIPATING HOW EASILY SOMEONE YOU CARE DEEPLY FOR COULD CATCH A BULLET.
SIR— WE HAVE MOVEMENT.
CRIIIK

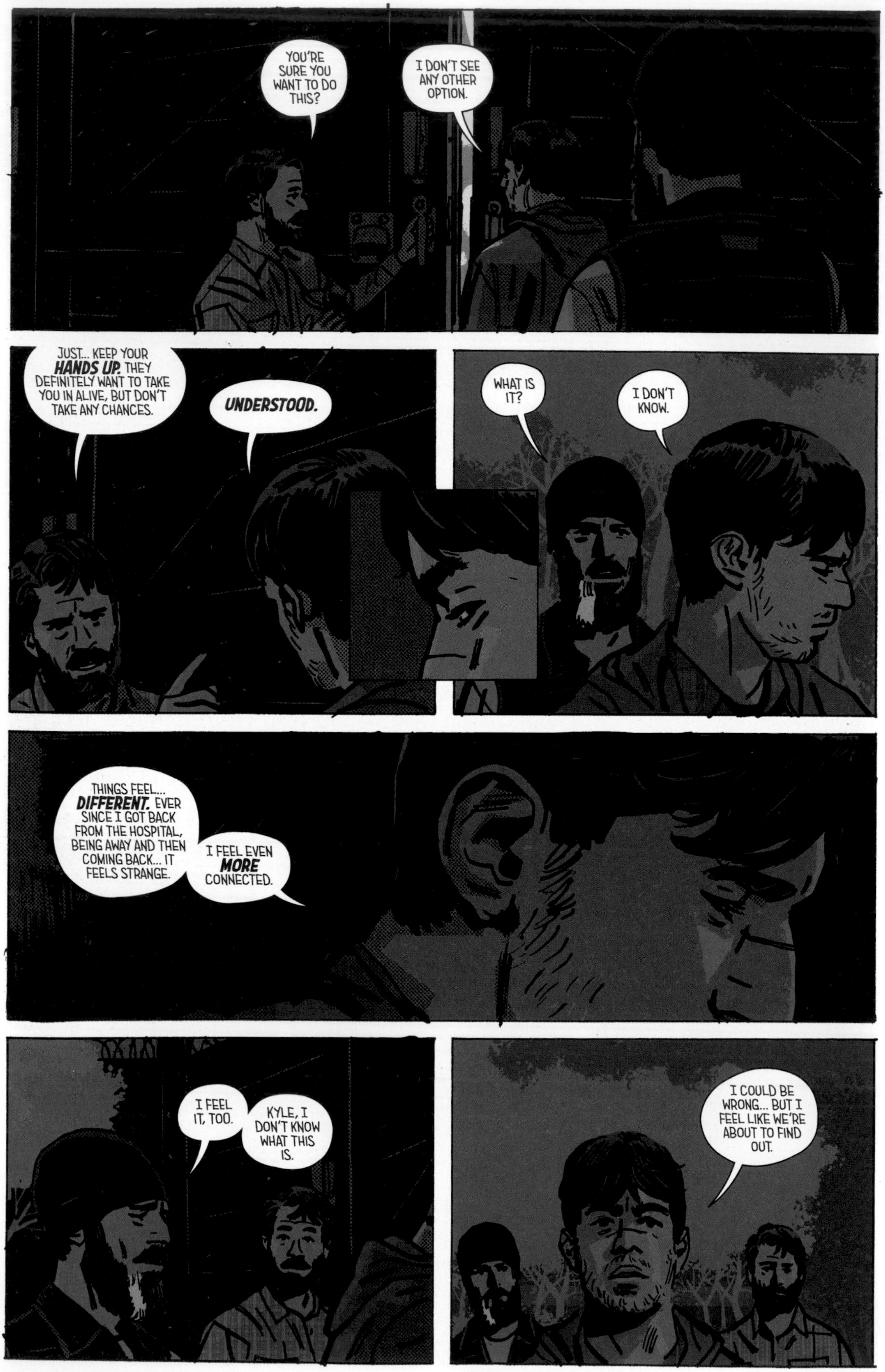
YOU'RE SURE YOU WANT TO DO THIS?
I DON'T SEE ANY OTHER OPTION.
JUST... KEEP YOUR HANDS UP. THEY DEFINITELY WANT TO TAKE YOU IN ALIVE, BUT DON'T TAKE ANY CHANCES.
UNDERSTOOD.
WHAT IS IT?
I DON'T KNOW.
THINGS FEEL... DIFFERENT. EVER SINCE I GOT BACK FROM THE HOSPITAL, BEING AWAY AND THEN COMING BACK... IT FEELS STRANGE.
I FEEL EVEN MORE CONNECTED.
I FEEL IT, TOO.
KYLE, I DON'T KNOW WHAT THIS IS.
I COULD BE WRONG... BUT I FEEL LIKE WE'RE ABOUT TO FIND OUT.

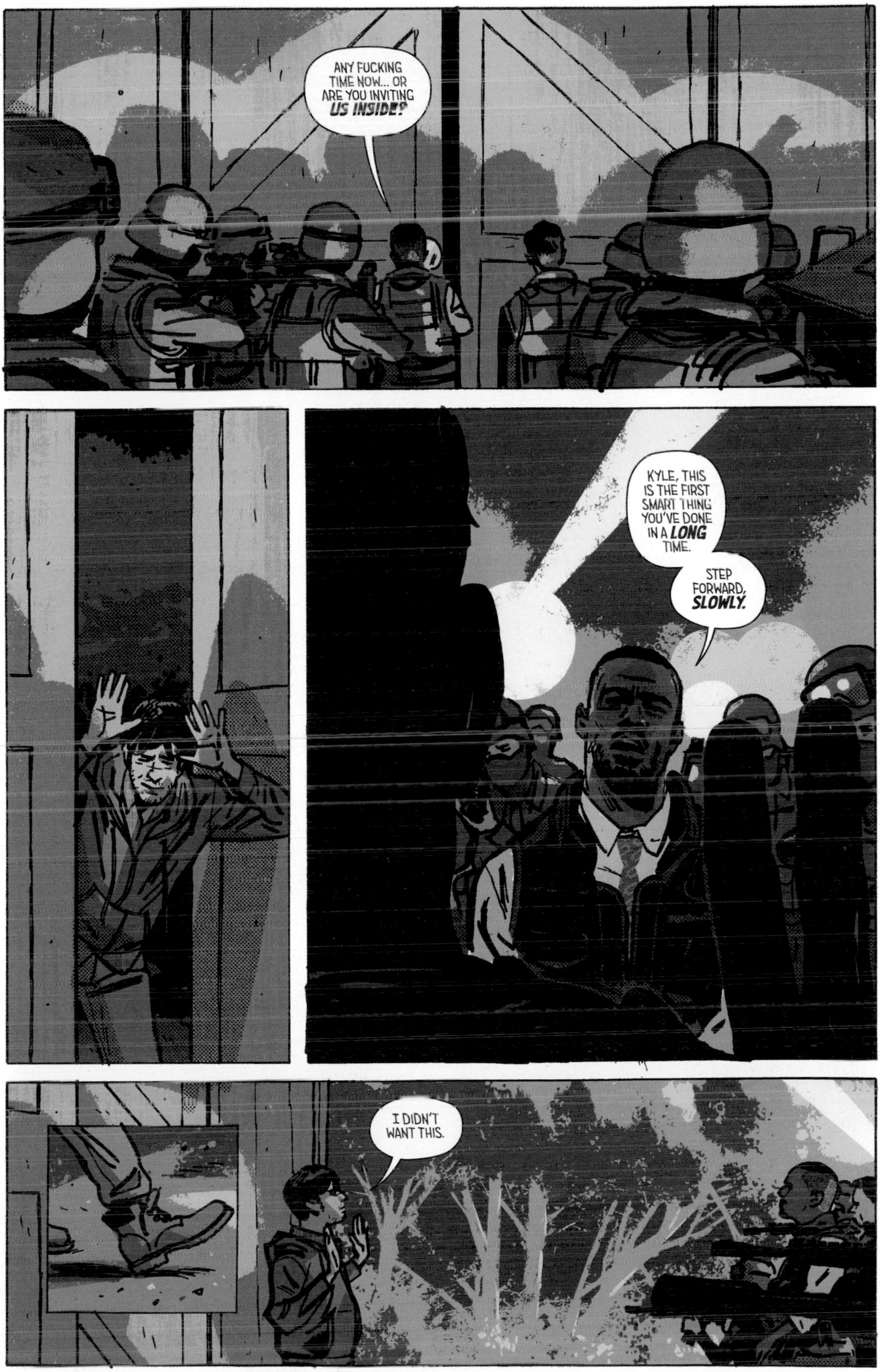
ANY FUCKING TIME NOW... OR ARE YOU INVITING US INSIDE?
KYLE, THIS IS THE FIRST SMART THING YOU'VE DONE IN A LONG TIME.
STEP FORWARD, SLOWLY.
I DIDN'T WANT THIS.

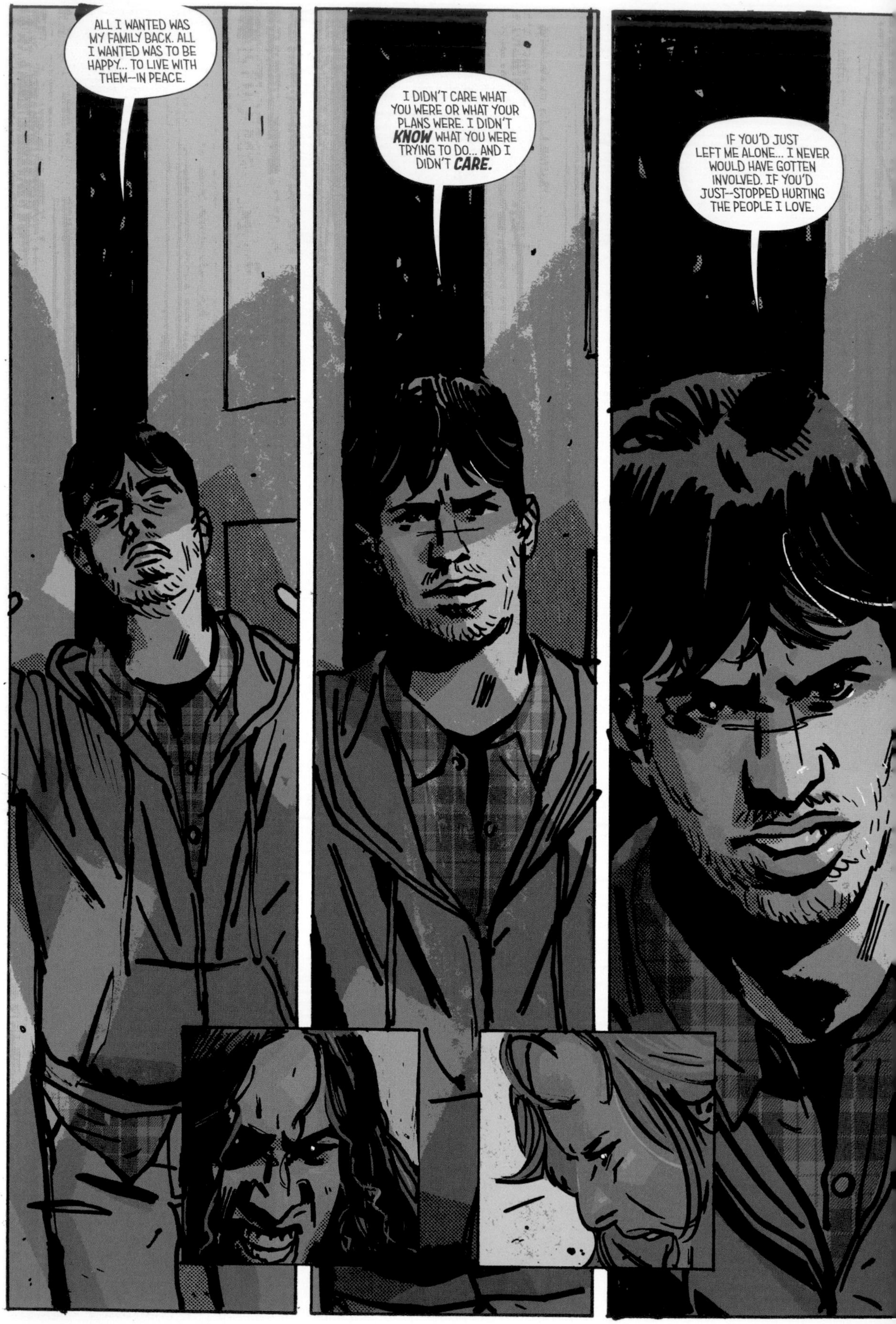
ALL I WANTED WAS MY FAMILY BACK. ALL I WANTED WAS TO BE HAPPY... TO LIVE WITH THEM--IN PEACE.
I DIDN'T CARE WHAT YOU WERE OR WHAT YOUR PLANS WERE. I DIDN'T KNOW WHAT YOU WERE TRYING TO DO... AND I DIDN'T CARE.
IF YOU'D JUST LEFT ME ALONE... I NEVER WOULD HAVE GOTTEN INVOLVED. IF YOU'D JUST--STOPPED HURTING THE PEOPLE I LOVE.

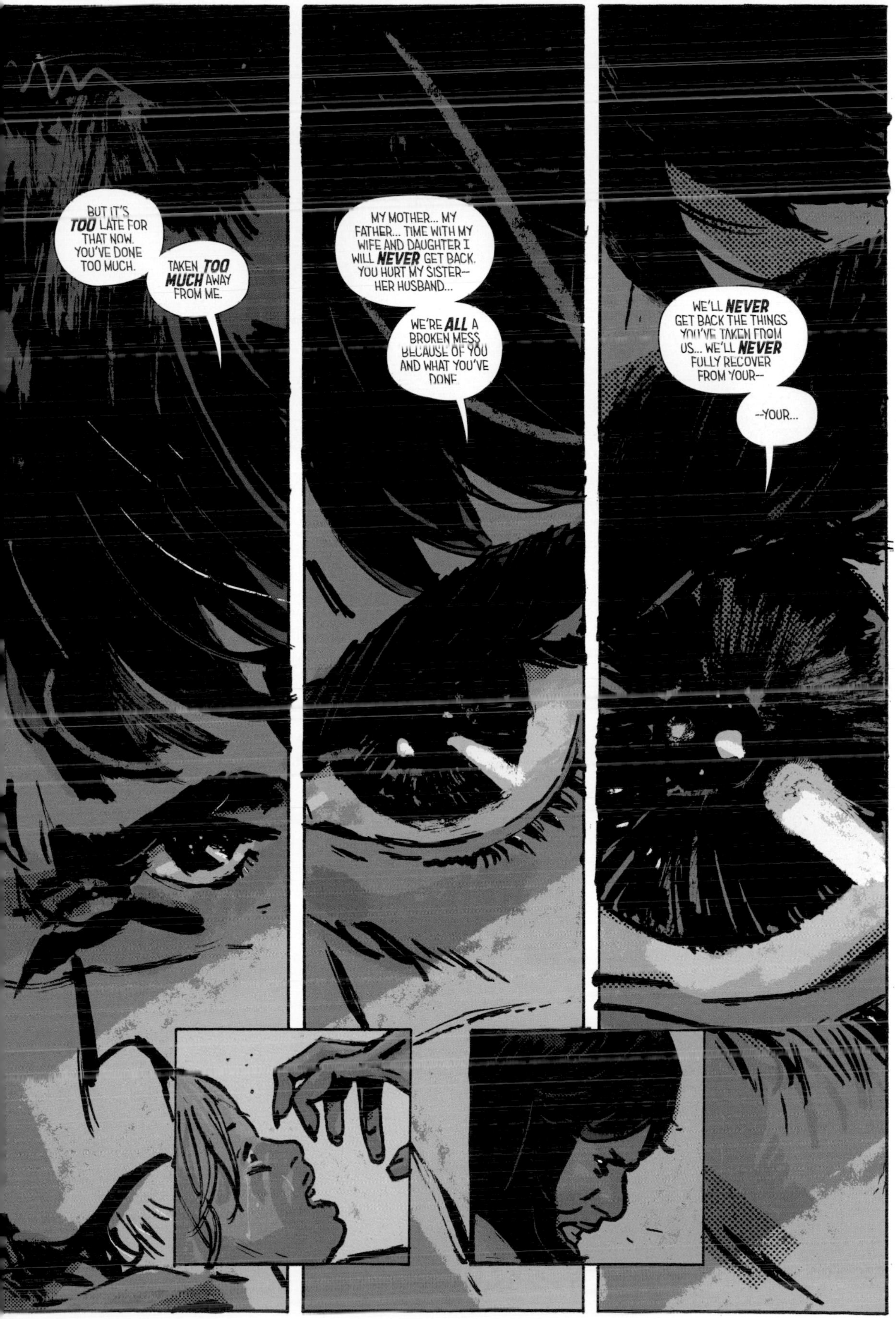
BUT IT'S TOO LATE FOR THAT NOW. YOU'VE DONE TOO MUCH.
TAKEN TOO MUCH AWAY FROM ME.
MY MOTHER... MY FATHER... TIME WITH MY WIFE AND DAUGHTER I WILL NEVER GET BACK. YOU HURT MY SISTER-- HER HUSBAND...
WE'RE ALL A BROKEN MESS BECAUSE OF YOU AND WHAT YOU'VE DONE.
WE'LL NEVER GET BACK THE THINGS YOU'VE TAKEN FROM US... WE'LL NEVER FULLY RECOVER FROM YOUR--
--YOUR...

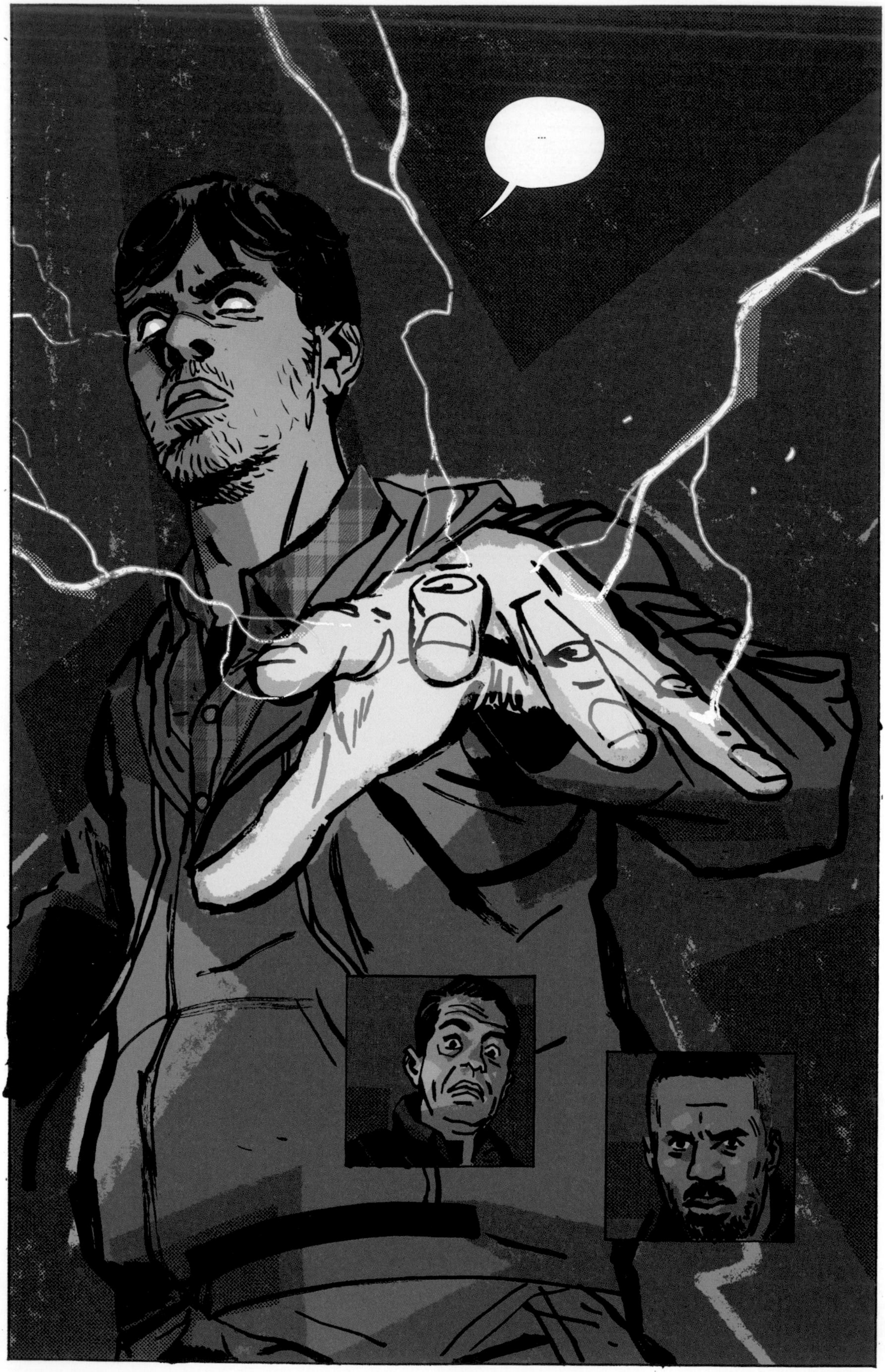
...

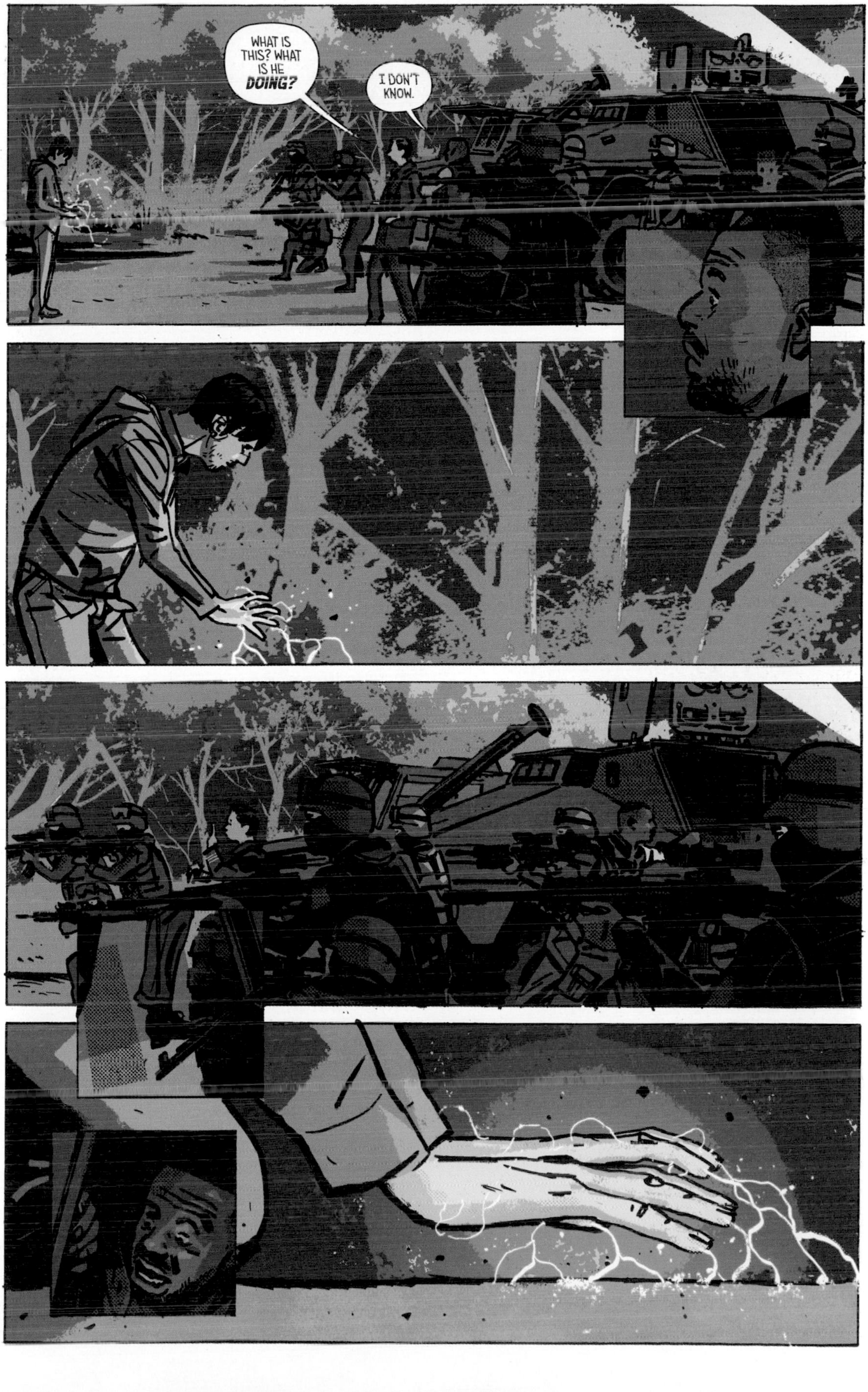
WHAT IS THIS? WHAT IS HE DOING?
I DON'T KNOW.

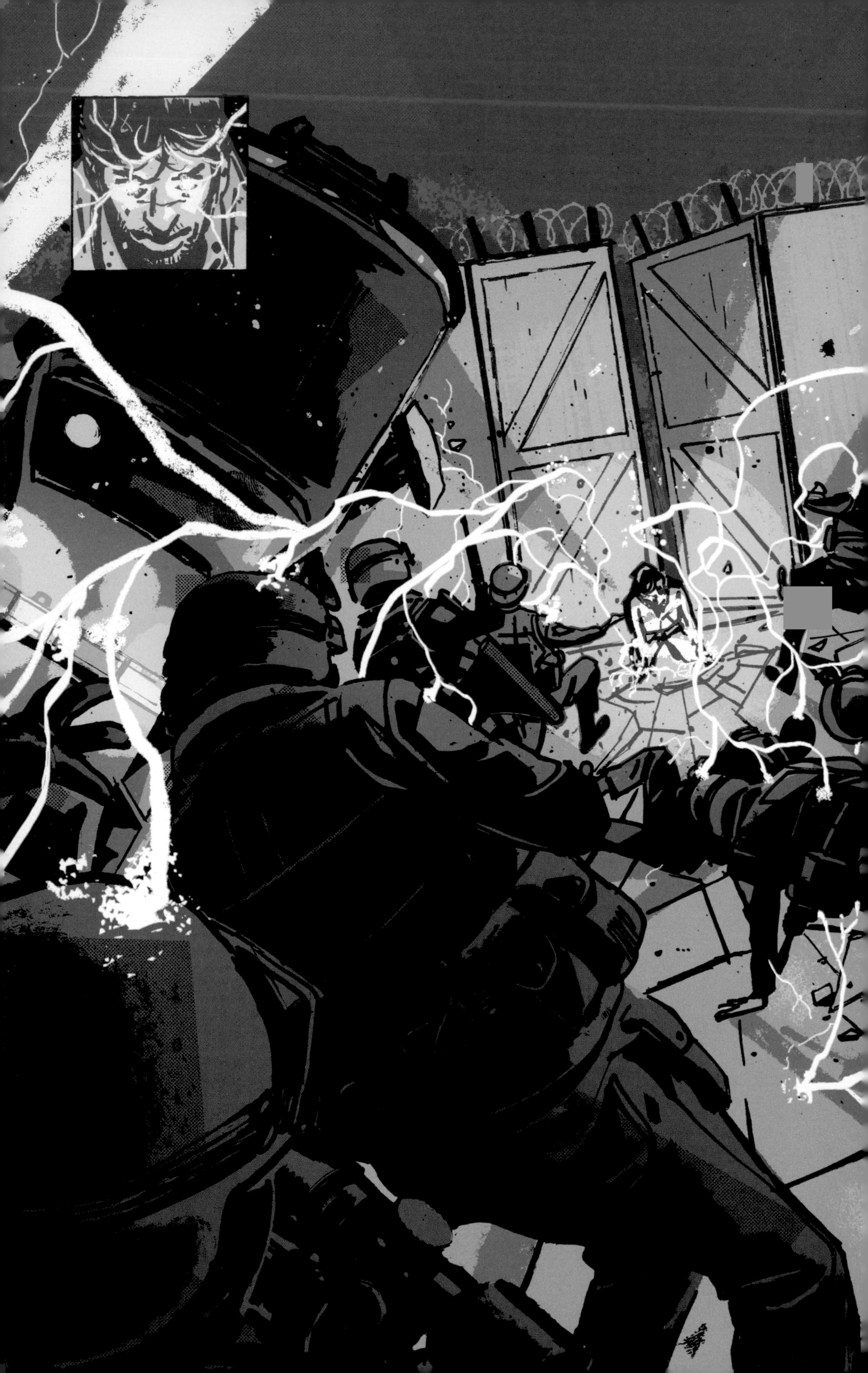

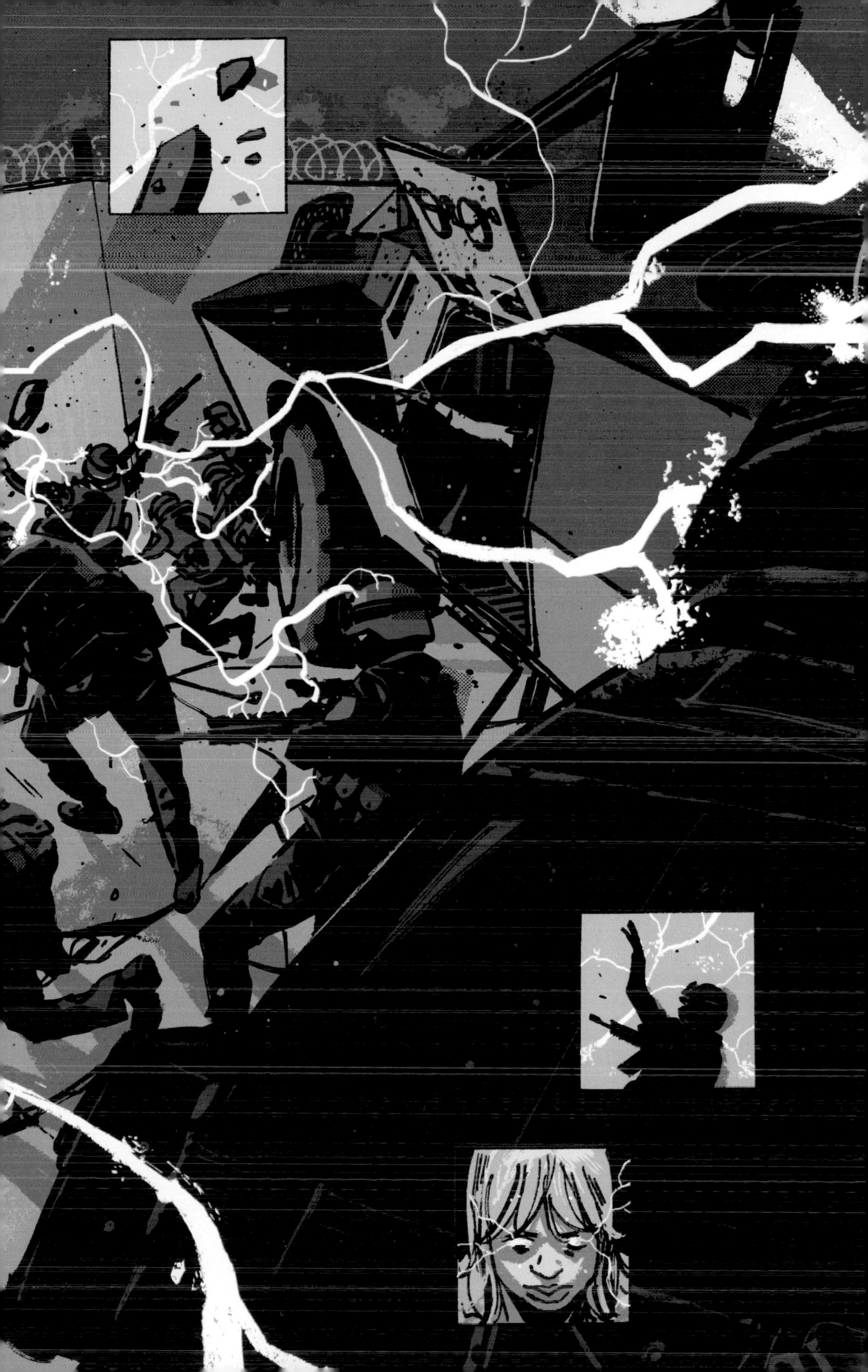

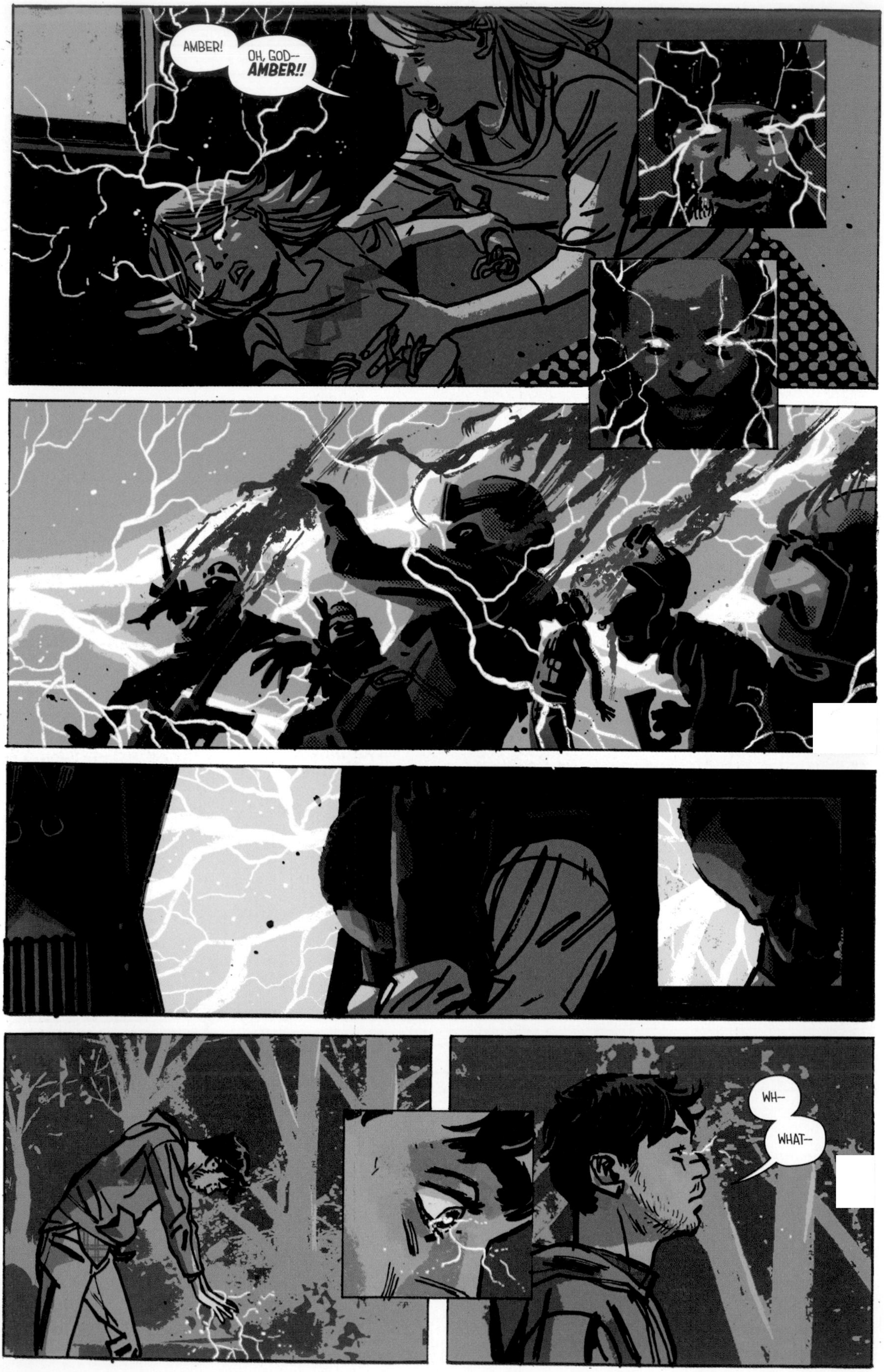
AMBER!
OH, GOD--
AMBER!!
WH-
WHAT--

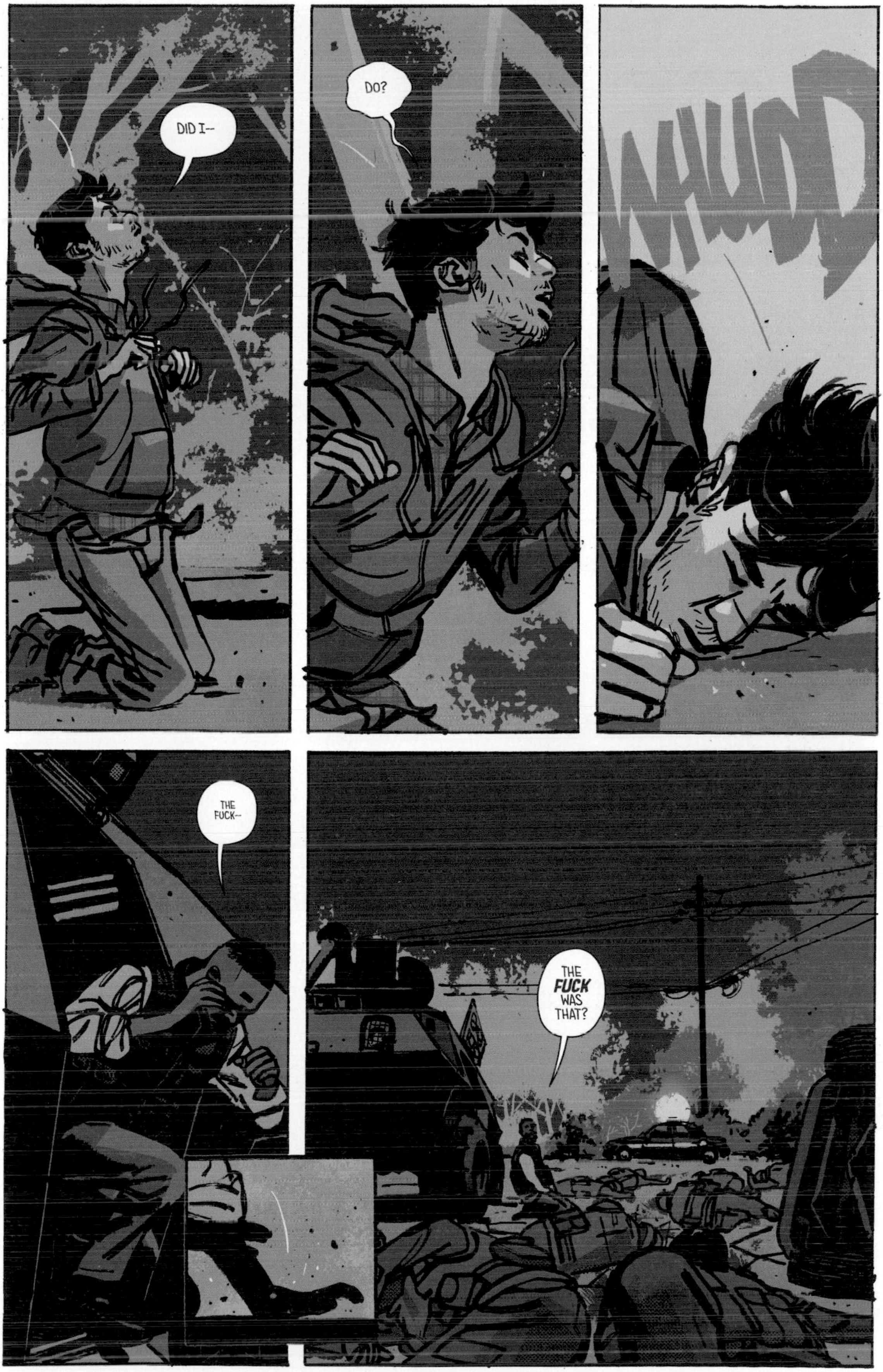

DID I--
DO?
WHUD
THE FUCK--
THE FUCK WAS THAT?

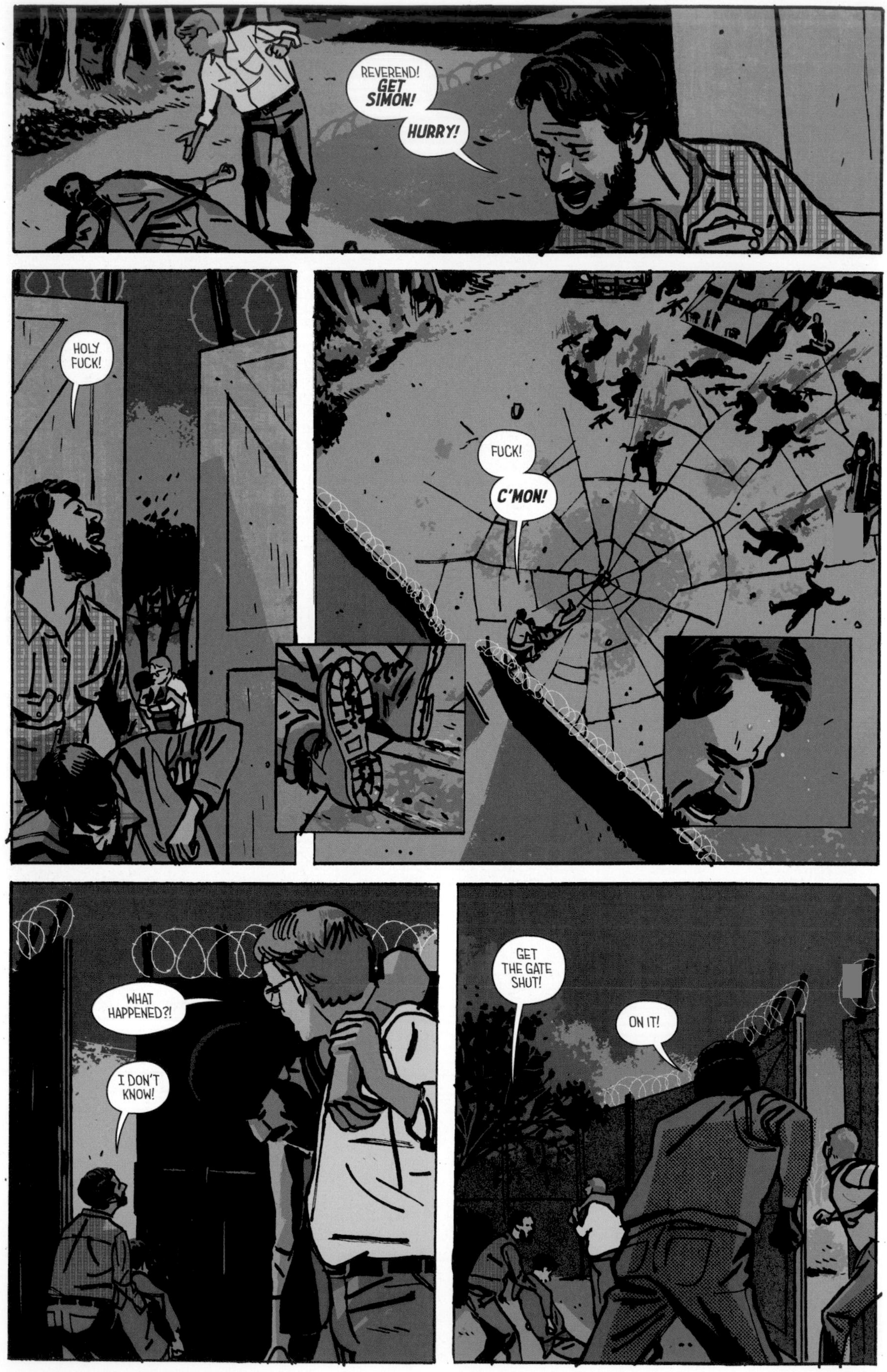
REVEREND! GET SIMON!
HURRY!
HOLY FUCK!
FUCK!
C'MON!
WHAT HAPPENED?!
I DON'T KNOW!
GET THE GATE SHUT!
ON IT!

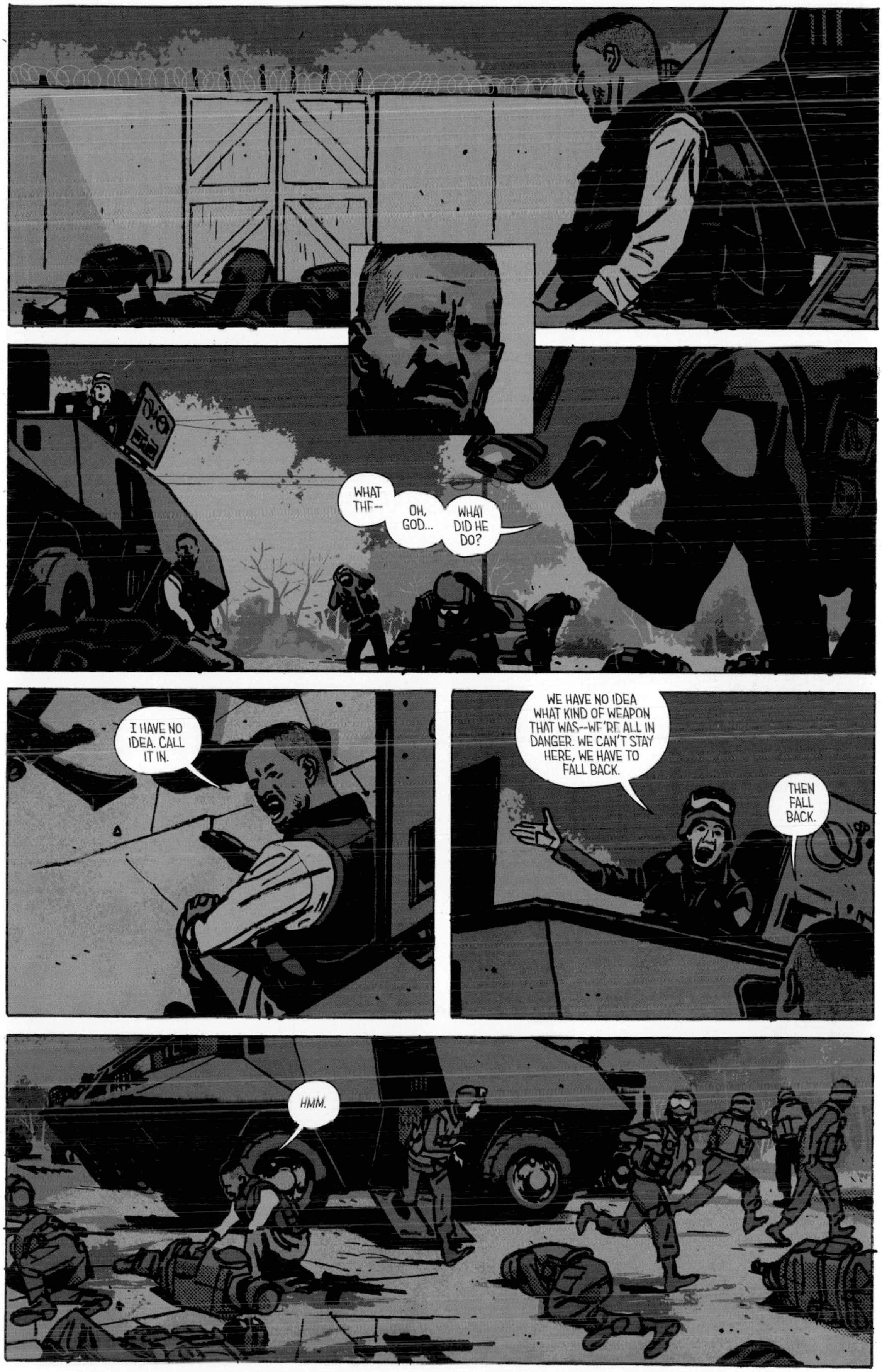
WHAT THE--
OH, GOD...
WHAT DID HE DO?
I HAVE NO IDEA. CALL IT IN.
WE HAVE NO IDEA WHAT KIND OF WEAPON THAT WAS--WE'RE ALL IN DANGER. WE CAN'T STAY HERE, WE HAVE TO FALL BACK.
THEN FALL BACK.
HMM.

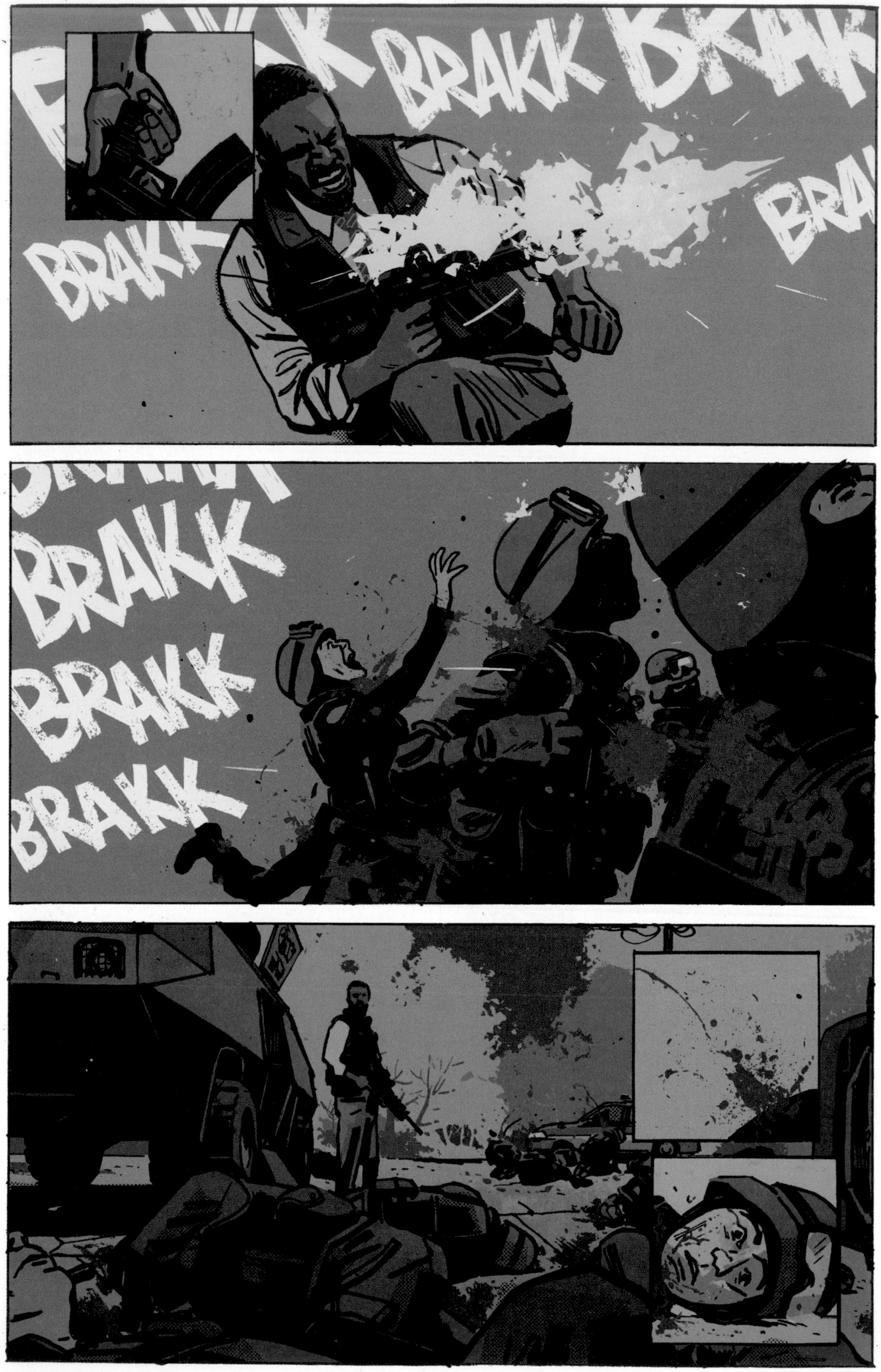
BRAKK
BRAKK
BRAKK
BRAKK
BRAKK

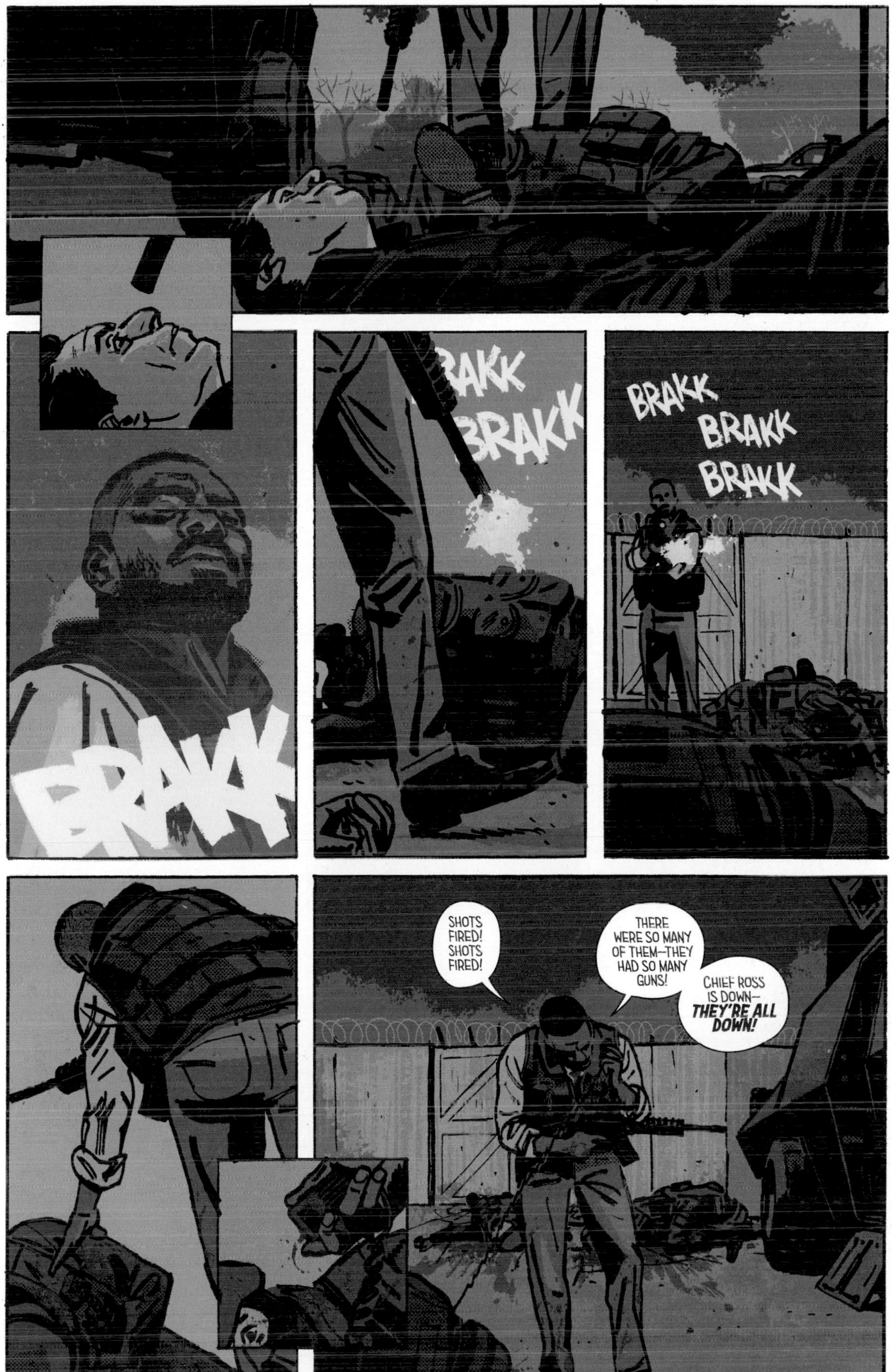
BRAKK
BRAKK
BRAKK
BRAKK
BRAKK
BRAKK
SHOTS FIRED! SHOTS FIRED!
THERE WERE SO MANY OF THEM--THEY HAD SO MANY GUNS!
CHIEF ROSS IS DOWN-- THEY'RE ALL DOWN!

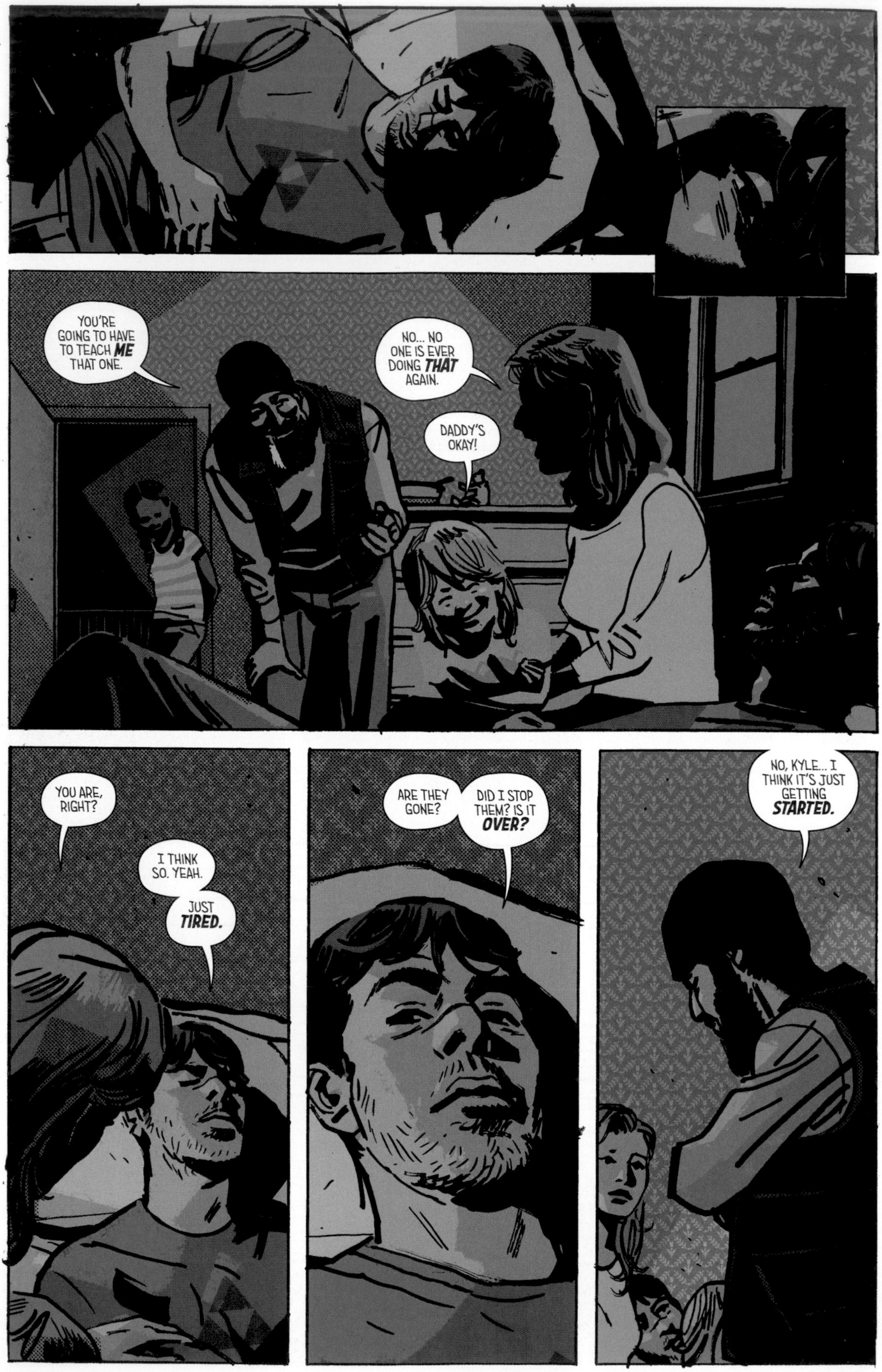
YOU'RE GOING TO HAVE TO TEACH ME THAT ONE.
NO... NO ONE IS EVER DOING THAT AGAIN.
DADDY'S OKAY!
YOU ARE, RIGHT?
I THINK SO. YEAH.
JUST TIRED.
ARE THEY GONE?
DID I STOP THEM? IS IT OVER?
NO, KYLE... I THINK IT'S JUST GETTING STARTED.

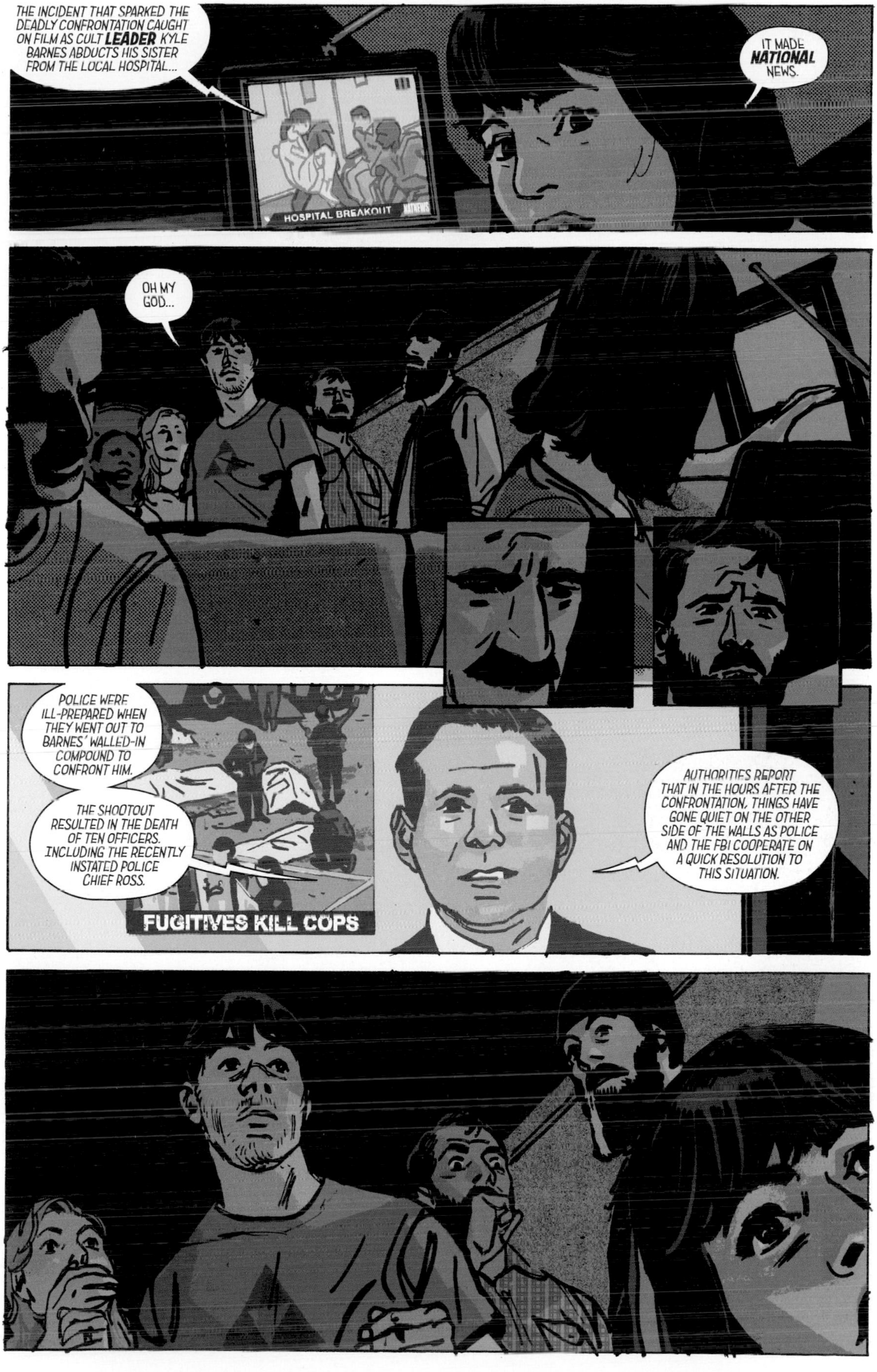
THE INCIDENT THAT SPARKED THE DEADLY CONFRONTATION CAUGHT ON FILM AS CULT LEADER KYLE BARNES ABDUCTS HIS SISTER FROM THE LOCAL HOSPITAL...
HOSPITAL BREAKOUT
IT MADE NATIONAL NEWS.
OH MY GOD...
POLICE WERE ILL-PREPARED WHEN THEY WENT OUT TO BARNES' WALLED-IN COMPOUND TO CONFRONT HIM.
THE SHOOTOUT RESULTED IN THE DEATH OF TEN OFFICERS. INCLUDING THE RECENTLY INSTATED POLICE CHIEF ROSS.
FUGITIVES KILL COPS
AUTHORITIES REPORT THAT IN THE HOURS AFTER THE CONFRONTATION, THINGS HAVE GONE QUIET ON THE OTHER SIDE OF THE WALLS AS POLICE AND THE FBI COOPERATE ON A QUICK RESOLUTION TO THIS SITUATION.

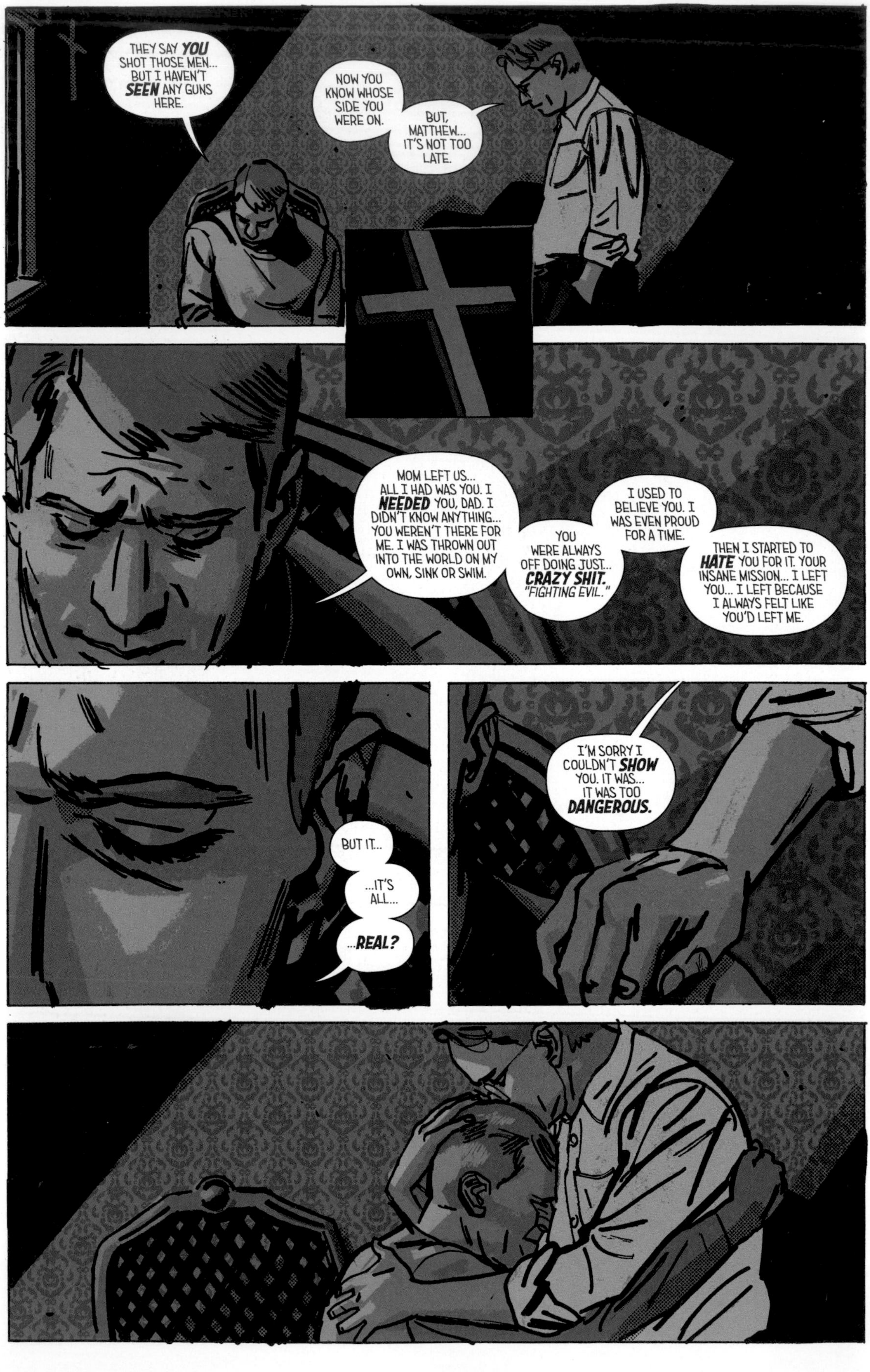
THEY SAY YOU SHOT THOSE MEN... BUT I HAVEN'T SEEN ANY GUNS HERE.
NOW YOU KNOW WHOSE SIDE YOU WERE ON.
BUT, MATTHEW... IT'S NOT TOO LATE.
MOM LEFT US... ALL I HAD WAS YOU. I NEEDED YOU, DAD. I DIDN'T KNOW ANYTHING... YOU WEREN'T THERE FOR ME. I WAS THROWN OUT INTO THE WORLD ON MY OWN, SINK OR SWIM.
YOU WERE ALWAYS OFF DOING JUST... CRAZY SHIT. "FIGHTING EVIL."
I USED TO BELIEVE YOU. I WAS EVEN PROUD FOR A TIME.
THEN I STARTED TO HATE YOU FOR IT. YOUR INSANE MISSION... I LEFT YOU... I LEFT BECAUSE I ALWAYS FELT LIKE YOU'D LEFT ME.
BUT IT...
...IT'S ALL...
...REAL?
I'M SORRY I COULDN'T SHOW YOU. IT WAS... IT WAS TOO DANGEROUS.

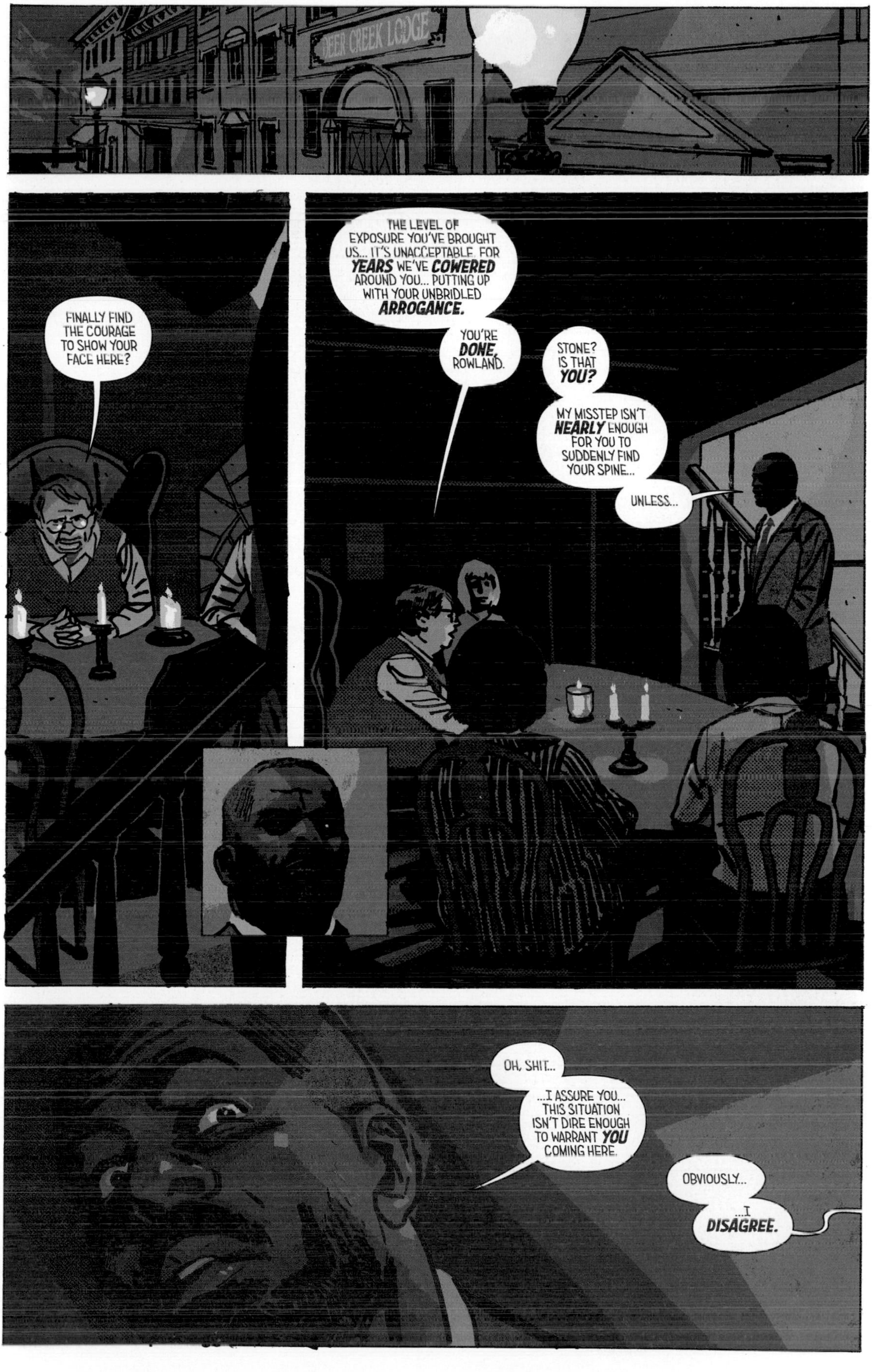
DEER CREEK LODGE
FINALLY FIND THE COURAGE TO SHOW YOUR FACE HERE?
THE LEVEL OF EXPOSURE YOU'VE BROUGHT US... IT'S UNACCEPTABLE. FOR YEARS WE'VE COWERED AROUND YOU... PUTTING UP WITH YOUR UNBRIDLED ARROGANCE.
YOU'RE DONE, ROWLAND.
STONE? IS THAT YOU?
MY MISSTEP ISN'T NEARLY ENOUGH FOR YOU TO SUDDENLY FIND YOUR SPINE...
UNLESS...
OH, SHIT...
...I ASSURE YOU... THIS SITUATION ISN'T DIRE ENOUGH TO WARRANT YOU COMING HERE.
OBVIOUSLY...
...I DISAGREE.

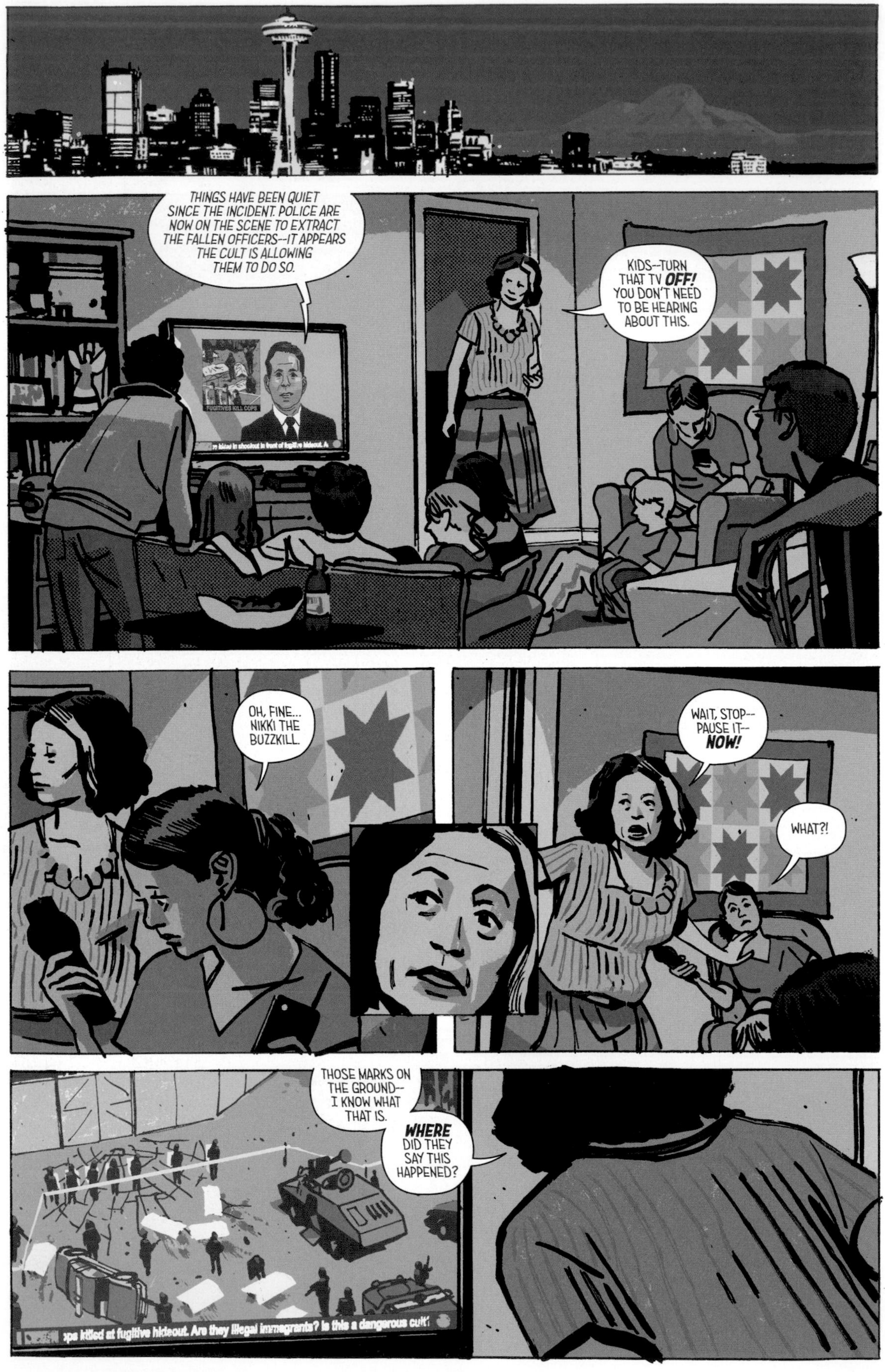
THINGS HAVE BEEN QUIET SINCE THE INCIDENT. POLICE ARE NOW ON THE SCENE TO EXTRACT THE FALLEN OFFICERS--IT APPEARS THE CULT IS ALLOWING THEM TO DO SO.
FUGITIVES KILL COPS
KIDS--TURN THAT TV **OFF!** YOU DON'T NEED TO BE HEARING ABOUT THIS.
OH, FINE... NIKKI THE BUZZKILL.
WAIT, STOP--PAUSE IT--**NOW!**
WHAT?!
THOSE MARKS ON THE GROUND--I KNOW WHAT THAT IS.
WHERE DID THEY SAY THIS HAPPENED?
ps killed at fugitive hideout. Are they illegal immegrants? Is this a dangerous cult

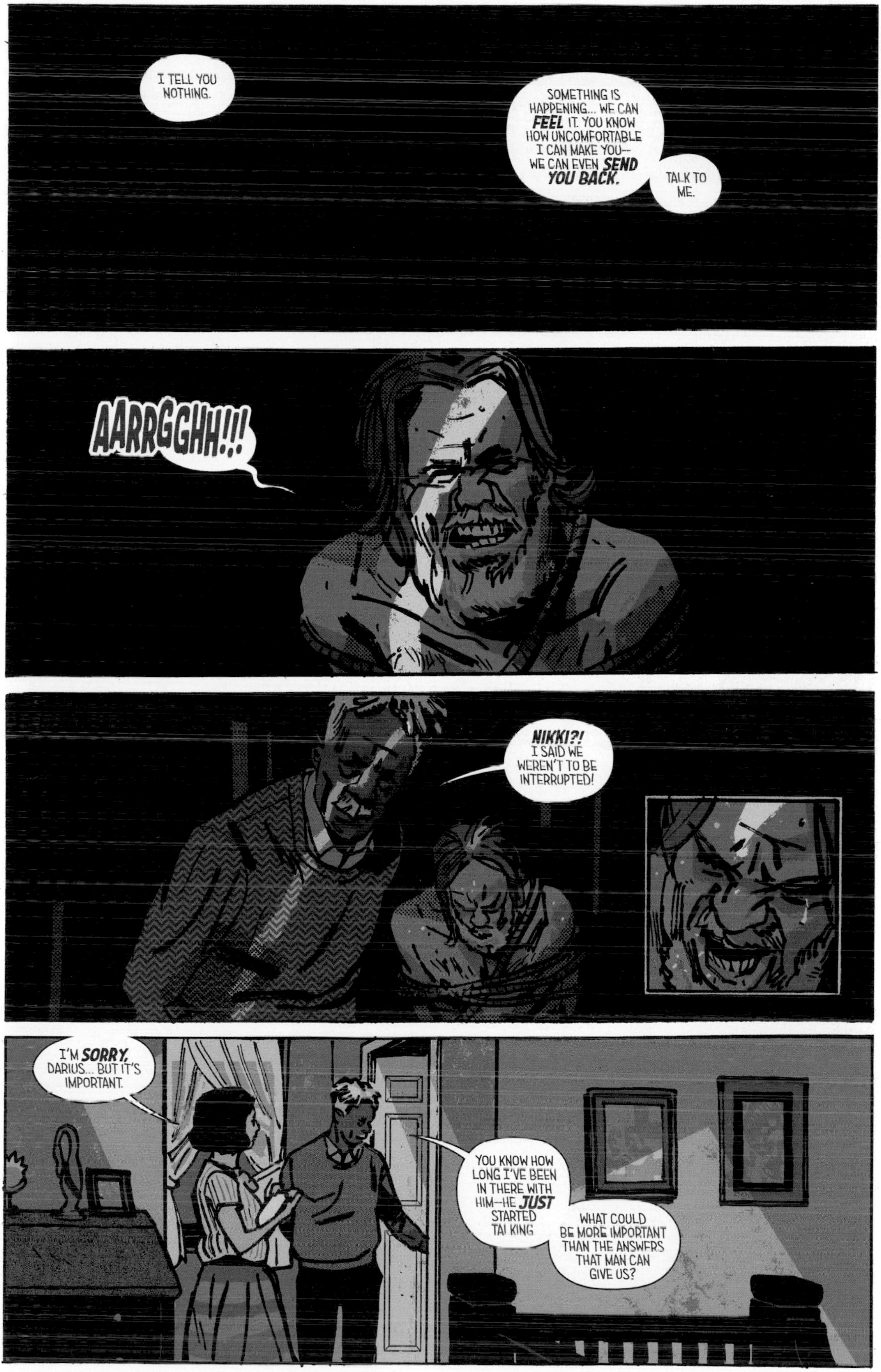
I TELL YOU NOTHING.
SOMETHING IS HAPPENING... WE CAN FEEL IT. YOU KNOW HOW UNCOMFORTABLE I CAN MAKE YOU-- WE CAN EVEN SEND YOU BACK.
TALK TO ME.
AARRGGHH!!!
NIKKI?! I SAID WE WEREN'T TO BE INTERRUPTED!
I'M SORRY, DARIUS... BUT IT'S IMPORTANT.
YOU KNOW HOW LONG I'VE BEEN IN THERE WITH HIM--HE JUST STARTED TALKING
WHAT COULD BE MORE IMPORTANT THAN THE ANSWERS THAT MAN CAN GIVE US?

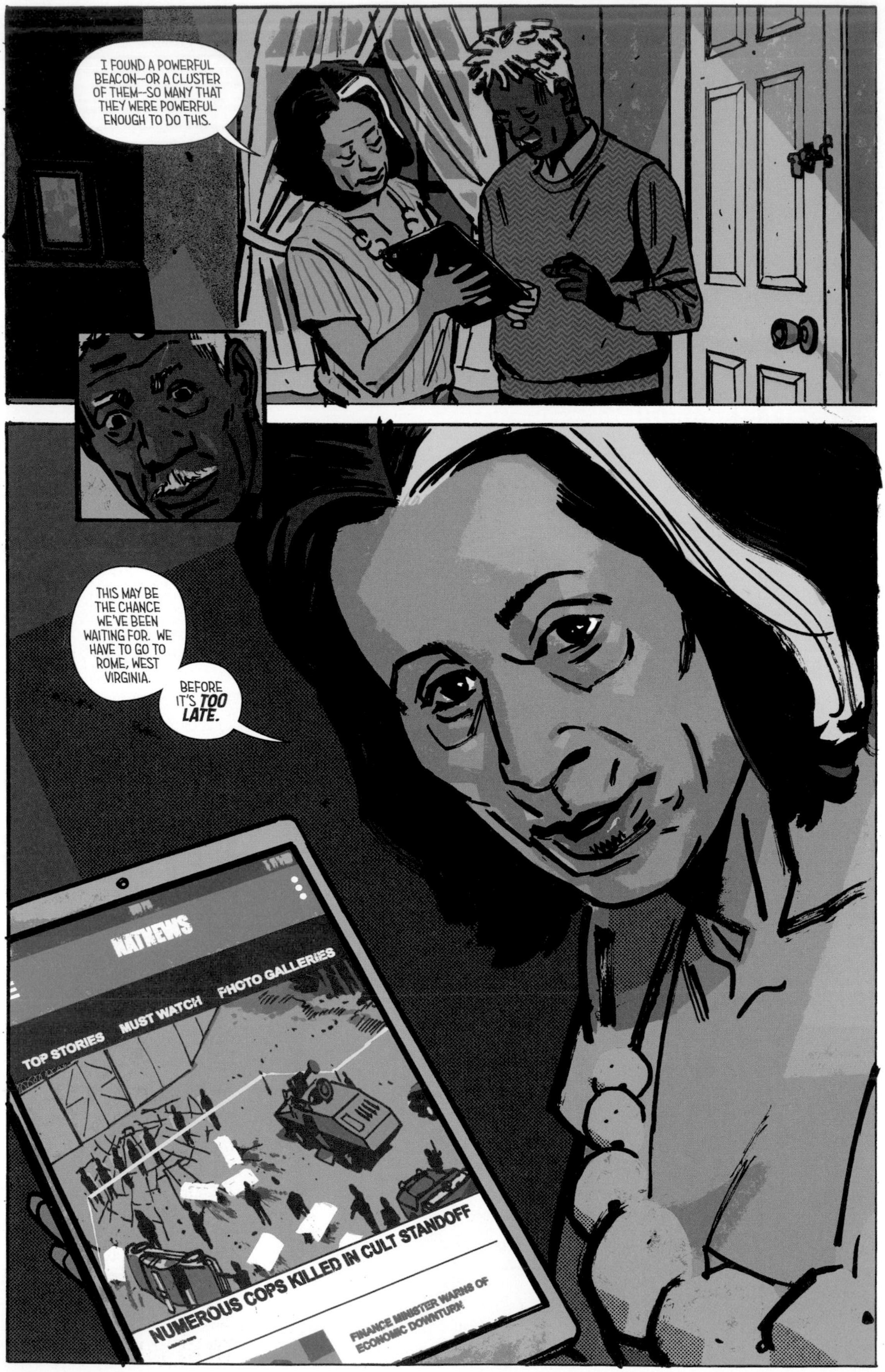
I FOUND A POWERFUL BEACON--OR A CLUSTER OF THEM--SO MANY THAT THEY WERE POWERFUL ENOUGH TO DO THIS.
THIS MAY BE THE CHANCE WE'VE BEEN WAITING FOR. WE HAVE TO GO TO ROME, WEST VIRGINIA.
BEFORE IT'S TOO LATE.
NATNEWS
TOP STORIES
MUST WATCH
PHOTO GALLERIES
NUMEROUS COPS KILLED IN CULT STANDOFF
FINANCE MINISTER WARNS OF ECONOMIC DOWNTURN

TO BE CONTINUED